Powerful and determined to have
their way, three sexy Australian
millionaires will purchase the
women they want to wed!

Bought *by the* TYCOON

Get hooked by this stunning, glamorous,
Sydney-based, wealthy bachelor trilogy
from bestseller Miranda Lee

Bought by the TYCOON

Miranda Lee

featuring

Bought: One Bride
The Tycoon's Trophy Wife
A Scandalous Marriage

*M&B™ and M&B™ with the Rose Device
are trademarks of the publisher.
Harlequin Mills & Boon Limited, Eton House,
18-24 Paradise Road, Richmond, Surrey TW9 1SR*

BOUGHT BY THE TYCOON
© by Harlequin Enterprises II B.V./S.à.r.l 2009

Bought: One Bride, The Tycoon's Trophy Wife and *A Scandalous
Marriage* were first published in Great Britain in separate,
single volumes.

Bought: One Bride © Miranda Lee 2005
The Tycoon's Trophy Wife © Miranda Lee 2005
A Scandalous Marriage © Miranda Lee 2005

ISBN: 978 0 263 86754 1

010-0209

*Printed and bound in Spain
by Litografia Rosés S.A., Barcelona*

Bought:
One Bride

Miranda Lee is Australian, living near Sydney. Born and raised in the bush, she was boarding-school educated and briefly pursued a career in classical music, before moving to Sydney and embracing the world of computers. Happily married, with three daughters, she began writing when family commitments kept her at home. She likes to create stories that are believable, modern, fast-paced and sexy. Her interests include meaty sagas, doing word puzzles, gambling and going to the movies.

PROLOGUE

THE lift purred its way up to the penthouse floor, coming to a quiet halt before the door slid smoothly open, revealing a marble-floored foyer underfoot, and a breathtaking view straight ahead. Sydney Harbour on a clear summer's day was always a sight to behold, with its sparkling blue water and picturesque surrounds, but more so from this height and this vantage point.

Richard shook his head as he walked from the lift towards the huge plate-glass window, his expression wry as he glanced over his shoulder at Reece, who'd hung back a little.

"I can see why you've had no trouble selling these apartments," he remarked to his friend and business colleague. "I've never seen a finer view."

Reece's handsome face showed satisfaction as he came forward to stand at Richard's shoulder. "I always abide by that famous old real estate saying. Position. Position. Position. Aside from being north-facing with a great view of the bridge, this point at East Balmain is just a short ferry ride from Sydney's Central Business District, and an even shorter ride across to Darling Harbour."

"It's certainly a top spot, especially being near to the CBD. Which is just as well," Richard added. "There were mutterings at the bank all last year that I'd used their money to back one too many of your projects. My new position as CEO could have been on the line if this had proved to be one big white elephant. The board were seriously worried when you wouldn't allow investors to buy off the plan.''

Reece smiled. ''Aah, but these apartments weren't directed at investors. They were designed so that people would fall in love with at least one of them and want to live here. As well as devoting two floors to a private gym, pool, sauna and squash courts, I had each apartment individually decorated and furnished, right down to the sheets, towels and accessories. It added between one and two hundred thousand to the cost of each apartment, but it's proved to be a most successful selling tool.''

Richard winced. Up to two hundred thousand, spent decorating each apartment. Good God.

''I'm glad you didn't tell me that earlier. The old fogies at the bank would have had a pink fit. I might have too,'' he added with a dry laugh. There were factions at the bank who didn't approve of Richard's promotion last year. A couple of the senior executives thought he was too young at thirty-eight to run a multibillion-dollar financial institution.

''That's why I didn't tell you till now,'' Reece said with a wry grin. ''I know when to keep a secret. But you've had the last laugh, dear friend,'' he said, clapping Richard on the shoulder. ''The building's only been open since last October and we already have a ninety-five per cent occupancy rate. Three short months, and there's only one penthouse left empty, along with a few apartments on the lower floors.''

''What's wrong with the penthouse you haven't

sold?'' Richard asked. ''Too expensive? Wrong colour scheme?''

''Nope. It's not on the market.''

''Aah. The developer has claimed it for himself.''

Reece's blue eyes twinkled. ''Come on. I'll show it to you.''

''I can understand now why you've kept this one,'' Richard said ten minutes later.

It was nothing like other city penthouses Richard had seen during his lifetime. And he'd seen quite a few. This was like a house up in the sky. A beach house, complete with garden beds, a lap pool and wide, cream-tiled terraces where you could stretch out and enjoy the view and soak up the sun.

Inside, the décor continued the promise of a relaxed, sun-filled lifestyle, with the same cream tiles on the floors throughout. The walls were painted either cream or a warm buttery colour. Most of the furniture was made of natural cane, with soft furnishings in various shades of blue. Rugs in blues and yellows gave warmth to the tiled floors.

No curtains or blinds blocked the view, though the glass doors and windows were tinted to reduce any glare. Naturally, the interior was fully air-conditioned and Reece proudly announced there was heating under the floor tiles to warm the place in the winter. Every room had a view and sliding glass doors that led out onto the terraces. A high cement wall separated the two top-floor penthouses, providing privacy and a courtyard effect to house the lap pool.

When Richard walked into the spacious master bedroom with its luxuriously large bed and built-in television screen in the wall opposite, a feeling of sheer envy consumed him.

He'd always admired Reece for his tenacity and resilience, admired how he'd picked himself up both professionally and personally a few years back and worked his way back from the brink of bankruptcy to his current position as the golden boy of Sydney's property development business.

But he had never, ever envied him.

Till now.

Suddenly, Richard wanted this penthouse. Wanted to live in it. Wanted to come home to it every night, instead of the cold, soulless apartment he'd occupied since his wife's death eighteen months ago. He even wanted to share it with someone, which was a surprise as well. Up till this moment, the thought of sharing his life—and his bed—with another woman had been anathema to him. He'd been in total emotional shutdown since he'd buried Joanna. Total sexual shutdown as well.

No wonder he'd been capable of putting in twenty-four-hour days at the bank. His male hormones had to be directed somewhere. It seemed, however, that his male hormones were about to emerge from their cryogenic state, for when Richard looked at the king-sized bed in front of his eyes, he didn't envisage sleeping in it alone.

His flesh actually stirred with the mental image of himself making love to a woman on top of that blue satin quilt. No one he already knew. An attractive stranger. Brunette. Soft-eyed. Full-breasted. And very willing.

His flesh stirred even further.

"You really like this place, don't you?" Reece said.

Richard laughed. "I didn't think I was that obvious. But, yes, I really do. Would you consider selling it to me?"

"Nope."

Frustration flared within Richard, alongside another surge of testosterone. "Damn it, Reece, you already own a mansion on the water just around the corner. What do you want this place for?"

"To give to you."

"What?" Richard's eyebrows shot ceiling-wards.

Reece smiled that disarming, charming smile of his. "Here are the keys, my friend. It's yours."

"Don't be ridiculous!" Richard exclaimed, though his heart was hammering inside his chest. "I can't let you do that. Hell, this place has to be worth a small fortune."

"Five point four million the other penthouse sold for, to be precise. But this one is bigger and better. Here." And he pressed the keys into Richard's right hand.

"No, no. You *have* to let me pay for it!"

"Absolutely not. It's all yours, in appreciation. You were there for me, Rich, when no one else was. And I'm not just talking about the money. You gave me your hand in friendship. And you had faith in my judgement. That's worth more than all the money in the world."

Richard didn't know what to say. Only twice in his banking career had he made personal friends of men he'd lent money to. It was generally advised against. But he'd never had any cause to regret either decision.

Reece, of course, was always a hard man to say no to, and impossible not to like.

Mike had been a different kettle of fish entirely. As dark in looks and personality as Reece was light and bright, the young computer genius had come to the bank several years ago for backing to start his own software company. A one-time juvenile delinquent who had a permanent chip on his shoulder, Mike had no ability to sell himself at all.

But he was creatively brilliant, cripplingly honest and unashamedly ambitious. Richard had been so impressed, he'd invested his own money into Mike's company as well as the bank's.

Over time, Richard had found himself really liking Mike as well, despite his gruff manner. He'd persuaded Mike to go along to one of Reece's famous parties and the three of them had soon become close friends.

Nowadays, Richard counted Reece and Mike as his best and only true friends. Other male colleagues in his life pretended friendship, but Richard knew that they had knives ready behind his back, to be used if he gave them a chance.

"You have no idea how much this means to me," Richard said, his hand closing tightly around the keys. "But to accept a luxury penthouse as a gift—especially *this* one—would put me in an impossible position at the bank. My enemies would have a field day. There'd be all sorts of rumours about corruption and paybacks and Lord knows what else. You *must* let me pay for it."

"You and that bloody bank and those pompous pricks you work with!"

Richard laughed. "Yes, I know, but it's *my* bloody bank now and I'd like to keep it that way. I'll give you the proper market value. What would that be? Six million?"

"Probably." Reece sighed. "Very well. Six million."

"Look, it's not as though I can't afford it," Richard pointed out. "I made a packet out of the house at Palm Beach I bought." And which he'd sold a week after Joanna's funeral.

Richard didn't add that in the eighteen months since Joanna's death, he'd also tripled his personal fortune in the stock market. Amazing what profits could be made when you were uncaring of the risks you were taking.

He could retire right now on his portfolio of property and shares.

But of course he wouldn't. He enjoyed the cut and thrust of the financial world; enjoyed the power of his new position, and the prestige that went with it.

Richard wondered momentarily what Joanna would have made of his success, if she'd still been alive. She would have liked the money, and the social life his new job required of him. But would it have kept her solely in his bed?

Richard doubted it. Any woman who took a lover within two years of her marriage had to be unfaithful by nature.

If it hadn't been for the autopsy report, he would never have known the awful truth about the woman he loved. He'd questioned the coroner at length about the age of the child Joanna had been carrying when the car accident had claimed her life, but he'd been told there was no mistake. Six weeks, give or take a few days.

Richard had been overseas on business for over a month surrounding the time of conception.

The child was not his.

Richard's hand closed even more tightly around the keys. He'd wanted a child with her so much. But Joanna had kept putting him off, saying she wasn't ready for dirty nappies and sleepless nights.

The thing that tormented him the most—now that he could bear to think about it—was the way she'd greeted him when he'd returned home that last time. As if she'd truly loved him. As if she'd missed him so much. She hadn't been able to get enough of him in bed, when all the while she'd been carrying another man's child.

Clearly, she'd been going to pass the baby off as his.

What kind of woman could do that?

Richard had buried both of them with a broken heart, then buried himself in his career.

They said time healed everything. Perhaps so. But Richard knew his life would never be the same, post-Joanna. He could never fall in love again for starters. That part of him had died with her.

But he didn't want to continue living alone.

And he still wanted a child.

It was definitely time to move on. Time to find himself a new wife, the way Reece had found Alanna after his fiancée had dumped him.

"You have that look on your face," Reece said, breaking the silence in the bedroom.

"What look is that?"

"The one you get when you're about to ask me endless questions, usually on the new project I've just come to you with."

The corner of Richard's mouth twitched. "You're a remarkably intuitive man. I do have some questions for you. And, yes, it's about a project of yours. But not a new one. One you completed last year. Shall we go out onto the terrace and sit down?"

"I've never known you to be so mysterious," he said as he followed Richard through the sliding glass doors out into the sunshine.

Richard pulled out one of the chairs of the nearest outdoor setting and sat down. There were several arrangements dotted around the various terraces. This was made in cream aluminium, with a glass-topped table and pale blue, all-weather cushions on the chairs.

Richard waited till Reece was settled opposite him before he spoke.

"I've decided I want to get married again," he began.

"But that's great!" his friend proclaimed. "I didn't realise you were seeing someone."

"I'm not. But I hope to be soon, once you put me in touch with the woman who runs Wives Wanted."

Reece's mouth dropped open before snapping shut again. "But you didn't approve when I told you about that."

"I was surprised, that's all." A reasonable reaction, in Richard's opinion. Reece was not the sort of man one would ever imagine using an introduction agency. His confession to his best man and groomsman just before his wedding last year that he'd found his beau-

tiful new bride via an internet website had come as a
shock.

The agency was called Wives Wanted, its aim being to match professional men with the kind of
women lots of them wanted to marry, especially those
of the ''once bitten, twice shy'' brigade. Apparently,
its database was chock-full of attractive women who
were only interested in one career. Marriage. Women
whose priority was not necessarily romantic love, but
security and commitment.

A lot of them had had previous marriages, or relationships, that had failed to deliver what they
wanted in life. Some were currently career girls, but
were prepared to relegate their careers to the back
seat, for the right man.

''It was Mike who didn't approve,'' Richard
pointed out. ''But don't forget, he hadn't met Alanna
at that stage.''

Thankfully, Richard had stopped Mike from re-
peating to Reece at the reception that he thought all
women who put themselves out like that were nothing
but cold-blooded gold-diggers, looking for a gravy
train to ride. He'd voiced that opinion to Richard,
however. More than once.

But no one who got to know Reece's wife would
believe such a thing of her.

Richard had initially been stunned when Reece had
confessed that he'd found his lovely Alanna through
this agency. He'd presumed Reece had met her so-
cially. After all, he had a very active social life. A
man of his looks and position could have had his pick
of women.

When Richard had asked him outright at the wedding reception why he'd gone to an introduction agency, Reece's reply had been very to the point, and extremely pragmatic.

"It was a question of time. I wanted a wife and a family, but I didn't want to be bothered with a traditional courtship. Far too lengthy a process. Whenever I want a property with certain requirements, I get my PA to narrow the field down for me before I look personally. I approached finding a wife the same way. I gave Wives Wanted a list of my requirements and they selected several suitable candidates for me to view via the internet. I chose three who appealed to me. I only had to date each one once and I knew straight away which girl I would marry."

Richard recalled naïvely asking Reece if it was a case of love at first sight, at which Mike had laughed.

"Reece isn't interested in love any more," Mike had drily informed him. "Not after that other bitch did the dirty on him. Isn't that right, Reece?"

Reece had confirmed that love certainly hadn't come into the equation, on either side, although he claimed he wouldn't have married Alanna without some sexual chemistry between them.

Some sexual chemistry?

Richard still considered this a rather outrageous understatement. He'd had several opportunities to observe Reece and Alanna together, both before and after their wedding. To his eyes, the sexual chemistry between them was quite electric, especially on Reece's part.

Richard had noted at a recent dinner party he'd attended at the Diamonds' place that Reece had spent an inordinate amount of time watching his beautiful wife talking to the male guest sitting next to her.

Admittedly, Alanna had looked extra stunning that night in a clinging white satin gown that made the most of her physical assets. There hadn't been a man sitting at that table who hadn't found his eyes coming back to her all the time, himself included.

Richard thought it was just as well that ethereal-looking blondes with porcelain skin, pale green eyes and tall, willowy figures didn't overly stir his male hormones. He preferred the more earthy kind of women, with stronger colouring and lush bodies.

Joanna had had black hair, black eyes and a voluptuous figure.

Not that Richard wanted to marry some clone of Joanna. Hell, no. He wanted the second Mrs Richard Crawford to be as far removed from the first as a woman could be. In personality and character, that was. Physically, he'd always been attracted to brunettes with curves. He knew, when he eventually studied the Wives Wanted database, he wouldn't be selecting any skinny blondes.

''Are you absolutely sure about this?'' Reece asked him.

''Absolutely.''

''I presume you're not looking for love, then.''

''You presume correctly.''

''You want a marriage of convenience. Like mine.''

''Yes.''

Reece frowned. ''I'm not sure you're cut out for a relationship like that, Rich. You're a bit of a romantic at heart.''

"Not any more, I'm not."

Richard wished he hadn't sounded quite so bitter. Reece looked startled. As well he might. Reece knew nothing about Joanna's betrayal. Men, even the closest of friends, didn't tell each other things like that.

"I've made up my mind about this," Richard stated firmly.

"Can I ask why?" Reece probed.

"It's not rocket science, my friend. Just the need for companionship. And some regular sex."

"You could get that from a girlfriend."

"I don't want a girlfriend. I want a wife."

"Aah, I get the picture. It's because of the bank. Your position as CEO would be consolidated if you were married."

Now it was Richard's turn to be startled. "It has nothing whatsoever to do with the bank. I simply want to be married. I want what you've got, Reece. A good-looking woman who's happy to be my wife, and to have my child."

"I didn't realise you wanted a family."

"Why on earth would you think that?"

Reece shrugged. "You were married to Joanna for two years, more than enough time to have a baby."

"That was not my doing," Richard informed his friend, doing his best not to sound cold.

Reece still frowned. "I thought you were happy with Joanna..."

"I was," he said truthfully enough. His unhappiness hadn't begun till after she'd died. "I was mad about her. But she's gone, and I'm here and I'm lonely, all right? I want a woman in my life. What I don't want, however, is romance. I've been there, done that.''

Reece nodded. ''Yes, I can understand where you're coming from.''

''You should. I know how you felt about Kristine. Which is why *you* went to Wives Wanted in the first place. Because you were still in love with her.''

''The way you still are with Joanna.''

Richard didn't deny it. If he had, he might have had to explain.

''Now that that's all settled, I'm going back inside to have another look at my fabulous new penthouse,'' he said, scraping back his chair and standing up. ''Which reminds me. Can I move in before contracts are exchanged?''

''Move in today, if you like.''

Richard was not an impulsive man by nature but, today, things were a-changing. ''You know what? I think I will.''

CHAPTER ONE

HOLLY glared for the umpteenth time at the FOR
SALE sign that had been taped on the shop window
less than half an hour earlier. Fury and indignation
warred inside her swirling stomach and whirling head.

How dared her stepmother do this? How *dared*
she?

A Flower A Day was at least half hers by rights.
She should have been consulted. Should have been
considered.

But any consideration for *her* feelings had clearly
ended with her father's death. Any hope of his beloved business one day being hers had died with him.

She'd been stupid to stay on. Especially stupid to
work for such a pathetic salary, considering she managed the shop now, and did the books as well. Every
Sunday, no less. Her day off!

Heck, Sara took home almost as much money as
she did. And Sara only worked from Wednesday till
Saturday as a casual. Sure, Sara was an excellent florist with loads of experience but Holly was every bit
as experienced. She might only be twenty-six but
she'd been working with flowers all her life. Her dad
had started training her to be a florist when she'd been
knee-high to a grasshopper. She'd joined him in the
shop soon after her fifteenth birthday.

Holly's heart twisted as she remembered how
happy they'd been back then. Just her and her dad.

And then Connie had come along.

Holly hadn't realised till after her dad had died two years back what kind of woman her stepmother was. Connie had been very clever during the eight years she'd been the second Mrs Greenaway.

But Holly had certainly known within weeks of her dad marrying the attractive divorcee that her stepsister was a nasty piece of work. Jealous, spiteful and devious. Unfortunately, Katie had been equally clever with her new stepfather as his new wife had.

Butter wouldn't melt in her mouth around him.

Holly bitterly resented the money Connie and Katie had wheedled out of her dad. Only the fact that he'd seemed happy had made her stay silent over the vicious things Katie had said to her in private.

Of course, after her dad had died, all gloves had been off. Connie had begun showing her true colours and Katie...well, Katie had gone from bad to worse.

Holly knew she should have moved out of their lives altogether right then and there, but she just couldn't bear to part company with her dad's flower shop. She still felt close to him there. So she'd moved into the flat above the shop and set about getting A Flower A Day back on track.

Business had fallen right off after her father's stroke, Holly having been so upset that she'd had to close the shop for a while. It had taken over a year to get all his old clients back and to start making a profit. Not that A Flower A Day would ever be a great money-making concern. Strip shopping wasn't very successful these days. The malls had taken over.

The shop and the flat, however, were still worth good money, despite being ancient and not in the best

of condition. Probably over a million. More if someone bought it as a business, along with the goodwill.

Holly glowered at the FOR SALE sign one more
time. She'd been crazy to work so hard for so little
when she'd known, deep down, that the only ones
who would reap the rewards were Connie and the
obnoxious Katie. Unfortunately, her father had left his
wife everything in his will, made soon after they'd
been married when Holly had only been sixteen. He'd
relied on Connie to look after his daughter. But the
merry widow had had other plans.

So had her rotten daughter...

But Holly didn't want to think about that. She'd
thought about what had happened over Christmas far
too much already.

If Dave had really loved her, Katie would not have
been able to steal him. But she had. She was even
going to marry him. That should have been the final
straw for Holly but, strangely enough, it hadn't been.

The final straw was that FOR SALE sign.

Holly decided then and there that she'd played
Cinderella long enough. The time had come for some
major changes and major decisions. She knew she'd
be very sad to walk away from her dad's pride and
joy, but it had to be done. Because it wasn't going to
be *her* pride and joy for much longer. It would soon
belong to someone else.

"I'm just ducking down to the station, Sara," she
said crisply. "I need this morning's *Herald*."

Sara glanced up from where she was finishing an
exquisite table setting of pink carnations. It was for a
local lady who was a pink addict.

"Looking for a new job?" Sara said.

"Absolutely."

"About time," Sara muttered.

A very attractive redhead in her midthirties, Sara had seen plenty of living and did not suffer fools gladly. She'd long expressed the opinion that Holly should strike out on her own.

"You're right," Holly agreed. "I'll be looking for a new place to live as well."

Sydney's Saturday morning *Herald* was always chock-full of job and flat-share advertisements. Holly had actually looked before; a few weeks ago, after Dave had left her for Katie. She just hadn't had the courage at that stage to totally change her life, and to leave everything that was so familiar to her.

But she'd found the courage now.

Sara smiled her approval. "Atta girl. And don't you go worrying about me. As soon as you're out of here, so am I. I wouldn't work for that cow Connie if this was the last flower shop in Sydney."

"She is a cow, isn't she?"

"Of the highest order. And so's the daughter. For what it's worth, Katie deserves Dave. I was pleased as Punch the day you got rid of him."

"Er…he dumped me, Sara."

"Only good thing he ever did for you. Now you can find yourself a really nice bloke, someone who'll appreciate your qualities."

"Thanks for the compliment, Sara, but really nice blokes are hard to find. They certainly haven't been thick on the ground in my life. Dave's not the first loser boyfriend I've had. I seem to attract the fickle, faithless type."

"Go get yourself a job in the city, love. Where the suits are."

"Suits?"

"You know. Men in suits. Executive types. I used to work at a flower stall in Market Place. There was an endless parade of male eye candy walking by there, I can tell you. Talk about yummy."

"Yes, but does wearing a suit to work equate with being a nice bloke?"

"Nope. But it often equates with money. Might as well fall for a rich guy as a poor guy."

"*You* didn't." Sara was married to a man who worked on the railways.

"Yes, well, I'm a romantic fool."

"I'm a romantic fool as well."

Sara pulled a face. "Yeah. Most of us girls are. Oh well, you'd better go get that *Herald* before they're all gone."

Holly bought the last paper in the newsagent's and hurried back to study the classifieds between customers, but the news was disappointing. There weren't very many jobs for florists advertised that weekend. And only two in the city. As for sharing a flat…

The reality of moving in with strangers after living on her own for two years made Holly shudder. Yet she couldn't afford to rent somewhere decent by herself, not unless her salary was pretty good. She certainly couldn't afford to buy a place. She had *some* savings but not much. A couple of thousand. Having Dave as a boyfriend had not been cheap. She'd ended up paying for most things, his excuse being he was saving up for their future together.

Like, how gullible could a girl get?

Facing her shortcomings was not a pleasant experience. But by the time Sara left to go home at four o'clock and Holly began closing up the shop, she'd come to terms with her own pathetic performance as a supposedly adult woman. She had no one to blame but herself if her life was a shambles. She'd taken the line of least resistance and allowed people to walk all over her.

But no more. Come Monday morning she would get in contact with one of the many services who did professional résumés. She'd never had to apply for a job before but she knew you had to present yourself well. Then she would apply for those two jobs in the city. Sara was right. The city was the way to go.

But she wasn't going to fall into the trap of accepting any job that paid poorly. She would need a good salary if she wanted to keep living by herself.

She didn't have to rush. Businesses like A Flower A Day did not sell overnight. She probably had a couple of months at least to make her plans and execute them.

Meanwhile, she wasn't going to breathe a word to Connie. And she would stash away every cent she could.

The sight of a huge bunch of red roses sitting in a bucket in the corner brought Holly up with a jolt. It was a phone order she had taken yesterday afternoon. Not one of her usual clients. A man, who'd promised to pick them up by noon today.

With a sigh, she checked her records, found his name and number, and rang.

An answering machine. Botheration. She hated answering machines.

After leaving a message saying she'd cancelled the order, Holly hung up with a sigh.

What a waste. Such lovely red roses. Expensive, too. He hadn't wanted buds, but open flowers. They wouldn't last more than a few days. Impossible to sell them to anyone else.

And then an idea came to her.

Mrs Crawford. She absolutely loved roses, and she wasn't due to leave on her overseas jaunt till the end of next week. Holly could call them a going-away gift. Plus a thank you for all the times she'd dropped into the shop for a chat and a cuppa.

Nice woman, Mrs Crawford.

If Holly's thoughts drifted momentarily to Richard Crawford, she didn't allow them to linger. Yet there was a time when she'd thought about Mrs Crawford's precious only son quite a bit. She'd even woven wild fantasies around him, about their meeting one day and his being bowled over by her.

Sara was right. Most women were romantic fools!

Flicking her address book over to the Cs, she checked Mrs Crawford's number and rang to make sure she'd be there.

Engaged.

Oh, well, at least she was home.

Holly bent to scoop the roses out of the bucket, wrapped them in some silver paper and tied them with a red bow the same colour as the blooms. She would walk up to Mrs Crawford's house and give them to her personally. It wasn't far and the day was still pleasantly warm. The sun didn't set till late and it was only four-fifteen.

When Holly set out, it never occurred to her that

Richard Crawford might be at his mother's house, even if it *was* the weekend. Mrs Crawford had told her just the other day that she rarely saw her son any more. Apparently, he'd been promoted to CEO at his bank—the youngest ever!—and was more of a work-aholic than ever.

Holly took her time, strolling rather than striding out, enjoying the fresh air and mentally running through her list of things to do in the coming weeks.

Number one. Find a job, preferably in the city.

Number two. Find a flat, preferably near the city.

Number three. Find herself a nice bloke. Preferably one who wore a suit and worked in the city.

Holly pulled a face, then struck number three off her list. That could definitely wait a while.

Regardless of how much of a two-timing rat Dave had turned out to be, he'd still been her boyfriend for over a year and she'd thought she loved him. Had thought he loved her as well. He'd said he did often enough.

Dave's dumping her for Katie had really hurt. Holly's self-esteem was still seriously bruised and she simply wasn't ready to launch herself back into the dating scene.

No, she would concentrate on the two things she could manage. A new job and a new place to live.

Finding a new boyfriend was not on her agenda, not for quite some time.

CHAPTER TWO

"I'M GOING now."

Richard looked up from his laptop, taking a few moments to focus on his mother, who was standing in the study doorway.

"You're looking very smart," he said.

"Thank you," she returned, her hand lifting to lightly touch her exquisitely groomed blonde hair. "Nice of you to notice."

Richard had noticed more than her new hair. She was a totally different woman today, all due to Melvin's arrival in her life, no doubt.

"I'm sorry I'm going out, Richard. But you could have warned me you were dropping by. I haven't seen hide nor hair of you for weeks."

"I've been exceptionally busy," he said, and let her think he meant at the bank.

In reality, he'd been busy, wining and dining his five final selections from Wives Wanted. So far he'd taken out four of them. The first three, on successive Saturday nights. Number four, however, hadn't been able to make it tonight, so he'd taken her out last night.

The evening had proved as disappointing as the three previous dinner dates.

Richard had been going to go into work today—he often worked on a Saturday—but he'd decided at the last moment, and in a spirit of total exasperation, to come and tell his mother about his quest for a new wife via Wives Wanted. He hadn't wanted to discuss his lack of success so far with Reece, and certainly not with Mike, who knew nothing of his wife-finding endeavours. Richard had even brought his laptop with him to show his mother the Wives Wanted database.

But when he'd arrived she'd been so excited about her own date with Melvin that Richard had abandoned that idea.

And now he was glad he had. Because she would never understand why he wanted a marriage of convenience. Not unless he told her the truth about Joanna. And he refused to bare his soul like that.

"I won't be back till late," she said. "We're going to the theatre after dinner. But there's pizza in the freezer. And a nice bottle of wine in the door of the fridge."

"Watch it, Mum. You're in danger of becoming a party girl."

Her face visibly stiffened. "And what if I am?" she snapped. "I think it's about time, don't you?"

Richard was startled by her reaction. Did she think he was criticising her?

Possibly. His father had been a critical bastard. He didn't know how his mother had stood being married to him. It had been bad enough being his son. Richard had learned to survive by excelling in all his endeavours. Difficult for a father to find fault when his son came first at everything.

After his father had died several years back, Richard had expected his mother to marry again. She'd only been in her late fifties at the time. And she was a good-looking woman. Reginald Crawford wouldn't have married any other kind.

But she hadn't married again. She'd lived a very quiet life, playing bowls once a week on ladies day, and bridge on a Tuesday night. Mostly, she stayed at home where she looked after her garden, watched TV and read. Then suddenly, at sixty-five, the travel bug had hit.

Not wanting to explore the world alone, she'd placed an ad on the community bulletin board at the local library for a travelling companion. Melvin had applied a fortnight ago and was found to be very agreeable. A retired surgeon, he was a widower as well. Not a man to let grass grow under his feet, Melvin had already organised their world trip to start this coming Friday.

"I wasn't being critical, Mum," Richard said carefully. "I think what you're doing is fabulous."

"You mean that, Richard? You don't think I'm being foolish?"

"Not at all. But I would like to meet Melvin personally before you leave."

"Check up on him, you mean."

"You are quite a wealthy widow, Mum," he pointed out. "And I'm your only son. I have to keep an eye on my future inheritance, you know."

This was a load of garbage and his mother knew it. Richard had made more money during his relatively short banking career than his father had in forty years of accounting. Reginald Crawford had always been too conservative with his own investments. He gave excellent advice to his clients but couldn't seem to transfer that to his own portfolio.

Still, by the time he'd dropped dead of a heart attack at the age of seventy, he'd been able to leave his wife their Strathfield home, mortgage-free, along with a superannuation policy that would keep her in comfort till her own death. Which hopefully wouldn't be for many years to come.

"You don't have to worry, Richard," she said airily. "Melvin is wealthy in his own right. Far wealthier than me. You should see his home. It's magnificent."

"I'd like to. So how old, exactly, is Melvin, by the way?"

"Sixty-six."

Only one year older than his mother. A good match. Better than with his father, who'd been twelve years older.

"He sounds great. Better not keep him waiting, then. See you in the morning. Have fun," he called after her as she headed for the front door.

He wasn't sure if he heard right, but he was pretty sure she'd muttered, "I intend to."

The front door banged shut, leaving Richard to an empty house, but not an empty mind.

Sixty-six, he mused. Was a man past it at sixty-six?

He doubted it.

One thing he knew for sure. A man wasn't past it at thirty-eight.

Ignoring his growing sexual frustration was proving difficult. His male hormones, now directed where they normally went, had been giving him hassle. Yet there was no hope for them in sight.

It had been six weeks since Reece had put him in touch with the woman who ran Wives Wanted, a

striking-looking but tough lady named Natalie
Fairlane. Six weeks, and he wasn't any closer to finding a woman he wanted to continue dating, with a
view to matrimony.

He returned to his laptop and brought up the photo
of his fifth selection. Another brunette. She was as
beautiful on the screen as the other four had been.
But not one of them had had any effect on him in the
flesh.

There'd been no chemistry, as Reece would have
put it.

They'd all been far too eager to please him as well.
He'd seen the lack of sincerity in their eyes. In a
couple of them, he'd sensed downright greed. They'd
chosen the most expensive food on the menu, *and* the
most expensive wine.

That had been one of his little tests. Letting them
choose the wine, of which he never drank much. No
way did he want any decision he made influenced by
being intoxicated. By the end of dinner, every one of
the four had made it obvious they would be only too
happy to accompany him home to bed.

Richard didn't think he was *that* irresistible to
women.

He was a good-looking enough man. Tall and well
built with strong, masculine features. His steely grey
eyes, however, were on the hard side, he'd been told,
and his manner was formidable.

Forbidding was the word one female employee had
called him.

He supposed his approachability was not helped by
his manner of dress, which could only be described
as ultra conservative. The board at the bank preferred

their CEO to look dignified, rather than sexy. The mainly pinstriped suits he wore *were* expensive, but not trendy. His dark brown hair was kept short. He shaved twice a day when necessary, and his after-shave was discreet. His only jewellery was a gold Rolex watch.

Women did not throw themselves at him as they did at Reece, or even at Mike, whose long-haired bad-boy image seemed to attract a certain type of lady. Probably the ones who liked to live dangerously.

No, Richard didn't think it was his natural sex appeal that had made his dates salivate by the end of each dinner. More likely the unlimited limit on his credit card.

So he'd sent each of them home in a taxi afterwards and returned home alone, where he'd filled in the questionnaire required after each date, ticking the box that said he didn't want to see the lady again and emailing it to Natalie Fairlane.

That was another of Wives Wanted's hard and fast rules. If either person didn't want to see the other again, that was it. *Finis.* If the female attempted fur-ther contact they were struck off the database. If it was the male doing the harassing, he was no longer a client of Wives Wanted.

No doubt this system was much better than going through a normal introduction agency or internet dat-ing service. For one thing, the weirdos were weeded out. Richard knew he'd been put through an extensive background check before being accepted as a client. Ms Fairlane had informed him of this necessary pro-cedure during his personal interview, at the same time assuring him that every girl on the database had been through the same security check, and was exactly what she purported to be.

Physically, at least, that was true. Each girl he'd dated had been as beautiful as they were in their photos.

But more and more Richard was beginning to think Mike was right. Most of these women were gold-diggers. Maybe Reece had just been damned lucky with Alanna.

But, having paid his money, he was determined to see the list through before giving up on the idea. He was planning to contact his fifth choice on the list when the front doorbell rang.

"Who on earth?" he muttered, standing up and making his way across the study and into the main hallway.

The Crawford family home was not a mansion, but it was spacious and solid, with the kind of character associated with houses built in Sydney's better suburbs in the nineteen thirties. Tall ceilings, decorative cornices, wide verandas, and wonderful stained-glass panels on either side of the front door.

As Richard strode towards the door the sunshine filtered through those panels, making coloured patterns on the polished wooden floor, then on the pale grey trousers he was wearing.

Wrenching the door open, the first thing he saw was a huge bunch of red roses. Followed by a face peeping around them.

A female face.

"Oh," the owner of the face exclaimed, her big brown eyes widening. "I wasn't expecting... I didn't realise..." She grimaced, then drew herself up straight, holding the roses at her waist, a bit like a nervous bride. "Sorry. I don't usually babble. Is Mrs Crawford home?"

"I'm afraid not," Richard replied, whilst thinking to himself that he already liked this girl much better than any on that damned database.

Yet she wasn't nearly as beautiful. Or as well groomed.

Her long dark brown hair was somewhat wind-blown. And there wasn't a scrap of make-up on her oval-shaped face. Her outfit of a wraparound floral skirt and simple blue T-shirt shouted department-store wear, not designer label.

But, for all that, he couldn't take his eyes off her.

"My mother's gone out for the day," he heard himself say whilst his hormone-sharpened gaze took in her ringless left hand.

Not that that meant much. She could still be living with someone, or be dating some commitment-phobic fool who hadn't snapped her up off the single shelf. That was one thing each of his Saturday night dates had bewailed over the dinner table. How many men these days didn't want to become husbands and fathers.

"She won't be back till very late tonight," he added. "Can I help you perhaps? I'm her son. Richard."

"Yes, I know that," she said, then looked flustered by her admission.

"In that case, you have the advantage on me," he replied smoothly. "Have we met before?" He knew damned well they hadn't. He would have remembered.

"No. Not really. I mean, I saw you at your wife's funeral. I…um…I did the flowers.''

She seemed embarrassed at having to mention the occasion. On his part, Richard was pleased that he could be reminded of that day without too much pain.

Yes, he was definitely ready to move on.

"I see,'' he said as he wondered how old she might be. Late twenties perhaps?

"Please forgive me if I say I don't recall noticing the flowers that day,'' he said ruefully. "But I'm sure they were lovely. I presume these are for my mother?'' he said, nodding towards the roses she was holding. Probably from crafty old Melvin.

"Yes. It's a phone order which was never picked up today. I know how much Mrs Crawford likes flow-ers—roses particularly—and I thought she might like them. I realise she's going away next Friday but they won't last that long.''

"You know about Mum's trip?''

"Yes, she…um…told me about it herself last week. And about her new doctor friend. Melvin, isn't it? It's a pity, really. If she'd still been looking for a travelling companion, I might have applied for the job myself.''

Richard was taken aback. "Why on earth would a girl like you want to travel anywhere with a woman old enough to be her grandmother?''

She shrugged. "Just to escape, I guess.''

If she'd said to travel the world on the cheap, Richard might have understood. But to escape screamed something much more emotional. So did the bleakness that had suddenly filled her big brown eyes.

"Escape from what?" he probed gently. "Are you in some kind of trouble? Man trouble perhaps?"

She wasn't a raving beauty but, the more Richard looked at her, the more attractive he found her. She had lovely eyes, a sexy mouth and a fabulous figure.

He fancied her. Other men would, too.

She shook her head. "No, no, nothing like that. Here. Give these to your mother when she gets home, will you? Tell her they're from Holly. Just say they're a little thank-you present for all the times she's dropped in at the shop for a chat. She's a really sweet lady, your mum."

Richard refused to take the flowers. "Why don't you come inside and arrange them in a vase for her?" he suggested before she could cut and run. Any girl who wanted to get away that badly sounded like a girl who wasn't very happy with her life at the moment. If she did have a boyfriend, he sure as hell wasn't doing the right thing by her.

She blinked, then stared at him.

Richard had no idea what she was thinking, which in itself was as intriguing and attractive as she was. He'd been able to read those women he'd taken to dinner like an open book.

"Look," he said with what he hoped wasn't a "big bad wolf" smile. "I have absolutely no talent with flower arranging, whereas you'd have to be an expert. So what do you say, Holly? You do the flowers and I'll make us both some coffee. I'm good at coffee."

She still hesitated, making Richard wonder if he was easier to read than she was. Maybe she could see his intentions in his eyes. Not that they were evil intentions. He just wanted the opportunity to learn a bit more about her. He wasn't planning to seduce her.

Not yet, anyway.

"Who knows?" he said lightly. "Maybe Melvin will prove to be an utter bore and Mum will come home early, still looking for that travelling companion."

She laughed. "I don't think there's much chance of that happening, and you know it. You're just being nice, like your mum."

Nice. She thought he was being nice.

Richard's conscience stirred. But he swiftly put aside any qualms.

Faint heart never won fair lady.

"We will adjourn to the kitchen," he said before she had time to think up some excuse to flee. "This way." And taking her arm, he ushered her inside.

CHAPTER THREE

"I'LL JUST get you some scissors from Dad's study first," Richard said as he closed the door behind them.

When he abandoned Holly's elbow to walk up the hallway into a room on the right, a small shudder of relief rippled through her.

Having Richard Crawford answer the doorbell had been a real shock. She'd been expecting his mother.

But there he'd been, as large as life, and more handsome than ever, even more so than eighteen months earlier, when she'd first seen him. Gone were the dark rings under his eyes and that pale, haunted expression.

How wicked Holly had felt, finding him so attractive at his wife's funeral. The man had been in deep mourning, for pity's sake, shattered by the tragic death of the beautiful woman he'd married two years before. She knew from Mrs Crawford how much her son had adored his beautiful Joanna.

But all Holly had been able to think of whenever she'd snuck a peek at Richard Crawford that day was how impressive he looked in black. Her eyes had returned repeatedly to him during the service. She'd even envied his dead wife for at least having known the love of a man like that. Holly had been feeling extra lonely and vulnerable at the time, her father having passed away only a few months earlier.

For several weeks afterwards, she'd dreamt up all sorts of romantic scenarios where the handsome widower and herself would meet. But, strangely, not one had involved his being home, alone, when she delivered flowers to his mother's house. Neither did any scenario anticipate how intimidating she might actually find him in the flesh.

Intimidating. But still disturbingly sexy.

When he'd taken her arm just now, she'd felt almost paralysed by his touch, and his commanding physical presence.

Richard Crawford was a big man. Very tall and broad-shouldered, with large hands and firm fingers, and a manner to match.

She was grateful not to be in his presence at the moment. It gave her time to regather her composure.

But he'd be back any moment.

When he didn't return after a couple of excruciatingly long minutes, an agitated Holly tiptoed along the floral carpet runner till she could see into the room he'd entered.

His father's study, he'd said it was.

The room resembled more of an English gentleman's club than a study, with wood panelled walls, rich maroon velvet curtains and large leather armchairs. The desk Richard Crawford was rummaging through was a huge mahogany antique, which looked at odds with the very modern laptop sitting down one end.

Which was plugged in and on, she noted.

That explained the engaged signal when she'd telephoned. He'd been working. His mother said he'd become a workaholic.

But what was he doing here when Mrs Crawford was out? And why was he dressed the way he was, in smart grey trousers and a crisp blue business shirt? Add a tie and jacket, he'd be ready for the office.

Not many Australian men would be dressed as he was on a summer Saturday afternoon. Most would be lounging around in shorts and thongs.

Dave would have.

"Shouldn't be much longer," he said with a quick, upwards glance at her from under his darkly beetled brows. "I know they're here somewhere."

"That's all right," she replied. "Take your time."

He smiled at her. Not a wide, warm, infectious grin that had been Dave's trademark. A rather restrained smile.

Richard Crawford was different from Dave all round.

Of course, he came from a different world from Dave. A more cultured, educated world. And he was a lot older. In his late thirties at least.

Holly frowned at this last thought. Normally, she wouldn't look twice at any man his age. She was only twenty-six. All her boyfriends to date had always been around her own age, give or take a year.

Dave, the rat, had been exactly the same age.

Holly's thoughts turned bitter as they always did when she thought of Dave. Her only comfort was her recent realisation that she hadn't been truly in love with the creep. She'd just been fooled by his flattering ways. He was a charmer, was Dave.

A sales rep for a company that made cheap cards, he'd talked her into stocking his entire range within five minutes of walking into the shop. Talked himself into her life and her bed a week later.

Not that he was all that good in bed. But then, neither was she.

Dave had insisted she was, of course. He'd never stopped paying her compliments. Holly had come to the somewhat depressing conclusion since the demise of their relationship that he'd probably lied to her about everything, but especially that.

The man was a liar and a louse. Lots of men were these days.

But not this man, she thought as Richard Crawford looked up from the final desk drawer in triumph, a pair of scissors in his left hand. He was a man of honour. And depth. According to his mother, he hadn't even looked at another woman since his wife's death. What Holly wouldn't give to be loved the way he'd loved his wife.

"Thought I'd never find the darned things," he said as he rejoined her in the hallway. "The kitchen's down here," he added, then took her elbow again.

Holly shivered when another jolt of electricity shot up her arm, the same as the first time.

"It's cool inside these old houses, isn't it?" he said, thankfully misinterpreting her reaction as he ushered her down the hallway.

"Very," she agreed. But she didn't feel cool. Suddenly, she felt very warm indeed.

"Your mother didn't say you were staying with her," she began babbling again. "That's why I was so surprised when you answered the door."

"Just popped in to visit for the weekend," he explained, steering her into a large, homey kitchen with a dark slate floor and lots of pale wooden benchtops. "Didn't know Mum would be going out. Mmm, I wonder where she keeps the vases?" he said, stopping in the middle of the room to survey the U-shaped array of cupboards. "You wouldn't happen to know, would you?"

Holly tried to will her heart to slow down. Useless exercise. It kept pounding away behind her ribs, regardless.

"Sorry," she said with a stiff little smile. "I've delivered flowers here before, but I've never been inside. I'll just put these in the sink and help you look."

"Good idea."

She was still half filling the smaller of the two sinks with water when he said, "Bingo! Vases galore down in here!"

Snapping off the tap, she turned to find him hunched down in front of one of the lower cupboards, the fine wool of his grey trousers stretched tight across his buttocks and thighs. His shirt was having a similar problem as it tried to house his broad shoulders and back.

Holly swallowed. This was crazy. She'd never been the sort of girl to ogle men's bodies. She'd never cared if her past boyfriends had muscles or not. She'd once filled in a survey in a women's magazine asking what it was that first attracted her to a man and she'd put eyes. Dave had had twinkly blue eyes to go with his winning smiles.

This memory had just entered her head when Richard Crawford's head turned and two wintry grey eyes lifted to hers.

A strangely erotic shiver ran deep inside her.

"Plenty of different sizes here," he said. "What do you prefer?"

It was testimony to her shocking state of mind that her thoughts immediately jumped to the size, not of the various vases on offer, but of the part of his anatomy that was thankfully hidden by his squatting position.

"I'll have that glass one there on the right," she said. How she didn't blush when he handed it to her, she had no idea.

Actually arranging the flowers was a blessing. She could concentrate on what she did best, and not even look at him as he busied himself making some truly mouth-watering coffee. Not the instant kind. The kind that percolated.

Unfortunately, he finished his job first, after which he settled on one of the kitchen stools to watch her work. She knew it was probably her over-heated imagination, but Holly could have sworn his eyes were more on her than the flowers.

"You really are good at that," he said.

"It's my job," she returned, pleased to hear her voice didn't betray her inner turmoil.

"Have you always worked with flowers?"

"All my life. My dad was a florist. He trained me."

"Was?"

"He died just over two years back. A stroke."

"I'm sorry. That must have been tough on you and your family."

"My mother's dead too," she told him. "She died when I was just a toddler. But Dad married again when I was sixteen. I have a stepmother and a stepsister, Katie, who's two years younger than I am."

Holly refrained from blurting out that both females were wicked witches, especially Katie. She didn't want to sound like a whinger. She'd cried out her sob story to his mother, though, when she'd come into the shop one day, soon after Dave had dumped her.

"How old are you?" he asked.

"What? Oh, I'm twenty-six."

"*That* young," he said in a way that indicated he had thought her older.

Holly's already battered self-esteem took this added blow quite badly. All of a sudden, tears welled up in her eyes. Thank God she wasn't facing his way, giving her the opportunity to blink them away and gather herself once more.

But the incident put a stop to her foolishly getting excited at being alone with Richard Crawford. Which she had been. No use pretending she hadn't. She'd been thinking all sorts of silly things in the back of her head, such as he'd been looking at her with admiration and asking her questions because he was attracted to her.

God, she was laughable. If and when Richard Crawford started dating again, it would be with a woman like his wife. A sophisticated stunner. Holly had seen a framed photo of Joanna Crawford at the funeral. Talk about gorgeous! She'd also been supersmart. A literary agent, working for an international publisher whose head office was in New York. Mrs Crawford senior had told Holly all about her daughter-in-law-to-be when she'd dropped into the shop to select a mother-of-the-groom corsage the day before the wedding.

What interest could Richard Crawford possibly have in a simple girl who arranged flowers for a living, was passably attractive at best and had never been further from Sydney than the Central Coast?

CHAPTER FOUR

RICHARD could not believe how much he was enjoying just sitting there in his mother's kitchen, watching this lovely girl put flowers in a vase.

And she *was* lovely.

He'd now had the opportunity to study her at length, noting the perfect shape of her profile, the lushness of her lips, the slenderness of her neck and arms. His eyes followed each graceful movement as she snipped the end of a rose, then lifted it into place in the tall vase.

Her figure continued to entrance him as well. Although only of average height, she was beautifully in proportion with the hourglass shape he preferred in a woman. Her breasts looked naturally full, with no artificial enhancement. Her bra was of the thin variety, her nipples clearly outlined against the soft blue material of the T-shirt.

He wondered momentarily if they were erect because she was cold, or because she was as sexually aware of him as he was of her. He had no way of knowing. She wasn't in any way flirtatious, which he liked. Joanna had been a terrible flirt.

But it would be good to have a sign that the attraction he felt was mutual. Were hard nipples a reliable sign?

''Are you still cold?'' he asked, and watched as she turned an annoyingly unreadable face his way.

46

"Cold?" she repeated blankly. "No. Not really."

Mmm. Maybe her nipples were always like that. His flesh tightened at the thought.

"I don't think I should put any more of the roses in this vase," she announced, tipping her head charmingly to one side as she surveyed the arrangement of richly coloured blooms. "It's perfectly balanced right now. Any more would spoil it."

"You're right," he agreed. "It's perfect."

Just like you, he thought, and wondered how soon he could ask her out. Obviously, not till he found out her boyfriend situation.

The phone began to ring, which annoyed him no end. For one thing, it was out in the hallway and not in the kitchen.

"Won't be a moment," he said. "Why don't you find another smaller vase for the rest of the roses whilst I'm gone?" he suggested. He knew how awkward it could be, standing round at a loose end whilst people chatted on the phone. He didn't want her finding any excuse to leave.

It was his mother on the phone, being uncharacteristically but blessedly brief, allowing him to get back to Holly before she'd finished doing the second vase.

"That was Mum. I've been invited to go to lunch at Melvin's place tomorrow. Sorry, but I'd say the travelling companion job has definitely been taken," he finished, thinking of how eager his mother had been to get back to the new man in her life.

Holly gave him a wan little smile. "I never imagined anything else. Well, I'll be off, then, Mr Crawford. I don't think I'll stay for coffee, but thank you for the offer."

Richard was taken aback. Had he been overly optimistic, hoping the chemistry he'd been feeling was mutual? Maybe he'd lost the knack of knowing when a woman fancied him and when she didn't. Yet he'd been sure he'd sensed something in Holly's body language whenever their eyes had met.

Maybe she was nervous of him. He knew he sometimes made women nervous.

"You have something you have to go home for?" he asked, and made eye contact with her again. This time he saw what he hoped he'd see. That flicker. That spark.

"There's always work to do when you run a business," she replied.

"Please don't go," he said with a smile that would have rivalled Reece's on the charm meter. "I was really enjoying your company."

She blinked. "Really?"

"Really. And whilst we're having our coffee, I want you to tell me what it is you thought you needed to escape from?"

It took him a good half an hour to get all the details out of her—and to get her to call him Richard. But once the full picture of Holly's position was clear, he felt furious on her behalf. The poor girl. Betrayed by her boyfriend with her stepsister. Betrayed by her stepmother with the business.

And no one to stand up for her!

No wonder she wanted to escape. Why would she want to stay with a family who clearly didn't love her? Or continue to work hard for no rewards? Such a situation was not only unjust, it was untenable.

"You could have contested your father's will, you know," he pointed out sternly.

Her velvety eyes showed surprise. "Really?"

"Yes, really. And it's not too late. If you like, I could put you in touch with a good solicitor."

"No," she said, pulling a face and shaking her head. "No, it's too late for that. Besides, Dad warned me never to take anyone to court. He said the only ones who got rich from suing people were the lawyers."

Richard had to smile. That opinion was widely held by lots of people, but not true in the circles he moved in.

"That depends on the lawyer," he said, "but it's your call."

She sighed. "If only Dad had changed his will and left me a controlling percentage of the business. I know that's what he intended to do. But, of course, he wasn't expecting to have a stroke at fifty-five, no more than my mother expected to be knocked down by a bus at twenty-five."

"You seem to have had some rotten luck in life, Holly."

"Things haven't been all that easy lately," she admitted.

"Why don't you tell your stepmother and stepsister to go to hell?"

"Trust me. I intend to one day. When the time is right. My plan is to stay on where I am till I've found a new job and a new place to live. That way I can go on living in the flat above the shop for nothing, and save some more money. I think I should keep my big mouth shut till I'm ready to move out, don't you?"

"No, I don't. I think you should tell them both exactly what you think of them right now," he ground out. "Along with your bastard of an ex-boyfriend!"

How he would have liked the opportunity to tell Joanna what he thought of her! Instead, he'd had to grieve for her with all that bitterness building up within him. Bitterness and bewilderment. Her betrayal still ate away at him, whenever he thought about it. Why *had* she been unfaithful to him? He'd thought she loved him. She'd said she did. And acted as though she did.

But she couldn't have. Which meant she must have married him for his money. And the prestige of being Mrs Richard Crawford. She'd certainly loved their multimillion-dollar home at Palm Beach, and the wardrobe of designer clothes she'd constantly added to. Joanna had always claimed you could never wear the same dress twice when mixing with the high echelons of Sydney society. Not a weekend had gone by that they weren't going to some fancy dinner party, or gallery opening, or the races. Or all three.

Richard hadn't been enamoured with that life, but he would have done anything to make her happy. Love really did make a man blind. Women too, he supposed. Clearly, Holly hadn't been able to see her ex-boyfriend's true nature. Reading between the lines, it was obvious that this Dave had thought Holly owned the flower shop, and had dropped her when he'd discovered it was the stepmother—hence the stepsister—who'd inherited everything.

"That's all very well for you to say, Richard," Holly pointed out, an indignant colour creeping into her cheeks. "You have a great job, according to your mother, and a great place to live, no doubt. You'd never have to live in a crummy bedsit, which is what I'd be relegated to if I shouted my mouth off prematurely. Connie would have me tossed out in the street.''

Richard almost offered her free room and board at his penthouse right then and there. His room, preferably.

For a few perverse seconds, he indulged in the erotic fantasy of taking Holly back home with him tonight, of his taking off all her clothes and taking her to bed for the rest of the weekend.

But that was all it was. A fantasy.

He could see she wasn't the kind of girl who jumped into bed with men at the drop of a hat. Easy women, Richard realised, behaved very differently from Holly. They flirted, for starters. Fluttered their eyelashes and stroked male egos with constant verbal flattery. Joanna had been brilliant at that, always telling him what an incredible lover he was.

How many other men, he thought bitterly, had she said the same thing to?

Richard wondered if Holly was still in love with that bastard who'd dumped her for her stepsister. Love didn't die just because someone had done you wrong. Richard knew that for a fact.

Still, he was now convinced that romantic love was not the best foundation for choosing a wife. Besides being based on emotion, it was a poor judge of character.

Joanna's true character remained a mystery to him, whereas he already knew Holly to be sweet and soft, without a greedy bone in her body.

She was also wonderfully vulnerable right now.
A quotation of Shakespeare's popped into his mind.

There is a tide in the affairs of men,
Which, taken at the flood, leads on to fortune;
Omitted, all the voyage of their life
Is bound in shallows and in miseries.
On such a full sea are we now afloat,
And we must take the current when it serves,
Or lose our ventures.

Richard decided then and there not to let the grass
grow under his feet where Holly was concerned. It
was clear he probably wasn't going to find a wife
from Wives Wanted. Which meant he had to find one
the old-fashioned way.

"You're right," he said. "There's nothing to be
gained by shouting your mouth off. Far better to out-
wit your enemies. I do that at the bank all the time.
So tell me, dear Holly, are you doing anything tonight? If you're not, how about letting me take you
somewhere nice for dinner?"

CHAPTER FIVE

HOLLY just stared at Richard.

"I've shocked you," he said.

What an understatement!

She continued to stare at him, her head spinning.

"Is there any reason why you can't come to dinner with me?" he went on. "Have you found a new boyfriend since Dave?"

"Heavens, no!"

"Then what's the problem? You don't like my company, is that it?"

"No, no, that's not it at all!" she blurted out before gaining control of her tongue. "I um...I'm just surprised, that's all."

Floored was a better word. Why on earth would a man like Richard Crawford want to take a girl like her out to dinner? She wasn't a total dimwit where men were concerned, even if Katie said she was.

It came to her then that maybe Mrs Crawford might have been wrong about her son not looking at another woman since his wife died. It had been eighteen months, after all. Eighteen months was a long time for a man of Richard's age—of any age, for that matter—to go without a woman.

Could sex be the answer to the puzzle of his asking her out?

Holly knew she was a pretty enough girl, with nice eyes and the kind of figure men had always been attracted to. She had never had any trouble getting boy-friends. The trouble had always been keeping them.

Not that Richard Crawford would want to be her boyfriend. The idea was ludicrous! He might, how-ever, be on the lookout for a one-night stand. A lot of men expected an after-dinner thank-you of sex these days.

Not that he would pressure her for it. Holly knew he wasn't that kind of man. But he was still a man, a man in his physical prime, a man with cold, sexy eyes and a great body and probably more sexual know-how than any man Holly had ever been with.

So why wasn't she jumping at the chance? Hadn't she fantasised about just this kind of scenario?

Actually, no, she hadn't. Her fantasies had been of his falling in love with her at first sight and wanting her till death did them part. Holly always gave her fantasies a happily-ever-after ending, not a ''thank you for the sex but I don't want to see you any more'' ending.

''What's worrying you?'' Richard asked. ''We're just talking dinner here.''

''Are we?'' she snapped before she could snatch the words back.

His eyes rounded slightly. Then he nodded. ''Yes,'' he said. ''We are.''

Holly sighed. But was it with relief, or disappoint-ment?

Still, she hesitated. Why, she wasn't sure. Maybe because she feared having a taste of something that she'd always secretly craved, but which had previ-ously been well beyond her reach, even for a few short hours. How would she feel when the evening was over and she never saw or heard from Richard again?

At the same time, how would she feel if she said no and was left wondering what even having dinner with a man like Richard Crawford was like? He was sure to take her to a top restaurant in town, somewhere elegant and expensive.

Dave had been the king of the take-away meal. Even then, she'd paid for most of them. Holly knew she wouldn't have to pay for a single thing tonight. Except perhaps emotionally.

But the temptation was too great. "All right," she said, a zing of adrenaline sending her heart into a gallop with her surrender.

"Wonderful," he said, and glanced at the gold watch on his wrist. "It's half-past five. Shall I pick you up at, say…seven-thirty?"

"Seven-thirty will be fine," she said, doing her best to sound all cool and sophisticated, now that she'd accepted his invitation.

"How are you getting home?" he asked. "I didn't see a car outside when I opened the door."

She didn't have a car. She had a van, which belonged to the business. "It's just a short walk."

"I'll walk you home," he offered.

"That's not necessary." She wanted to run home. She'd need every second of the time left to be ready. She'd have to wash her hair and blow-dry it, and do her nails and Lord knew what else.

"I'll walk you home," he repeated, his gaze as uncompromising as his voice.

My, but he could be masterful when he wanted to be. Holly wondered if he was just as masterful in bed. Not that she'd find out. Richard had said to-night was just dinner and he struck Holly as a man of his word. Darn it. Despite never having been a one-night-stand kind of girl, there were always exceptions to the rule, and, for Richard Crawford, Holly might have made an exception.

The Crawford house was on top of a hill, about half a kilometre from Strathfield railway station. Holly's shop was in a small block of three not far from the station, a reasonably good position for pass-ing trade. There was a café, a hairdresser and her flower shop, right on the corner, all ancient brick buildings with awnings over the pavements and a sec-ond floor upstairs.

"Where does your stepmother live?" Richard asked as they walked down the hill together.

"About a kilometre away," she replied. "On the other side of the railway."

"So how long have you lived in the flat over the shop?"

"I moved in not long after Dad died."

"And why was that? Couldn't stand the wicked witches any longer?"

She smiled. That was what Sara had called them. "Partly," she agreed. "But I also felt closer to Dad there."

"Understandable," Richard sympathised.

"I dare say Connie will sell Dad's house too, if and when the business sells. She's always wanted to live on the North Shore."

"So how much would the business be worth?" he asked.

"I'm not sure. I was too angry to ask Connie what

price she'd put on it. But over a million at least. It's a freehold property.''

"That's a lot of money to give up without a fight, Holly.''

"Yes, I know that. But it isn't the money so much as the business itself. Dad loved it. And I love it. I love working with flowers, you see. It makes me feel good. Flowers make people happy.''

"I still think you should take your stepmother to court. The shop should be yours. It's not fair.''

"Life's not always fair, Richard. Surely you must appreciate that,'' she added, then wished she hadn't. A sidewards glance saw that the muscles in his face and neck had tightened.

"You're right,'' he bit out. "It isn't always fair, but you can't allow the injustices of life to beat you down. You have to fight back.''

"I *am* fighting back,'' she countered, stung that he might think her weak. "In my own way.''

He smiled over at her. "A quiet achiever,'' he said. "Yes, I can see you are that, Holly. I apologise. I have no right to criticise. Or force my opinion down your throat. What's your second name, by the way?''

"Greenaway.''

"An apt name, for a florist.''

"You're not the first person to say that.''

"Sorry again. Is it a sore point?''

"No. Not really. But Dave used to tease me about it.''

"The dastardly Dave. God help me from ever being like him.''

"You're not. Don't worry.''

They walked on, Holly increasing the pace a little.

"I haven't walked down this road in years," Richard said as they finally reached the front of A Flower A Day, the large FOR SALE sign even more glaring from the outside. "I used to catch the train to and from high school so I came past here every day. I actually bought some flowers in here for Mum one year when I was about seventeen. Did your dad own it back then?"

"I'm not sure," Holly said as she retrieved the key from where she always hid it behind a drainpipe. "How long ago was that?"

"Twenty-one years."

"I think so. He bought it when he was about thirty. Look, I'd better get myself inside if you want me to be ready in time. I'm a female, you know."

"I did notice that," he said, and suddenly his grey eyes weren't cold at all. They travelled slowly over her body, telling her in no uncertain terms that he did find her attractive. *Very* attractive.

But as quickly as his gaze had heated up, it cooled, making her wonder if that imagination of hers had been playing tricks on her again.

"You'd better give me your phone number, in case I'm delayed for any reason," he went on. "I'm not dressed for dinner. I'll have to dash home and change."

Holly almost panicked at this point. Not dressed for dinner? He looked fine to her. What was he going to change into, a dinner suit? She didn't have a lot of seriously dressy clothes in her wardrobe. None, actually, now that she came to think of it.

"Where's home?" she asked as she pushed the shop door open, her mind busily searching her wardrobe for possibilities. If only she had one of those little black dresses, the kind that took a girl anywhere. But the only black outfit she owned was the suit she wore to funerals. Besides being very tailored, black was not her colour.

"East Balmain," he replied as he followed her inside the shop. "I bought a new apartment on the point there a few weeks ago."

"Oh, right," she said, not really listening to him. What on earth was she going to wear?

"I shouldn't be late," he went on, "but give me your number, just in case."

"What? Oh, yes, my phone number." She hurried over to the long table that served as a reception desk and work station, picking up one of the business cards from the stack that sat in a plastic stand on the corner.

"Jot down your cell-phone number on it as well," he said before she could hand it to him. "You must have a cell phone," he added when she lifted blank eyes to him.

"Yes, but..." She was about to say why would he want that when she wouldn't be seeing him again after tonight. But then she thought, why be so negative? He might be at a loose end another night and think of her. Who knew?

"Okay," she agreed, picking up a Biro off the table and writing the number on the back of the business card.

"See you at seven-thirty," he said after she handed him the card.

"Could you make it closer to eight?"

He nodded. "Eight it is, then." And he was gone. Holly watched him stride past the shop window on

his way up the hill, watched him and tried to come
to terms with the fact that in two short hours Richard
Crawford would return to take her out. Richard
Crawford. Mrs Crawford's son. The CEO of a bank.
A man, not only of impeccable background and
breeding, but impeccable dress sense.

"Oh, hell," she squawked, and dashed for the
stairs.

CHAPTER SIX

BY FIVE to eight, Holly's nerves had reached lift-off.

She'd done the best she could with her appearance, but typically, when you were in a state, things went wrong from the start. She'd spent far too long trying to put together the semblance of a classy outfit, discarding everything in her wardrobe till finally she'd come across an outfit she'd bought for a wedding at least four years back, a three-piece number in pale blue.

It had a straight, calf-length skirt, a beaded camisole with a highish round neckline and a filmy overjacket with three-quarter sleeves that shouted "wedding guest" at her when she put it on, but at least it didn't look cheap. If she'd had the time, she might have taken the hem up on the skirt, but an hour had skipped by before she could blink. It had been seven by the time she'd jumped into the shower.

Putting her hair up, as she'd mentally planned, had been out of the question. She always took ages to do it that way. So she'd blow-dried it dead straight, then hurriedly put the sides up with some clear combs.

By then it had been seven thirty-five, leaving only twenty-five minutes to do her make-up and nails. Not nearly enough time to do a good job. In the end, she'd settled for a fairly natural look with her face. Fortunately, she could get away without foundation, having clear skin that always tanned to a nice honey colour by the end of summer. A hint of blue eye shadow, a few strokes of black mascara, some coral lipstick and her face was done.

Her nails had presented a real problem, however. You needed steady hands to do your nails properly. Hers had been shaking like a leaf. After a couple of attempts Holly had given up, wiping the smudged coral polish off and leaving her nails totally au naturel. Fortunately, she always took care of her nails. She had to, with her job, so they were always neat and clean and well filed to a nice shape.

But she wasn't happy. She'd wanted to be perfect.

A swift glance at her bedside clock now showed two minutes to eight. She almost wished Richard would be late. She still had to put some perfume on, plus her earrings, if she could decide which ones looked best. The pearl drops, or the gold. She held a different one up against each ear but wasn't sure. Neither looked quite right, perhaps because the camisole was beaded.

The shop doorbell ringing made up her mind for her. Neither.

"Oh, God," she muttered as she shoved her feet into the ivory high heels that had been bought to go with the outfit, and which hadn't seen the light of day since. The same with the ivory evening bag. Sweeping it up from her bed, she headed for the stairs, totally forgetting the perfume till she reached the bottom. Too late, then. She could see Richard standing outside the shop window, not wearing a dinner suit, but looking sensational all the same in a superbly tailored black suit with one of those collarless shirts underneath. A steely grey, it was, the same colour as his eyes.

Taking a deep breath, she plastered a smile on her face and swept the door open.

Richard hadn't known quite what to expect. He knew girls of Holly's age tended to dress sexily these days, especially on a Saturday night. He'd seen them around town, wearing short tight skirts and even skimpier tops. Anticipating this, he'd teamed his new black suit with one of the trendier shirts Joanna had bought for him, and which he'd never worn. He hadn't wanted to look like an old fuddy-duddy next to his twenty-six-year-old date. It had been different when he'd taken the women out from Wives Wanted. They'd all been older.

When Holly emerged onto the pavement, dressed elegantly and very modestly, Richard breathed a sigh of relief. With that delicious body of hers nicely covered up, he wouldn't suffer too much physical torture this evening.

When he'd been showering earlier, his aroused body had regretted his earlier reassurance that he would keep his hands off. A lot of people went to bed on their first date these days, he tried telling himself. It wasn't frowned upon, nor seen as evidence of loose morals.

In truth, Richard liked it that Holly wasn't a flirt or a sexpot. As he watched her lock the door then turn to face him he decided he couldn't have his cake and eat it too.

"You look lovely," he said. "Blue suits you."

"Thank you. You do, too. I mean…you look very handsome."

Her blush was delightful, and perversely provocative. When the time came, he was going to thoroughly enjoy taking this innocent to bed.

And she *was* a relative innocent. Not a virgin, of course. He understood Holly had undoubtedly slept with Dave, and probably other boyfriends over the years. Girls who looked like Holly didn't stay virgins for long.

But she lacked the kind of sexual confidence that had oozed from Joanna. That was why Holly didn't flirt. Or dress to tease.

More and more Richard believed he'd found the right girl to marry. All he had to do now was make sure Holly would say yes, when he asked her. Which meant he had to make her fall in love with him. Or think she had.

The restaurant he'd chosen to take her to tonight was a good start, Richard reasoned as he opened the passenger door of his navy BMW. Nothing impressed women as much as an intimate dinner by candlelight in a five-star establishment. This place had certainly impressed the first of his dates from Wives Wanted.

High up in a building overlooking Circular Quay, Hal's Hideaway restaurant had everything. A magnificent view. A relaxing ambience. Discreet, but prompt service. A wonderfully diverse menu. And a cellar to die for.

"So where are you taking me?" she asked once they were on their way.

"To a restaurant in town, overlooking the harbour."

"What kind of food do they serve? I mean, is it Italian, or Chinese, or what?"

"The cuisine is international."

"Oh, dear, it sounds posh."

He smiled. "It is posh. But you don't have to worry. You look absolutely gorgeous."

"I look like I'm going to a wedding."

"Not at all. You look divine."

She laughed. "You know how to make a girl feel good, I'll say that for you, Richard."

He aimed to make her feel even better by the time the night was out. They chatted away amiably during the twenty-minute drive into the city, but by the time he'd parked the car in one of the spots especially reserved for Hal's clientele, then steered her up to the restaurant, she'd gone all quiet and stiff.

"I've never been to a place like this," Holly whispered after they'd been settled by the maître d' at one of the best tables in the house. Next to one of the wide windows that gave an uninterrupted view of the opera house and the bridge. "I won't have a clue what to order," she added with worry in her voice as she glanced at the menu, which was, admittedly, a bit daunting.

"Would you like me to order for you?" he offered. "I've been here before and I have a pretty good idea what the chef does best."

Her eyes showed relief. "Yes. Yes, I think that would be a very good idea. I'm not a fussy eater. I'm sure I'd like anything you like."

Let's hope so, Richard thought privately as his flesh stirred and his mind filled with the things he'd like to do to her.

"What about the wine list?" he went on. "Is there anything on it you especially prefer?" And he held it out to her.

When she took it, he noticed that she didn't have painted nails. Neither was she wearing jewellery, or perfume. Whilst this pleased him tonight—her lack of feminine artifice showed she didn't have any secret agenda where he was concerned—Richard was already looking forward to the nights when she would wear nothing else for him *but* perfume. She would look magnificent naked, he thought as his eyes surreptitiously raked over her. He could see her now, stretched out on top of his blue satin quilt, her dark hair spread over his pillows, her soft brown eyes slumberous from his lovemaking.

"I can't believe these prices," she said as she studied the wine list, a frown on her pretty forehead. "I do like wine, but I always buy it at a discount liquor shop. I've never paid more than twelve dollars for a bottle. I know they bump up the prices in these fancy restaurants, but there isn't a bottle here under seventy-five dollars. Most are over a hundred! Some of them are over two hundred!"

One of which his first date from Wives Wanted had chosen, Richard recalled.

"They're specialist wines," he told her, "from wineries all over the world. You won't find them on any shelf in liquor shops, especially discount ones."

She handed him back the list. "I'm sorry, Richard, but I wouldn't feel comfortable drinking wine at fifteen dollars a glass. That's outrageous. No wonder they didn't put any prices on the meal menu. I'll bet the food here costs a bomb as well."

Richard felt gratified that his character assessment of Holly had been correct. She was nothing like Joanna, or any of the women he'd dated from Wives Wanted. ''Why don't you let me worry about the prices, and the choices? You just sit back and enjoy.''

She opened her mouth, possibly to protest further, but then closed it again with a resigned shrug. ''All right. I guess I can manage to ignore my suburban mentality for one evening. It will be something to tell my grandchildren about one day.''

Richard smiled. He could live with that, provided they were his grandchildren as well.

The evening progressed nicely from that point. Holly seemed to relax—even if Richard didn't entirely. Difficult to be totally relaxed when he felt so aroused. But he discovered lots more to like about Holly during their four-course meal and almost two bottles of wine. She was remarkably well read, and even played bridge, which would make her popular with his mother. Apparently, her father had taught her and they had played together at a local bridge club. She also liked to keep fit and went to a gym three or four nights a week.

Richard thought of the many hours he'd spent in the private executive gym at the bank since he'd buried Joanna, working out his bitterness.

In future, he would work out for a different reason. To look good for this delightful girl. And to be extra fit. He wanted his body to be able to keep up with his mind.

And his mind had him making love to Holly for hours on end.

Midnight rolled around before he knew it. The

waiter offered them a complimentary cognac to follow their after-dinner coffee, but Richard declined.
Although Holly had consumed more than half the
wine, a cognac would surely tip him over the driving
limit. So he ordered another coffee and they sat talking for another half an hour before he called for the
bill.

"I think I'm a bit tipsy," Holly confessed when
she stood up and swayed on her high heels.

"No worries," he said, and took her elbow.
"You're with me."

"Yes..." Something like dismay flashed through
her eyes. "Yes, I'm with you."

Richard thought about that moment during the
drive home. Was she still pining for Dave? Wishing
she'd been with him?

He resented that idea. A lot.

As much as he admired and desired Holly, there
was no point in pressing on with a relationship if she
was pining for some other man. If and when he married again, it would be to a girl who gave him her
undivided attention and loyalty. This time, his wife
would be the one madly in love with him, not the
other way around.

"Thank you so much for tonight, Richard," she
said rather primly as he angled his car into the kerb
outside the flower shop. "Like I said earlier, it was
an experience I will never forget."

Richard switched off the engine and turned to her.
"Was it an experience you'd like to repeat?" he
asked.

He could see her face quite clearly, his car parked
underneath a corner street light.

Surprise zoomed into her eyes as she twisted in the seat to face him.

"You want to take me out to dinner again?"

"Dinner. Lunch. The theatre. The races. You name it, I'd like to take you there."

"Oh…" Her mouth fell open. And stayed open.

"But I only want to take you, Holly," Richard said as he reached over to place a gentle hand on her cheek.

Damn, but it was soft. *She* was soft. How he ached to bury himself in that softness, to feel her flesh close tightly around his, to lose himself in her.

"I don't want any third party coming along with us," he said, his eyes narrowing on her lush mouth. "No ghosts from the past. No wishing I was Dave."

"Dave!" she exclaimed. "I haven't given Dave a single thought all night."

"Good," he said, then abruptly closed the short distance between their mouths.

She sucked in sharply, but didn't pull back, letting his lips move over hers without protest. But without obvious pleasure as well.

His head lifted to find her staring at him with eyes like saucers.

"Don't you know how beautiful you are?" he said. "And how much I want you?"

She blinked and said nothing. She seemed frozen.

His hand stroked her cheek, then moved along her stiffly held jaw, drifting downwards to find the pulse that was throbbing wildly at the base of her throat.

Not frozen there, Richard realised, and kissed her again, this time slipping his tongue between her still-parted lips.

She came to life with a low moan, showing him with her own tongue that she liked that kind of kissing.

A raw triumph claimed Richard when she tipped her head back for him to kiss her even more deeply. He knew then that Dave was history.

It proved difficult to wrench his mouth away from hers. Clearly, she didn't want him to stop. On his part, his long-denied body was screaming at him to continue, to carry her inside the shop and ravage her on that work table.

But Richard wasn't going to risk ruining his long-term plans for any short-term pleasure. Holly was a woman. When sanity returned afterwards, she would remember that he'd promised to keep his hands off tonight. She might not be overly impressed.

He could wait one more week before satisfying his carnal urges. It wouldn't kill him.

Besides, he didn't really want a quickie. He wanted her in his bed at the penthouse for hours and hours.

"I'm sorry," he said swiftly. "I know I promised not to do that. I lost control for a moment," he added, which was almost true.

"It's all right," she said. "I...I didn't mind. Truly."

He stared hard at her. "Are you sure?"

She nodded, her eyes still dilated, her face flushed.

"Then you'll go out with me again?"

"Yes, of course," she said, her voice low and husky.

He touched her cheek again whilst he stared down at her mouth.

What wonderfully lush lips she had. He craved to have them all over him.

"I'd really like to take you somewhere tomorrow," he said, "but I have to go to Melvin's for the day. Then this coming week I'll be away, interstate, on business." Not a total lie. He did have to fly to Melbourne on the Monday for a few days. But he could easily have taken her out on the Thursday night. "Friday, I'm driving Mum and Melvin to the airport."

No. Richard wanted her to wait. Waiting would make her more susceptible to his desires, and her own. She might not be a woman of the world, but she was a healthy twenty-six-year-old girl who, till recently, had had a boyfriend. She was used to being made love to on a regular basis. It was obvious from the avid way she'd responded to his kiss that she was attracted to him.

"A friend of mine is having a party next Saturday night," he told her, his hand finally dropping away from her face. "You might have heard of him. Reece Diamond, the property developer?"

"No, no, I haven't," she said, confirming his earlier opinion that she'd led a rather insular life.

"It doesn't matter. You'll like him. Everyone does. And his wife, too. Her name is Alanna and she's a doll. Anyway, it's a house-warming party. Not of the casual kind, however. It'll be black tie. Reece doesn't know how to throw any other kind. He likes dressing up because he knows how good he looks in a tux. You'll need to wear something on the glamorous side if you don't want to feel under-dressed. Alanna usually goes for broke on these occasions."

Holly's eyes showed worry.

"If you don't have a suitable dress to wear," he said, "I'll buy you one."

"You certainly will not!" she said quite indignantly. "I can afford my own dress."

"Fine." Again, Richard was pleased. No fortune hunter here. Not like that piece he'd taken out on Friday night. He'd practically been able to see the dollar signs clicking away in her eyes.

"That's all settled, then," he said. "I'll walk you to the door." Which he did, resisting the temptation to kiss her again. Enough was enough. He wasn't a saint.

"I'll call you," he promised. "Tomorrow..."

And then he left her, without looking back. But he could feel her gaze on him all the way to the car. Once behind the wheel, he shot her one last glance through the passenger window.

She was still standing there at the door, looking forlorn.

Good, he thought, then gunned the engine. She wouldn't sleep much tonight.

There again, neither would he.

CHAPTER SEVEN

HOLLY was doing two hospital orders the following Monday morning, day-dreaming about Richard's call the previous night at the same time, when the bell on the shop door tinkled and his mother walked in.

Holly tried not to panic. Richard had warned her last night during his two-hour-long phone call that he'd told his mother about taking her out to dinner on Saturday night. Mrs Crawford had been surprised, apparently, but pleased.

The look on Mrs Crawford's face, however, was not the expression of a woman who was pleased. More like one who was perplexed.

''I came to thank you for the lovely flowers,'' she began with a puzzled frown wrinkling her high forehead. ''And to tell you how pleased I was to hear that Richard had taken you out somewhere nice on Saturday night. But I just noticed the FOR SALE sign on the window. Richard never mentioned that. Why are you selling, dear? Isn't the business going well?''

Holly heaved a great sigh of relief that this was what was bothering Richard's mother, *not* Holly's social or educational status. For a second there, she'd worried that Mrs Crawford thought a suburban florist wasn't good enough to date her precious son.

''It's not my idea, Mrs Crawford,'' she said. ''The business is actually doing quite well nowadays.''

''Don't tell me. I can guess. It's your stepmother.''

"Afraid so."

"But that's terrible. She has no right. I knew your father. He wanted *you* to have the business. You have to take that woman to court, Holly. Get what's rightfully yours."

Holly winced. Like mother, like son.

"I'd rather not, Mrs Crawford. Going to court is always so time-consuming. And nasty. And expensive."

"Richard has an excellent legal team at the bank. I'm sure he could help. I could ask him for you."

"He's already offered," she confessed, "and I refused."

Mrs Crawford rolled her eyes. "You're just like I used to be. Too soft. Life is cruel to soft women, Holly. You have to stand up and be counted. Act like a man, sometimes. I used to kowtow to Richard's father all the time. Frankly, I used to kowtow to everyone. But not any more. I don't intend spending the rest of my life turning the other cheek, or staying at home all the time. I've always wanted to travel, but I was too nervous to go alone. But I feel perfectly safe with Melvin. He's such a sweetie, and so knowledgeable about the world."

Holly didn't want to douse the woman's excitement by saying that she'd already had a detailed report about Melvin's good points from Richard last night, including his opinion that, the sooner the pair of them got married, the better.

"Sounds like Melvin might become more than just a travelling companion," Holly ventured.

A self-satisfied expression zoomed into Mrs Crawford's blue eyes. "Maybe. I'm not about to rush into anything. But you know, Holly, there's no better way to find out a couple's compatibility than to go away together somewhere. Being together twenty-four hours a day finds out the flaws in a relationship, I can tell you. I can still remember my honeymoon,'' she said, and actually shuddered. ''If Melvin and I are still happy with each other after two months, then we might tie the knot. I have to confess that I have liked what I've seen so far. Melvin is a very good-looking man. And he has the most beautiful home. It's in one of Strathfield's best streets.''

''Yes, but can he play bridge?'' Holly asked, rather mischievously.

Mrs Crawford laughed. ''You know me well, don't you, my dear? Yes, of course he can play bridge. It was the first thing I asked.''

''In that case, you have my seal of approval. I…'' The phone suddenly ringing made Holly forget what she was going to add.

''Would you excuse me a moment?'' she said.

''A Flower A Day,'' she answered.

''Won't keep Richard at bay.''

Holly immediately went hot all over. For a man who was on the conservative side in the flesh, he was quite the flirt on the phone. By the time he'd hung up last night she'd been as turned on as she'd been the previous night, tossing and turning in her bed into the small hours of the morning. And he hadn't even touched her. Just talked to her.

How would she react when he started making love to her? And he was going to. Next Saturday night. She just knew it.

''I'm sorry,'' she said, a shiver running down her

spine, "but I have a customer and I can't talk right now. Could you possibly ring back a bit later?"

"Can't. I'm off to a board meeting and then off to the airport. Just wanted to ring and warn you before you went shopping for a new dress that Reece said there's going to be lots of dancing at the party."

"What makes you so sure I'll be buying a new dress?" she retorted in a teasing tone. She'd become a bit of a flirt on the phone as well.

"I'm thirty-eight years old, Holly. I know women. You wouldn't be seen dead next Saturday night in any old dress. Just don't buy a long one. I have a hankering to see you in something sexy and short, with a swishy skirt."

"Swishy?" she repeated, though her mind was still on sexy.

"Yes, swishy. Look, I won't keep you and I won't go bothering you with late-night phone calls for the rest of the week. I, for one, need some sleep before next weekend if we're going to be dancing the night away. See you next Saturday night, beautiful. At eight."

"Don't you dare be late," she blurted out before he could hang up on her.

"I won't be," he returned with a dry laugh. "Don't worry."

Holly gripped the phone for a few seconds after he hung up, then slowly, and with a ragged sigh, placed the receiver back on its cradle.

When she turned back to Mrs Crawford, the woman was staring at her with a very thoughtful look on her face.

"That was Richard, wasn't it?" she said.

"Yes," Holly admitted. "Why? What's wrong? Oh, I get it. You don't really approve of my going out with him, do you?"

"You're going out with him *again*?"

"He's taking me to a party next Saturday night."

"I see," the other woman said, then frowned some more.

"So can I. You don't think I'm good enough for him, do you?" Holly threw at her.

Mrs Crawford shook her head, her expression anguished. "It's not that, dear. Please don't think that. You're a lovely girl. It's just that you're not long over Dave and I...well...I wouldn't want you getting hurt again."

"You think Richard will hurt me?"

"I don't know what to think. All I know is that Richard has never gotten over his wife's death. It shattered him totally. You are the first girl he's taken out in any way, shape or form since Joanna's death."

"Forgive me for saying this, Mrs Crawford, but how do you know that? He doesn't live with you. He could be picking up a different woman every weekend and you'd be none the wiser. He's still a young man. You don't honestly think he's been celibate all this time, do you?"

Holly watched the cold, hard logic of her words sink in.

But the woman still shook her head. "I know my son. He has not been with any other woman since Joanna died and I can tell you why. He's still in love with her. He was crazy about her. You went to her funeral, Holly. You saw his grief. Don't go there, love. She spoilt him for any other woman."

"I don't believe that," Holly argued, thinking of the way Richard had kissed her. There'd been passion in that kiss and with passion came the possibility of love. Holly had been able to think of nothing else but Richard Crawford since the moment his lips had met hers.

"Your son genuinely likes me, Mrs Crawford, and I like him back. I fully intend going out with him next Saturday night and nothing you say will stop me."

The older woman's blue eyes softened on her. "I wouldn't dream of trying to stop you. You're one of the nicest girls I've ever met, Holly. Frankly, I like you much more than I ever liked Joanna. If by some miracle you and Richard find a future together, I would be the happiest mother in the world. But be careful. Promise me not to rush into anything. Will you promise me that?"

"Are you talking about sex?" Holly retorted, flustered and angry by the woman's interference. The last thing she wanted to hear was how much Richard had loved his wife. Or that he was still in love with her. "Are you asking me not to go to bed with your son?"

"No. No, I'm not asking you that. It might do Richard the world of good to go to bed with a girl like you."

"What do you mean, a girl like me?"

"I mean a girl who's a giver instead of a taker."

"His wife was a taker?"

Mrs Crawford shrugged. "Joanna was…greedy. Greedy for life and greedy for Richard."

But I'm greedy for him, too, Holly wanted to cry out.

She *had* to go out with him next Saturday night. Had to feel his lips on hers again. Had to let fate take her where it willed. Or wherever Richard willed.

"Maybe he's just lonely," Holly said in an attempt to defuse this conversation, which was in danger of getting out of hand. "We all get lonely, Mrs Crawford. *I'm* lonely. It's not as though Richard and I are about to get married. We just enjoy each other's company."

"You're right. I'm being melodramatic. I should be grateful to you for making Richard see that life is still to be lived. Please don't tell my son about this conversation, Holly. I won't, either. Promise?"

"I promise."

"Forget what I said about his wife, too. He's awfully sensitive about Joanna. Clams up whenever I mention her."

"I certainly won't be bringing his wife up," Holly said, unable to ignore the stab of jealousy over Richard still being obsessed with his wife.

But she could see that it was probably true. Probably true what *she'd* said as well. Richard was taking her out because he was lonely.

But that didn't make her own feelings any less intense. Holly couldn't recall ever losing this much sleep over Dave, not till *after* he'd dumped her. She couldn't recall any of Dave's kisses doing what Richard's kiss had done to her last Saturday night, either. She'd been mindless within seconds. Lord knew what would have happened if he'd pushed the matter further.

Instead, he'd stopped, leaving her more turned on than she'd ever been in her life. She hadn't wanted him to leave. She'd wanted him to stay and make love to her. Wanted him to bypass all those feelings of sexual inadequacy that had always plagued her.

"I...I have to get back to these flowers now, Mrs Crawford," she said, agitated by her thoughts. "I hope you have a wonderful trip."

"Thank you, dear. And take care."

"I will. I promise."

Famous last words.

A swishy skirt.

Well, it had that all right.

Holly stood back from the full-length mirror and twirled around once. The skirt flared out, but stopped short of showing her white satin G-string to the world. Which was just as well because the darned dress showed more of her body than any dress Holly had ever owned.

Made in pale pink chiffon, it was halter-necked in style, with a V-shaped cleavage slashed down past her breasts. Her already small waistline was cinched in tightly with a wide silver chain belt, making her full bust look even more voluptuous.

Of course, wearing a bra was out of the question. They didn't make frontless bras. Thankfully, the dress was fully lined, and draped in soft folds over her breasts, which minimised the visual impact of her naked nipples.

She'd bought the dress last night, at an expensive boutique in the city, driven to the extravagance by her desire to knock Richard dead when he picked her up tonight.

The salesgirl had raved, of course, saying it looked simply fab on her.

"Not many girls can carry this dress off," she'd said. "Most don't have the curves for it. Or the skin."

Holly knew what she meant. She did have smooth, honey-coloured skin with no freckles. To be honest, she'd thought she looked pretty fab in the dress, too.

But now that the moment was almost at hand—it was five to eight—her confidence was wavering. Had she gone too far with the dress and accessories, along with her hair and make-up? Would Richard like her dressed to thrill? He'd asked for sexy but maybe, once he saw her, he would prefer the more au naturel Holly of last Saturday night.

The phone ringing startled her. Oh, no, please, not Richard calling off our date, she prayed as she picked up the receiver with a shaky hand. She couldn't bear it.

"Yes?" she choked out.

"I'm outside," Richard said, "I can see a light upstairs, but the place is in darkness down here. Are you ready?"

"Ready as I'll ever be."

"No need to be nervous," he replied. "Reece and Alanna are very nice people."

"It's not them who make me nervous."

He laughed. "You don't have to be nervous of me. Now come downstairs this minute. I want to see what you look like."

The moment she came through that door out onto the pavement, Richard realised she *did* have to be nervous about him. Very nervous.

He'd expected her to doll herself up tonight. What he hadn't expected was to be totally blown away by the results. One glance at her in that provocative pink dress and Richard was consumed with a desire so hot and strong that his already-frustrated body was in danger of spontaneous combustion.

As he watched her lock the door he vowed then and there that she would not just stay the night with him. But all of Sunday as well. If he had his way, Holly would not be going home till Monday morning.

At last, she turned and walked towards where he was standing by the open passenger door, trying not to look too gobsmacked. Or too lustful.

"You look ravishing," he complimented, stepping forward to take her free right hand in both of his. Her left hand was swinging a cute little pink evening bag, which matched her dress. Her lips were pink, too. A slightly darker, brighter pink, the vibrant lipgloss making her mouth look wet and inviting.

A decidedly X-rated thought zoomed into Richard's mind. Not the first X-rated thought he'd had about her this week. He really was in a bad way.

He dropped his gaze swiftly downwards, lest the darkness of his desires showed in his eyes. Her high heels were silver, he noted, the same as that decadent-looking belt.

More appalling thoughts.

His eyes shot back upwards, past her braless breasts and that sinful-looking mouth.

Not much peace there, either.

Her hair was up in one of those sexy styles where loose strands fell around her face, covering half of her eyes and brushing sensually against her neck when she walked.

For a second he wondered if she was wearing panties, then decided that of course she was. Holly was not the kind of girl who would go without panties.

When he lifted her fingers to his lips she actually trembled.

"I'm going to be the envy of every man at the party tonight," he said as he straightened. "Shall we go?"

Holly did her best to pull herself together once she was in the car and they were on the way. But she could not seem to get her head around the way Richard had just looked at her. As if he wanted to eat her alive.

She hoped she hadn't looked at him quite so lasciviously.

But, dear heaven, black did become him.

She'd thought him handsome last Saturday night, dressed in that other black suit. In a black tuxedo, however, he looked not just handsome, but supersuave. Like James Bond on his way to an international casino.

Thank the Lord she'd gone to the trouble she had. And that he liked the way she looked. Nevertheless, Holly didn't believe Richard would be the envy of every man there tonight. She understood full well that this was going to be a party full of genuinely glamorous and beautiful women. It was being held at Reece Diamond's home, a waterside mansion in East Balmain not far from where Richard lived.

Richard had told her quite a bit about Reece

Diamond during his phone call last Sunday night, making Holly curious to see what kind of man he was. The most fascinating part had been how he'd met his wife, apparently through an introduction agency called Wives Wanted, a computer matchmaking service that catered for rich men who wanted beautiful wives, and beautiful women who wanted rich husbands.

Love was not precluded, but it was not high on the list of priorities with the clients of Wives Wanted.

Holly didn't like to criticise Richard's best friend, but privately she thought the whole deal sounded too much like legalised prostitution for her liking. She could not understand, either, why a man like Reece Diamond would need to employ such a service to find a wife. Richard had described him as charming and good-looking and highly successful. That didn't sound like the type of man to need help in finding a wife. It was a strange situation. But fascinating, in a way.

Holly was very curious to meet the wife as well. Alanna. What kind of woman put herself out there like that? If she was as lovely a person as Richard said, then why wouldn't she want to be loved?

Holly knew she could never marry a man she didn't love and who didn't love her.

Thinking of love and marriage reminded her of Mrs Crawford, and Melvin.

"Did your mother's plane leave on time last night?" Holly asked when they stopped at the first set of lights.

"Yes, thank goodness. I've never seen her so excited. Melvin, too. Truly, they were acting like giddy teenagers together.''

''You really like Melvin, don't you?''

''Very much so. He's just what the doctor ordered for Mum, if you'll pardon the pun.''

Holly laughed. Richard had a wonderfully dry sense of humour, rather like her dad.

''How did your business go this week?'' she asked.

''It would have gone better,'' he replied ruefully, ''if I'd been able to put my mind on it.''

His head turned and their eyes met. Holly's heart stopped beating for a few seconds, before it lurched on.

''I...I know what you mean,'' she said huskily.

''I wonder if you do.''

''I'm not a child, Richard.''

His eyes dropped to her breasts, making her nipples tingle as they tightened.

''I can see that,'' he said.

''The...the lights have gone green,'' she told him shakily.

He said nothing in reply, just turned his eyes back onto the road and continued on, almost as though nothing had happened between them.

Lord, but she felt out of her depth with this man. His mother's warning popped back into her head, urging her to be careful. But she didn't want to be careful. She wanted to be reckless, and wicked. And she wanted *him* to be wicked.

She wanted his eyes back on her again. And his mouth. And his hands.

The wanting was acute and intense, a hunger that wasn't going to go away till it was satisfied.

Holly sucked in a deep breath, glancing at the clock on the dash as she slowly exhaled. Ten past eight. It wouldn't take all that long to get from Strathfield to East Balmain. Both were on the western side of the city. Balmain was a lot closer to the CBD than Strathfield, of course. A very trendy suburb these days. Very "in".

She needed to be there, to be surrounded by other people, to not feel the way she was suddenly feeling, as if she was in danger of losing total control of her life.

There she'd been last weekend, trying so hard to make sensible plans for the future, and along had come Richard Crawford, blowing them all out of the water. She couldn't think about a new job or a new place to live when all she could think about was him. She hadn't had her résumé done yet, let alone applied for any position. Instead, she'd gone out and blown nearly two thousand dollars on what she was wearing tonight.

Her perfume alone had cost over a hundred dollars, an exotic scent that was supposed to be irresistible to men. That was what it was called. *Irresistible.* She'd resisted the temptation to practically bathe in it, but she'd sprayed it in places she'd never sprayed perfume before.

Oh, God, some conversation was definitely called for.

"How many people know about Reece finding his wife through that introduction agency?" she blurted out.

"Only myself and Mike. So please don't spread that around. Reece told me in confidence."

Holly felt flattered now that he'd told her. He must really like her, and trust her, to tell her such sensitive information.

"I won't breathe a word. Who's Mike?"

"A computer genius friend of mine," Richard said. "And a very bad boy. So you keep right away from him, beautiful."

"I don't think there's any danger of my going off with some other man," she said rather ruefully. Didn't he realise how crazy she was about him? And how much she wanted him?

"You haven't met Mike."

"He must be a real charmer for you to be worried."

Richard laughed. "Mike has no charm whatsoever. Which for some weird and wonderful reason is his charm. I'm not sure what the attraction is for the ladies. He's not a pretty boy by any means. Looks like an escapee from the Russian Mafia. Always needs a haircut. Usually sports a five-day growth on his chin. But, for all that, there are some women—usually the oddest ones—who take one look at Mike and literally throw themselves at him. Maybe it's the challenge. Maybe they think they can change him. Little do they know, but he'll never change. Women are just rest and recreation to Mike. His life is his work, and making money."

"So why do *you* like him?"

"I guess it's because he's dead honest. And damn hard-working. You always know where you stand with Mike."

"Honesty *is* a good quality in a man," she admitted. "And rare as hen's teeth. But, from the sounds of things, I don't think you need worry about my going off with this Mike."

"Any man would be worried with you looking the way you look tonight," he said with a searing glance that set her skin breaking out into goose-bumps. "That *has* to be a designer dress."

"It's an Orsini," she confessed.

"Expensive?"

"Horribly."

"You *should* let me pay for it," he said. "You shouldn't be out of pocket, just because of me."

"I told you before, Richard. I like to pay my own way."

"I'll bet you let Dave buy you things."

Laughter burst from her lips. "You have to be joking. Dave never bought me a darned thing. No, I won't lie. He did buy me something once. A gold-plated pendant for my birthday last year. Must have cost him all of twenty dollars."

"The more I hear about this Dave, the worse he sounds. Whatever did you see in him?"

Holly shrugged. "Dave's a good salesman. As the saying goes, he could sell ice to Eskimos. He sold himself to me at a time when I was very lonely. My dad hadn't long died and I was beginning to see that my stepmother wasn't as fond of me as she'd pretended whilst he was alive. I'd always known Katie didn't like me, but I honestly thought Connie did. More fool me. I guess you could say I was ripe and ready to be conned."

"We all get conned at one time in our lives."

"I can't see *you* getting conned."

"Can't you? Well, you don't know me very well yet, do you?"

The moment the words were out of his mouth Richard regretted them. Talk about stupid! He was supposed to be seducing her tonight, not putting seeds of worry into her head.

If tonight worked out as well as he hoped it would, he would soon be asking her to marry him.

One of the reasons he'd chosen this party to bring Holly to tonight was to show her the kind of life she could have as his wife. A life of luxury and security, of pampering and privilege. She would never have to worry about money. She could have anything she wanted, and so could her children. *Their* children.

His second goal tonight was to give Holly pleasure. Sexual pleasure.

Admittedly, he was keen to have some sexual pleasure himself. More than keen, actually. The situation was close to desperation level. Dancing with her was going to prove damned difficult. Just the thought of taking her into his arms and holding her close made his groin ache. Hell on earth, maybe he should have come to visit her on Thursday night. Then things might not have been so…hard.

Reece's address came into view, the street lined with parked cars. Reece did not throw small parties.

"We'll have to park down the road a bit," Richard said, driving slowly past the house, "then walk back."

He had to drive for quite a way, eventually finding a spot.

"Sorry about the walk," he said as he turned off the engine and retrieved his car keys. "Will you manage in those shoes?"

He reached over to unsnap her seatbelt, bringing his face close to hers. Temptingly close. Before he could stop himself, his hand had lifted to encircle the soft skin at the base of her throat, sliding slowly upwards till it cupped her chin. Her eyes—what he could see of them—had definitely widened, her mouth falling open a little as well. Her perfume wafted up from that incredible cleavage, teasing him with its incredibly sexy scent.

One kiss, he thought. Surely one little kiss wouldn't hurt at this stage.

Her lips were ready for him. Ready and eager, flowering further open under his with a sound that was half sob, half moan. His tongue had slipped past them before his brain could stop it.

The rest of his body wasn't obeying him, either.

The desire for more than one little kiss kicked in with a vengeance and he found himself pressing her head back against the car seat, keeping her firmly captive there with his mouth whilst the hand that had been holding her chin slid down into the deep V of her neckline, finding its way like a homing beacon under the soft pink material and over one exquisitely naked breast.

Her back arched away from the seat, her mouth gasping under his. His tongue withdrew, his head lifting to watch her eyes dilate whilst he moved his palm back and forth across her already hardened nipple.

She seemed to have ceased breathing, her eyes round, their pupils hugely dark.

''Oh, please,'' she choked out when his hand stilled.

Her abject plea evoked a dark sense of triumph.

Later, he promised himself as he removed his hand. Later, he would make her beg again. But next time, she would be totally naked. And there would be no stopping. Not till she was crying out with one release after another. Not till she was entirely, totally his.

CHAPTER EIGHT

HOLLY closed the door of the ladies' powder room behind her.

What ordinary house, she thought agitatedly as she washed her hands, had two guest powder rooms, one for the gentlemen and one for the ladies?

But of course this wasn't an ordinary house. And these weren't ordinary people. The rich and the famous abounded out there. The wheelers and dealers of this world. Aside from her ultraglamorous host and hostess, Holly had already been introduced to two top politicians, a well-known television anchor-man and a famous actor with his new third wife, a gorgeous young thing twenty years his junior.

Holly felt she'd held her own, despite the company and despite being totally rattled by what had happened out in the car less than fifteen minutes earlier. But as soon as she'd been able to, she'd excused herself and asked directions to the powder room.

Now here she was, alone for a few precious moments, desperately trying to stop herself from thinking she'd fallen wildly in love with Richard Crawford.

Okay, so he was a good kisser. Lots of men were good kissers. Dave had been a pretty good kisser.

But once again, Holly could not remember responding to any of Dave's kisses the way she responded to Richard's kisses—with such utter abandonment of her own will. She would have let him do anything to her. Right there in his car. In a public street, for pity's sake.

She cringed when she recalled how she'd practically begged him to keep caressing her breast, which was still throbbing inside her dress. *Both* breasts were throbbing, even the one he hadn't touched.

What bewildered her the most was how cool Richard had been about it all. Cool and composed. Yet he was the man, wasn't he? Weren't men supposed to be turned on more easily than women? Weren't they the ones who usually lost control first?

Dave had been very impatient at times to get her into bed. Holly had quite enjoyed his lovemaking— when she wasn't worried about her own performance—but had never even come *close* to desperation, let alone begging.

Her face flamed with the memory. Was that why she wanted to believe she was in love with Richard? Would she feel better—less slutty—if it was love making her act so...so...

The door of the powder room opened and in walked her hostess, Alanna Diamond.

Richard hadn't exaggerated when he'd said Mrs Diamond was lovely. She was. A natural blonde, if Holly was any guess, her fine creamy blonde hair was styled into soft waves that framed a face that almost defied description. An angel's face. Delicate features. Huge green eyes. A soft mouth. And skin that was as fair and silky smooth as the rest of her.

Her dress was not the dress of an angel, however. Made in champagne-coloured satin, it was long and slinky, with spaghetti straps and a neckline that might have looked tacky if she hadn't had small, firm breasts. Her nipples were prominent, however. Round and hard. Like pebbles.

Age-wise, she was possibly around thirty. From a distance she looked younger, but up close Holly could see life's experience in and around her eyes.

"Hi there," Alanna said. "I'm so glad I caught you in here by yourself. I wanted to speak to you about something and I couldn't in front of the others. Reece would have killed me. Richard, too, I imagine."

"Oh?" Holly was at a loss.

"Reece told me a few weeks back that he'd put Richard in contact with the Wives Wanted agency and…well…you see, you might not know this, but I was one of Natalie's girls too, and… Oh, dear! I can see by the look on your face that you're embarrassed that I've brought this up. You're right. I shouldn't have. I'm sorry."

Holly wasn't embarrassed so much as stunned. *Richard* had been seeking the services of Wives Wanted? *Her* Richard, the one who'd just been making love to her in the car? The same Richard whose mother had proclaimed had never even *looked* at another woman since his wife died?

Holly couldn't think straight for a moment. If Richard was on the lookout for a wife of convenience, then what was *she*? A potential candidate, or a sexual stopgap to tide him over till he found the right woman to marry?

She opened her mouth to indignantly deny that she was one of Natalie's girls, whoever Natalie was. But at the last second, Holly bit her tongue. Whatever

Richard's agenda was where she was concerned, *he* obviously wasn't going to tell her the truth.

His mother sure didn't know her precious son as well as she thought she did.

Holly had to find out what was going on here.

"Please don't apologise," she said. "The thing is, I'm not…um…one of Natalie's girls. I do know about the Wives Wanted agency, though," she added swiftly. "Richard told me about it the other day. And, yes, he did mention that was how you and your husband got together."

"Oh, dear, now I feel even worse. I wish Richard had told Reece all this. But you know men. They just don't communicate the way we women do," she added with an exasperated shrug of her slender shoulders. "So how *did* you and Richard meet?"

"I was delivering some flowers to his mother's house last weekend. He happened to be home on a visit. Mrs Crawford was out and Richard answered the door. I'm the local florist."

"Oh, how romantic! There again, Reece says Richard's always been a romantic. He wasn't at all convinced that Wives Wanted was the right way for Richard to find a wife, but Richard was adamant at the time. Of course, after what happened to Joanna, you could understand why he might not want to fall madly in love again. Oh, Lord, there I go again! You do know his first wife was killed in a car accident, don't you?"

"Yes. I did the flowers at her funeral, actually. I've known Richard's mother for years. I just didn't meet Richard himself till the other day."

"Phew! Thank God I didn't put my foot in my

mouth twice in five minutes. So tell me, what do you think of Richard? I can see he's very taken with you.''

''We've only been out once together before to-night,'' Holly said. ''For dinner last Saturday night. But what I know, I like. Still, I would never consider marrying any man I didn't love. Or who wasn't madly in love with me.''

''Yes, well, we women all think that at some time in our lives,'' Alanna remarked ruefully. ''Sometimes it's better to settle for something less...intense. Something less dangerous.''

Holly blinked. ''Dangerous? What do you mean by dangerous?''

''Men who are madly in love can become very jeal-ous, and irrational. Even violent. I prefer a less vol-atile relationship, especially in a marriage. Reece and I have a wonderful understanding of each other's needs. He gives me what I want and I give him what he wants. We're a darned good team, even if I say so myself.''

She looked Holly up and down with thoughtful eyes. ''You're a very attractive girl, but a few years younger than most of the women at Wives Wanted. When you get older, you might think differently. But if you want my advice, you could do a lot worse than to marry Richard. He's a good man.''

''He hasn't asked me to marry him. I'm not sure he ever will.''

''Oh, I think he will.''

Holly didn't know whether to feel flattered, or fu-rious.

''If he does, then I'll be saying no,'' she said firmly, and told herself she meant it. ''Especially if he's still in love with his wife. Which his mother warned me is the case.''

''Does that bother you?''

''Yes, it does.''

''In that case, definitely don't marry him,'' Alanna said with a hint of coldness in her voice. ''Jealousy is a curse. Now, I must get back to my guests. I'll just make sure I'm still decent first.''

When she turned around to check the back of her dress in the long mirror hanging on the powder-room door, Holly's eyes widened. She'd thought her own dress was borderline in modesty but the back of Alanna's dress—which she hadn't seen earlier—left absolutely nothing to the imagination.

Mainly because there *was* no back. The only thing stopping the entire creation from sliding off her slender curves were the spaghetti straps that crossed at her shoulder blades and attached at the sides just above her waist.

What had Holly really staring, however, was how low the dress was cut at the back, plus the way it clung to Alanna's well-toned buttocks. No way could she be wearing any underwear at all!

''Reece likes me to dress sexily, but I think he's gone a bit too far this time,'' Alanna remarked as she tried to hitch the dress higher, all to no avail. ''I'm going to start choosing my own evening gowns in future. Are you finished in here, Holly? If so, we can go back together. But not a word about this conversation to the men.''

''Absolutely not,'' Holly agreed.

But Alanna had given her plenty to think about.

She still wasn't convinced Richard ever intended

asking her to marry him. It seemed more likely he just wanted some sex from her. Surely, he would marry someone more like his wife. Someone older and more sophisticated and better educated. Someone from this Wives Wanted agency.

And if you're wrong, Holly? What if he *is* targeting you as the next Mrs Richard Crawford?

A tiny shiver rippled down her spine by this thought. So much for her declaration that she wouldn't marry a man who wasn't madly in love with her!

Still, Alanna's marriage to Reece seemed to be successful, she reasoned. Maybe a loveless marriage *could* work. Provided the sex side of things was all right.

No doubt Alanna didn't mind sleeping with her very handsome husband.

But for how long? Yes, how long before Alanna began to feel as if she was just being used, till she realised that her role in her husband's life was little more than that of a trophy wife?

Was that what Richard wanted of her?

Holly wished she felt more repulsed by the idea of being Richard's trophy wife. She'd talked holier than thou to Alanna, but would she really say no to marriage, if he ever asked her?

Holly was quite grateful to return to the party with her hostess by her side. With all these thoughts tumbling through her head, she needed someone with her as a buffer. She didn't want to say anything to Richard to spoil their night together and she was afraid she might do that. Her temper was already simmering at his not being open and honest with her.

Logic came to her rescue before her resentment could boil over. Why *would* Richard have told her about his being a client of Wives Wanted? A man of his personality and pride would keep such a thing a secret.

But what on earth *was* the attraction of a match-making service with these two men? They could have their pick of women. Surely.

Holly could only conclude that neither of them wanted love, or romance. They just wanted a beautiful woman to share their lives, and their beds. Not such a terrible crime, she supposed. But rather cold-blooded.

She shivered again.

Holly and Alanna found Richard and Reece standing out on the magnificent back terrace, which over-looked a resort-style pool and the water far below. The two friends were deep in conversation as they approached, giving Holly the opportunity to study both men. To compare them physically.

Reece Diamond was a flashy-looking individual, handsome in a decidedly Hollywood style, with bed-room blue eyes and streaky blonde hair that flopped sexily across his forehead. In a way, he had every-thing. The face. The body. The outgoing personality. He was drop-dead gorgeous to look at. Eye candy of the highest order.

But for all that, Holly infinitely preferred Richard's looks, with his dark hair, deeply set grey eyes and strongly masculine features. Maybe he wasn't quite movie-star material, but he was extremely attractive and very well built. He also had subtle layers to his persona whereas Reece was all out there, with everything he was and everything he owned on show.

Which included his trophy wife.

Alanna said she gave her husband everything he wanted.

Holly only had to look into that man's eyes as his wife walked towards him to see what it was Reece wanted from her. Holly imagined Alanna would be "on call" every single night.

Holly's insides tightened at the thought of being "on call" for Richard on a daily basis.

"Mike's just rung," Reece said straight away to his wife. "He's not coming. He sends his apologies."

"That's a shame," Alanna replied as she slid her hand through the crook of her handsome husband's arm. "I was looking forward to giving his latest girlfriend the once-over. You said she was a stripper, didn't you, darling?"

"Yes. That poor boy has no taste in women," Reece purred, bending to press his lips against his wife's bare shoulder. "Not like us, Richard. But I dare say he'll be happy enough with her, for the short time she'll last."

"I don't like men who treat women as sex objects," Holly said before she could think better of it.

"Some women don't seem to mind," Reece returned silkily, extracting his arm from Alanna's, then snaking it snugly around her waist, his hand coming to rest just under her right breast.

Holly found herself staring at it and wanting, not Reece's hand on her, but Richard's. And not *under* her breast, but right on it.

Her eyes lifted to Richard's, only to find them fixed on her cleavage.

Maybe he'd been wanting exactly the same thing.

When their eyes finally connected, Holly swallowed. Richard was looking at her exactly the same way Reece Diamond had been looking at his wife. With naked desire, not tenderness or affection.

Yet her heart flipped over just the same.

"I'd like to show Holly around the grounds," Richard said suddenly, his eyes not leaving hers. "The view is wonderful from the jetty."

"Why not take a bottle of champers and a couple of glasses with you?" Reece suggested. "If you wait a sec, I'll dash in and get them for you." And he did just that, returning in no time to hand everything to Richard, whispering something to him at the same time.

"What did Reece say to you just now?" Holly asked tautly before they'd even made it down the first flight of flagstone steps.

"He told me where he hides the key to the boat-house."

A boathouse. A much more private spot than a jetty.

"I don't want to go into the boathouse," she said rather sharply. She didn't trust herself to be that alone with him right now. Or vice versa.

"That's fine," he returned affably enough. "What do you want to do, then?"

"Can't we just walk? And talk?"

"Absolutely," he said, and they moved off again, making their way slowly down more flagstones.

"I would never want the kind of marriage Reece

and Alanna have,'' Holly said, and waited nervously for Richard's reaction.

''What's wrong with their marriage? They're very happy.''

''Maybe, but how long can it last, especially without children?''

''What makes you think they won't have children?''

''Oh, come on, Richard, just look at the way Reece dresses his wife.''

''What do you mean?''

''Alanna told me he chooses a lot of her clothes. If tonight's dress is any guide, he doesn't give a damn how much of her is on display. It probably turns him on to make other men jealous of him. She's like a married mistress, not a real wife. He won't want to risk spoiling her figure with a baby.''

''You're entitled to your opinion, but you're wrong. Reece was saying to me the other day they were going to try for a baby soon. As far as Alanna's dress is concerned, lots of women wear sexy evening clothes nowadays.''

''But she didn't have any underwear on!''

''Now that's the pot calling the kettle black, don't you think, beautiful?''

She hated the colour that zoomed into her cheeks. ''I'm wearing panties. And my top is lined. Unlike you-know-who.''

He laughed. ''You-know-who is an adult woman who went into her marriage with her eyes well and truly open. Look, I suggest you stop getting yourself so het up over Reece and Alanna's marriage. It has nothing to do with us.''

Richard was right. She *had* been getting all het up about Alanna's marriage. Perhaps because she was afraid Richard would talk her into a similar marriage. Afraid that she might like the idea of being his married mistress.

She could see him now, taking her into the kind of boutique that sold sexy dresses and outrageously erotic lingerie. She would have to parade everything for him. In her mind's eye she could see herself in a black satin corselette with suspenders and black stockings and shockingly high heels. And no panties, of course.

He would command her never to wear panties once she was his wife. She was to be always accessible to him, even when she visited him at the bank. She would be in a permanent state of arousal, always ready for him.

Always…

Holly sucked in deeply, then let out a long, slow, shuddering breath.

This has to stop, she told herself, but remained shaken by her fantasies.

"That view is pretty spectacular," she said as her eyes lifted to focus on the bridge, and the city beyond.

Richard laughed. "What an understatement. That view cost Reece ten million dollars."

"My God," she exclaimed. "He must be very rich."

"He is," Richard said. "At the moment. His fortune tends to fluctuate. A few years back, he was practically bankrupt."

"What happened to turn things around?"

"Two things. There was this savvy banker who

backed him when he wanted to borrow more money to buy land and houses. Then there was the property boom.''

''Aah. So that's how you two became friends.''

''Yes. I lent him some of my own money as well. Not just the bank's. Same with Mike, when he wanted to start up his software company. Both were very rewarding investments.''

''So you're as rich as Reece?''

''Actually, no,'' he said, then added as cool as you please, ''I'm a lot richer.''

CHAPTER NINE

FOR the second time tonight, Richard regretted his words, plus his moment of vanity.

The look Holly gave him was not the same kind of look his dates from Wives Wanted would have responded with, if he'd outlined his wealth to them.

Not that Richard could read exactly what Holly was thinking. The only time he could do that for certain was just after he'd been kissing her. He knew what she was thinking at those moments.

Nothing at all.

Right now, however, her far-too-intelligent brain was ticking over. Richard suspected his character was being assessed, and possibly found wanting.

"Of course, money isn't everything," he went on, going into damage control. "But it can make life a little easier."

She laughed. "Oh, I'm sure it can. But I would imagine it could be very corrupting, to be able to buy whatever you want."

Richard wondered where this edge had come from that he was suddenly hearing in her voice. It occurred to him that he should never have told her the truth about Reece's marriage. Holly was far too young and inexperienced to understand where a man like Reece was coming from. She certainly would never appreciate what had made *him* the man he was today. Holly might have been hurt by that Dave bloke, but she hadn't been devastated.

Bringing her here tonight was a mistake. He'd been hoping to impress her. Instead, he might have ended up alienating her.

The thought that the night would not end the way he wanted it to end had Richard's hands closing tightly around the bottle of champagne and the two crystal flutes he was holding.

"Do you want to leave?" he asked abruptly.

"Leave?" Her eyes flared wide. "Why would I want to leave?"

"You don't seem happy here. You obviously don't like Reece and Alanna, or this kind of party."

"But I do! I mean…I think Reece is a bit much, but I do like Alanna. Truly, I do. I think their house is fabulous. This party, too."

"Then what is it? What's wrong? Is it me? Are you angry with me for some reason? Are you upset over what happened out in the car?"

This was her chance to tell him, to bring the issue out into the open. But if she told him she knew about his connection with Wives Wanted, she would be breaking the promise she'd made to Alanna.

Holly did not break promises.

"No," she said. "No, I'm not upset over that. I guess I just feel a little out of my league here, Richard. Everyone is so sophisticated and I'm…" She broke off with a shrug.

"You are not out of your league," Richard insisted. "You are beautiful and intelligent and as good as any person here."

She stiffened. "Don't flatter me, Richard. I had enough false flattery from Dave to last me a lifetime."

"I'm not flattering you. I mean every single word. You're a very special girl, Holly."

She stared into his eyes, trying to see what he saw when he looked at her. Was he sizing her up as a potential wife, or buttering her up for his bed later tonight?

Thinking about actually going to bed with Richard after this party was over brought Holly up with a jolt. Oh, Lord, now that was where she would be *way* out of her league!

Yet she knew that was what Richard wanted. What she wanted, too. She'd thought about little else all week.

But if he was expecting an accomplished lover, then he was in for a shock. She supposed she wasn't utterly hopeless in bed. But she did feel a failure, the way she couldn't seem to lose herself in sex like some people seemed to. There'd never been any bells ringing for Holly, or stars exploding in her head, or whatever happened when you had an orgasm.

Still, maybe things would be different with Richard. It had certainly been different each time he'd kissed her. Very different when he'd touched her bare breast earlier on.

A shudder of remembered pleasure ricocheted through her.

"It's a little fresh out here," she said. "Perhaps we should go back inside. I can hear dancing music."

"Do you like dancing?" Richard asked as they turned and headed back up to the house.

"Yes, I do. What about you?"

"I'm no Fred Astaire but I can hold my own."

"I'll bet you can. I'll bet you're good at everything."

He laughed. "Now who's using flattery?"

"But you are good at everything, aren't you?"

Their eyes met, and his were extremely confident. "I always do my best."

Richard didn't drive her home after the party. He drove straight to his nearby apartment block, using his key-card to gain entrance to the private car park in the basement. He slid the BMW into one of his three allotted parking bays, turned off the engine and withdrew his car keys before glancing over at Holly, who hadn't said a single word since Reece and Alanna had waved them off.

He understood why. The time for small talk was over.

Any momentary worry earlier on that the evening would not end as he'd hoped had long disappeared. She hadn't been able to hide her own desire when they'd danced together. She'd pressed herself against him, her body language much more telling than her eyes ever were.

"We'll be more comfortable here than your place," he told her, his own tension on the rise.

Her head turned slowly towards him. If she was shocked by his presumption, she didn't show it. She did, however, seem somewhat dazed, or drugged, like someone about to go in for a major operation. Possibly she was a little drunk. She'd consumed the majority of that bottle of champagne over the eve-

ning. He'd restricted his intake, since he was driving.
Still, he'd made sure she ate as well, not wanting her
plagued by feeling sick tonight, or having a hangover
in the morning.

"Stay where you are," he commanded. "I'll come
round and help you out."

"All right," she replied, then sighed a deep sigh.

Richard frowned as he hurried around to the passenger door. He hoped she wasn't exhausted. They'd
danced quite a bit. When he yanked open the car door
and bent to release her seat-belt, their eyes connected.

"Don't kiss me down here," she warned him huskily.

Richard smothered a sigh of relief. She wasn't
drunk. Or exhausted. Just turned on.

He knew exactly how she felt.

Straightening, he took her nearest hand and helped
her out, slamming the door behind them and zapping
the car locked.

"My...my purse," she said shakily when he
started guiding her towards the lift well. "It's on the
back seat."

"Leave it."

"But..."

"Leave it, Holly."

Holly left it, her mouth drying appreciably as Richard
led her over to a lift door, which quickly opened when
he pressed the up button. As he ushered her inside
she felt his fingers tighten on her flesh a little.

"Not...not in here, either," she said in a sudden
panic.

"Absolutely not," Richard returned, and indicated the security camera up in the corner.

She stared at him as he went about inserting his security key-card, her eyes widening when he pressed the penthouse floor.

"You live in the penthouse?"

"One of them. There are two in this building."

My God. A penthouse. She would never have thought Richard a penthouse type of man. It seemed he'd been right when he'd said earlier tonight that she didn't know him very well.

The lift started to rise so smoothly she was barely aware of movement. Holly hadn't taken much notice of her surrounds on the short drive here. She'd been too worked up with a distracting mixture of nerves and excitement.

In truth, she hadn't needed to see where they were going. She already knew Richard had recently bought an apartment on a point at East Balmain, not far from the Diamonds. He'd told her so.

He hadn't told her it was a penthouse, however.

Would a man planning to remarry buy a penthouse to live in? A penthouse was more of a bachelor playground, a place for girlfriends and mistresses, not wives. Good Lord, maybe Richard was planning to set her up as his mistress! Maybe he already had some other woman lined up to be his wife.

The lift eased to a supersmooth halt before the door whooshed open and Holly gasped. For straight ahead, across an expanse of shiny marble floor, was a huge window that had the most spectacular night-time view, with the bridge on the right and the skyscrapers of North Sydney straight ahead. As she walked towards it the harbour below came more into view, the reflection of lights dancing in the darkened waters.

"In here, Holly."

She whirled to find that Richard had opened a door she hadn't noticed. She saw then that there was another door in the wall opposite, clearly the entry to the second penthouse.

Holly walked into Richard's penthouse, expecting one thing but being confronted with something totally different.

"Oh!" she said with surprise as she glanced around.

"What were you expecting? Black leather and bear rugs?"

"Something like that."

"Are you disappointed?"

"Heavens, no. It's…fantastic. Nothing like a penthouse at all. More like a holiday house," she said as she walked slowly around the open-plan living areas, admiring the easy living layout and the relaxed furniture.

"I'll give you a grand tour in the morning," Richard said, and started coming towards her across the blue-and-yellow rug she was standing on. "For now, the only room I want to show you is my bedroom."

All the breath zoomed from Holly's lungs as he pulled her into his arms.

"Can I kiss you now?" he asked, his voice soft but his eyes hard. So was his body.

Holly was seized by a mad, mischievous moment. "What if I said no?"

His eyes made her shiver.

"Don't tease me, Holly. I'm not in the mood for games."

His mouth closed off any further conversation. His arms encircled her back, his hands settling at opposite ends of her spine, his huge palms keeping her pressed against the full length of him.

She'd known he was a big man. A powerful man. Now she felt his power, and his passion, his kiss going on and on and on. His head didn't lift till she was dizzy from lack of air.

His sweeping her up into his arms was a welcome move. It saved her from falling. As he carried her from the living room down a long hallway she buried her face into his chest, trying desperately not to think, or worry.

Strangely, this time, his kiss hadn't totally addled her brains. Maybe because she knew the moment of truth was at hand. The mind was a terrible thing. Cruel and merciless. And sometimes perverse.

By the time Richard carried her through an open doorway into what was obviously the master bedroom, the butterflies in Holly's stomach had reached epidemic proportions. Her head lifted from his chest and darted nervously to the bed, which was huge, with a white cane headboard and a shiny blue satin quilt.

Holly took some comfort from the fact that it was at least a new bed. No way did she want to share some bed with Richard that Joanna had slept in. Which was pretty silly, really. What did it matter? Alanna was right. Jealousy was a curse.

But she couldn't seem to help it. She was jealous

of Richard's love for his beautiful wife. And fearful that *she* could never measure up, either in bed or out.

He lowered her down, down onto the satin quilt, pressing light kisses to her mouth all the while, nothing like the wildly hungry kiss he'd given her in the living room. It seemed that, now he had her in his bedroom, he didn't want to hurry. He wanted to savour the moment. Savour her.

For a minute or so he kept her captive under his mouth, but then he rolled onto his side next to her, propping himself up on one elbow whilst his free hand began to explore her body.

At last her mind was merciful, spinning her out into another world where she no longer worried about her own performance. Her focus was all on what Richard was doing to her and the wonderful ways her body kept responding, as though it had been waiting for him to come along to show her what she was capable of feeling. When he slipped his hand in over her right breast, the nipple became even more erect. When his outstretched palm slid back and forth over it, everything inside her contracted fiercely.

She moaned with the exquisite pleasure of it all, and the desire for more. Much more.

"As delicious as this dress is," he murmured, taking his hand away, "it has to go. But first, this very sexy belt."

The belt was not unlike a large silver watchband that expanded and contracted. Its clasp was strong, but very simple to undo.

"Interesting," he said as he slid the belt from her waist, placing it beside him on the bed before returning his attention to the dress. He quickly found the

clasp that anchored the halter around her neck, unsnapping it, then peeling the top down over her
breasts.

"Beautiful," he murmured, and bent his mouth to
the same nipple he'd been playing with, licking it at
first, then nipping it with his teeth before sucking it
deep into his mouth.

Holly moaned again, the sensations of his suckling
seeming to have some secret connection to that area
between her legs. When his lips tugged on her breast
there was a corresponding tug down there. No, not a
tug. An exciting tightening. She didn't want him to
ever stop.

He did stop, but not for long, his mouth moving
over to her other breast whilst his right hand took
possession of the bereft nipple, squeezing it quite
hard.

She cried out, writhing against the rather confusing
combination of pleasure and pain. Did she like it, or
not?

He took an agonisingly long time before releasing
her burning nipple, yet as soon as he did she wanted
him to do it again. He obliged, and when his head
finally lifted his normally cold eyes blazed down at
her like molten steel.

Lord knew what she looked like. Her face felt hot
and her heart was going so fast she could very well
be heading for a coronary. Her mouth fell open and
she was panting like a marathon runner on a hot day.

His stripping her of the rest of the dress was
achieved with considerable speed, along with the re-
moval of her white satin G-string. He left her silver
high heels on, however, then stunned her by picking

up the silver belt and refastening it around her naked waist.

"The chains of love," he said, his hand sliding down over her stomach and between her legs.

His fingers on her breast had made her writhe. His fingers inside her body propelled her to a place infinitely more intense, a place she'd never been to before. Any pleasure seemed overlaid with an agitating tension that made her grimace and groan. She wanted to tell him to stop. But she couldn't, and he didn't.

Holly came with a rush, a cry bursting from her lips as she was propelled headlong into her first full-blown orgasm. She squeezed her eyes tightly shut, wallowing in the pleasure as her flesh spasmed over and over.

So this was what it was like. No wonder people became addicted to the experience.

Finally, the contractions stopped, followed up by the most delicious feeling of abandonment.

Richard's hand did not abandon her, however, Holly's eyes flying open on a gasp when it continued to probe and to play with her down there, even more intimately. At first, she wasn't sure if she wanted him to, but he must have known what he was doing, because eventually her first climax became a dim memory and she began craving another. Quite desperately.

When her hips started to lift from the bed, he did abandon her. Totally.

"Wh...where are you going?" she cried when he rose from the bed.

"Not very far," he returned, his eyes remaining hot on her as he began to strip off his own clothes.

Holly didn't know whose gaze was more intense.

His or hers. She could not believe how magnificent his body was. Clearly, he worked out a lot.

He seemed to like her shape as well.

"You look incredibly sexy with that belt on," he said.

She flushed wildly, having forgotten about the belt. A downwards glance reminded her of what he'd said when he'd put it back on her.

The chains of love.

Holly didn't think it was love making Richard look at her the way he was looking at her. She suspected it didn't have much to do with her own feelings at that moment, either.

All she cared about was having Richard back on this bed with her. And soon.

When he yanked open the top drawer of his bedside chest and picked up a box of condoms, Holly blinked. Having that much protection on hand was hardly the act of a man who hadn't looked at a woman in the last eighteen months. Richard's mother didn't know him any better than *she* did.

But Holly was beyond caring at this moment. Desire had a very narrow focus.

"You don't need to use protection," she blurted out. "Not unless you think it's necessary. I…I'm on the pill."

"You're not at any risk from me," he reassured her as he tossed the box back into the drawer and pushed it shut.

"Don't…don't you think I'd better take these shoes off?" she said when he went to climb back on the bed. "They have very sharp heels."

"If you like. But not the belt. The belt stays. No, let me…"

She gasped when he took her by the ankles and pulled her crossways on the bed. He removed the left shoe first, dropping it onto the floor before bending her knee up and placing the sole of her foot flat on the edge of the bed. Then he did the same thing with her right foot, placing it so that her legs were far enough apart for him to see every secret, glistening part of her.

Her heart started thudding as he stared down at her. One part of her wanted to close her legs. But it was not the strongest part.

Finally, he came forward to kneel between her legs, his hands reaching to run up and down the front of her thighs. Her belly tightened, then trembled. Heat flooded her face as he continued to stare at her down there.

"Don't," she choked out. "Don't look at me like that."

"I want to look at you like that. I like seeing how much you want me. You do want me, Holly, don't you?"

"You know I do," she cried, shaken by the force of her wanting. "Oh, please…don't tease me, Richard."

"Tell me what you want."

"Just you."

"So easily pleased," he muttered, then did what she craved, entering her with a single, forceful thrust.

Her mouth fell open on a raw cry, her buttocks contracting fiercely. He scooped them up high with his hands and began driving into her with a long, slow, relentless rhythm, his eyes narrowing on hers as he did so.

"Oh, God," she gasped.

Her head began to twist from side to side on the bed, her eyes squeezing shut in an effort to hide the wild pleasure in them.

"No, don't close your eyes," he commanded gruffly. "Open them. Look at me!"

She opened them and stared up at him.

Did he want to watch her climax? Or did he want her to watch *him* climax?

Both prospects excited her.

What kind of girl was she to like lovemaking like this?

"Stop thinking," he ordered her. Then, before she could protest, he rolled over onto his back, taking her with him, like a yacht tossed in a storm. Suddenly, she was on top of him, swaying like a mast.

Her knees dug into the mattress on each side of him to steady herself, the action automatically lifting her hips, her internal muscles contracting to stop him from slipping out of her body. He grunted, then pulled her down hard onto him so that he was buried inside her to the hilt.

Holly blushed when he reached for her breasts, which were oh, so accessible to him now.

"No need for you to be shy," he said as he stroked his hands down over her breasts, each action ending with a tug on her nipples. "You have truly magnificent breasts," he said in a desire-thickened voice, doing the same action over and over, each tug on her nipples pulling her forward till she was leaning over him, her breasts dangling close to his lips, her nipples harder than they had ever been.

"Put one in my mouth."

His erotic request evoked another flood of heat in Holly. But there was no thought of denying him. Unlike with Dave, she didn't feel Richard was lying to her when he complimented her body. His eyes reflected true admiration as he touched her. True excitement, too. His flesh felt even fuller inside her. Harder. Thicker.

When she directed one of the aching nipples between his lips, he drew the whole aureole into his mouth, sucking on it and playing with her at the same time. Not her other breast this time, but her buttocks, stroking them, then cupping them, lifting her bottom up and down, up and down, up and down.

Holly's moans reflected the sensations that began bombarding her body.

As much as she wanted to please Richard, it wasn't long before she needed to sit up, to ride him, to pursue release from the tortuous feelings building up within her belly. Her pleasure had turned dark, and desperate.

Wrenching her breast out of his mouth, she began to ride him, quite frantically. She was dimly aware of his hands grabbing her hips, of his urging her on, of his hot hungry words of encouragement.

But she didn't really need any help. She was now in command of the situation. In control. No, not in control, she thought with a hint of hysteria when her hair fell down and her mouth fell open.

He came before her, but it was only a matter of a few seconds. Perhaps his release triggered hers.

Whatever, the sensation of coming with Richard deep inside her blew Holly away. She could not get over the way he felt, the way *she* felt. Even before her contractions began to fade she knew she could never walk away from Richard after this. She would be whatever he wanted her to be. Girlfriend. Mistress. Wife.

Slave.

"Oh, God," she cried as she collapsed across his chest, unable to stay upright any longer.

Another ragged sigh puffed from her lungs.

"Is that a good sigh or a bad sigh?" he asked softly.

She didn't lift her head or answer him for a while, amazed to find that, once her orgasm was totally over, some common sense came back.

"Holly?"

She dragged her head up a few inches, pushing her hair out of her face at the same time. "Don't be silly. How could it be a bad sigh? That was incredible."

"*You* were incredible," he said, looping her hair behind her ears for her.

"I…I'm not normally like that," she said truthfully, putting her head back down on his chest.

"Maybe it's this belt," he murmured, stroking down her back till he reached it. He began rubbing his hand back and forth across the links, touching her skin at the same time, making her break out into goose-bumps.

"Maybe," she said with a shiver.

"In that case, you're not allowed to take it off tonight," he said. "In fact, you have to keep it on all weekend."

Holly's head jerked up. "What do you mean, all weekend?"

"You don't honestly think I'm going to let you go home in the morning, do you? Not after that performance just now. You're going to stay here. With me. Till I take you home Monday morning."

"But…"

"No buts. And no clothes. Just that belt, and wall-to-wall sex."

She blushed wildly, both shamed and excited by what he was proposing.

"But for now," he swept on, "I think it's time for a shower together. Or would you prefer a bath? You choose."

She stared up at him.

You choose.

Such a simple choice, really. But either answer carried potential danger. Holly wasn't the sort of girl who could separate sex and love indefinitely.

He'd called the belt around her waist the chains of love. If she wore it for him all weekend—and nothing else—the chains of love would surely slip around her heart.

Holly wasn't sure what Richard wanted from her ultimately, but she knew one thing. Love wasn't on *his* agenda.

If only he hadn't chosen that moment to withdraw from her body, showing her what her world would be like without him.

"Come along," he said, and scooped her up out of the bed. "I can see I will have to make all the decisions where you're concerned."

Holly didn't like the sound of that. If she was going to be weak, she was going to be weak on her terms.

"A shower," she pronounced as he carried her into the all blue bathroom. "And this belt comes off first."

He ground to halt. "Why? I like it on you."

So did she. Too much.

"It's only cheap silver plating," she told him as she struggled to unhook it. "It might tarnish if it gets wet."

"I'll buy you a new one if it does," he pronounced, then carried her, belt and all, into the shower.

CHAPTER TEN

HOLLY woke with her silver belt still encircling her waist, and Richard's hand over her right breast. Fortunately, he was sound asleep. Totally dead to the world.

As well he should be, she thought with remembered awe as she very carefully lifted his hand off her breast, placed it palm down on the mattress, then slid out from under the sheets.

She'd been spot on when she'd said he would be good at everything. But he wasn't just good at sex. He was absolutely fabulous. He also had amazing stamina. My God, anyone would think he *hadn't* had sex in yonks. She couldn't count the number of times he'd made love to her. And not in the same way twice!

She now knew he was also a good kisser in places she'd never imagined being kissed before. She'd also been educated in a couple of positions she had never tried before.

Holly shook her head as she tiptoed into the bathroom. Even before she shut the door behind her, the memories of what had happened in there flooded back. Richard hadn't been the only one last night who'd surprised her. Her own sexual shenanigans had been wickedly uncharacteristic.

She'd been more than willing to use her hands on

him, and her mouth. And very happy to lean wantonly back against the tiles whilst he'd returned the favour.

Holly shivered at the memory.

When she returned to the bedroom and glanced at his gloriously naked form once more, Richard's proposal for the rest of this weekend swirled back into her mind.

"No buts. And no clothes," he'd said. "Just that belt, and wall-to-wall sex."

God, but she was tempted. Just the thought turned her on.

But to *really* do that, to walk around Richard's penthouse in the nude all day, to obey his every sexual command, was simply not on. It was not only shaming but demeaning. She would not do it.

Holly twisted the corrupting belt around so that the clasp was at the front. Her hands actually shook as she unclipped it, as though they didn't want to obey her, but once they did a huge sigh of relief rippled through her.

Next, she looked for something to put on, shuddering when she spotted her pink dress on the floor, along with her panties and shoes.

No way would she be putting those on, either.

She had noticed a robe hanging up on the back of the bathroom door, but that had to be the one Richard was currently using. She quickly found the door that led into his walk-in closet and started searching for a spare robe, or something suitable to put on after she had a shower.

Everything in there was very neat and organised, just as she would imagine Richard's wardrobe to be. All his suits were hanging up neatly in a row, along with a large number of business shirts. All white or blue. Along the opposite wall was a long row of casual clothes. Trousers, shirts, tops and jackets of all kinds, even leather.

But there were no spare robes.

After dithering for a while, Holly went back to his business shirts and selected a blue one. It was very good material, she noted. Soft and uncreasable. Expensive. Of course the darned thing would swim on her, but that was okay. She wanted to be well covered up when Richard woke.

Taking the shirt with her, she tiptoed back to the bathroom.

Richard woke to the sound of the shower running.

He smiled as he stretched. God, but he felt marvellous. Last night was exactly what he'd needed.

Holly was what he'd needed. Not just for one night, either. Or even one weekend. It might be a bit too soon to propose marriage, but there was no reason why he couldn't ask her to move in with him. When the flower shop sold, she'd have to find somewhere else to live. Why not here, with him?

How wonderful it would be to come home to Holly every night. The memory of what she'd done to him in the shower popped back into his mind, making his flesh twitch back to life. She'd proved to be somewhat more experienced, sexually, than he'd imagined, but he'd surprised her, too, a few times. He was sure of it.

Still, she'd wanted him as much and as often as he'd wanted her. Hopefully, by the end of this weekend, she'd be more than willing to do *whatever* he wanted.

Unfortunately, her flower shop probably wouldn't sell for ages. Property in Sydney was proving hard to shift at the moment. Maybe he could help things along.

Richard was planning a rather ruthless move on his part when the phone rang.

He wondered who it could be, calling him this early on a Sunday morning. A glance at his watch showed it was only twenty past nine.

Richard leant over and swept the phone off its cradle.

"Richard Crawford," he answered crisply.

"Richard, it's Reece."

"Reece! Now what are you doing up at this hour? I thought you and Alanna would sleep in till noon at least. You—"

"Is Holly there with you?" Reece cut in brusquely.

"Er...she's in the shower."

"I think you might have a problem."

Richard's stomach tightened. "What kind of problem?"

"You know how you told me at the party last night that Holly wasn't from Wives Wanted."

"Yes…"

"It's a pity you didn't tell me that earlier."

"What do you mean?"

"When you rang Alanna earlier this week to say that you were bringing a date to our party, she assumed she would be one of Natalie's girls."

Richard sucked in sharply. "You *told* Alanna I signed up with Wives Wanted?"

"Sorry, mate. There didn't seem any reason not to tell her, considering *she* was one of Natalie's girls."

"I guess not. So what are you saying? That Alanna said something to Holly? She told her that I'd been looking for a wife through an introduction agency?"

"Afraid so. When they were in the powder room together. Alanna said Holly seemed okay about it, other than being somewhat surprised. Anyway, the girls promised each other not to say anything to either of us last night. They were worried we might be angry. But this morning, Alanna decided you should know that Holly knows. She also said you should know that Holly said she would never marry without love, especially a man who was still in love with his dead wife."

Richard clenched his teeth. He wasn't still in love with Joanna. He hated her. But he supposed his hate was just as much of an impediment to falling in love again. Once bitten that badly, a million times shy.

"I see," he said, his brain ticking away with the implications of what Reece had just told him. At least this news explained why Holly had become stroppy with him at the party for a while.

But she'd still come home with him, hadn't she? And still gone to bed with him.

That said a lot in his favour.

"You could lie to her, of course, Richard. Tell her you love her. Tell her you're totally over Joanna. Lots of women will believe whatever they want to believe."

"I won't do that, Reece. Did *you* tell *Alanna* you loved her?"

"No, but then Alanna's a very unusual woman. She

doesn't want to be loved. She's even more pragmatic than I am. But blind Freddy can see that your Holly is nothing like us. She's quite young, for starters. And idealistic. A bit like you used to be. I wasn't keen on your going to Wives Wanted to find a wife. Most of those women on that database are out for what they can get. But I still think you might have pulled the wrong straw with Holly.''

''I don't think so. She's what I want. And I mean to have her, one way or the other.''

''You've already had her, mate, by the sounds of things. That doesn't mean you have to marry her.''

''I know that, Reece. But I'm going to, if she'll have me.''

''What will you do about the Wives Wanted business?''

''The only thing I can do. Tell Holly everything, of course.''

Up to a point. He wasn't about to spill his guts over what Joanna had done to him. He would concentrate on his need to move on with his life, the same way Holly was moving on with hers. Why not move on together? he would argue. They liked each other and desired each other. He would also tell her he thought she'd make a wonderful wife and mother. It wasn't flattery. It was the truth.

''Thanks for telling me, Reece,'' Richard said. ''I appreciate it. And tell Alanna not to worry. Everything will be fine.''

''I hope so.''

''I'd better go. The water went off in the shower some time ago. She'll be coming out of the bathroom any time now.''

He hung up just in time. Holly emerged, her hair down and damp, her face scrubbed of make-up, her beautiful body totally covered by one of his blue business shirts.

For all that, she looked incredibly sexy.

When she saw that he was awake, she halted with a small gasp, a delightful pink zooming into her cheeks.

Richard smiled, thinking how nice it was that she was susceptible to some "morning after" embarrassment, that she wasn't the kind of girl who was totally blasé about getting up to what they'd got up to last night.

"And good morning to you, too," he said softly. "You're wearing one of my shirts, I see."

He loved the way her blush was quickly replaced by a saucy toss of her head. She had spirit, this girl he'd chosen to marry.

"You didn't honestly think I was going to go around with no clothes on today, did you? Or wear that silly belt."

His dark brows lifted. He'd actually forgotten about saying that. "A man can always hope."

"Sorry," she said with a haughty sniff. "If you want a sex slave, you'll have to go elsewhere."

He had to laugh. "You are unique, Holly, I'll give you that. And intriguingly unpredictable. After last night a man could be forgiven for thinking you might have enjoyed acting out the sex-slave fantasy."

"Well, you'd be wrong."

"I often am," he said. "Especially about you. So what's on the agenda for today? I am yours to command."

She rolled her eyes. "Very funny. You might be a man of leisure today but I have to go home. I always do the books on a Sunday."

"You will not be doing the books today, madam," Richard said sternly. "Or any other Sunday, for that matter. Let your stepmother do them. Or let her pay for an accountant."

"You're right. I'm mad. No more books. In that case, I suppose you could take me out to brunch somewhere. I'm hungry as a horse. But you'll have to drive me home first. I will need to change."

"Oh, I don't know. You look very fetching, dressed like that. Alternatively, we could eat in. I could go get us some videos and a pizza."

Already, Richard was changing his mind about bringing up the subject of Wives Wanted today. Why spoil the moment?

"Not on your life!" she retorted. "I spent twelve months having pizzas and videos every weekend. And paying for them myself. I wouldn't let you buy me a dress, but I don't mind you paying to take me somewhere nice to eat. That's perfectly acceptable."

Richard could see she wasn't going to let him drag her back to bed for the rest of the day, damn it. If he was going to get up and take her out somewhere, he might as well clear the air on the subject of the Wives Wanted agency right here and now.

"Somewhere nice it will be, then. But before I get dressed and run you home," he said, "could you come over here and sit down on the bed next to me?" He patted the side of the bed with one hand as he dragged a sheet over his lower half with the other. "I have something I want to discuss with you."

"What?" she asked a bit nervously as she did as he asked. But as she sat down and crossed her legs his shirt parted across her thighs and he had a tantalising glimpse of the dark triangle of curly hair that arrowed down between her legs.

"I've just had a call from Reece," he said before he succumbed to temptation and pulled her into the bed with him.

"Oh?" Her hand lifted to finger-comb her hair back from her forehead.

"Alanna told him what she'd said to you in the powder room last night."

"Oh!"

Was that alarm in her eyes?

Damn it all, but she could be hard to read at times.

"Why didn't you mention it last night?" he asked, watching her face closely.

Definite guilt in her eyes this time. Though Lord knew what she had to feel guilty about.

"I...I didn't want to spoil anything," she said.

Aaah, now he got it. She'd wanted him to bring her home and make love to her. That had been her priority at the time.

"But you were still angry with me," he pointed out.

"Not really. More like...bewildered. I...I couldn't understand why you would want to go to that kind of agency, or why you would think you had to buy yourself a wife, the way Reece did."

"Reece didn't buy Alanna."

"Oh, come now, Richard. Do you think she'd have married him if he'd been poor?"

"No. But Reece's wealth was not the whole picture. They connected straight away. And the chemistry was right. The way we did.''

Now she definitely looked alarmed. Or was it shock?

''What is it you're saying, Richard? Surely you're not asking *me* to marry you?''

''Would that be so surprising?''

''Yes! I mean…I thought…I just…I… For pity's sake, we've only known each other a little over a week. And please don't go saying you've fallen madly in love with me.''

''I don't intend to,'' he said, and watched her eyes widen.

''Wow. You can be brutally honest when you want to be, can't you?''

''Would you prefer I did a Dave on you?''

''Lord, no,'' she said with a shudder.

''In that case, hear me out,'' he said, throwing back the sheet and climbing out of the bed. ''Wait here.''

Holly remained rooted to the spot, her head spinning. So he *had* been targeting her as a marital candidate.

Holly couldn't deny she felt flattered, but, goodness, what was the rush? It couldn't be because he wanted sex. She'd slept with him last night and would undoubtedly sleep with him again, whenever he wanted. Her insistence earlier that she wouldn't be his sex slave was just so much rubbish. Being Richard's sex slave was exactly what Holly would like to be.

But his wife?

No, thank you very much. She might have toyed with the idea last night, when she'd been turned on to the max. But the cold light of morning had a way of making her see common sense.

Holly refused to play second fiddle in any man's life! If and when she got married, she definitely wanted a man who was in love with her. A deep and everlasting love. She deserved to be loved and was not going to settle for anything less!

The bathroom door opened and out he came.

Thank God, he'd put something on. Though what he was wearing wasn't much of a covering, the navy silk robe only loosely sashed around his hips. Most of his massive chest was on display, the matted curls in the centre giving him a cavemanish look. Adding to his primal appearance was his stubbly chin and his slightly messy hair.

"Come with me," he said, taking her by the hand.

"Where are we going?" she asked as he practically dragged her along the hallway.

"My study," he answered.

The room he took her into was nothing like his father's study back at Strathfield. Bright and sunny, the walls were a pale yellow, the floor covered in the same cream tiles that seemed to run through the whole penthouse. One wall was almost entirely of glass, with sliding doors leading out onto a huge terrace. Another wall had built-in shelves, housing a colourful array of books. A blue-and-yellow rug stretched out in front of the desk, which was sleek and modern. The desktop was clear, she noted, except for a phone and a laptop.

"Sit," Richard said, and indicated the blue office chair behind the desk.

She sat, wondering what on earth he was about to

show her. Richard grabbed the arm of the chair and pulled it down in front of the laptop. He stayed standing next to her and started clicking the mouse. In no time, he'd brought up a photograph of a brunette who would have given Catherine Zeta-Jones a run for her money.

"She was the first woman from Wives Wanted I took out," he said. "She's a television producer. Thirty-four and divorced."

He clicked up another raven-haired beauty.

"Took her out next," Richard said. "She's a pathologist. Thirty-five. Never been married."

Two more stunning brunettes filled the screen with successive clicks, each one accompanied by a succinct report from Richard. Each one had higher education, as well as incredible physical beauty.

At last he switched the computer off, pushed it over a little and perched on the edge of the desk, facing her.

"To answer your first question, you wondered why I would go to such an agency. I'll tell you why. I'm thirty-eight years old, Holly. I've been in love, I've been married and I've been horribly hurt. For eighteen months I could hardly bear to go out, let alone date. But life does move on and the time came when I wanted a woman in my life, and in my bed again. As well as that, I want a child. And not when I'm in my dotage."

Holly sat up straighter in the chair. A *child*! So that was the reason behind his urgency. Now why hadn't she thought of that?

"I know people have children all the time these days out of wedlock," he went on, "but that's not me. I wanted my child to be legitimate. And I wanted a wife for myself, too. I'd been lonely and celibate for long enough. But I couldn't see myself cruising singles bars every weekend, or signing up for speed-dating night.''

''But don't you meet a lot of women at work, and in the course of your social life? A man in your position would go to lots of dos.''

''Like I said, I'm thirty-eight. Most of the women around my age that I meet are married, or divorced. The married ones are out of bounds and the divorced ones are carrying too much emotional baggage for me. I have enough of my own. I saw how successful Reece's marriage was using Wives Wanted and I thought, Why not give it a try?''

Now that she had heard his explanation, Holly could see it was reasonable.

''So what happened?'' she probed.

''It didn't work out.''

''But all those women were incredible. And brilliant!''

''Gold diggers, every one of them.''

''How do you know that?''

''Trust me,'' he said drily.

''But isn't financial security part of the deal?''

''I guess so. But I suspect Reece was very lucky, to find a real diamond amongst the paste jewels on offer.''

''But they were all very beautiful.''

''In a skin-deep fashion.''

''Did…did you sleep with any of them?''

Holly hated herself for asking, but she had to know.

''Not a one. There was no chemistry. Not for me,

anyway. Every one of them left me cold. You, how-ever, my sweet darling Holly,'' he said, yanking the chair up between his legs, ''you heated my blood from the first moment I saw you.''

Holly was already melting from his endearment when he cupped her face and bent down to kiss her.

Not a hard kiss. Or a hungry one. A soft, tender, loving kiss that rocked her soul, and her belief that she had not fallen in love with Richard.

What a fool she was. A silly fool. Didn't she know she'd been half in love with him before she'd even met him? He was everything she'd ever wanted in a man. The trouble was, as perfect as he was in her eyes, in his heart of hearts he would always belong to someone else.

Tears pricked at her eyes, bringing panic. She didn't want him to know how she felt about him. And he might add two and two together, if she started crying. He might use the knowledge against her. Make her do things she knew she shouldn't do, like say yes to marrying him.

So she cupped *his* face with her hand and deepened the kiss, all to hide her tears. He slid off the desk and pulled her up out of the chair at the same time, yank-ing her hard against him.

Their mouths burst apart and he glared down at her.

''You shouldn't have done that,'' he growled.

''Why not?''

''Because I've been wanting to do this ever since I woke up.''

He wrenched his robe apart before his hands scooped up under his blue shirt, spanning her waist and squeezing tightly, rather like the silver belt had done. She gasped when he lifted her and sat her on the edge of the desk. Moaned when he pushed her legs wide. Cried out when he plunged into her.

None of their matings the previous night had been anything like this. This was wild and primitive. The sounds they both made. The lack of finesse. The roughness of it all.

He came quickly, his back arching, his mouth falling wide with a primal cry as his flesh exploded inside hers. Holly could not believe it when her body swiftly followed with a climax just as intense. She clutched at his shoulders, sobbing as the spasms twisted at her insides.

He swore and scooped her up off the desk, holding her close. Her legs automatically wrapped around his hips, her arms around his back.

''Sorry,'' he muttered. ''Sorry.''

She buried her face into his chest and surrendered to the need to weep.

''I'll take you home now,'' he said gently when she finally quietened.

''Yes, please,'' she said, feeling calmer. And resigned.

So she loved him. There wasn't much Holly could do about that.

She would undoubtedly continue to go out with him. And sleep with him. But she would not—absolutely not—agree to marry him!

''Do you still want me to take you somewhere nice to eat?''

No use pretending she didn't. So she nodded and he smiled, and her fate was sealed.

CHAPTER ELEVEN

"RICHARD! So it *is* you!''

Richard knew the identity of the woman before he lifted his eyes from the chicken and mushroom risotto he'd been thoroughly enjoying.

It had been a mistake, he accepted as he finally looked up, to bring Holly to one of the trendy eating places he and Joanna used to frequent. Despite the time lapse, he should have realised that some of his wife's old crowd might still go to their regular haunts. The Cockle Bay Wharf at Darling Harbour was a favourite of the rich and idle on a Sunday summer's afternoon.

"Hello, Kim," he said.

Of all Joanna's girlfriends, Kim was probably her closest. She'd been the chief bridesmaid at their wedding. Richard had quite liked her to begin with. Most of Joanna's friends were of the bright, bubbly kind. Good fun to be with. But he'd changed his mind when she'd made a serious play for him one night, uncaring that she'd been in her best friend's home, or that her own husband had been just a room away.

Since then, she had divorced that particular husband, after he'd served his purpose, of course, which was to provide her with an income for life. Kim was a bitch through and through. A beautiful bitch, though.

Birds of a feather, he now realised.

"It's great to see you out and about again," she gushed. "And looking so trendy! Do you know I was with Joanna when she bought you that outfit. It suits you, darling. There again, Joanna's taste was impeccable, especially in men. But I am blathering on, aren't I? Would you and your little friend like to join us? We're just sitting over there." And she indicated a long table full of people across the way. Richard glanced over but didn't recognise anyone else from his past life.

"Holly's not my little friend," Richard informed her coolly. "She's my girlfriend. And, no, thank you, Kim, we'd prefer to be alone."

"How romantic. There again, you always were a romantic, Richard. We'll catch up some other time, shall we?" she said, and actually had the temerity to bend and kiss him on the cheek before undulating off back to her companions.

Richard felt as if his face were suddenly carved in ice.

Poor Holly was not looking too comfortable, either.

Damn Kim for going on about Joanna and the stupid clothes he was wearing. He'd only put them on because Holly had picked them out of his wardrobe, not because Joanna had bought them for him.

But Holly wouldn't believe that now. Which was a shame.

Less than five minutes earlier, he'd been thinking how happy she looked sitting there in her simple but very pretty lemon sundress, her skin glowing and her long brown hair gleaming in the sunshine.

"Sorry about that," he said abruptly. "Kim's an old friend of my wife's. Her best friend, actually."

Even as he said the words, a thought occurred to him. Kim would probably know the truth about Joanna. Female friends always confided in each other. But how much did she know, exactly?

Richard decided he would ask, as soon as he got the chance. He probably wouldn't like the answers but he had to know. Had to put the past behind him once and for all.

Till then, he wasn't going to let the memory of his wife, or her so-called friends, spoil his afternoon with Holly.

And it could, if the frown on her face was anything to go by.

"I'm not upset, if that's what you're thinking," he said.

Holly stared at him across the table. Who did he think he was kidding?

She'd been flattered by the way he'd set Kim straight about her status in his life. Holly had taken an instant dislike to the woman. Maybe because she was drop-dead gorgeous, one of those slim, cool blondes who always looked as if they'd just stepped out of a beauty salon.

But anyone with half a brain could see that Richard running into his wife's best friend had thrown a dampener over proceedings.

His eyes, which had been bright and sparkly all day, were now the colour of a wintry lake under a cloudy sky. The muscles around his jaw looked stiff and his mouth was pressed into a thin, hard line.

He certainly hadn't got over his wife. Not in the slightest. His mother had been right. Any last lingering hope that some miracle might happen and Richard might fall in love with *her* eventually went straight down the gurgler.

Holly's dismay was acute, and telling. She was setting herself up for another personal disaster with this man. One far worse than Dave, because this time she was going into things with her eyes well and truly open.

Richard didn't love her. He would *never* love her.

Face it, Holly, and deal with it.

Facing it was very depressing. Dealing with it quite impossible. Because she could not walk away from him. She loved him.

"Thank you for calling me your girlfriend," she said, trying her best not to sound the way she was suddenly feeling.

"I would have preferred to say fiancée," he returned.

She stared at him, then shook her head. "Please don't."

"Please don't what?"

"Don't keep on about that. I'm happy to be your girlfriend, Richard. But I won't marry you."

"You know, Holly, it's only in the western culture that people marry for love. Romance is all very nice, but it's not all that reliable. Look at our divorce rate. Most of those couples thought they were in love when they tied the knot. Being *in love* doesn't last. Caring and commitment are what makes a marriage last. That, and common goals. And children. You want children, don't you?"

"Yes, of course I do."

"There is no *of course* about it. Some women these

days don't want children. And lots of men, according to the ladies from Wives Wanted. I will give you children, plus the security to raise them right. I will also give you caring and commitment. If this weekend is anything to go by you won't have any complaints about our sex life, either. Our compatibility in bed is better than lots of people who are in love.''

Holly sighed. ''That all sounds very reasonable, Richard, but you don't *love* me. I'm all alone in the world. My parents are gone. So are my grandparents. I have an aunt in Melbourne I might have seen three times in my lifetime. And a gay uncle who moved to San Francisco when I was a teenager. That's it. I have no family who loves me. I *need* to be loved by my husband.''

''That's romantic ideology,'' he said sharply. ''What a wife and mother needs is a husband who can provide and protect you and yours. Who will always be faithful. Who will never deliberately hurt you or let you down. I will deliver all that, Holly. I give you my solemn word.''

His eyes bored into Holly's, the passion in his voice making her doubt her resolve to resist his proposal. Maybe he was right. Maybe they could be happy together.

But then she remembered that photo of Joanna, which she had seen propped up against her coffin.

She would always be there, coming between them. The beautiful first wife. The love of Richard's life.

''Just think about it,'' he went on. ''That's all I ask.''

''All right,'' she agreed, knowing she would probably think about little else.

"Shall we go?" he suggested.

"Why not?" They'd eaten most of their risotto and drunk all of the excellent bottle of white wine Richard had ordered with it.

Richard called for the bill.

Five minutes later they were strolling across the old iron bridge that took them to the other side of Darling Harbour, her hand enclosed tightly in Richard's. They hadn't spoken since they'd got up from the table.

"Would you like to go into the casino?" he asked.

"Would you?" she countered, glancing up at the Star City complex.

"Not particularly. I'm not a gambler. I have a bet on the Melbourne Cup each year but that's about it."

"I have a flutter on that as well. But I never win."

He smiled. "Neither do I. What shall we do, then?"

"Whatever you like," she returned, perhaps a little thoughtlessly. Her mind was just so full with tortured thoughts.

"Right. See that taxi rank over there? Let's go!"

They hadn't driven here. They'd taken a taxi, Richard explaining that parking at Darling Harbour on a Sunday afternoon was difficult.

"Where are you taking me?" she asked breathlessly as he pulled her along the pavement at power-walking pace.

"Where do you think?"

Holly ground to a halt once she realised what he was talking about.

"No," she said, panic-stricken at the idea of going back to that penthouse and being seduced over and over. Her mind was already in a mess. "I don't want to do that, Richard."

His eyes bored into hers. "Yes, you do."

"Well, yes, I do, but I'm not going to. You don't understand. I...I've never experienced anything like I experienced with you last night. And again this morning. It's sent me into a tail-spin."

"What's wrong with my making love to you?"

"It's confusing. And corrupting. I mean...I know you might laugh at this, but I...I've never had an orgasm before. Then, in the space of a few hours I had about twenty. With you."

He just stared at her. "Are you serious?"

"Of course I'm serious! Why would I lie about something as embarrassing as that?"

His eyes softened on her. "I don't think that's an embarrassing admission at all. I think it's sweet. You're sweet."

"I'm a silly, naïve little fool!" she snapped.

"No. Not at all. You just haven't had the right lovers. I'm flattered that I gave you such pleasure. But why not have more where that came from?"

"I knew you'd say something like that. I should never have told you. I *am* a fool."

"Would all women be such fools, then," he muttered. "Okay, I'll take you home, if that's what you want. But I'll be over to visit you tomorrow night."

"Tomorrow's one of my gym nights."

"Then cancel it."

"No."

"There's a gym in my apartment block," he pointed out. "A private one for the owners and their guests."

"You're not going to leave me alone now, are you?"

He smiled. "I just want to give you more pleasure."

"You just want me to marry you."

"That, too."

Holly groaned. "You're a wicked man, Richard Crawford."

"Not really," he returned. "Just a very determined one."

CHAPTER TWELVE

RICHARD sat in his office at the bank the following morning, thinking about Holly.

As determined as he was to marry her, she was just as determined to marry only for love.

Love, Richard thought scornfully. If only she knew what kind of hell love could create. He'd been in hell ever since he'd read that coroner's report.

Thinking about that reminded Richard of his thoughts after running into Kim yesterday. Maybe if he knew the truth, he might be able to find closure on the subject of Joanna once and for all.

Richard pressed the button that connected him with his PA.

Five minutes later he had what he wanted. Kim's phone number. It seemed she was still living in the Kirribilli apartment she'd lived in with her husband. No doubt it had been part of her lucrative divorce settlement.

He rang straight away, experience telling him women like Kim didn't go to work. They did charity work occasionally. Other than that, they had their hair done, went to health spas, shopped at Double Bay and lunched at Doyles. Oh, and they seduced other women's husbands.

"Hello, Kim," he said when she picked up on the seventh ring. Clearly not an early riser by the sound of her groggy greeting. "It's Richard. Richard Crawford."

"Richard! My God. Fancy you calling me. I got the impression yesterday you weren't too pleased to see me."

"Whatever gave you that idea?" he returned drily.

"Sarcasm, Richard?"

"I won't lie, Kim. I wasn't pleased to see you. I don't like you. I never did. Not after the way you tried to come on to me that night."

"You really are pompous, Richard. Most men would have been flattered. But not you. You wanted to keep yourself for your one true love. Your beautiful Joanna. If only you knew the truth about your darling wife," she sneered down the line.

"The truth is why I'm ringing, Kim. You and Joanna were always as thick as thieves. After seeing you yesterday, I began to wonder if you knew the name of Joanna's lover, the one who fathered the child she was carrying when she died."

"Well, well. Looks like I kept mum for nothing. You knew all along."

"Not till after the autopsy."

"Ri...ght. I see."

"Was this man her first affair?"

"You want to know the absolute truth?"

Richard's hand tightened on the phone. "That's why I'm ringing you."

"No. It wasn't her first affair."

Richard closed his eyes for a long moment.

"Which didn't mean that she didn't love you, Richard. She actually did, as much as Joanna could ever love anyone. She used to say you were the best she'd ever had. I guess that's why I did what I did that night. I wanted to see what she was always raving about. Joanna knew I was going to try to get you into bed. She said I wouldn't succeed and she was right.''

Richard could hardly believe what he was hearing. What kind of woman had he married?

Perhaps he would have come to realise her true nature in time. The clues had been there, he supposed, with the type of people she'd hung around. At the time, however, he'd been blinded by her beauty. And her obsessive need for him in bed. His male ego had made a fool of him.

In hindsight, however, he should have seen that her sexual greediness had reflected a greediness in her whole character, an inability to ever do without anything she'd enjoyed.

''The trouble was you weren't around enough,'' Kim flung at him almost accusingly. ''You worked such long hours. And you were always going away. She was lonely, and bored. Her job didn't involve her twenty-four seven, like yours did. She used to brag about her long lunches, most of them taken at a hotel room in town. I couldn't count the number of aspiring young writers she had a fling with.''

Richard wanted to be sick.

''But really, Richard,'' Kim raved on, ''you shouldn't feel short-changed. She was good to you, wasn't she? She was always there when you wanted her. And like I said, she loved you in her own way. Why should it worry you now if she slept around on the side? That was just sex, not love. Trust me, she wasn't having some torrid affair with the bloke who got her pregnant. She didn't even know who it was.

You were away on business and she threw this party, which developed into a bit of an orgy. She was usually very careful about using protection but things got out of hand that night. When she found out she was pregnant, she was so angry at herself. No way was she going to have a baby. She was on her way to the abortion clinic when the accident happened."

Richard had to get off that phone before he did something incredibly humiliating, like cry.

"I have to go now, Kim."

"Look, I'm sorry, Richard. But you did ask. She wasn't a bad person. Just very needy. And she did love you. Truly."

"Yeah, right. Bye, Kim."

He hung up, then just sat there, trying to make sense of it all, trying to find himself again through the wall of bitterness that had cloaked his soul for far too long.

But it was no use. He wasn't there any longer.

He stood up and walked across to the window of his office, staring down at the city below, not really seeing anything. What was the point of going on when the world was full of such wickedness?

And then he thought of Holly.

Nothing wicked about her. Even when she thought she was being wicked, she wasn't really.

If he had her in his life, he might find himself again. His spirits lifted when he thought of her being there, waiting for him, when he came home from work.

He couldn't let her run away from him. Which was what she was trying to do. She was afraid of him, because she liked being with him too much. Liked the sex too much. If only she would agree to move in with him, he could use the sex to bind her to him, to break her down and make her need him as much as he needed her.

He had to get her to move in with him. Sooner rather than later.

Whirling round, he strode over to his desk, picked up his phone and pressed Reece's number.

"Reece Diamond," Reece answered promptly.

"Reece, it's Richard. I have something I want you to do for me."

"Anything, Richard. You know that."

"I want you to act as my agent in buying a flower shop."

"A *flower* shop? That's not your usual style. Aah…I get the picture. This is for Holly, isn't it?"

"In a roundabout fashion."

"So where is this flower shop?"

"In Strathfield. It's called A Flower A Day. It's on the market with L.J. Hooker. Offer the full price they're asking, but with conditions attached to the sale."

"What conditions?"

"A very fast settlement date. This Friday."

"Can't be done that soon, mate, not if you want the books checked and proper searches done."

"I don't. Put down a substantial deposit today. I want vacant possession of the place, contracts to be exchanged this coming Friday."

"The owner might not go for that."

"If she doesn't, offer her more. Just make sure she doesn't know either your name or mine. Use my investment company name to do the deal."

"*She?* Holly owns this shop, is that it?"

"Nope. Her stepmother does."

"I don't get it."

"Holly manages the shop and lives above it."

"Now I get it," Reece said ruefully. "My God, Richard, this is not like you. You've become obsessed with this girl."

Obsessed. Yes. Obsessed just about described his condition at the moment.

"Just do what I've asked, Reece," Richard bit out. "And ring me back when they've agreed to the deal."

Reece sighed. "Okay. But be it on your head if you end up with a flower shop and no girl as well."

"I don't think that will happen."

Mondays were always slow days in the floristry industry. Holly hadn't had a customer all day. She was sitting behind her work table just after three, trying to write out a word-grabbing résumé when the doorbell tinkled.

Holly jumped to her feet just as her stepmother walked in.

Connie had always been an attractive woman. But she'd turned the clock back ten of her forty-seven years since Holly's dad had died, courtesy of a facelift done before he'd even been cold in his grave, paid for with his life insurance policy. Katie had had a few things done as well. Her big nose made smaller and her small breasts made much larger.

Holly had long been aware of the fact that Katie envied Holly her breasts. *And* her boyfriends. It was no surprise, in hindsight, that Katie had stolen Dave. Though Holly suspected it wasn't Katie's new big boobs that Dave wanted so much, but her source of money. Connie had never been able to deny her daughter anything she wanted. She was already talking about a big, fancy wedding.

Holly could only hope that, some day, some fortune-hunting man would come along and con Connie, as she'd conned Holly's Dad. The woman had never loved him. Holly could see that now as well.

Holly looked at her stepmother with genuine distaste as the woman walked towards her with a plastic smile on her plastic face. Even her blonde hair looked plastic.

"Hello, Holly," Connie said breezily. "I have some wonderful news."

"Really?" She couldn't imagine what.

"The shop was sold today, and I didn't have to drop the price I was asking at all."

Holly's heart started thudding. "But...but...nobody's even been in here to inspect it. Or looked at the books!"

"The buyer probably isn't interested in it as a flower shop. I dare say he just wants the property. He also wants a quick settlement. Contracts will be exchanged this Friday. Unfortunately, you have to be out of here by then. It's a vacant possession deal."

Holly felt as if someone had just punched her in the stomach. She'd thought it would be ages before the shop sold. Months and months.

"But you don't have to worry, dear," Connie continued in a sickly sweet, pseudo-conciliatory tone. "I've signed a cheque for you for ten thousand dollars. Here it is." And she placed the slip of paper on the table Holly was now holding onto for dear life.

"That should be more than enough for you to live on while you find another place and another job. Which won't present a problem, I'm sure, since you're such an excellent florist."

Holly picked up the cheque, staring down at it before glancing up at her stepmother.

"You think this is enough to compensate for all the work I've put into this business?" she ground out. "I've worked six days a week since Dad died. I've taken a pittance of a salary and done the books as well. I deserve half the business, Connie. You know that."

Connie drew herself up straight, her tautly unlined face growing haughty at the same time. "I know no such thing. You've been paid quite adequately. After all, you've had a free flat to live in. Not to mention unlimited use of the delivery van. Free flowers as well!"

Free *flowers*! That did it. That absolutely did it!

"If you don't give me what's due to me, Connie, I'll take you to court."

Connie laughed. "Do that and you'll end up with nothing. Or less than nothing, once you've paid your lawyer and court costs. I was married to your father for eight years, missie. Judges are very sympathetic to widows, not vindictive young daughters who have the means to make their own way in life. For pity's sake, Holly," she spat, "don't be a fool!"

"I am not a fool. You're the fool if you think I'm going to let you sell my dad's business and give me nothing. You're a greedy bitch. You never loved my dad. You only married him for what you could get out of him."

"I held up my part of the bargain. Your dad wanted a sexy, good-looking wife. Well, he got one. It wasn't easy going to bed with a man I wasn't attracted to, but I did. I earned every cent I got from him and I aim to keep every cent, so don't you threaten me, Holly Greenaway. I'm a lot tougher than the likes of you. If you take me to court I'll have Katie up on the witness stand telling the judge how much of your dad's money you wasted on clothes and boys and drugs and God knows what. You want to play dirty, girl, then just watch me!"

Holly gaped at the woman. My God, she was more than a mercenary bitch. She was evil.

Connie's face turned ugly as it twisted into a sneer. "I suggest you take that money and run, because that's all you're going to get!"

Holly looked the woman straight in the eye as she tore the cheque into little pieces. "You think so? I'm going to get my dad's shop," she said with a bitter resolve. "*All* of it. And I won't even have to take you to court. Just you wait and see."

"In your dreams, girlie. Katie always said you were a dreamer. Be out of this place by Friday morning, or I'll have you thrown out." Spinning on her heels, Connie stormed out without a backward glance.

When Holly felt tears begin to threaten, she forced them back. No tears. Not this time. This time she was going to do what Mrs Crawford said a woman had to do sometimes.

Act like a man!

Flipping over her phone and address book, she memorised the number she'd entered under C just that morning, and which Richard had given her yesterday.

"Ring me any time," he'd said.

Her hand only shook a little as she picked up her phone, then punched his number in.

"Richard," she said when he answered. "It's Holly. I...I need to see you." Darn, but that didn't sound at all as a man would sound.

"Now," she added swiftly. "I need to see you *now*!"

Much better.

"My God, Holly, what's wrong? What's happened, my darling?"

Oh, dear. He shouldn't have called her his darling.

"I...I..."

"Yes?"

She tried again. "The thing is, Richard..."

"Yes?"

No use. She burst into tears.

Richard gripped the steering wheel of his BMW as he threaded his way through the city traffic, heading for Strathfield, and Holly.

"Damn and blast," he swore when he struck another set of red lights.

But it wasn't the driving delays that were distressing him the most, but his own disgusting self. What had possessed him to think he could play with a person's life as he had just played with Holly's?

There was no excuse. Buying the flower shop and having her chucked out, just so she would run to him, was the behaviour of an out-and-out bastard. When she'd broken down on the phone and sobbed out her confrontation with her stepmother, Richard had wanted to cut his own throat.

Holly's pain had been palpable, even over the phone.

Richard could not believe how insensitive he'd been to do something like that.

At the same time, he could not deny that there was a part of him that felt satisfaction. She had turned to him. Straight away. Without any hesitation.

No matter how cruel his strategy had been, it had worked.

For the rest of the drive to Strathfield, he tried convincing himself that the end justified the means. He would be good to her. Very good. He'd help her move, help her find a new job. He might even buy her another shop, if she'd let him. A better shop. Her life would be better, with him.

She'd stopped crying by the time he arrived, her face surprisingly composed as he hurried in through the door.

"I'm glad you came," she said, in a very odd voice for a girl who'd been beside herself less than half an hour earlier.

Richard slowed his step.

"I had planned to talk to you about this on the phone," she went on, again in that strangely cool voice. "But it didn't work out that way. We dreamers take a while to get our heads out of the clouds and into the real world."

Now she sounded bitter. And terribly hard!

"Anyway, I have a proposition for you."

Richard ground to a halt. "A proposition?"

"Yes. Do you still want to marry me?"

He blinked. Crikey!

"Of course," he said immediately.

"Buy me this shop and I'll marry you."

Buy her this shop. Hell, he already owned the damned thing.

"The contracts haven't been exchanged yet," she went on. "All you have to do is contact the real estate agency and gazump the bid. My stepmother will drop that other buyer like a hotcake. Contracts haven't been signed so it's still up for grabs."

Richard could not believe things had turned out this well.

And yet...

"You said you wouldn't marry for any reason other than love," he threw at her.

Her eyes softened, reminding him of the warm, loving, sensual girl he'd spent the weekend with. But then, suddenly, they hardened again.

"Don't argue with me, Richard. Will you do this for me, or not?"

"I'll do it today."

She breathed in deeply, then let it out in one long, shuddering sigh. "Good. One other thing."

"Yes?"

"Take me away somewhere. I...I have to get away from here for a while."

He saw it then, the fragility behind the superficial hardness. She was like a thin sheet of glass. One little shake and she would shatter. Getting her right away would be a good idea. He wouldn't mind a break himself.

"Where would you like to go?" he asked gently.

"I don't care," she said, desperation in her eyes. "Anywhere, as long as it's a long way from here."

"Do you have a current passport?"

"Of course not," she said with a bitter laugh. "You're looking at a go-nowhere nobody. A fool and a dreamer."

"I don't think you're a fool," he said, making his way slowly towards her. "And I don't think there's anything wrong with being a dreamer, as long as you dream nice dreams."

"I dreamt of owning Dad's flower shop," she said, her voice breaking off with a sob.

"I know, darling," he said softly, and gathered her into his arms. "I know."

"Oh, Richard," she cried, and buried her face in his chest, her hands clutching at the lapels of his suit jacket. "She was so horrid. So hateful! I don't understand people like that."

"Don't think about her any more, Holly. Put her out of your mind and out of your life. People like that are poison. And don't worry. This shop will be all yours by the end of the day. I promise."

"And I'll be all yours," she returned on a whisper, then began to cry again.

Richard tightened his hold on her, telling himself that he was doing the right thing. But he knew he wasn't.

She'd once said how corrupting it must be to be able to buy anything you wanted. It seemed it was. He'd wanted Holly as his bride. And he was about to buy her, even though he knew it was wrong.

"I'm sorry, but I'm going to have to love you and leave you, Holly," he said, putting her at arm's length. "I have to get onto the real estate agent before they shut up shop today. I suggest you get busy as

well. You said you have a girl who comes in sometimes to help you?''

''Yes, Sara. She comes from Wednesday till
Saturday.''

''Would she look after the shop for you if you went
away tomorrow?''

''I'm sure she would. Did you say *tomorrow*?''

''Yes, I'm going to see if I can get tickets on the
Spirit of Tasmania. I know it leaves Sydney for
Tasmania every Tuesday afternoon.''

''Tasmania!'' Her lovely eyes lit up. ''Oh, I've always wanted to go there. I saw a segment on a holiday programme on TV about that trip. You can take
your car on the ferry and they have proper cabins and
everything. It'll be like a mini cruise.''

''I'm glad you like the idea.'' Richard was struck
with a momentary crisis of conscience. ''Are you absolutely sure you want to do this, Holly? The shop,
and the marriage, and everything.''

Her eyes cleared. Her chin lifted. ''Absolutely.''

''So be it,'' he said.

CHAPTER THIRTEEN

"LOOK, Richard!" Holly exclaimed. "We're going under the Harbour Bridge! Doesn't it look fabulous from down here?"

"It sure does," he agreed.

They were standing out on the back deck of the *Spirit Of Tasmania*, along with several other passengers, enjoying the warmth of the afternoon sunshine and the wonderful sights of the city as the ferry made its way slowly from the wharf at Darling Harbour towards Sydney Heads.

"I still can't believe how quickly you did everything," Holly said, with an awed glance up at the handsome man next to her. "The shop. This trip. My ring..." She looked back down at her left hand, and the glorious diamond engagement ring sparkling on her ring finger.

"My mother says I'm an overachiever."

Holly smiled up at him. "In that case, I *like* overachievers." She would have preferred to say love. But overnight, Holly had come to terms with her one-sided love for Richard. He did care about her. And he was totally committed to their marriage. That meant a lot. And who knew? In time, the memory of his wife would surely fade. Joanna was dead and Holly was here, in the flesh, to look after him, and love him.

Miracles did happen. After all, who would have

believed she'd shortly be the proud owner of A Flower A Day? Or living in that incredible penthouse? Or having a man like Richard as her husband and the father of her children?

On the other hand, there was no getting round the fact that her impulsive decision to let Richard buy her as his wife was no miracle. It had been partly inspired by fury. A fury that hadn't yet abated.

"By the way, Richard," she said. "I want Connie to know that the shop was bought for me by my fiancé. Can you arrange that?" She liked imagining the looks on Katie's and Dave's faces as well, when they heard the news. She hoped they all choked on it.

"Of course," Richard returned. "But best leave such a surprise till after the contracts are exchanged, don't you think?"

"Yes, you're right. That bitch might pull out of the sale, if she thinks I'm going to get the shop. You *are* a wise man."

Wise, and wonderfully passionate. Holly could forgive Richard for not loving her, if his passion for her remained intact. Last night he'd been especially passionate.

A sudden thought occurred to her. Oh, dear, oh, dear. How could she have been so stupid?

"Richard," she whispered urgently.

"What?" he whispered back, bending his head down sidewards.

"In all the hurry to pack, I…um…I forgot to bring my pills."

"Is that such a problem? I mean, we both want children, Holly. And I, for one, don't want to wait too long. Why not just forget the pill from now on?"

"No, you don't understand. I'm happy to have your

baby. But first, I'm sure to get a period in a day or two. And the thing is...I don't like...I mean..."

"I understand, Holly. Truly."

"Are you sure?"

"Please don't stress, darling. I'm not here with you just for sex. Besides, we still have tonight. Though I'll probably have a bad back in the morning if I attempt too much in that teensy-weensy cabin of ours with its teensy-weensy bunks and teensy-weensy shower."

"They certainly didn't choose those beds with a man like you in mind," Holly agreed, relieved that Richard wasn't annoyed with her.

"I'll manage," he said. "I noticed a nice firm little table between the bunks, and another one under the mirror. Not as good as my desk, or your work table in the shop last night, but necessity is the mother of invention."

"Shh," she warned, glancing over at the elderly couple standing next to them.

"You're right," Richard murmured. "Wouldn't want our fellow passengers to hear too much about our X-rated love life. The shock might do them in."

Holly knew what Richard meant. Most of the people on the ferry were on the older side. Retired couples going to Tasmania on holiday together. She supposed it was a good way to travel, taking their own cars with them. But she wondered if some might have been better on bus tours, especially the ones using walking sticks!

"Do you think we'll still be going away on holidays together when we're their age?" she said a bit wistfully.

"Absolutely," he replied.

"We'll have to keep fit."

"We'll keep fit running after our children. Look, the Heads are coming up," Richard said, pointing towards the impressive promontories that guarded the entrance to Port Jackson. "It's calm here in the harbour but things might get a bit rougher once we're out to sea. Do you get seasick?"

"I don't know."

"You'd better come with me, then. I brought some tablets, just in case."

Typical of Richard, she thought as he took her arm and led her inside off the deck. He was a planner, as well as a doer. She would always feel safe with him at her side.

Making their way back to the cabin took a few minutes. The cabins were located on a different level at the front of the boat, with lots of narrow hallways going every which way, rather like a rabbit warren.

Still, Richard seemed to know where they were going.

"No, it's this way," he said when she went to turn in the wrong direction at the end of a long corridor.

Holly realised she was going to learn a lot about her husband-to-be during the ten days they would be away. Their return ticket was for Thursday week, docking back at Darling Harbour on the Friday.

"You know your mother told me recently that the best way for two people to find out if they can get along is to go away together."

"In that case, we're doing exceptionally well so far. Already an hour on the boat and we haven't argued once."

"You're obviously on your best behaviour. But can you keep it up?"

"It'll be a challenge," he said with a devilish twinkle in his eye. "But I'll do my best."

Holly punched him on one of his rock-hard biceps. "Your mother didn't tell me you were so bad. She always said you were such a good boy."

"Never believe anything mothers say about their sons," he said as they reached their cabin. "But speaking of my mother," he added once they were inside, "I got an email from her this morning. Clever Melvin took a laptop with him and gave me his email address. So I sent them an announcement of our engagement."

"Oh, Richard, you didn't!" Holly had assumed he'd keep that a secret for a while. "I hope you didn't tell her about the shop business. I *like* your mother, Richard. And she likes me. The last thing I want is for her to start thinking I'm some kind of fortune hunter!"

"Trust me, she doesn't. I *did* tell her I'd bought the shop for you and she was very happy about it. I also told her that I was crazy about you and that I was taking you away to Tassie for a well-needed break. I also informed her that we were getting married as soon as she got back."

Holly blinked. "And…and what did she say?" Holly couldn't help wondering how Mrs Crawford interpreted Richard saying he was crazy about her. Did she think that meant he'd fallen in love with her; that he was finally over Joanna's death?

Holly supposed it didn't matter if the woman thought that. Other people would. To be honest, Holly preferred that they did. She didn't want people thinking their marriage was like Reece and Alanna's.

"Mum was tickled pink. She said we might have a double wedding."

"She and Melvin?"

"Yep. He popped the question and she said yes."

"That's wonderful!"

"Yes, they're well suited, that pair. Just like us."

Holly could see that she and Richard *were* quite well suited. But he *was* twelve years older than she was. Older and much more experienced. She wondered if he was like a father-figure to her. If that was his main attraction for her.

"You're thinking again," Richard said. "I hate it when you do that. I never know quite *what* you're thinking."

"Don't you?" That surprised her. She imagined he'd always read her every thought and move. "You mean I'm a woman of mystery?"

"Irritatingly so at times."

"What am I thinking now?" she said, her eyes raking down over his body.

"Now *that*, I can read," he growled.

"Be careful now," she said laughingly when he pulled her down onto the narrow bed with him.

"Why don't you shut up, woman?" And he kissed her.

It was a good hour later before Holly got round to taking the seasickness tablet.

"What would you like to do now?" Richard asked after they'd both straightened their clothes and combed their hair.

"We could pop along and check out that café we came past," she suggested. "Or, even better, we could go along to the bar and have a drink? We don't have to drive anywhere."

"We?" he said, his eyes narrowing on her as he moved very close.

The smallness of the cabin plus his looming over her by some inches reminded Holly of what a big man Richard was. He was intimidating in size, as well as in manner.

But she wasn't afraid of him any more. Not one little bit.

"You don't think I'm going to let you do all the driving during this trip, do you?" she tossed up at him saucily.

"Hmm. Perhaps we should get one thing straight, madam. I like to do the driving in my own car."

"Is that so?" she returned, arms crossing. "Methinks we're just about to have our first argument."

"No, no," he said, lifting up his hands in swift surrender. "No arguing. You can drive. Sometimes. If you're extra careful."

"Typical male."

"Yes," he agreed. "I'm a typical male. Sorry about that. But when we get back to Sydney I'll buy you your own car. What would you like?"

Holly was taken aback. Just like that. A new car. One part of her thrilled to the idea of driving round in her own new car. But there was another part of her that worried Richard was buying her again.

Silly, really. They were going to be husband and wife. Why shouldn't he buy her a new car? But as much as she tried to be logical about it, she still didn't like it.

"I...I don't know," she said. "I'll think about it."

CHAPTER FOURTEEN

SUNDAY saw them driving into Hobart, Tasmania's capital city. Situated on the estuary of the Derwent River, on the lower east side of the island, Hobart was one of Australia's oldest and most beautiful cities.

"Reminds me of some of the large port towns in the south of England," Richard said as they drove slowly along the harbour foreshore, which was only a stone's throw from the CBD.

"I've never been overseas, so I wouldn't know," Holly said. "All I can say is that it's very picturesque, with almost as good a harbour as Sydney."

There were lots of boats of all shapes and sizes moored against the many piers, from small runabouts to expensive-looking speedboats and racing yachts. In the distance, a massive, grey-painted catamaran was churning across the wide expanse of water, looking quite magnificent, but rather menacing. Richard speculated that it had to belong to the armed forces.

"Could even be American," he said.

Further along, a white ocean liner was anchored against a jetty, glistening in the sunshine. It made the ferry they'd travelled down on look small, yet Holly had thought the *Spirit of Tasmania* very large when she'd first seen it docked at Darling Harbour.

"Did you know Hobart has the second deepest harbour in the world?'' Richard said when she commented on the size of the liner.

''What's the deepest?'' she asked, curious.

''Rio.''

''How do you know such things?''

He shrugged. ''I read a lot. I also have a photographic memory. Made studying for exams a lot easier, I can tell you.''

''I never had to sit for any proper exams,'' Holly said without thinking. ''I never even sat for my school certificate. I left school at fifteen to work with Dad in the shop.'' That feeling of inferiority flooded Holly with her admissions. ''You must think me very ignorant.''

''I don't think you're at all ignorant. Just the opposite. I think you're a very smart girl. Look at the way you did those books without any formal training. Passing exams is no gauge to a person's intelligence, Holly. Simply their ability to recall facts and figures.''

''You might think that way, but a lot of people don't. They think a degree is the be-all and end-all.''

''It isn't.''

''That's easy for you to say. You have your degree. It's a bit like people saying money isn't important when they already have it. Try not having any money and see how important it suddenly becomes.''

Holly had no idea how she got onto this subject. But she regretted it immediately. Regretted her sharp tone as well.

The past few days had been so wonderful. The first night of their trip—the night before she'd got her period—they'd stayed at this lovely historical house. It had originally been a doctor's residence before it had become a hospital during the late nineteenth century. Now, it was a B & B.

The owner had taken them for a tour when they'd arrived, telling them its history and showing them all the rooms with their many antiques, pointing out that the spacious suite they were sleeping in had been where the babies were born.

It had been decorated in blue with a big brass bed and a wonderfully romantic atmosphere.

That night, Richard had made love to her in the big brass bed for ages. Really made love to her. Very tenderly, telling her all the while that soon *they'd* be making a baby. The next morning, when she'd looked at him over breakfast Holly had felt more confident than ever that their marriage would work.

They'd driven across the north-eastern part of Tasmania on the Thursday and Friday, exploring the countryside by day, and relaxing over a fine meal each night, discovering that they didn't need to be having sex to enjoy each other's company. They'd stayed at a different place every night, another historic home that had been converted to a boutique hotel on the Thursday, a B & B in Swansea on Friday and a guest-house in Richmond last night.

Holly had never realised till she came here just how beautiful and interesting Tasmania was. Very rich in history. Richard thought the same. Every night, both of them had devoured the travel brochures they'd picked up on the ferry, seeing where they could go and what they could do the next day. Next Tuesday they planned to drive down to Port Arthur, the famous old convict jail, after which they would follow the highway up the east coast before crossing to Devonport for the ferry's departure on Thursday.

Holly had been very excited about their plans. So why had she risked spoiling everything with such provocative comments? She might not be ignorant, but she was a complete idiot!

"I'm sorry, Richard," she said swiftly. "I wish I hadn't said any of that. It sounded petty. And bitter. I'm a bit touchy about education. Connie used to lord it over Dad that she had some fancy arts degree. Katie went to university as well, and of course Dad paid for it all."

"I can well understand why you would feel resentful, Holly," he said. "Don't apologise for your feelings. You're a human being, not a saint. But higher education can be highly overrated. As far as money is concerned, everyone likes having money and I'm no exception. I've worked very hard accumulating lots of it and I enjoy the power it gives me. It *is* satisfying to be able to buy just about anything you want. I won't deny that, either. You wouldn't be sitting here with me now if it wasn't for my money."

"Don't say that!"

"Why not? It's true."

Clearly, from his point of view, however, he *had* bought her. Lock, stock, and barrel.

"There were other considerations," she felt forced to say. "I would not have made my proposition in the first place if I hadn't liked you as much as I do."

"And if the sex wasn't as good," Richard added with a dry laugh, even whilst his heart twisted.

It was his own silly fault, of course. He'd set out to bind her to him through sex.

He seemed to have succeeded all too well.

How perverse it was to find that he now resented Holly liking his lovemaking as much as she obviously did. No doubt the reason for her stroppiness this morning was frustration. Three whole days without an orgasm! Underneath, she was probably panting for him to take her straight to the hotel, and to bed.

The thought both repelled and excited him.

"You said it would be all systems clear for a resumption of relations today, didn't you?" he asked with a long sideways glance, noting the instant pink in her cheeks.

Yet it was very cool in the car, the air-conditioning doing a good job of keeping the heat out. Outside, the temperature was thirty degrees, the sun very bright.

"Yes," she said tautly.

"Just as well we're not far from the hotel then," he muttered, his own body already stirring.

Richard had chosen the Wrest Point Casino to stay in, not because of the gambling facilities, but because it was one of Hobart's top hotels. Situated on a point overlooking the water, the circular tower building boasted five-star rooms, all with magnificent views of the river, which was as wide as it was deep.

A circular driveway led up to the entrance of the hotel, a smartly dressed parking valet jumping to attention as soon as Richard stopped. The reception staff was just as efficient, and they were soon riding the lift up to their allotted floor. Their luggage was just being delivered as they reached the door, Richard giving the young man a tip, even though he didn't have to. Australia was not large on tipping, but Richard had found it was never a bad idea.

Money did smooth one's path in life, he thought ruefully as he ushered Holly into their five-star room. It bought you the best of accommodation, and the most accommodating of women.

Despite his throbbing erection and Holly's admission that his lovemaking was one of the reasons she was here, Richard resisted the temptation to pull her into his arms as soon as the porter departed. Instead, he strolled across to the window, pretending that he found the magnificent water view much more interesting than Holly.

When he slowly turned, he found her standing there in the middle of the spacious room, looking slightly confused, and incredibly sexy.

Not that she was dressed sexily. Her white shorts were a modest length and her simple pink blouse didn't cling. Her long tanned legs were bare, however, and her hair was down, the way he liked it. Her make-up was zilch, other than a touch of red lipstick.

"Are you angry with me for some reason?" she asked at last.

"Not at all," he lied.

"Then why are you acting like this?"

"Like what?"

"Like you don't want to make love to me."

"You want me to make love to you?" he said, hating himself for being such an idiot.

"I thought that was what you wanted, too."

"I need to have a shower first. We've been travelling all day and I feel hot and sticky. Of course, you're welcome to join me, if you like…"

Let *her* make love to *him*, if that was what she wanted so much. With her hands and her mouth.

She stared at him the way she'd stared at him the first day he'd met her, her eyes totally inscrutable. If only he knew what she was thinking...

Her smile blew him away.

"You know I like," she said, her eyes going all soft and smoky.

Richard had often read about women going weak at the knees with desire. He'd never imagined being afflicted in a similar manner. He leant back against the wall and gripped the window-sill.

"You'll have to be gentle with me," he drawled, hoping to hide his unexpected vulnerability with humour. "All that driving has made me exhausted."

"Poor Richard," she purred. "Perhaps a bath would be a better idea. I'll go and run one for you." And she was gone.

Richard closed his eyes at the sound of the water running.

A bath. With her, naked. Her, washing him. All over. Her, kissing him and caressing him in the water.

His knuckles whitened on the sill as he envisaged what would happen after that. He'd have her dry him but leave herself wet. Then he'd carry her to bed where he'd lick her dry. All over. He'd make her cry out under his mouth. Then cry out under him.

He wanted her to lose herself entirely. Lose control. He needed to see that she was totally his. At least in bed.

"Are you coming?"

His eyes opened, his breath catching to find her

standing in the doorway of the bathroom, already naked.

He'd never seen her look more beautiful, or more desirable.

"Absolutely," he said, laughing with dark humour as he propelled himself towards her.

CHAPTER FIFTEEN

"I SHOULD never have let you buy me all those clothes," Holly muttered over the rim of her coffee-cup.

Richard glanced up from his cappuccino in surprise. It was Monday, and they were sitting together in a cosy little coffee shop in Sandy Bay, the Hobart suburb that boasted the casino and lots of trendy boutiques. Richard had thoroughly enjoyed himself all morning, taking her to the most expensive dress shops, having her try on outfits for him, choosing only the best to buy. He'd got over his irrational burst of resentment yesterday, telling himself not to be such a fool. It was great that she liked him making love to her, that she wasn't at all inhibited, or prudish.

"What on earth are you talking about?" he demanded to know. "Why shouldn't I have bought you those clothes? They're classy clothes, nothing like that dress Reece bought Alanna."

She shook her head, her eyes worrying him. "I'm sorry, Richard."

"Sorry? What do you mean you're sorry? Sorry about what?"

Her coffee-cup clattered back into its saucer. "I can't marry you. I thought I could, but I can't."

Richard tried not to panic.

"Why?" he grated out.

"It simply won't work," she said.

"Why won't it work?"

"You know why. I told you once. I need my husband to love me. *Me*, Holly Greenaway. I'm a living, breathing person, Richard, not a possession. You made me feel like a possession this morning. Like a trophy wife, to be made over into what you want. When we go back to the hotel after this and you…you want me to do the kind of things you like, I'll feel I *have* to, not because I *want* to. Those clothes feel like payment for services rendered, as well as services yet to be rendered. Same with the new car you offered me. Same with the shop, too."

"The shop was your idea," he bit out, an emotional storm building up inside him. "So was the marriage proposal."

"Yes. Yes, you're right. I let your wealth corrupt me into getting what *I* wanted. That, and your skill in bed. But it has to stop now, before I get pregnant. I'm sorry about the shop. But you won't lose by buying it. I'm sure it will be a good long-term investment. All I ask is for you to let me stay on there till I can find another job and another place to live." She wiggled the engagement ring off her finger and placed it in the middle of the table.

He could not believe it. She was rejecting him. Running out on him.

The need to strike out at her, to hurt her as he was hurting, was intense.

"I'll be selling that bloody shop," he growled. "I should never have bought it in the first place. Which I did, you know. There never was any other buyer. It was me all along."

She stared at him, and for the first time Richard

had no doubt about what he was seeing in her eyes. Total shock. And then, the most dreadful dismay.

"Oh, Richard," she said brokenly. "How could you? I always thought you were a man of honour."

"Nice men finish last, sweetheart," he threw at her, talking tough, but inside he was disintegrating.

A sob broke from her throat. "Oh, God. I have to get out of here."

She jumped up, her chair falling back. She almost tripped over the bags at her feet as she fled. Richard hesitated only a moment before he was up and after her, leaving everything behind. The ring. The clothes. None of them mattered. All that mattered was Holly. He had to get her and tell her how sorry he was. He would try to explain and beg her to forgive him.

"Holly!" he called after her as he pushed through the coffee-shop door in her wake.

She halted at the kerb just long enough to send a distressed glance over her shoulder at him. Then she dashed out into the road.

The loud screech of brakes assaulted Richard's ears as he saw a white van hurtling down the hill towards her.

They said your life flashed before you the moment before you died. The *truth* flashed before Richard's eyes the moment before he thought Holly would die.

He loved her. Loved her as he'd never loved Joanna.

The thought of burying Holly gave him a strength and a speed that was inhuman. Some guardian angel must have lifted him and propelled him across that road, because before he knew it he was diving into mid-air, taking her with him out of harm's way.

She screamed as they crashed into the gutter on the other side, Richard's body buffering hers against the fall. Richard didn't scream. He was thanking God for his mercy.

People quickly milled around them, helping them to their feet, asking if they were all right. The driver from the white van, which had stopped. People from the coffee shop. Passers-by.

"I...I think so," Holly said shakily. "Richard? Are you all right?"

"I'm fine," he insisted, even as his leg throbbed with pain under his trousers. Thank God the weather had turned cool that day and he'd been wearing a leather jacket, or all his arms would have been grazed.

"Your face is bleeding," Holly said, reaching up to touch his cheek.

Someone produced some tissues, which he dabbed against his cut cheekbone.

"Come back into the coffee shop," the lady proprietor insisted. "You've had a bad shock. A sit down and a hot sweet drink is called for."

Holly knew the woman was right. She also knew Richard had just saved her life. But to go back and sit down with him. To have to *talk* to him.

"Please, Holly," he said, perhaps guessing that she still wanted to flee.

She closed her eyes rather than look at him. He took her arm and led her back across the road to the coffee shop. She finally opened her eyes after she'd been settled back in the chair she'd occupied earlier. The sight of her engagement ring still in the middle of the table brought back the reasons for her fleeing in the first place.

Richard's admission to buying the shop behind her back.

Why? The reason was obvious. He'd wanted her to be evicted. Wanted her to have nowhere else to go, but him.

Two new cups of milk coffee arrived, into which the waitress heaped some sugar.

"Drink up, dears," she advised before leaving them to it.

Holly just sat there, saying nothing.

"You shouldn't have run like that, Holly," Richard said quietly at last. "You could have been killed."

"Better dead than wed to a man like you."

"Don't say that," he choked out, his face ashen. "I love you, Holly. I know you won't believe me, but it's true."

"How dare you?" she snapped under her breath. "It's despicable to lie about something like that! But then you *are* despicable."

"I couldn't agree with you more. What I did was despicable. But I do love you."

"You simply can't accept defeat, can you? You don't love me," she said bitterly. "Everyone knows you're still in love with Joanna. Your mother. Your friends. I'm just a means to an end."

"That's not true."

"Don't you dare try to tell me what's true and what isn't. I *know* the truth."

"No, you don't," he bit out. "And neither does anyone else. You think I'm still in love with Joanna? Well, you're wrong. I hate her. No, that's wrong. I don't even hate her any more. She's not worthy of being hated. Because that would mean she was worthy of being loved.''

Holly gaped at him.

''Yes, well you might be surprised. But I couldn't let anyone know I was married to an unfaithful bitch, could I? Not me. Mr Successful. Impossible to tell anyone that she'd been expecting a child when she was killed, especially when that child definitely wasn't mine. Ever since she died I thought she'd been having an affair and that she'd been going to pass the child off as mine. But Kim finally filled in the gaps for me when I rang her the other day and demanded to know the truth. Joanna was going to have an abortion on the day she was killed. She didn't even *know* who the father of her child was. It could have been any of half a dozen men she let screw her at a party she threw when I was away. Isn't that a lovely thought? My wife, a slut!''

Holly could not think of a thing to say as shock warred with sympathy for Richard. How dreadful to discover that the person you loved was so…sick. She'd been shattered when Dave had dumped her for Katie. What if she'd been married to Dave and discovered he'd been sleeping around like a tom-cat and had made some other girl pregnant?

''Oh, Richard,'' she said at last, feeling truly sorry for him.

Holly was appalled when tears glistened in his eyes.

''Don't cry, Richard,'' she pleaded. ''Please don't cry.''

''I'm not crying for her, Holly. Let the devil take her. I'm sure he has. But I feel like crying over losing you,'' he choked out. ''You have no idea how much I love you.''

''Do you, Richard? Do you, really?''

''More than words can say. You brought me back from the edge of darkness. You gave me hope for a future. You showed me that love doesn't have to be selfish.''

''Then why did you buy the shop?''

He shook his head. ''It was a mistake. I'd just found out from Kim how truly wicked Joanna was and I was afraid for my sanity. I needed you, Holly. Needed your warmth and your kindness. And, yes, the comfort of your body. I was too blind with bitterness to see that my feelings for you had already deepened to love. It wasn't till I saw that car coming towards you a little while ago that the truth hit me. I do realise that you will still find it hard to forgive me. But give me another chance, Holly. You must feel something for me. Maybe, one day, you might learn to love me.''

''I don't think so, Richard,'' she said quietly. When she picked up the ring and slipped it back onto her finger, his head snapped back with shock.

Her smile was soft and loving. ''You see, I've been in love with you for quite a while, my darling,'' she said, reaching over to take one of his hands in hers.

His eyes filled with tears again, and this time she wasn't appalled. There was something about a man who could cry over her that was very lovable indeed.

CHAPTER SIXTEEN

"THANK you so much for giving me away, Melvin," Holly said sincerely.

"My pleasure, sweetie," Melvin replied.

Holly thought *he* was the sweetie. He was such a nice man. So kind and considerate. Melvin and Mrs Crawford had surprised everyone by tying the knot whilst they were overseas. But they'd been home for a few weeks now and Holly had never known a happier couple.

Not counting herself and Richard, of course, she amended with a sigh. They were so happy together, even more so since she'd found out last month that she was expecting a baby. Already, Richard had given Reece the job of finding them the right family home. No way, he said, was he going to raise a child of his in a penthouse.

"Not nervous, are you?" Melvin whispered as he took her arm.

"Just a little," Holly returned. The day so far had been somewhat nerve-racking, trying to get everything right, making sure she looked as good as she could possibly look.

"No reason to be," he said, and patted her arm. "You look divine. And you're marrying a fine man."

Holly had no doubts about that. But she still felt a bit jittery as she glanced up the aisle.

Her eyes landed first on Alanna and Sara, who were slowly making their way towards the front of the church, both of them looking extremely svelte and elegant in red. Their long satin dresses were the same colour as the bouquet of red roses Holly was holding, a sentimental choice because of the way she and Richard had met.

Her bridesmaids' bouquets, however, were of white roses, matching Holly's dazzlingly white gown. She hadn't wanted to wear cream or ivory. Her satin gown was also not straight, like theirs, but had a traditionally large skirt, gathered out from a tightly boned bodice that showed her hourglass figure. The neckline was wide and low, the sleeves long and tight. Her tulle veil stretched out into a train, seeded with small pearls around the edges.

Alanna and Sara had said she looked like a princess. But what they thought didn't really matter. All Holly really cared about was what Richard thought of her.

Her agitated gaze finally reached the three men standing up near the priest who was to conduct the ceremony.

Each one of them looked very handsome in their black dinner suits, even Mike, who'd scrubbed up remarkably well after a shave and a haircut. He really was an unusual man. Very intense, with a darkly brooding nature, which could be interesting, if you liked that kind of thing.

Fortunately Sara, who was partnering him today, wasn't one of those women who'd taken an instant fancy to him. Her husband wouldn't have been too pleased if she had.

Reece, of course, looked as glamorous as usual. He and Alanna would always be a striking couple. Holly had finally warmed to Reece, and she *really* liked Alanna, who'd taken her under her wing and been such a help with all the wedding preparations, which had been considerable.

Finally, Holly allowed her eyes to move over to Richard, who was looking absolutely gorgeous but just a little nervous too, she thought with a relieved smile.

No one else would have noticed. They would just see a tall, handsome man with steely grey eyes and a dignified expression.

But Holly knew him better than anyone by now. His hands were clasped just a little too tightly together down in front of him for true composure. And his lips were pressed into a firm line as well.

She liked it that he loved her so much that he would be nervous on his wedding day. Richard was not a man who ever showed nerves.

Holly suspected she would never see him cry again, as he had that day in Tasmania. But the memory of that day would always stay with her. Thinking of it right now reassured her.

Richard loved her. Truly loved her. Her, Holly Greenaway.

You would have liked him, Dad, she whispered in her mind as she walked up the aisle to marry the man she loved.

Mrs Crawford beamed at her from where she was

sitting in the front pew, looking amazingly young in lemon silk.

They hadn't told her about the baby yet, but she was going to be thrilled when she found out. But not as thrilled as Holly.

She was going to have a baby. She and Richard were going to be a family. Holly's heart turned over with happiness. She hadn't been part of a family for so long.

Finally, Alanna moved away from the aisle to the side and Richard had a clearer view of his bride.

He sucked in sharply.

"I admit I was wrong, Rich," Reece murmured by his side. "She's definitely the girl for you."

"Too young for him, I reckon," Mike muttered, and Reece jabbed him in the ribs.

Mike grunted. "Okay, okay, she does love him. I can see that. Even worse, I think he loves her."

"What's wrong with that?" Reece said sharply.

"Hush up, you two," Richard commanded. "I'm getting married here."

Really married this time, he thought as his lovely Holly reached his side. This is the real thing. This is *real* love.

His heart squeezed tight as he reached out his hand to her. She smiled as she took it, a warm, loving smile that made him relax for the first time that day.

"You look incredible," he whispered, still in awe of her. "Exquisite."

"Thank you," she whispered back.

I should be thanking you, my darling, he thought

as they turned to face the priest together. For loving me. And forgiving me. And trusting me again.

I won't ever let you down, he promised her silently as the priest started talking about the sacredness of marriage. I will protect you with my life. And I will love you to my dying day...

The Tycoon's Trophy Wife

PROLOGUE

Sydney. September. Spring.

ALANNA hesitated at the entrance to the cemetery, dismayed to find that her stomach had begun to churn.

Just butterflies, she reassured herself, and forged on.

The churning increased by the time she stood in front of his headstone. But she remained determined to do this. To say what she had come to say. To find closure once and for all.

'It's been five years since I stood here,' she said to the man buried there. 'Five long, incredibly difficult years. I've come here today to tell you that you didn't win, Darko. I have survived.

'Time does have amazing healing powers and I finally found the will to go on, a will much stronger than I ever believed I had. I have taken my life in my hands. *My* hands,' she repeated quite forcefully as those same hands gripped her handbag in front of her.

'I've remarried, Darko. Yes, you heard me. I am now another man's wife. How you must be turning in your grave to hear that,' she bit out between clenched teeth.

'Of course, I did not choose a love match. Would I be so foolish as to marry another man who loved

5

me? But we like and respect each other, Reece and I. Best of all, Reece doesn't try to own me, or control me. He trusts me and wants me to be happy. He doesn't mind if I go out with my girlfriends. He doesn't mind if I wear sexy clothes. He even buys them for me. He bought me the suit I have on today. It's the kind of outfit *you* would have ripped off me. But Reece loves me to wear clothes like this.'

With a defiant tilt of her head, she spread her arms wide and turned around, showing off her eye-catching figure, encased that day in a cream silk suit that had a short, tight skirt and a figure hugging jacket with a deep V neckline.

'Did I mention that my husband is a very rich, very handsome man?' Alanna went on. 'Very sexy, too. He might not be crazy in love with me, but he wants to make love to me almost every night. To satisfy me. Which he does. Do you hear me, Darko?' Alanna threw at the headstone in a challenging tone, which didn't totally mask the underlying hurt and pain that twisted at her heart.

Tears threatened but she dashed them away. The time for tears had long gone.

'One final thing before I go,' she continued more calmly. 'Reece and I are going to try for a baby. Not every man is like you, Darko. Reece won't see a child as competition. Or something else to be suspicious of. Or jealous over. Reece doesn't have a jealous bone in his body.

'You will say that means he doesn't care about me. But you know what? I don't want to *ever* be cared for the way *you* cared for me. And you're wrong, anyway. Reece *does* care for me in his own way. And I care for him. He makes me feel good, something you never did for all your supposed loving.'

Alanna scooped in a deep breath before letting it out slowly, relieved to find that the churning in her stomach had finally subsided. 'My mother said I should forgive you, that there were excuses for your behaviour. But I can't do that. What you did was unforgivable. I am going now, Darko, and this time, I am never coming back. You are now firmly consigned to the past. And I will do my best not to think of you any more.'

CHAPTER ONE

THE organ player breaking into the wedding march signalled the bride was ready at last. She was only fifteen minutes late, Reece realised as he glanced at his gold Rolex. Long enough, however, for the groom next to him to get fidgety.

'It's showtime!' Reece said, smiling over at Richard who'd gone ramrod straight at the change of music, his hands clasped tightly in front of him.

'Have you got the rings?' Richard whispered out of the side of his mouth.

Reece patted the right pocket of his black dinner jacket. 'Of course. Relax, Rich,' he said, and reached out to touch him reassuringly on the arm. 'I've done this before.'

'So has he,' Mike muttered under his breath from the other side of Reece.

Reece's head whipped round to throw him a reproachful glare. Mike was a good bloke at heart, but his eternal cynicism over romance and relationships could be exasperating. It was also out of place today. Blind Freddie could see that Richard and Holly were deeply in love. This would be a much better marriage than the one Richard had had with Joanna, who, quite frankly, had not been Mrs Perfect.

Reece would never forget the night she'd made a

8

play for him, something he'd never told Richard, but which had bothered him greatly at the time.

He'd avoided Joanna after that.

When she'd been killed in a car accident a couple of years back, he'd felt very sorry for Richard. But Reece sometimes wondered if it was a case of fate being cruel to be kind.

Whatever, Richard's first marriage was past history. Today was a new day and Reece finally felt optimistic for his best friend's choice for his second wife.

Despite an initial concern that Holly, at twenty-six, was too young and naive for a man of Richard's age and status—Richard was thirty-eight and the CEO of a merchant bank—Reece could now see that Holly was exactly what Richard needed after Joanna. She was a genuinely sweet, caring, loving girl. Very pretty, too.

She was going to make a lovely bride.

Reece's eyes narrowed as he peered down to the back of the church, curious to see what the girls were wearing. But the church doors were open and the late-afternoon light was streaming in. All he could see were silhouettes.

The first bridesmaid eventually came into view, looking elegant in a long, straight red dress and carrying a bouquet of white roses. She was tall, with auburn hair, a nice enough figure and an attractive face.

Reece didn't know her. She was a florist friend of

Holly's. In her thirties. And married, Alanna had told him last night.

Reece hoped happily so, given she was being partnered by Mike today.

Reece glanced to his left at Mike, who was looking surprisingly debonair, a far cry from his usual dishevelled self. Amazing what a haircut, a shave and a tuxedo could achieve. Most days, Mike looked as if he'd walked out of a spaghetti western. Acted like that, too. Very tough and gruff.

Strangely, some women seemed to fancy him like that. Lord knew why. Reece thought Mike's clean-cut image today was infinitely more attractive. But what was one woman's trash was another woman's treasure, he supposed.

On Mike's part, he went for any good-looking female who made the chase easy for him and who agreed with his rules, his rules being he would take her out for one reason and one reason only. Sex. There would be no real relationship. No romance. The only promise he gave was not to be a two-timer.

But when it was over—meaning when he got bored—it was over.

Mike was an obsessively compulsive computer genius with a very low boredom threshold. His last girlfriend..an exotic dancer..had lasted all of a month.

It still never failed to astonish Reece just how many takers Mike got. And how many of his ex-girlfriends remained friendly with him, afterwards. Damned if it made sense to him.

'Behave yourself with your partner today,' he whispered in Mike's direction. 'She's married.'

'That never seems to stop *them*,' Mike returned drily. 'But don't worry. I avoid married women like the plague. They're nothing but trouble.'

'Sounds like you've had some experience.'

'Only once. It was a close call, but I managed to escape.'

'Anyone I know?'

'I don't think this is the time to discuss it,' he bit out.

Reece stared at Mike, who gave a slight nod in Richard's direction. Fortunately, Richard wasn't taking any notice of them, his eyes fixed straight ahead.

'Joanna?' Reece whispered.

'Yep.'

'She hit on me, too,' Reece admitted.

'No kidding. What a bitch.'

'Stunningly beautiful, though.'

'It's always the stunningly beautiful ones you have to worry about,' Mike muttered.

Just then, the chief bridesmaid came into view, dressed exactly the same as the girl walking a few metres in front of her.

Every male hormone in Reece moved from stationary into overdrive. Now *that* was one stunningly beautiful woman.

But, of course, he already knew that. He'd been married to her for nine months.

Reece struggled with a perverse jab of jealousy as he watched the eyes of all the male wedding guests slavishly following Alanna's graceful progress down the aisle.

Perverse, because he'd never felt jealous before, not even when she was showing off her model-slim figure in one of the revealing evening gowns he liked her to wear.

By comparison, Alanna was very modestly dressed today. Yet for some reason, the effect was sexier. Maybe it was true that what was hidden and hinted at was more provocative than what was on open display.

Or maybe it was the colour.

Alanna had never worn red before. She preferred softer, paler shades. But Holly had chosen red for the bridesmaids for some sentimental reason. Something to do with a bunch of red roses having brought her and Richard together.

The colour actually looked magnificent against Alanna's porcelain skin and creamy blonde hair.

The style was quite simple. A full-length sheath, it skimmed rather than hugged Alanna's figure. The neckline was wide. Almost off the shoulder, but not low-cut. The sleeves were straight and long, no doubt in deference to the weather. It was, after all, June. And June in Sydney was winter time.

The day outside was pleasant enough, but inside this rather old church the air was crisp and cold.

The first bridesmaid reached the end of the aisle and turned away to the side, giving Reece an even better view of his wife, especially her face.

And what an exquisite face it was. Classically

sculptured, with a delicately pointed chin, high cheek-bones and a fine, fair complexion. Her eyes were a smoky green, almond-shaped and lushly lashed. Her nose was small and straight with an elegant tip. Her mouth was full, her lips looking even fuller painted scarlet.

Reece's gaze moved down further, his mind stripping her of that dress and seeing her as he liked seeing her best of all.

Alanna had the kind of body that had always attracted and aroused him. Slender and firm, with long legs, a tight butt and small, high-set breasts.

Body-wise, she was very similar to Kristine.

That was one of the reasons Reece has chosen Alanna for his wife. He would never have considered marriage to a woman he wasn't physically attracted to, regardless of his motivations. The other, more vengeful reason for choosing Alanna was that she was even more beautiful than his ex-fiancée.

Her willingness to have his children was merely a bonus.

As these thoughts tumbled through Reece's head he tried to revive the vengeful feelings that had inspired his marriage to Alanna last year.

But astonishingly, they just weren't there!

Reece's shock was soon replaced by an overwhelming sense of relief as he realised he didn't give a damn about Kristine any more.

Let the devil take her, which he would.

The only woman he cared about these days was the woman in red, coming down the aisle. His wife. The

stunningly beautiful, extremely enigmatic, very intriguing Alanna.

A few years ago, Reece might have believed his
uncharacteristic jealousy a minute ago meant he'd
fallen in love with Alanna.

But Reece had turned thirty-six this year, past the
age when an intelligent man mistook male posses-
siveness for love. He did like and respect Alanna. A
lot. But love?

No. Love wasn't what he felt when he looked at
her.

Which was just as well, because love hadn't been
part of their deal. In fact, it had been the one thing
Alanna had been very adamant about. *No love.*

She'd been madly in love before, she'd explained.
With her dead husband. The love of her life, killed in
a tragic road accident.

She didn't want to tread that path again.

During their first dinner date Alanna had confided
that she'd once believed she would never marry
again, but as she'd approached thirty she'd realised
she still wanted a family. What she didn't want, she
insisted repeatedly, was romantic love, and all the
emotional torment that went with it.

Which was why she'd become a client of Wives
Wanted, an introduction agency that specialised in
matching professional men of substance with attractive, intelligent women who were happy to be career
wives. Although falling in love sometimes happened—according to the woman who ran the
agency—on the whole, these were marriages made

with heads and not hearts. Marriages of convenience, they were called in the old days.

A marriage of convenience was exactly what Reece had in mind when *he* had become a client of Wives Wanted a year ago. Love hadn't been on his agenda, either.

At the time, he'd got exactly what he'd wanted in Alanna. The ultimate trophy wife for him to display on his arm. The perfect salve for his bruised male ego. A visible token of his professional survival as well as a none-too-subtle weapon of personal revenge.

To this end, he'd made sure that photographs of his wedding had been printed in every paper and glossy magazine in Australia.

Not a difficult thing to arrange. He was a high-profile property developer, after all. What he did and whom he married made the news. Photos of every glamorous party he'd held since his wedding—and there were many—had found their way into the media as well, with Alanna always dressed to show off her physical assets.

For quite some time it had given Reece perverse pleasure to think of Kristine thinking of him with his beautiful blonde wife whilst she was having to service her ageing sugar-daddy, the one she'd dumped him for. He liked imagining his ex-fiancée feeling regret that she'd bailed out of their relationship prematurely. No doubt she hadn't expected him to go from near bankruptcy to billionaire status within three short years of her desertion.

Poor Kristine, came the caustic thought. If only

she'd had some faith and loyalty, she could have had her cake and eaten it too. Instead, she'd thrown her lot in with an ageing playboy film producer who had a reputation for replacing his starlet girlfriends every year or so.

There'd been a time when Reece had waited to hear such news with baited breath. Somewhere along the line, however, he'd stopped thinking about—and caring about—what happened to Kristine.

In hindsight, Reece could not put a date on this miracle. But it had to be some months ago. He supposed it was difficult to keep pining for another woman when you were married to someone as fascinating as Alanna.

Aside from her breathtaking beauty, Alanna was an amazing woman to live with. She never nagged at him or questioned him. There were never any scenes when he came home late, or had to go away unexpectedly on business. She kept his house beautifully, was an accomplished hostess and never said no in bed. What more could a man in his position want? When you thought about it, their marriage was perfect.

Frankly, falling in love would have spoilt it.

But as he continued to gaze at his beautiful wife Reece recognised that he *had* fallen in lust with her.

He'd always desired Alanna. Right from the moment he'd set eyes on her. But his desire seemed to have taken a darker, more intense turning today.

It was that damned dress's fault, he decided.

Not the style. The colour. It *had* to be the colour.

Red was the devil's colour. The colour of desire, and danger.

Whatever, Reece could not wait for Richard's wedding to be over. Could not wait to get that dress off her.

What a pity he was the best man and she was the chief bridesmaid. They would have to attend the reception afterwards, plus stay till it was finished. There was no excuse they could give to leave early.

Not that Alanna would. She would think him mad to suggest such a thing. She'd been helping Holly with the wedding preparations for weeks and had been very excited this morning.

Another dark thought intruded. Maybe he'd be able to persuade her to slip away with him somewhere for a few minutes. A powder room perhaps?

Reece had never done anything like that with her before. Their lovemaking had always been confined to the house. Actually, now that he came to think of it, it had also been confined to their bedroom.

Time to widen their sexual horizons, Reece decided with a rush of blood. *Before* she got pregnant.

They'd been trying for a baby for three months now. Surprisingly, with no success. But sooner or later, he'd strike a home run.

Reece imagined that once Alanna was having a baby, she might not be overly keen on having sexual adventures.

Suddenly, Reece became aware of Alanna frowning at him as she approached the end of the aisle.

Had his darker thoughts been reflected in his face?

Probably.

He swiftly summoned up one of his warmly winning smiles, the kind he used at work every day and which had become second nature to him.

'You look incredible,' he mouthed to her.

When she beamed back at him, his flesh tightened further.

Reece gritted his teeth and kept on smiling till she turned away to join the other bridesmaid, at which point his sigh of relief was swiftly followed by a jab of guilt. Damn it all, he was here today to be Richard's best man. Not to think and act like some depraved roué, consumed by uncontrollable lust.

The trouble was Reece had always been given to strong emotions. People thought he was an easygoing man, but underneath his charming façade he was often a maelstrom of emotion. Ever since he was a boy, his needs and wants had ruled his life. When he'd wanted something, he'd wanted it too much. When he'd fallen in love, he'd loved too much.

When Kristine had first left him, he'd gone wild with despair and jealousy. To the world, he'd presented a coolly positive, never-say-die image, whereas underneath he'd been eaten up by a compulsive need to strike back in whatever way he could; to have his revenge on the woman who'd spurned him. First, by regaining his wealth. Secondly, by marrying.

It had been sheer luck that his marriage to Alanna had worked out as well as it had. It could very well have been a complete disaster.

Now that Reece realised Kristine was out of his head and his heart for ever, no way did he want to risk spoiling things. He decided that, no matter how frustrated he was feeling at this moment, sex with Alanna could at least wait till they were home. Whether they got as far as the bedroom, however, was another question. He rather fancied the idea of undressing her in the living room. Or perhaps not undressing her at all.

He began to wonder what she was wearing underneath that red dress...

The arrival of Holly walking down the aisle was a well-timed distraction, dragging Reece's mind back from the erotic possibilities of later tonight to the sweetly romantic present.

He'd been right. Holly *did* look lovely.

Hearing the groom suck in sharply at the sight of his beautiful bride brought a wry smile to Reece's lips. Underneath his ultra conservative, buttoned-up, banker façade, Richard was a total softie. A romantic and an idealist.

A visionary, as well.

For which Reece was grateful. If it hadn't been for Richard's ability to think outside the box, *he'd* be stony-broke today. Richard had backed Reece when not one other financial institution would touch him. He'd given him every loan he'd needed till the slump in the real-estate market had changed to a property boom, extending his hand in friendship as well.

Reece thought the world of him.

'I admit I was wrong, Rich,' he murmured to his friend. 'She's definitely the girl for you.'

'Too young for him, I reckon,' Mike muttered, grunting when Reece jabbed him in the ribs.

'Okay, okay, she does love him,' Mike grumbled. 'I can see that. Even worse, I think he loves her.'

'What's wrong with that?' Reece said sharply.

'Hush up, you two,' Richard commanded. 'I'm getting married here.'

Reece gave Mike another savage glare. Mike just shrugged.

When Richard stepped over to take his bride's hand, Reece caught a glimpse of Holly's face through her veil.

The expression he saw in her eyes should have pleased him. For it was undoubtedly the look of a girl very much in love. Why, then, did Reece suddenly feel out of sorts? Surely he didn't envy Richard, did he?

Perhaps.

No woman had ever looked at *him* quite that way, with such gloriously blind adoration. Not even Kristine when she'd supposedly been in love with him. And certainly not Alanna.

Alanna, again...

Reece glanced over to where his wife was standing on the other side of the bride. But he couldn't make eye contact. Holly's veil was getting in the way.

Maybe it was just as well, he thought. Because he knew he'd never see anything like that expression in *her* eyes. The most he could hope for was a degree of mindless desire.

There was no doubt Alanna got carried away sometimes when Reece made love to her.

Reece vowed he would at least see *that* in her eyes later tonight. It wouldn't be quite as good, but it would have to do.

CHAPTER TWO

'YOU see?' Alanna said, smiling up into Mike's face. 'You *can* dance. In fact, you have a great sense of rhythm.'

Alanna had become tired of Mike always making excuses not to come to their parties, having suspected it was because he couldn't dance. When she saw him sitting down by himself at the bridal table, looking glum whilst everyone else was up on their feet, she'd decided to take matters into her own hands. So she'd sent Reece off to dance with Sara whilst she'd dragged Mike onto the dance floor.

The function centre Richard and Holly had chosen for their wedding reception was a converted Edwardian mansion that was simply huge, with polished wooden floors just made for dancing.

'You're a good teacher,' Mike said, glancing up from his feet at last.

'You're a fast learner. Now you can take your girl-friend out dancing.'

'Don't have one at the moment.'

'Oh? That's not like you.'

'Been working too hard.'

'On anything special?'

'A new anti-virus, anti-spy program. It's going to make me a fortune. Or it will,' he added, 'if and when

I can get the right company to market and distribute it.'

'What about your own company?' Alanna knew that Mike's software company had been very successful. Reece had shares in it. So did Richard.

'Not big enough. I need a top international company. American, preferably. With plenty of clout. I'll ask Richard to do the negotiating for me, once I decide who to approach. He's much better at that type of thing then I am.'

'But he'll be away on his honeymoon for the next month,' Alanna pointed out. 'He's taking Holly to Europe.'

'No sweat. The program's not quite ready. It needs more testing. Make sure there aren't any bugs.'

'I see.' Sort of. Alanna was no dummy, and she was competent enough on a computer. She used to use a computer every day at work. Although she'd given up her job in public relations after marrying Reece—being Mrs Reece Diamond was a full-time career—she still paid all the housekeeping bills over the internet. Nevertheless, she had no idea how computers really worked.

'I don't think Reece is too happy with you dancing with me,' Mike suddenly muttered under his breath.

'What?' Surprise sent Alanna's eyes darting around the room till she found her husband, who was still dancing with Sara. Even with his back towards her, he was easy to spot with his being so tall and having fair hair. When he turned around enough for their eyes to meet, Alanna was taken aback by the angry expression on his very handsome and usually cheerful face.

'Yep. He's jealous,' Mike repeated.

Alanna's hackles rose instinctively. 'Don't be ridiculous,' she snapped. 'Reece doesn't have a jealous bone in his body.'

'Come on, Alanna. Get real. You are one drop-dead gorgeous woman. If you were my wife, I'd be jealous of you being in another man's arms. Just because you two have a different sort of marriage doesn't mean a damned thing. You're Reece's wife and I'm a single guy with a certain reputation. It's only natural for him to feel threatened, even though it doesn't say too much for our friendship. He should know that you'd be the last woman on earth that I'd hit on. You and Holly.'

Despite Mike's explanation, Alanna still could not conceive of Reece being jealous of her in any way, shape or form. She'd danced with lots of men in front of him before, *and* wearing a whole lot less than she was today.

Not once had Reece ever criticised, commented, or cared.

As for feeling threatened by Mike…

That idea was equally ludicrous. Alanna had never met any man as confident or as self-assured as her husband. And he had every reason to be. Not only was he very good-looking and very successful, his personality outshone everyone else's. When Reece walked into a room, he became the sun around which the rest of the world revolved. Frankly, Alanna had never met another man quite like him.

'I don't believe he's jealous at all,' she pronounced firmly. 'Sara must have said something to annoy him.'

'Want to put it to the test?'

'What do you mean?'

Mike's hand in the small of her back suddenly pressed Alanna close against his hard male body, making her gasp.

The reaction in her husband's face was instantaneous.

His nostrils flared. His blue eyes narrowed.

Alanna's reaction to her husband's jealousy was also instantaneous. Chaos, inside. Chaos and panic.

'I don't believe this,' she whispered shakily. 'Reece is *never* jealous.'

'He's a man, Alanna. It comes with the territory.' Mike abruptly lifted the pressure on his hand and Alanna moved back to a more discreet distance.

'But he's never been jealous before!' she protested. 'You've seen some of the dresses he likes me to wear. Would a jealous man buy such dresses for his wife?'

'That depends.'

'On what?'

'On why he wanted you to wear such dresses in the first place.'

'I don't know what you're talking about.'

'Don't you?'

Alanna was taken aback. 'You'll have to be a bit more specific.'

'What do you know about your husband's past?' came the blunt question.

Alanna frowned. 'A fair bit. I know he's the eldest son of a family of three boys. I know his father died in an electrical accident when he was in high school. I know he worked weekends selling real estate from the time he was seventeen and was so successful he abandoned his plans to go to university. He told me he made his first million by the time he was twenty-one.'

'That's not what I meant. What do you know about his more immediate past, the years just before he met and married you?'

'Well, I know he went through a horror patch, financially, a few years back. He told me he would have gone to the wall if Richard hadn't helped him out. But I suppose you're referring to his ex-fiancée, Kristine. Reece told me how she dumped him for some wealthy older guy during that time.'

Which was why, Reece had explained the first night they'd met, he was no more interested in romance than she was. He'd been madly in love, and been hurt, as she had. And he didn't want to go there any more.

Of course, Reece thought her hurt came from her beloved husband's tragic death in a car crash. Alanna couldn't bring herself to tell him the truth about Darko.

Which made her wonder if Reece had been totally honest with her as well. Did Mike know something she didn't know?

'So Reece did tell you all about Kristine,' he said.

'He told me *everything* about her.' How beautiful she was. How she desperately wanted to be an actress. How they were only three weeks from their wedding when she left him.

'I doubt it, Alanna. No man tells his wife everything, especially about a previous woman who did the dirty on him the way she did. Men have their pride, you know.'

So do women, she wanted to throw at him.

'What did she do?'

'You'll have to ask your husband that. I've already said more than I should have.'

'But I can't ask Reece something like that. *You* have to tell me.'

'Tell you what?'

Alanna whirled to find her husband standing right behind her, looking daggers at Mike.

'Your wife wants me to explain how my new program works,' Mike said without missing a beat. 'But she's much better at teaching dancing than I am at teaching computer-speak. Do you want her back now? I gather by that he-man look on your face that you do. Time for me to go, anyway. I'll just have a word with the bride and groom first. See you around, folks. Thanks for the dancing lessons, Alanna. They might come in handy one day.'

Alanna felt new respect for Mike as he walked away. Whilst she was aware he was a genius in his field, she'd never thought much of his social skills.

That little display, however, had been very clever. It wasn't easy to think on your feet like that.

As she turned to face her husband Alanna decided to tackle his seeming jealousy head-on. She knew she would worry if she ignored it. As for her curiosity over what Kristine had done to Reece... That would have to remain unsatisfied for now. No way could she broach such a subject with Reece. He would be angry with her for discussing him with Mike behind his back. And rightly so.

'Why were you glowering at me just now?' she demanded to know. 'Mike said you were jealous.'

For a moment, Reece's face stiffened, his square jawline looking even squarer with his neck muscles all tight like that. His nicely shaped lips, usually relaxed and smiling, were pressed tautly together. As for his eyes... Alanna had never seen them so hard. And so cold.

But then he laughed, and the Reece she knew and felt safe with was back. 'Aren't I allowed to be a bit possessive of my beautiful wife?'

'Being possessive is too close to jealousy for my liking,' she chided, but gently. 'I don't like jealousy, Reece.'

Reece pursed his lips, but his eyes were smiling at her. 'Don't you, darling? Sorry. Blame that dress you have on.'

'*This* dress? That's silly. This is a very modest dress.'

'It's the colour. It does things to me. If you must know, I've been thinking wicked things ever since I watched you walk down that aisle,' he said, his voice dropping to the low, sexy timbre that he used during foreplay.

Reece was a talker in bed, giving her head-turning compliments and calling her 'Babe' whilst he caressed her and turned her on.

Her breath quickened just thinking about those times. He was suddenly thinking about them, too. She could see it in his face, and in his eyes.

'I want you badly, Babe,' he muttered under his breath. 'I don't think I can wait till we get home.'

His calling her Babe at this stage was not only telling, but instantly arousing, as if he'd turned a switch on inside her. Alanna opened her mouth, then closed it again, finding herself speechless under his by now smouldering gaze.

Reece had looked at her with desire before. Many times. But this was a different type of desire tonight. Darker. And infinitely more exciting.

Suddenly, the room around Alanna began to recede, till she was aware of nothing but her husband's eyes on her. Her lips fell slightly apart. Her mouth went dry. Her skin broke out into goose bumps.

Very dimly, she heard the music change to a slow, moody number.

Without saying another word, Reece drew her into his arms, his eyes not leaving hers as he let them do his talking for him for a while. As he pressed her stomach against his stark arousal the most exquisite sensations gripped Alanna's body. Her nipples hardened. Her belly quivered. Her insides contracted.

Her arms slipped up around his neck and their bodies melded even closer together.

'I need to kiss you,' he whispered into her hair.

'You…you can't,' she answered shakily. 'Not here.'

'Where, then?'

She knew what he was asking her. It wasn't just a kiss he needed. The thought of him taking her somewhere relatively private sent the blood rushing to her head.

Even as she flushed possible places jumped into her mind. There were several powder rooms, a couple of them well away from everyone, on the first floor. Alanna had been upstairs with Holly the previous day, delivering her going-away outfit, so she knew the layout of the place quite well.

The temptation to go up there with Reece was acute. She wanted to. Far too much.

When she'd married Reece last year, Alanna had vowed to keep a tight rein on her highly sexed nature. No good ever came from a man thinking his wife was a whore.

She'd been quite content with their sex life so far. And happy in her marriage. Reece liked and respected her. Would he continue to respect her, however, if she let him do this? It worried her where such a surrender might lead. She wanted to be his wife and the mother of his children, not his married mistress, catering to his every sexual whim, regardless of time or place.

No. She had to resist temptation.

'I can't, Reece,' she said tautly. 'I have to go help Holly change into her going-away outfit.'

'She's dancing away happily at the moment,' Reece pointed out, nodding towards the bride and groom who were wrapped in each other's arms, gliding slowly around the dance floor. 'Come on. Let's go.'

'Go where?'

'You know where,' he ground out. 'I saw it in your eyes.'

She drew back and stared up at him, her heart pounding. Was she that easy to read?

'We're married, Alanna,' he went on brusquely. 'Whatever we do together is perfectly acceptable.'

'Being married doesn't make everything acceptable,' she countered heatedly. 'I'm sorry, Reece. You'll just have to wait till we get home.'

His face darkened with frustration. 'This is bloody ridiculous. You want to. I know you do.'

When his fingers tightened on her arm, Alanna wrenched her arm out of his hold and glowered up at him.

'Don't ever presume what I want to do, Reece,' she bit out. 'I said no. That means no. I don't know what's got into you tonight but, whatever it is, I don't much like it. Now I'm going to take Holly upstairs to change. Hopefully, by the time we get home you will have gotten over your caveman impulses and gone back to being the sophisticated man I married.'

CHAPTER THREE

THE strained silence in the car during the drive home gave Reece plenty of time to wonder, and to worry. He'd soothed his earlier frustrations with the surety Alanna wouldn't knock him back when they got home. But had his thinking been correct?

Alanna wanted a baby. Quite desperately, judging by her disappointment over not conceiving yet. She'd started reading books on the subject, and had circled the days on the kitchen calendar when she was most likely to conceive. Tonight was not optimum but it was close enough.

Back at the reception, he'd reasoned that no way would Alanna let this day end without sex, especially since they hadn't made love last night. She'd been busy with Holly on last minute wedding preparations whilst he'd been out having a few drinks with Richard and Mike. When he'd finally come home around one o'clock, Alanna had been in bed, sound asleep.

So he felt quite confident that some of his desires would be satisfied tonight. Although not all.

For a few seconds tonight he'd glimpsed a different Alanna, one who'd almost agreed to have a quickie. Her gorgeous green eyes had glittered wildly with the idea.

He wanted that Alanna to surface again. He also

wanted a wife who didn't lock the bathroom door after her any more. One who wasn't so darned protective of her privacy.

Such thinking revived his frustrations. All of a sudden, he wanted to snap at her. Taunt her. Challenge her.

Do you only let me make love to you because you want a baby? he felt like flinging at her. *Do you fake your orgasms? Do you care for me at all, or am I just a means to an end?*

Actually, Reece didn't believe she faked her orgasms. But there was *something* fake about Alanna. He just didn't know what. Up till this point, it hadn't bothered him how much of herself she'd kept to herself. As long as he'd got what he wanted, he hadn't made waves.

But everything had changed tonight. Reece wanted more from Alanna now, and, by God, he aimed to get more!

Alanna sat in the passenger seat of Reece's red Mercedes sports, her face turned away from him, her hands clasped tightly in her lap.

She knew Reece was angry with her. She could *feel* it. If there was one thing Alanna had become adept at over the years, it was sensing a husband's anger.

Not that Reece's anger was anything like Darko's. She'd trembled with fear when *he'd* been angry.

Alanna wasn't even close to trembling at that moment. But she was agitated. And upset.

She hated having made Reece angry. Hated herself

for her silly overreactions. He'd hardly behaved badly. So he'd been a little possessive of her. A forgivable sin, considering he'd been turned on at the time and she'd been off teaching another man to dance.

In hindsight, however, Alanna suspected most of his anger came from the fact that he'd witnessed her momentary willingness to go along with what he'd wanted. Seen it in her eyes, he'd said.

She'd acted like a tease. Going hot, and then cold, on him. No wonder he was mad.

She should apologise. She knew she should. But the words simply wouldn't come, and before long Reece was turning into their driveway and braking abruptly to a halt. He zapped the automatic gate-opener, then waited, his fingers tapping impatiently on the steering wheel till they opened.

Once again, Alanna tried to force herself to say something. She turned her head in his direction, but still could not find her tongue, gazing past him instead at the impressive façade of their home.

Every now and then—usually at the oddest moments—Alanna took a mental step back from her present life and tried to see it as others saw it.

All of her girlfriends thought her a very lucky woman. Which she was. She lived in an extremely beautiful home. Drove a snazzy car, and had a fabulous wardrobe.

But it wasn't any of these material things that were the main subject of her girlfriends' 'you-are-so-lucky' remarks.

No, it was Reece himself they envied Alanna the most. Her charismatic and very handsome husband.

Admittedly, he was a dream of a husband. Hardworking, cheerful, complimentary and generous. A great lover, too, who, till tonight, had not been at all demanding where their sex life was concerned. He seemed content with fairly straightforward lovemaking. In bed. Tonight had been the first time he'd wanted something different.

So, yes, on the surface, she was a very lucky woman.

But all that would mean nothing, she realised with a pang in her heart, if she never had a child.

Reece hadn't been the only person to feel unexpected jealousy tonight. When she'd accompanied Holly upstairs to help her change out of her wedding dress, Holly had confided to Alanna that she was already pregnant.

Alanna had done her best to express delight at the news, but, down deep, she'd been worried. Reece had been making love to her very regularly since she'd come off the pill three months ago, but still no baby. Was there something wrong with her? It was possible. You couldn't throw yourself out of a speeding car and not sustain some internal damage.

The doctors had assured her that she would be fine, that her recovery would be complete in time.

But maybe they were wrong.

Perhaps she should go for some tests…

'I presume you *are* coming inside.'

Reece's sharp words snapped Alanna back to the

present, where she was surprised to see they were already parked in the garages, the door had shut behind them and Reece had taken his keys out of the ignition.

'Yes, of course,' she said, and opened her door with a weary sigh. Clearly, Reece was still angry with her. 'I was day-dreaming,' she added as she levered herself up onto her red high heels.

'What about?' he asked as he climbed out also, banging the car door after him. 'Becoming a dancing teacher?'

His nasty crack shocked Alanna. He was never like this. 'You're not still going on about that, are you?'

'Why not? A man doesn't like his wife to enjoy another man's company more than his own.'

She stared at Reece over the roof of the Mercedes. 'I usually don't. But if you keep acting like this, I just might in future.'

'Meaning?'

'Nothing,' she muttered. 'I meant nothing.'

When she came round the front of the car and went to walk past him, heading for the internal access to the house, Reece grabbed her arm and spun her round to face him.

'I won't tolerate you sleeping around on me, Alanna,' he ground out. 'We might not love each other but we promised before God to be faithful.'

'I would *never* break my marriage vows,' she denied fiercely. 'But I might ask for a divorce if you keep manhandling me.'

He didn't let her go. Just glared down into her face, his own flushed and frustrated-looking.

'That won't get you a baby,' he snapped. 'Which is the only reason you married me, isn't it?'

'It was one of the reasons,' she threw at him. 'I told you I wanted a family.'

'What were the other reasons? My money, I presume.'

'I wanted security. Yes. But if you must know, I had no idea you were as rich as you were when I agreed to marry you. Now let go of my arm.'

He did so, but remained standing in front of her, blocking her way. When she stepped back a little, the front bumper bar of the car contacted her calves.

'What about sex?' he ground out. 'You said at our first meeting that you discovered you weren't cut out for celibacy. You implied you wanted a man in your bed every night for the pleasure he could bring you. Have I brought you pleasure, Alanna?' he demanded to know.

When she went to move sidewards, his hands shot out to grab her shoulders, holding her and forcing her to look up at him.

'Have I, Alanna?' he repeated harshly, giving her a little shake.

'You know you have,' she choked out.

It was cold in the garages, but her sudden shivering had nothing to do with the air temperature.

He yanked her hard against him, his blue eyes blazing like a pitiless summer sky. His mouth was just as pitiless.

Reece knew exactly the kind of kissing she liked. Right from their wedding night she hadn't been able to resist his kisses. By the time his head lifted, she was no longer shivering.

'Lie back across the bonnet of the car,' he commanded, his voice rough and thick.

Her eyes flared wide with shock. 'But...'

'Damn it, don't argue with me,' he ground out, then kissed her some more till all her defences were gone.

No protest came from her lips when he lowered her back across the engine-heated bonnet and started pushing her dress upwards. Up. Up to her waist.

Her heart pounded. Her skin flamed. Her head spun.

'Oh, Babe,' he groaned when he saw what she was wearing underneath her dress.

A red strapless corselette, with suspenders holding up her stockings, and only a wisp of a red lace covering her.

Her underwear had been a present from the bride. Not that she didn't like sexy underwear. She did. She just didn't usually buy red.

Reece ripped the lacy thong off her with a single yank, leaving her totally exposed. When he pushed her legs apart and leant forward, Alanna bit her bottom lip and squeezed her eyes tightly shut.

She tensed in anticipation of his mouth making contact, but it was his hands she felt first, touching her, exploring her, teasing her.

'So wet,' she heard him say, and knew it was true.

He made her wet so easily. Made her want to be made love to, even when she thought she didn't.

His fingers continued to play with her till she almost cried out to him to stop. She wanted his lips. And his tongue.

When he finally did what she wanted, her head twisted from side to side, her face grimacing as the exquisite sensations he evoked brought with them an equally exquisite tension.

His sudden abandonment had her eyes flying open.

'You...you can't just stop!' she cried out.

He laughed as he scooped his hands under her bottom and swept her up from the bonnet. 'Oh, yes, I can.'

'You bastard.'

His eyes glittered wildly down at her, his smile devilishly sexy. 'Tch tch. You're a lady, remember?'

'I don't feel much like a lady at this moment.' Her frustration was at fever pitch, making her almost violent with need.

'*Tell* me what you feel like,' he challenged her as he carried her inside the house. 'Tell me what you want me to do to you.'

Her already heated face must have gone bright red.

'You can say it,' he whispered wickedly in her ear. 'There's no one here to hear you but me. And I *want* you to say it, just the way you're thinking it right now. Go on. Say it!'

She said it.

'Don't worry, Babe,' he muttered, his arms tightening around her as he began mounting the stairs that led up to their bedroom. 'It'll be my pleasure to do that, and more.'

CHAPTER FOUR

REECE stared down at his still-sleeping wife, in two minds whether to wake her or not. It was Sunday and they had nothing planned for the day, knowing that they'd be tired after Richard's wedding.

But it was approaching noon, and she'd been asleep for a good eight hours.

Reece wanted her company.

Wanted her, too. The *new* her. The one who'd emerged last night.

His flesh prickled at the memory of the woman he'd unleashed with that episode in the garage. She'd become quite aggressive after they'd reached the bedroom, stripping him of his clothes almost angrily, wanting to be on top, wanting all sorts of things.

They'd had their first shower together some time later—now *that* had been a mind-blowing experience!—after which he'd refused to let her grab a towel, or a nightie, to cover her beautiful body. After a momentary hesitation, she'd stayed naked for him.

But it was like having sex with a stranger. She was nothing like the Alanna he'd become used to, his elegant and coolly composed wife who had to be almost seduced at times. This Alanna had been totally different.

Which Alanna would it be, he wondered, who woke up this morning?

Maybe last night was a temporary aberration. Maybe she'd had more to drink at that wedding reception than he'd realised. The champagne had been flowing and there'd been a lot of toasting.

Reece didn't like to think her passion had been alcohol-induced. He'd really enjoyed her reaching for him so avidly. He'd been thrilled that she'd kissed him for a change, and had wallowed in watching her make love to him with her mouth.

Damn, but he had to stop thinking about that. If he didn't, he'd be jumping back onto that bed with her.

Possibly, she wouldn't object if he did. But maybe she would. Reece's well-honed people instinct warned him to take it easy with her today; not to presume that there would be more of the same just yet. Alanna could be surprisingly touchy. She hated him to presume anything about her.

No, best he get himself out of here and go have some breakfast. The sun was up and it would be pleasant out on the back terrace at this time of day.

Rather reluctantly, Reece picked up the top sheet from where it was scrunched up at the foot of the bed and pulled it up over his wife's beautifully bare body. *Very* reluctantly, he let it drop onto her shoulders. A sigh whispered from his lungs as he wrapped his heavy towelling robe more tightly around his own naked body, then headed for the kitchen.

*   *   *

Alanna's first thought on waking was how great she felt.

Then she remembered. Everything.

'Oh, God,' she groaned aloud, clutching at the sheet as she glanced around the bedroom, wondering where Reece was.

Shock joined her agitation when she saw the time on the bedside clock. Twelve-fourteen! It was afternoon! She'd never slept in so late in all her life.

Admittedly, it had to have been the early hours of the morning by the time she'd passed out last night. Through utter exhaustion.

Alanna grimaced, then shuddered. What on earth had she been thinking about to act the way she had?

Of course, she hadn't been thinking at all. That was the problem. For the first time since their marriage Reece had broken through all her personal and sexual defences, whisking her away to that wild, wanton place that a much younger Alanna had enjoyed so much, but which she had subsequently learned could be a dangerous place for a wife to go.

When she'd married Reece, she'd vowed not to make the same mistake twice. Any man could fall victim to sexual jealousy, she'd worried, even a laid-back husband who wasn't in love with you.

And she'd been right! Look what had happened with Mike at the wedding reception. Reece had reacted, if not jealously at that stage, then very possessively. And that had been *before* her performance last night.

What would he start thinking now? Might he start imagining she was having affairs behind his back. She did have a lot of spare time with Reece working such long hours.

Alanna groaned aloud. What a fool she was to have let her husband open her Pandora's box. A stupid, stupid fool.

Alanna shook her head in dismay over the possible consequences of last night. No way could she live with any man who started acting even remotely like Darko. If Reece began questioning her about her movements, or doubting her word, or—God forbid—having her followed, then their marriage was history.

Maybe it was as well she hadn't fallen pregnant yet. She was still a couple of days away from entering her most fertile time so she doubted last night would have changed the status quo.

As much as the thought of leaving Reece distressed Alanna terribly, she refused to tolerate any scenario where her hard-won self-esteem and much valued independence was threatened. She'd come too far back from the abyss to be propelled back in that direction again.

But maybe she was worrying for nothing. Maybe Reece would be quite happy with the way things had turned out last night. After all, he was totally opposite to Darko, both in looks and personality. *And* he didn't profess to love her.

Now why didn't she find that last thought comforting?

Shaking her head, Alanna tossed back the sheet and made a dash for the bathroom. Afterwards she wrapped a towel around herself and returned to her walk-in wardrobe where she gathered together some clothes. Just jeans and a light jumper today. They weren't going out anywhere. Or entertaining, which might be good news or bad news, depending on Reece's reaction to her this morning.

Fifteen minutes later—Alanna never bothered with make-up or an elaborate hairstyle when alone at home—she was showered, dressed and on her way downstairs to the kitchen for some much needed coffee. At the bottom of the stairs she made a brief detour to peek in Reece's study, but he wasn't in there. Possibly he was out on the back terrace. That was his favourite place when the sun was shining.

As soon as Alanna entered the foyer, she could see that she was right. Reece was out on the terrace, semi-reclining on a banana chair, wrapped in his white towelling robe, sunglasses on, sipping a glass of orange juice and reading the Sunday paper. At his elbow sat an empty cereal bowl and spoon, along with the various inserts from the paper.

Alanna momentarily toyed with the idea of boldly going out there and saying good morning to him as if nothing had changed. But she was low on boldness this morning. She must have used all of her boldness quota last night.

Her stomach tightened as another memory assailed her. Had she really said those words to Reece when he'd first carried her from the garage to the bedroom?

Oh, yes, she definitely had. Maybe it was a rebellion thing. Darko would have washed her mouth out with soap. Literally.

But Reece had just laughed. Oh, how she loved him for that laughter.

Reece must have finally sensed her standing there, watching him, for his golden head suddenly whipped round. He waved the glass of juice up at her, then waved at her to come outside.

Taking a gathering breath, Alanna proceeded down the wide step that separated the foyer from the living area, bypassing the kitchen on the right as she headed for the sliding glass doors, and the terrace.

'Have a good sleep?' Reece asked as soon as she stepped out onto the flagstones.

'Wonderful, thanks. And you?' Oh God. She sounded awfully polite. As if they were hotel guests, meeting over breakfast.

He smiled up at her as he removed his sunglasses. 'Never better,' he said, tossing the sunglasses onto the side table. 'Pull up a chair.'

'I need to go get some coffee first. You know I can't think straight till I have my morning coffee. You want some?'

'I'll have whatever you're having,' he said, then threw her one of his megawatt smiles.

Alanna tried not to let the relief show on her face. But she felt almost overwhelmed by the realisation that everything was going to be all right.

'Just coffee to begin with,' she said, smiling back at him.

'You can't live on just coffee, darling. You'll start fading away to a shadow.'

'I'll have a proper breakfast later.'

'Would you like me to take you somewhere for brunch? We could catch the ferry over to Darling Harbour.'

'Haven't you just eaten breakfast?' she said, nodding towards the side table.

'Only juice and muesli. That's nothing. I seem to have worked up quite an appetite after last night. Lord knows why,' he added, his blue eyes sparkling.

He was teasing her, as he sometimes did. But never before had the teasing been about sex.

'If anyone should have an appetite this morning, it's me,' she retorted. '*You* hardly did a thing.'

She'd floored him for a moment. He knew she had. But then his sexy mouth widened into the wickedest smile.

'You saucy minx! But you seem to have a case of selective memory this morning. I distinctively recall you begging me to stop at one stage.'

'If that's so, then your hearing is defective, Mr Diamond,' she replied haughtily, thoroughly enjoying their repartee. 'I definitely *didn't* beg you to stop.'

'Oh? What were you begging me to do, then?'

'I *never* beg.'

'Every woman should be made to beg at some stage,' he said, his voice dropping low as it always did when his focus became sexual. 'It releases them from the women their mothers taught them to be, turning them into the women their husbands want them to be.'

'And what kind of woman is that?'

'The woman you were last night.'

'Not all men like that type of woman,' she said before she could think better of it.

'Such men are fools.'

'You...you didn't mind the way I was, then?' Alanna hated herself for sounding so vulnerable, but that was how she felt, all of a sudden.

Reece looked genuinely bewildered. 'Why on earth should I mind?' He put down the orange juice and rose to his feet, resashing his robe as he did so. 'I think I'll come inside with you whilst you make that coffee. I want to find out why you would think I would mind. And don't imagine you can lie to me, madam,' he said sternly as he took her arm and started ushering her inside.

'Would I lie to you?' she quipped, sounding cool and casual, whereas inside she was a mess.

Would she lie to me?

Too damned right she would, Reece decided.

For some reason, she hadn't allowed her real self to emerge till last night. He wanted to know why. And why last night? What had happened last night that was different?

The answer to that last question popped into Reece's head as he accompanied Alanna to the kitchen.

He'd been different. First at the wedding reception,

when he'd become all primal and possessive, and then in the garage, where his sensitive, new-age-guy persona had fled totally in the face of the most intense frustration he'd ever known.

It came to him that Alanna was one of those women who claimed not to like the caveman type, but who were actually turned on by them.

He would remember that in future.

'Well?' he said as he let go of her arm and slid up on one of the breakfast bar stools.

She ignored him for a few seconds as she went about turning on the kettle and getting herself a mug from the overhead cupboard.

'Well what?' she said at last, deliberately making her face a blank mask as she looked at him.

He rolled his eyes at her. '*Why* did you think I'd mind about last night?'

Her shrug was nonchalant. 'I guess because I'm not usually like that.'

'No,' he said. 'You're certainly not.'

She stared at him, and he could have sworn he glimpsed a flicker of fear in her lovely green eyes.

'But it was great, Alanna,' he went on. '*You* were great.'

She visibly winced, as though the memory of her behaviour offended her in some way. 'You really mean that, Reece?' she asked him, her expression touchingly unsure.

He wasn't used to seeing Alanna in any way but coolly confident, and it touched something deep inside him. He'd never imagined she was a woman who needed reassuring, or protecting, but it seemed she did.

'Of course I meant it,' he said warmly. 'Like I said last night, darling. We're married. Whatever we do together *is* acceptable.'

Her eyes flared wide. 'What…what do you mean…?'

'What about a mild bit of bondage?' he said, wanting to find out exactly what made Alanna tick, sexually.

Her immediate reaction showed him he was way off target.

'I would hate that,' she said sharply, and turned her attention to her coffee-making. 'The thought of being tied up makes me feel sick.'

'But it would only be in fun.'

'It wouldn't be fun for me.'

Reece was taken aback by her attitude. He would have thought the woman who'd made love to him last night would have been into erotic games. Clearly, he was wrong.

'I wasn't suggesting it,' he was quick to say.

'Good. Now, can we talk about something else besides sex? I would have thought you'd have had enough sex to last you the whole weekend.'

Reece didn't know what to say to that. It seemed that his plans for an interesting afternoon, expanding their new sexual horizons even further, was now out of the question.

Alanna was in full sexual retreat.

Reece decided he could react two ways. He could let her, and do his best to hide his already simmering arousal. Or he could stop her, the same way he had last night. Caveman style.

CHAPTER FIVE

ALANNA turned away to switch off the jug and pour the boiling water into her coffee.

Dear heaven, but she wished Reece hadn't followed her in here and started this particular conversation.

She'd begun overreacting again. Being touchy and silly, snapping at him and even implying that sex was out, which was crazy. Aside from it getting closer to the right time of the month for conceiving, she really wanted him to make love to her.

He'd looked startled by her attitude, and rightly so. She'd been lighthearted and flirtatious out on the terrace, then all prickly and prudish in here. Alanna found it frustrating that Darko was dead and buried, yet she was still letting him spoil everything for her.

The atmosphere in the room was suddenly thick with tension. She could *feel* Reece's frowning eyes on her. He must be wondering what kind of weirdo he'd married.

And I *am* a weirdo, she thought unhappily as she picked up the mug and moved over to the sink. A screwed-up, emotionally scarred, seriously warped weirdo!

Alanna was adding some cold water to the steaming brew and wishing she could take back the last couple of minutes for an instant replay when her husband's arms snaked around her waist.

'Oh!' she cried out, hot coffee slurping over the rim of the mug into the sink.

'Reece, what on earth are you doing?' she gasped.

A rather silly statement. She knew exactly what he was doing, his hands by this point having successfully slipped up under her jumper and over her braless breasts.

'Just ignore me, darling,' Reece murmured as his palms skimmed over her instantly hardening nipples. 'Drink your coffee.'

Ignore him! How could she possibly ignore him when he was doing what he was doing?

Oh, God.

Alanna's head went into a spin when his thumbs and forefingers took firm possession of her stunningly erect nipples.

Drinking her coffee was quickly out of the question. She just gripped the mug like grim death with both hands and tried not to drop it.

Finally, a moan broke from her lips, her head dropping back against his shoulder. His hands immediately released her by-then burning nipples to take the shaking coffee mug and drop it into the sink, returning to lift her jumper upwards till her arms went with it and the garment was gone, tossed carelessly aside onto the kitchen bench.

'No,' Reece commanded when she went to turn around. 'Stay right where you are.'

'But...'

'Hush up, Babe,' he said thickly, unsnapping the waistband of her hipster jeans and sliding the zipper downwards.

'But...'

One of his hands cupped her chin and turned her head around just far enough for him to kiss her mouth, his other hand sliding down over her tensely held stomach, then under the elastic of her panties. By the time he let her mouth go, Alanna was leaning back against her husband's chest and shoulders, wallowing in the sensations his right hand was producing so expertly.

By then, all her earlier worries about there being consequences to her behaviour last night had dissolved to nothing. Clearly, Reece *liked* her like this. *She* liked herself like this, too.

How wonderful it felt to be finally free of the past, to be able to totally let herself go when her husband was making love to her.

Reece's left hand returned to play with her breasts, his outstretched palm skimming back and forth over the sensitised tips. She quivered with pleasure. Quivered and tightened.

Finally, what he was doing just wasn't enough. She wanted *him*, not his hands.

'Reece,' she choked out.

'Yes?'

'Oh, please... No more of that... Just...just do it. Please...'

'Are you begging, Babe?'

'Yes, yes, I'm begging.'

'Here?'

'Yes, here. Now.' And she began dragging at her clothes herself, pushing her jeans down her legs. Her panties as well. Soon, she was totally naked, her face flushed, her body trembling.

But when she went to reach for him, he would not let her turn around, keeping her facing the sink.

'Oh, God,' she moaned when his hands stroked down over her bare buttocks, squeezing them before moving down to push her thighs apart. She moaned again when his fingers stroked her open, making her slicker and even more desperate. Her bottom pouted back at him in the most primal invitation.

She cried out as he pushed into her, his flesh feeling thicker and harder than it ever had before. His hands gripped her hips as he set up a gentle yet sensual rhythm, making her whole body rock slowly back and forth.

Her head swam. Her heart thudded. She tried to catch her breath but could not. She began panting wildly. Her own flesh tightened around his, searching for release.

'Yes, Babe,' he urged. 'That's the way.'

She cried out when the first spasm struck, her knuckles turning white as wave after wave of pleasure swept through her. His orgasm was quick to follow, Alanna gasping when she felt the flood of heat deep inside her.

This was how lovemaking should always be, she thought dazedly. A man and a woman coming together as one. Passionately. Spontaneously. Uninhibitedly.

Reece was right. They were married. What did it matter where or when or how they made love?

When Reece wrapped his arms tightly around her and drew her back upright against him, Alanna's sigh carried total satisfaction with the experience, and the moment.

'You are never to hide this side of yourself from me again,' he said, gently stroking down the front of her spent body. 'Never. This is who you are, Alanna. A highly sensual women who needs to be made love to well.'

'Am I?' she said, still somewhat stunned by the experience.

'You know you are.'

The phone ringing splintered apart the atmosphere of tender intimacy that had wound around them like a warm blanket.

'We don't have to answer it,' Reece said straight away.

'But it might be important,' Alanna said after a few seconds. 'Your mother hasn't been well lately, Reece.' Reece's mother had developed type two diabetes, and had been having some health problems.

'Damn it, you're right,' he muttered.

'You have to answer it,' she said, already easing away from him.

He sighed as he wrapped his robe around his hips and resashed it. 'Yes, all right. But it had better not be one of your girlfriends, wanting you to go some-where today.'

Alanna scooped her jumper up from the nearby benchtop and pulled it over her head, thankful that it reached down to the top of her thighs. As liberated as she was feeling, there was still something embar-rassing about being stark naked in the kitchen in the cold light of day.

'If it is,' she said hurriedly, snatching up the rest of her clothes from the floor, 'tell her I'm indisposed and have decided to spend the day in bed.'

Reece grinned at her. 'Wicked woman,' he said, and reached for the wall phone.

'Reece Diamond,' he answered cheerfully.

Alanna watched and waited to see if there was some problem.

'Hello, Judy,' he went on, Alanna's eyes shooting ceilingwards at her mother's name. 'To what do we owe this pleasure at this time of day?'

Alanna's mother often rang on a Sunday, but never during the day. Always at night. It was cheaper to call after seven. The country town of Cessnock was hardly the other side of the world, but her mother was a careful budgeter.

'Now you're being mysterious,' Reece said. 'Yes, yes, I understand. She's right here. Just hold on.'

'Your mum,' he mouthed softly, his hand over the receiver. 'With news for you which just couldn't wait.'

Alanna's stomach contracted. The last time her mother had had news for her that couldn't wait, it had been to tell her her father had died, killed in a brawl outside his favourite pub one Friday night. That had been ten years ago, soon after Alanna had turned twenty.

'Is it good news or bad news, do you think?' she asked as she reached for the phone.

'She sounds pretty chipper to me. And very coy.'

Alanna frowned as she took the phone from Reece's hand. Now that didn't sound like her mother at all.

'Yes, Mum?' she said worriedly.

'I have some wonderful news. Bob asked me to marry him last night.'

'Wow!' Alanna exclaimed. 'That's great, Mum. Bob's a really nice man. Bob's asked Mum to marry him,' she relayed to Reece, who was standing there, an expectant expression his face.

'Tell her congratulations from me,' Reece replied, looking delighted at the news.

Alanna was genuinely delighted too, but surprised as well. Her mother had been dating the high school maths teacher for some time, but Alanna had always thought remarrying wasn't on her mother's agenda.

Alanna knew full well how hard it was to revisit a way of life that had previously brought you nothing but hurt and unhappiness. Her father had been a seriously neglectful husband, an uncaring, unloving man who had lived for his work mates and the pub. When drunk, he'd been very verbally abusive, putting his wife down, calling her names and generally being a foul-mouthed pig.

Alanna had despised and hated him, leaving home to move to Sydney as soon as she'd finished school at eighteen. She hadn't had much time for her mother back then, either. It wasn't till much later that she'd understood why her mother had stayed with her father all those years. Her own marital experience had taught her never to judge a person till you walked in their shoes.

'Tell her they'll have to come down to Sydney soon,' Reece called over his shoulder as he turned and headed off for their bedroom. 'We'll take them out somewhere special to celebrate.'

'Yes, I heard that,' her mother said down the line. 'And, yes, we'd love to. When?'

'I'll have to check my diary, Mum. You know Reece. He has a very active social life. I do know we're going to a party next Friday night, and an art exhibition on the Saturday night.'

'My, how do you keep up with him?'

Alanna laughed. 'Easily. I like to keep busy as well.' Which she did. Although no longer working, Alanna made sure her days were full. Of course, a lot of her activities were somewhat on the superficial side, but once she had a baby to look after that would change.

'You know, Alanna, your marriage to Reece has worked out much better than I thought it would. When you told me you were marrying a man you didn't love and who didn't love you, I was very worried. But once I met Reece, I knew you were in good hands.'

'*Very* good hands,' Alanna replied, thankful her mother couldn't see the erotic images that had instantly popped into her head. A wave of prickly heat washed over her skin, making her hotly aware of her still-erect nipples.

'Mum, I hate to love you and leave you, but I really have to go. Could I call you tonight? We can have a long chat about your wedding plans and everything.'

'I'd like that. You can tell me all about yesterday's wedding as well.'

'Yes, I'll do that, Mum. Around seven o'clock. Bye for now.'

Alanna hung up, then went to the nearest powder room, wondering as she washed her hands afterwards on how long it would be before she fell pregnant. She hadn't consciously thought of having a baby this time, which might be exactly what she needed to do. To stop thinking about it and hoping for it too much. Some experts said that stress and tension were some of the main reasons for infertility amongst couples. Often, there was nothing physically wrong with them. Some were just trying *too* hard.

When Alanna emerged, she wandered upstairs to the master bedroom in search of Reece, finding him in front of the vanity in their *en suite* bathroom, combing his hair. His bathrobe had been replaced by jeans, joggers and a pale blue windcheater that matched the colour of his eyes.

'That was a short call for your mum,' he said, smiling at Alanna in the mirror.

'I promised to ring her tonight. I couldn't stand there talking for ever.'

'Great. You're all ready to go, then?'

'Go where?'

'Out to lunch.'

'I...er...I thought we might stay home all day today,' she said, trying not to blush or feel wicked. He *liked* her bold, didn't he?

'That's a very tempting offer, Babe, but I doubt I'd survive staying home *all* day. I simply wouldn't be able to keep my hands off you and I'd be wrecked in no time. So I've decided we're going to drive into the city for something to eat.'

'The city? Why not Darling Harbour? And why drive? We could grab the ferry like you suggested earlier.'

'The city has more shops. I thought after lunch we'd look for an engagement present for your mum and Bob. That's why I want the car.'

Alanna's eyes lit up. She just *loved* going present shopping with Reece. He was not like any man she'd ever known in that regard. He loved buying things for people and didn't mind how long it took or how much money he spent. Christmas had been simply fabulous.

'We could buy your mum a little something at the same time,' Alanna suggested happily. 'Make her feel better.'

'Good thinking. Okay,' he said, giving his watch a quick glance. 'Now don't go getting thingy about your hair and face. You look great and we're not going anywhere fancy to eat. Just slap some lipstick on and grab a jacket.'

Alanna rolled her eyes at him. 'Oh, come now, Reece. No way am I going anywhere looking like this. Give me ten minutes at least.'

'Ten minutes and not a second more, madam.'

Twelve minutes later Reece's red Mercedes was heading for the city, the driver and his passenger in high spirits.

As they approached the first intersection at the bottom of their road the lights, which had been red, abruptly turned green. Reece could not have anticipated that the driver of a small green sedan coming along the street on his left would either ignore.. or not see.. his red light. A truck, parked illegally too close to the corner, blocked Reece's view.

His first sight of the car was out of the corner of his eye, registering a flash of green heading straight for Alanna. Reece yelled a warning as he pulled the wheel wildly to his right. But the green car still clipped the back of the Mercedes, spinning it right round and pushing it over into the path of traffic going the other way.

Suddenly, another car was heading straight for the passenger side, this one big and black and powerful.

Brakes screeched and Alanna screamed, Reece's arms stiffening on the wheel as he heard metal crunch with metal. When the side air bag exploded he prayed it had done its job.

But when silence finally came upon the scene and

Reece looked frantically over at his wife, his cry was the cry of desolation and despair.

For his lovely Alanna was unconscious, her head tilted sideways at an awkward angle, her skin deathly pale.

CHAPTER SIX

FOR one horrifying moment, Reece thought Alanna was dead. But then her head moved and a small, whimpering sound whispered from her lips.

Grabbing his mobile, Reece punched in the emergency number and screamed for an ambulance. By the time he finished the call, people had started crowding around the car, opening his door, asking him if he was all right.

'I'm okay,' he insisted. 'It's my wife who's been hurt.'

'Better not touch her, mate,' a man advised when Reece started to crawl over to her. 'Wait for the paramedics.'

Reece stopped and glanced back over his shoulder at the grey-haired man who looked around sixty.

'But..'

'I know, mate,' the man went on, his eyes soft and understanding. 'You love her. But there's nothing you can do for her right now. Best to wait.'

Reece slumped back into the driver's seat. He had never felt so impotent in all his life. Or so shocked.

Dear God, please don't let her die.

Reece kept on praying till the ambulance finally arrived, making bargains with God, promising all sorts of things in exchange for Alanna's life.

When the paramedic pronounced her in reasonable condition and not paralysed, Reece struggled not to burst into tears on the spot. Instead, he concentrated on helping them get her out of the car.

Prying open the crumpled passenger door proved impossible, so Alanna was carefully manoeuvred out through the driver's door and stretchered towards the waiting ambulance. Reece retrieved her bag from where she always dropped it at her feet, then followed her unconscious form into the back of the ambulance, leaving instructions behind for his car to be towed away.

By then, six tow trucks had arrived. So had the police, who were busily taking statements from witnesses, especially the drivers of the other two cars involved in the accident, neither of whom had been injured. One of the two sergeants involved, a big bloke named Frank, kindly told a distraught Reece to go with his wife and they'd catch up with him later.

Once the ambulance arrived at the hospital, Alanna was whisked away for X-rays and further diagnosis. Reece refused to be checked over himself, claiming he was perfectly fine..despite an appalling headache and some pain in his right elbow. No way was he going to give anyone an excuse to separate him from Alanna.

But the doctor in charge of Casualty—a harassed-looking chap in his late twenties—was equally adamant. No one was to be allowed in with his patient at this moment. Reece would be called once his wife had been properly assessed and treated. He was advised to calm down and wait.

'Calm down, be damned,' Reece muttered to himself as he paced the waiting room.

But then he remembered his promises to God, and forced himself to get a grip of his increasingly wayward emotions. After making himself some coffee from the ancient machine in the corner of the less-than-salubrious waiting room, he sat down on one of the grey plastic chairs and waited.

The next hour and a half was unbearable. Three times, Reece surrendered to impatience and stormed out to grill the dour-faced triage nurse about Alanna's progress. Each time, he was firmly told there was no news as yet, and the doctor would send for him in due course.

By the time this happened, Reece was almost beside himself with worry, having convinced himself God hadn't believed his promises and something had gone terribly wrong. The look on the doctor's face only increased his concern.

'What is it?' Reece demanded to know. 'She's not paralysed or anything, is she?'

'No, no, nothing like that. Your wife has come round. She must have knocked the side of her head during the accident. She has a rather large lump in her hair above her left temple.'

'Then what's the problem?'

'The problem, Mr Diamond, is that your wife became hysterical when I said I was going to call you in to see her. She insists you tried to kill her in the car.'

'*What?* But that's insane! Why would she say something like that? Let me talk to her.'

'I'm sorry, Mr Diamond, but till I speak to the police I can't let you do that.'

'But I would never hurt Alanna!' Reece proclaimed heatedly, feeling both offended and confused. 'She knows that. Look, something's very wrong here. Maybe that blow to her head did something to her brain.'

'She's very convincing, Mr Diamond. Whatever the truth is, she *believes* you tried to kill her. And your unborn baby.'

Reece gaped at the doctor. 'But we're not expecting a baby.'

'She said she's only a few weeks gone.'

'I tell you,' Reece said firmly, 'Alanna is *not* pregnant. Give her a test. Find out for yourself.'

The doctor speared him with a long, assessing look, perhaps trying to weigh up who and what to believe. Reece knew then he would have to stay calm to get to the bottom of this madness.

'Very well,' the doctor said at last. 'Come with me. You can wait in my office while I do just that.'

'Fine.'

Another wait. Another test of patience. Another abysmal failure on Reece's part. Patience was not one of his virtues.

If he had any virtues at all, he began to wonder after a while.

When he'd been making his bargains with God back at the accident site, Reece had realised there were a lot of areas in his life where things could be greatly improved. Admittedly, he *had* baulked at promising to be a regular church-goer. The doer in Reece couldn't see that praying in a church every Sunday would be any great benefit to either himself, his family or the community at large. He had promised, however, to be a better man in general. In particular, he'd promised to spend more time with his ailing mother, to be kinder to his two idiot younger brothers, and give a decent amount of money to the poor and underprivileged.

Reece did already donate to several charities, but, to be honest, his donations were modest, unlike Mike, who spent a huge percentage of his earnings funding summer camps and buying computers for less-advantaged kids. Mike's obsessive drive to be successful had never been self-centred, unlike Reece's.

In the beginning, Reece had wanted to earn money to support his mother and his family, but somewhere along the line he'd begun wanting money for himself. Lots of it.

Okay, it *was* great to have money. He could not deny that. But Reece had found it meant nothing when faced with the possibility of losing the one thing of real value in his life.

Alanna. His wife.

'Damn, but where is that infernal doctor?' Reece grumbled aloud, jumping to his feet and pacing agitatedly around the doctor's small office.

When the door burst open a few minutes later, Reece whirled.

'Well?' he flung at the doctor, whose intelligent eyes betrayed bewilderment.

'You're right,' he said. 'She's definitely not pregnant. Not that I told her that. I suspect she wouldn't be too pleased with the news. I've given her a sedative and called the resident psychiatrist in to talk to her. His name is Dr Beckham and he's coming in straight away. Meanwhile, I really think you should go home, Mr Diamond. There's nothing you can do here.'

Reece reeled back from the suggestion. How could he just go home, without seeing for himself that Alanna was all right?

'Can't I just see her for a second?' he pleaded. 'From the doorway. Or through a window. Just a glimpse. You can be right by my side all the time.'

'I suppose that would be all right.'

The weirdest feeling of unreality gripped Reece as the doctor led him along the polished hospital hallway. He'd prayed for Alanna's life. He hadn't thought to pray for her mind.

The doctor stopped him at an observation window on his right.

'She's in there,' he said, nodding to the private room beyond.

Reece stood there, staring at the blonde head in the bed, using all his will-power to make her look at him.

His heart leapt when her head slowly turned in the direction of the window, his whole insides squeezing tight when their eyes made contact. If fear zoomed into her eyes, he didn't know what he'd do.

But no fear entered those somewhat glazed green eyes as she gazed steadily at him. Maybe a slight curiosity. But nothing else. *Nothing* else.

'She doesn't know me,' he said in shocked tones to the doctor. 'Did you see that? She doesn't *know* me!'

'Yes,' the doctor replied with a frown crinkling his high forehead. 'I did. Tell me, Mr Diamond, has your wife been married before?'

'Yes. Yes, she has. Why?'

'I wonder…'

'What? What do you wonder?' he demanded to know.

'Wait here for me. I won't be long.'

The doctor left Reece to go into the room and speak to Alanna. Soon, he was back, shaking his head in disbelief.

'I've never come across a case like this before,' he said, drawing Reece away from the window. 'I asked your wife for the name of her husband so that I could tell the police. That's who she thinks you are, by the way. The police. She says her husband's name is Darko. Darko Malinowski. Was that her first husband's name?'

'I don't know,' Reece was almost ashamed to say. 'I only know she was married.'

'Mmm. I'm going to have to call in another doctor as well as Dr Beckham. Your wife is going to need a neurologist.'

'I told you something must have gone wrong with her brain,' Reece said.

'You're quite right. Your wife, Mr Diamond, is suffering from a type of amnesia. She hasn't lost her entire memory. Just a big chunk of it.'

'Obviously the bit which includes me,' Reece said, his emotions swinging from dismay to a perverse kind of relief.

At least she didn't think he was the one who'd been trying to kill her.

But it did mean that she thought her first husband had. This Darko fellow. Reece couldn't remember the second name. But it had sounded foreign. Whatever, he'd supposedly been the love of Alanna's life. Yet she believed he'd tried to kill her and their unborn baby.

A relevant thought suddenly jumped into Reece's head.

'He was killed in a car accident,' he blurted out. 'Alanna's first husband.'

'Ah,' the doctor said, rubbing his chin. 'That could explain it, then. Was she with him in the accident?'

Reece grimaced. 'I don't know.'

The doctor's glance was sharp, plus a touch disapproving. 'You don't seem to know all that much about your wife's past,' he said, reinforcing Reece's discomfort.

Because he didn't.

But was that his fault, or Alanna's?

Probably both of them, Reece conceded. They'd gone into their marriage with their own private agendas which hadn't included confessing all to their prospective partners. Possibly because that kind of deep and meaningful discussion was associated with romantic courtships. People madly in love wanted to know everything about each other from day one.

Reece hadn't wanted to know anything much about Alanna's past at the time. She fulfilled his requirements for a wife and that was all he was interested in.

But everything had changed now.

'I suspect my wife kept secrets from me,' he tried excusing himself, whilst thinking he hadn't been much better.

He'd never told Alanna about that last awful day with Kristine; how the things she'd done and said had been like a knife in his guts afterwards, twisting and turning for such a long time. He certainly hadn't told Alanna that he'd initially married her as an instrument of revenge, that he hadn't even cared in the beginning whether she ever had a baby or not. He'd shown her off to the world..and Kristine..in a wickedly ruthless fashion, not caring a hoot for the real woman beneath the bright and beautiful façade.

Yet, somehow, Alanna had still crept under his skin, making him forget Kristine, making him care about her.

And now...now, she didn't even know him.

This knowledge was an even sharper knife in his guts, and his heart. What if she *never* remembered him? What then?

Last night, he'd craved to have her look at him with

mindless desire. And she had. More than once. Today, he would settle for her to just look at him with remembrance in her lovely green eyes.

'For pity's sake, tell me this is just a temporary condition,' he said with a despairing look at the doctor.

'I wish I could,' came the considered reply. 'I did study amnesia, of course. The textbooks say that most trauma-based amnesiacs do recover their memories in time. But not all of them. On top of that, I have no actual experience in the field. You'll have to speak to someone with more expertise than myself. Dr Jenkins is the chief neurologist at this hospital. I'll have him called in to see to your wife and to talk to you. Now I am sorry, Mr Diamond, but I do have to get back to Casualty. I would suggest that you go home till Dr Jenkins calls you. It could be several hours before he arrives. If I recall rightly, he went down to the snowfields this weekend.'

'Go home! You have to be kidding. Look, Alanna thinks I'm the police. Why can't I go along and sit with her till Dr Beckham arrives? She must be frightened being all by herself and thinking her husband just tried to kill her.'

The doctor didn't look entirely convinced.

'Isn't it better I be with her than nobody?' Reece argued reasonably. 'If she thinks I'm the police, I would be a reassuring presence. I could say I'm protecting her. I promise I won't say or do anything to upset her.'

The doctor looked frazzled, possibly because he was needed back in Casualty.

Reece's frustration bubbled over. 'Damn it all, man, what harm could it do?'

'All right. But I'll be telling the nurses to keep a close eye on things. Your wife is in a very fragile state right now, Mr Diamond. If she starts getting distressed for any reason, you're out of there. Right?' he snapped.

'Fair enough.'

CHAPTER SEVEN

ALANNA was struggling to keep awake. Her eyelids were drooping and her brain was going fuzzy. That doctor had given her something.

But going to sleep was far too dangerous. Darko was out there somewhere, waiting for his chance to get to her and finish off what he'd tried to do in the car.

She kept her eyes fixed on the door and forced herself to stay awake, certain that any moment it would open and her husband would appear. Her only weapon of defence against him in here was her voice. She could still scream. But she couldn't even do that if she were asleep.

The doctor had tried to reassure her earlier that she was safe. But Darko was not a man to be easily stopped. She could see him in her mind's eye, convincing the police and the medical staff that his wife was the crazy one. Somehow, he would get to her. Somehow.

He wanted her dead. Her and her baby.

Alanna's heart almost jumped out of her chest when the door knob began to turn.

Her mouth opened to scream when one of the nurses walked in, followed by the fair-haired policeman she'd seen earlier with the doctor.

Sheer relief brought a small sob to her lips.

The nurse hurried over to the side of the bed, her expression caring and kind.

'This gentleman is going to sit with you,' she said. 'You don't have to talk, Mrs Diamond. Just close your eyes and go to sleep.'

Alanna frowned up at her. '*What* did you just call me?'

Worry catapulted into the nurse's eyes. 'Oh, dear. I forgot.' And she threw the handsome detective a frantic glance.

'It's all right, Sister,' he replied. 'A perfectly reasonable mistake. Don't worry. I'll take it from here.'

'Are you sure?' she returned.

'Absolutely.'

Reece shepherded the nurse from the room, having already decided that the best medicine for Alanna was to be told that she had lost part of her memory and that her obviously violent ex-husband was dead and buried. Much better all round than her worrying herself sick that he might come in at any moment for a second go at killing her. He'd seen the total panic in her eyes when they'd first come in.

The Casualty Doctor might think he had his patient's best interests at heart, but he obviously hadn't thought this situation through. Which was better? A shock or two, or gut-wrenching fear?

There was safety in the truth. Safety and security. Reece closed the door of the hospital room and returned to draw a chair up to the bed, his eyes scanning Alanna's face as he sat down.

How pale she looked. Pale and frightened and, yes, fragile.

Only then did he hesitate. Was she ready for such news? Could she cope?

The woman *he'd* married could. But this wasn't that same woman. Still, she had to know the truth. Anything else would be even more cruel.

'Are you feeling all right?' he asked her softly, thinking how beautiful she still looked, even with her skin an ashen colour and her fair hair all a-tangle around her face.

'I'm a bit sleepy. But you must tell me what's going on. What was it the nurse forgot?'

'Firstly,' he began in a gentle tone, 'let me assure you that you are not in any danger. Your husband can't harm you in any way any more.'

'You…you have him in custody?' she asked, her voice shaky, her eyes haunted.

Reece's hands balled into fists in his lap. If that bastard hadn't already been dead, he would have killed him himself.

'Let's just say he has no way of getting to you.'

'You might think that because you're here,' she said, her eyes still flashing with fear. 'But you don't know Darko. He's very strong and very clever. If he's still out there, he'll find a way.'

'He's not out there, Alanna,' he said, noting her slight surprise when he used her first name. But what else could he call her? 'Darko is dead.'

'Dead…' The word whispered from her lips, her eyes going oddly blank for a moment.

'Dead,' she repeated, then groaned as her hands whipped up to cover her face.

Her shoulders started shaking.

'He's not worth your tears,' Reece said, stunned that she would cry for such a man.

'I'm not crying for him,' Alanna choked out between her fingers. 'I'm crying because I'm safe.' Her hands raked down her tear-stained cheeks to clasp together in a prayer-like gesture below her chin. 'And so is my baby. I knew when I jumped out of the car that it was a terrible risk. He was going so fast. He said he was going to drive straight into a telegraph pole and kill us all. He didn't believe the baby was his, you see, even though it was. I wouldn't have minded him killing me, but not my baby.'

Reece's heart squeezed tight. Oh, dear God, he'd forgotten about the baby.

What was she going to do when she found out her baby *had* died? Because it must have. The Alanna he'd married had no child.

Which perhaps was why she wanted one. Quite obsessively.

The enigma that was the woman he'd married last year was finally coming clearer. Reece didn't have the entire picture yet, but lots of pieces were beginning to fall into place.

He watched with increasing concern as she bravely dashed the tears from her face, her mouth breaking into a travesty of a smile.

'The doctor says there's nothing wrong with me except a bump on my head. I can't believe how lucky I've been. I..'

She broke off abruptly, her eyes searching his.

'What is it?' she said. 'What's wrong?'

Reece didn't know what to say. The doctor had been right after all. He shouldn't have said anything. He was way out of his depth here.

She was staring at him, her eyes clearing from their earlier dullness to focus quite sharply on him. They travelled down over his clothes.. hardly the clothes of a policeman, he realized.. then back up to his face.

'You're not with the police, are you?' she said, her voice betraying bewilderment, and concern.

'No,' he confessed.

'Then who *are* you?'

'My name is Diamond. Reece Diamond.'

'Diamond,' she repeated. 'But that's the same name that the nurse called me.'

'That's right. *Mrs* Diamond.'

'But that doesn't make sense. I'm Mrs Malinowski, not Mrs Diamond.'

'You *were* Mrs Malinowski, Alanna. But you're not any more.'

'I...I don't get it.'

'You *were* in a car accident this morning. But it wasn't the accident you thought it was. You didn't jump out of the car on this occasion. A car hit us.'

'*Us?* You mean...you and me?'

'Yes.'

'But that isn't right. I've never been in a car with you. I don't even know you.'

God, but that hurt.

'I know you don't. Not at the moment. But you did and will again, in time,' he said, and hoped with all his heart that she would. 'You're suffering from a type of amnesia. That blow to your head seems to have temporarily eliminated a few years of your memory.'

Her eyes rounded like saucers on him.

'I know this has come as a shock to you, Alanna. I'm sorry there wasn't a gentler way to tell you. How old do you think you are?'

'I'm twenty-five,' she replied. 'Aren't I?' she added, suddenly looking very unsure.

'No, Alanna. You're thirty. And you're not Mrs Darko Malinowski any more. Like I told you, your first husband *is* dead, killed in a car accident some years ago.'

'My *first* husband?'

'Yes, you remarried. Last year. You're now Mrs Reece Diamond. That's who I am, Alanna. Your husband.'

She blinked, then just stared at him, her eyes still holding no recognition whatsoever, just one hell of a lot of shock. Plus total rejection of the idea.

Reece had had some low points in his life, but this had to count as one of the lowest.

What if she never remembers you? came the terrible thought. What if she doesn't like you the second time around? What if she wants a divorce?

'No,' she said, shaking her head in agitation. 'If Darko is dead.. and I suppose I have to believe you about that.. then I would never get married again. *Never!*'

The bitter certainty in her declaration told Reece that her marriage must have been sheer hell.

'I wouldn't,' she insisted fiercely. 'I *couldn't*. I..' She broke off, something even more appalling having catapulted into her head.

'My baby!' she burst out. 'What happened to my baby?'

Reece smothered a groan. He couldn't bear to be the bearer of such news. But there was no one else.

'I'm not sure, Alanna,' he said with a heavy sadness blanketing his heart. 'You've never mentioned a baby to me. Till we can check your medical records, or your memory returns, I have to assume you must have miscarried when you jumped out of that car.'

Her cry was the cry of a wounded animal. Loud and primal, her pain echoing through the room. It tore right through Reece, making him long to take her in his arms and comfort her. But when he reached for her, she reeled back from him, rolling over and curling up into a foetal ball, sobbing a tormented *no* over and over.

The nurse burst into the room, looking daggers at him before rushing to her patient's side.

'You were not supposed to upset her,' she bit out. 'I think you'd better leave.'

'You can think what you like,' he threw back at her. 'I'm her husband and I'm staying!'

'No, you're not,' a male voice pronounced as its owner strode through the open doorway.

He was possibly thirty-five, with a lean face, penetrating blue eyes and longish brown hair. He was wearing stonewashed jeans, a dark blue shirt and a black leather jacket.

'I'm Dr Beckham,' he said by way of introduction. 'The resident psych. Nurse, sit with the patient. You!' His finger stabbed towards Reece. 'You come with me.'

Reece's first reaction to such a brusque order was defiance. But then he remembered his desperate promise to God to be a better man.

It was still a somewhat disgruntled Reece who followed the psychiatrist out of the room. He'd barely reached the corridor before he whirled and stood his ground.

'I'm getting pretty sick and tired of doctors telling me I can't stay with my wife. Look, I'm not going home and that's final!'

A wry smile crossed the psychiatrist's face. 'Nice to see a husband who actually cares for his wife. You can go back to her after you've filled me in on exactly what's going on. Meanwhile, try not to worry. Dr Masur gave your wife a sedative earlier. She won't be able to hold out for too long before dropping off to sleep. Okay, now give!'

CHAPTER EIGHT

ALANNA'S return to consciousness was slow, her eyelids fluttering up and down several times before they finally stayed open. Her brain was just as slow to register where she was. Even slower to remember what had brought her there.

'You've been in a car accident and lost your memory,' she told herself shakily, her hand coming up to feel the lump in her hair.

It was huge. And very sore to touch.

Yet, oddly, she didn't have a headache.

'Darko is dead,' she murmured, then shook her head in amazement.

But, dismayingly, so was her baby. Her precious, darling baby.

Five years ago it had happened, they said, but it was like yesterday to Alanna, the pain of loss very fresh and sharp. Tears threatened once more when suddenly, out of the corner of her eye, she glimpsed a pair of bejeaned legs.

'Oh,' she cried, her head whipping round to the right.

By the time Alanna realised that the man stretched out in the chair in the corner was fast asleep, she had her tears under control. Not so her quickened heartbeat.

Reece Diamond, he'd said his name was. Her husband. Her second husband.

No way, was her immediate reaction. No way!

Yet there was no reason for him to lie. No reason for him to still be here, if it wasn't true.

She stared at him again. He was incredibly handsome, with the type of chiselled features you saw on male models and movie stars. His hair was a sandy blond, wavy and worn slightly long at the front. His eyes, she recalled, had been blue, and strikingly beautiful. His body wasn't half bad, either. What she could see of it. Broad shoulders. Long legs. No visible flab.

Alanna could well understand lots of women falling for him. He was a sexy-looking man, as well as classically good-looking.

But not her.

After what she'd been through with Darko, Alanna knew she would never fall in love again. Or marry again.

Unless…

Her heart contracted fiercely. Was that the answer to this puzzle? Would she have married, just to have another baby?

Again, her reaction was negative. How could she have risked putting her life into the hands of another man? The notion was untenable. If she'd wanted a baby so much she would have found some other way. By artificial insemination. Or by asking a friend to be a sperm donor.

This last thought sent a bitter laugh bubbling up in her throat. A friend? She didn't have any friends.

At least she *hadn't* five years ago, when she'd been Mrs Darko Malinowski.

Alanna frowned, forcing herself to project ahead five years, trying to see what might have happened to her during that time interval.

Five years was a long time. Who knew what kind of person she had become after five years?

She tried to picture herself married to the man in the armchair. But whilst he was a very attractive man, her mind automatically baulked at the hurdle of actually sleeping with him. Yet she must, if she was his wife.

Did she enjoy it? she began to wonder as she gazed at him.

Her stomach flipped over at the thought. There'd been a time when she *had* enjoyed sex. But Darko had fixed that.

Had she somehow found pleasure again in a man's body?

Had she married for love, perhaps?

Again, Alanna refused to believe that could possibly be the case.

Darko had won her with love, the kind of love she'd never known a man could bestow upon a woman. But his love had been fool's gold and she had been the fool, mistaking his excessive attentions and constant gift-giving for genuine affection. She'd had no experience with that kind of sick obsession, so hadn't been able to recognise the warning signs. She'd thought his wanting to wait till their wedding night to make love for the first time had been incredibly romantic. She hadn't realised he'd be disgusted by her not being a virgin, or that he would feel threatened by her enjoying sex.

Their marriage had started to go horribly wrong long before their honeymoon had been over. But by then she'd felt trapped. Trapped by *her* love for *him*. Though of course it hadn't been love that had *kept* her tied to him. Eventually, it had been fear.

No, she decided bitterly. Love would not have made her marry this man.

So why had she become Mrs Reece Diamond?

The answer was a total mystery to her.

When she looked at him, nothing flickered in her brain. There were no flashes of *déjà vu*. Nothing.

'Reece,' she said, not to wake him, but simply to try out his name on her tongue.

He stirred immediately, his chin jerking up, his hands reaching to grab the arm rests of the chair as his eyes shot open and went straight to hers.

'Are you all right?' he asked anxiously, then seemed annoyed with himself. 'Stupid question. Of course, you're not all right. I'll go get the nurse.' He was on his feet in a flash and moving towards the door.

'No. No nurse!' she blurted out, stopping him midstride. 'Not yet,' she added more calmly.

'Are you sure?'

'Yes,' she said, surprising herself. Because she *was* sure.

Yet the twenty-five-year-old Alanna hadn't been

sure of anything. She'd been totally broken, with little will left of her own.

The alien decisiveness in her voice just now had to be the thirty-year-old Alanna talking, the one her brain couldn't consciously remember.

'Has any of your memory returned?' he asked rather anxiously.

'Unfortunately, no. But I *can* sense a difference in myself now that I'm calmer. I mean…I can see I'm not the same desperate creature who threw herself out of her husband's car five years ago.'

'That's good,' he said, nodding. 'Now, I really should go and call the doctor. He wanted to see you as soon as you came round.'

'What doctor are you talking about?'

'Dr Beckham. He's the resident psychiatrist here. Nice man. A neurologist has been called in as well to see about your memory loss. Dr Jenkins. But he has to drive back from the snowfields and won't be here for a while yet.'

Alanna gave a rueful shake of her head. 'A psychiatrist and a neurologist. I'm a right mess, aren't I?'

'You look pretty good to me,' he said. 'But then, you always do.'

Alanna blinked, startled by the compliment, plus her instant reaction to it. A warmth spread through her body, bringing a tingle to the surface of her skin and a faint flush to her cheeks.

Her brain might not remember Reece Diamond, but her body seemed to. There was a degree of relief and reassurance in her physical response to him. And a huge amount of curiosity.

'I have some things I have to ask you,' she said.

'Anything.'

'Could you please sit back down? You look like you're about to bolt.'

When he laughed, her eyes widened. Because she knew that laugh.

'You've remembered something, haven't you?' he immediately pounced.

'Yes. No. I don't know. Your laugh…'

'You often said you liked my laugh. And my sense of humour.'

Alanna mulled that statement over. After Darko, a sense of humour would certainly appeal to her. But it did not answer the most vital question in her mind. Till she got her memory back, only this man standing in front of her could do that.

'The thing I have to ask you,' she said tautly. 'It's very important. I simply must know.'

'What?'

'*Why* did we get married? I mean…I'm finding it hard to believe I ever got married again at all, but it seems that I did. The question still remains…*why* did I?'

He just stared at her, those beautiful blue eyes of his showing great reluctance to answer her.

'Please don't feel you have to say the supposed right thing, just because I've lost my memory. I don't want to be told lies. I'm not looking for empty words of love. God, no. That's the last thing I want you to tell me: that you love me. Darko spent our entire marriage telling me how much he loved me, then showing me how much he didn't. I want to know why we got married. It wasn't for love, was it?'

Reece raked his fingers through his hair, his frustration acute. What could he possibly say to her?

The truth again, he supposed. Yet the truth was not the truth any more. At least, not on his part. He *did* love her now. Hell, he loved her so much, his heart ached with it.

But she didn't want to hear that. She wanted to be told that their marriage had been made with their heads and not their hearts. Clearly, she was afraid of love. Did not trust it. Could not risk it again.

So he sat down on the side of the bed and told her the truth as it had been, up till today.

She listened, saying nothing, but frowning when he explained that their marriage had been a marriage of convenience, entered into for companionship and children. When Reece confessed he knew very little about her first marriage, not even her first husband's name, her face betrayed confusion.

'I must have said *something* to explain why I would enter a loveless marriage.'

'You led me to believe your first husband had been the love of your life and that you could never fall in love again after he died,' Reece explained. 'Since I'd had a similar experience, I didn't question your reason.'

'A similar experience?' she echoed, her eyes startled.

He told her about Kristine, though once again not revealing the events of their last day together. There really didn't seem any point at this stage. By the time he finished talking, a heaviness of spirit had taken hold of Reece. He found the true cause of Alanna's not wanting to be loved infinitely depressing. Because it meant her capacity for falling in love had been ir- reparably damaged. Even if she remembered him, her heart would never be his. He could see that now.

Suddenly, he couldn't take any more. He was tired, and his whole body was aching.

When he levered himself up onto his legs, he winced.

'You're hurt,' she said.

Reece found the concern in her voice frustrating in the extreme. He didn't want her concern. He wanted her love and her passion!

'I'm feeling a bit sore and sorry for myself,' he admitted brusquely. 'But nothing a hot bath and a few painkillers can't fix. Look, I really must go get the doctor now. Then I might go home. But I'll be back first thing in the morning.' Hopefully, by then, she might remember him.

'What about my mother?' she suddenly asked.

'What about your mother?' he returned, taken aback by the question.

'Is she still…alive?'

Now Reece was seriously taken aback. Alanna's mother was only fifty-one, unlike his own mother, who was in her late sixties. Why would Alanna think her mother might not be alive?

'Absolutely,' he said. 'Healthy as a horse. She's just become engaged to be married again.'

Her green eyes widened. 'You're kidding. Who to?'

'Bob. He's a maths teacher at Cessnock high school. They've been dating for some time.'

'Good Lord. This is unbelievable.'

'You were going to ring her tonight. Do you want me to do that for you, explain what's happened?'

'Are you saying we ring each other regularly, Mum and I?' Alanna asked with scepticism in her voice.

'All the time.'

'I'm finding this all a bit hard to take in.'

'I'll call her and get her to come down to Sydney.'

Panic filled her face. 'No, no, please don't do that. I don't want to see her just now. I…I need some more time by myself, to think, and to try to remember.'

'But she'll be hurt that you don't want her with you.'

'Will she?' Alanna said quite sharply. 'I doubt that.'

'You're living in the past, Alanna,' Reece said quite sternly. He really liked Judy and didn't want to see Alanna hurting her, however unintentionally. 'Whatever happened once between you and your mother has been smoothed over. You are very close now. She will want to be with you in this difficult time.'

Again, Alanna shook her head. 'I know what

you're saying is probably true. You have no reason to lie to me. But I just don't want to see her right now. I won't!' she said stubbornly.

Reece rolled his eyes. 'All right. I'll try to make her understand. Now, I really *have* to go get the doctor.'

'And then you definitely should go home,' came her unexpectedly solicitous advice. 'You look awfully tired.'

Reece couldn't help it. He smiled. 'That sounded like a wife talking.'

She smiled a small smile of her own. 'Yes, it did, didn't it?'

Their eyes connected, hers searching his with an anxious expression.

'Am I a good wife to you?' she asked, her voice heartbreakingly hopeful.

'The best,' he said, a lump having formed in his throat.

She shook her head. 'I find that hard to believe. Everything is so hard to believe.'

'Believe it,' he said, but through gritted teeth.

She stared at him for a long time before slowly nodding. 'I can see that it wouldn't be hard to be a good wife to a man like you. You're very patient. And very kind.'

Reece had to struggle not to laugh. Patient was the last thing he really was. As for being kind... People often called him kind and generous. But they were very superficial virtues when you were rich and successful. It was damned easy to throw your money around.

Reece momentarily toyed with the idea of making even more promises to God in exchange for Alanna's memory. If she went back to being the woman she'd been just before the accident, he could at least express his love for her in bed. And out.

That was better than nothing. But if she *never* remembered him, Reece feared he might never get to touch her again, let alone make love to her. He didn't yet know everything that bastard had done to her during their marriage, but he knew none of it had been nice.

Clearly, Mr Darko Malinowski had caused a lot of emotional damage to Alanna. Sexual damage as well. Reece understood now why she'd been the way she was during the early months of their married life. She'd been afraid to express herself sexually. Afraid of her true self, which was a very passionate and sensual woman.

Talking to a psychiatrist might do her the world of good.

'I'll go get Dr Beckham,' he pronounced firmly, and strode from the room.

CHAPTER NINE

'WHAT a lovely day it is,' Alanna said.

Lovely, weatherwise, Reece thought ruefully as he glanced across at his passenger. Not so lovely in other ways.

It was Wednesday morning, three days since the accident. He was taking Alanna home, and she still didn't remember a single moment of the last five years.

Physically, however, she was fine. The swelling on the side of her head had subsided. She had suffered some mild concussion, but a brain scan yesterday had shown no lasting damage.

Dr Jenkins.. and Dr Beckham as well.. had come to the conclusion that her memory loss was more of the psychological kind. The car accident had momentarily propelled her back to the previous car accident, a time of severe emotional and physical trauma. In defence, her brain had shut down her memory from that point in time, which was perverse in Reece's opinion. Far better if it had shut down her first twenty-five years, rather than the last five.

Both doctors believed her memory would return in time, especially once she was in her own home, surrounded by her own things.

Reece sure hoped so. Living with a wife who didn't

remember him wasn't going to be easy. He'd already decided to sleep in another room for a while, giving Alanna total space and privacy.

Reece now knew what her first husband had done to her. Alanna's mother had filled him in on the gross details when he'd rung her on the Sunday night.

Apparently, Darko Malinowski had been a refugee from abroad. An orphan, whose family had been massacred back in his home land, he had been an intense young man. Extremely good-looking in a tall, dark and handsome fashion. He'd been doing an engineering degree part-time at Sydney University and driving taxis to make ends meet when he'd met Alanna and fallen madly in love with her.

He'd pursued her avidly, showering her with little presents and poems, treating her like a princess. Alanna hadn't been able to resist such treatment, which was the total opposite of the way her own father had acted.

Judy had confessed to Reece that Alanna's father had been a pig of a man with no caring for his family at all. Alanna had never understood why she'd stayed with him. Judy's putting-up with such treatment had been the reason why mother and daughter had become estranged. They hadn't been reconciled till Darko had been killed and Alanna had gone home to Cessnock, a broken mess after miscarrying her baby. By then, she'd been much more understanding of why a woman stayed with a man she no longer loved and who treated her badly.

Judy had explained to Reece over the phone that

Darko had been a very possessive and jealous husband. He'd made Alanna's life a misery, questioning her all the time over her movements, following her, making scenes if Alanna wanted to go anywhere by herself. When Alanna had tried to defy him one Friday night, he'd tied her to a chair for the whole weekend.

Reece had been appalled when he'd heard that, more so when he thought of the time he'd suggested bondage to Alanna. No wonder she'd shrunk back from that idea. Reece vowed never to bring the subject up ever again. Or do anything that might remind Alanna of her ghastly first husband.

'He was a mentally sick man,' Judy had said. 'But physically very strong. Alanna told me she was terrified of him. When she fell pregnant, she said she hoped he'd be happy. But he wasn't. He accused her of having an affair. He was convinced the baby belonged to some other man. When he threatened to kill them all in the car, she knew he meant it. He always carried through with his threats. So in a last-ditch attempt to save her baby, she jumped out of the car.'

With this last thought in mind, Reece snuck a sidewards glance at Alanna and wondered if she was afraid to be in a car. After all, this would feel to her like the first time she'd been in a car since that original accident.

He recalled how she'd hesitated to get into the BMW this morning back at the hospital, claiming surprise that he drove such an expensive car. He swiftly told her that this was a rented car, but his adding that he usually drove a Mercedes had sent her eyebrows lifting once more.

Up till then, they hadn't talked about what he did for a living, or how much he earned, so he'd thought her surprise quite reasonable. He hadn't imagined for one moment that she might be afraid.

But she was sitting very still, he noted, with her hands clasped tightly in her lap. Her face was extra pale, but that could have been because she didn't have any make-up on. She was wearing the same jeans and cream jumper she'd been wearing last Sunday, though he'd brought her in fresh underwear. A matching pink bra and panties, which she'd frowned over... complaining that they were on the skimpy side.

Skimpy and sexy.

Reece scowled at himself when an image flashed into his mind of Alanna sitting there in nothing but that pink bra and panties.

Damn, but that was the last image of her he wanted in his head, especially now with no chance of their making love. He wouldn't even dare kiss her.

But the image stayed. And so did the desire that came with it.

Reece gave vent to a sigh. Life had turned very difficult indeed.

When Alanna heard the weary-sounding sigh she turned to look at Reece.

Poor man, she thought, being married to her.

But as her eyes moved over him Alanna realised her husband was anything but poor.

He was wearing a suit today, a superbly tailored grey single-breasted that shouted designer label. His business shirt was blue, which made his blue eyes look even bluer. His tie was gold. So was his wristwatch. A gold Rolex.

Reece Diamond was no rough diamond. He drove expensive cars and dressed like a prince.

Clearly, she'd married money.

Was that the reason behind her marriage of convenience? she now wondered. Had she turned into a mercenary woman during the last five years?

As Mrs Darko Malinowski she'd never had much money. Darko had dropped out of university after their marriage. He'd claimed he could make more money driving cabs, but she suspected he'd spent most of his time following her. She'd secured a good job in a city hotel with her degree in leisure and hospitality, but within a year of their marriage Darko had been demanding she hand over her entire salary to him.

And poor frightened fool that she had been, she'd obeyed with only a token protest. Then, when he'd finally demanded she quit work to stay home and be a 'good' wife to him, she had. By then, she'd been close to having a nervous breakdown, anyway.

'We're nearly home,' Reece said, putting a halt to her trip down memory lane. What she had of her memory, that was.

'We live in Balmain?' she said, glancing at the street signs. At least she still knew Sydney and its suburbs.

'East Balmain,' he answered. 'On the water.'

One of the most exclusive areas west of the city.

Even before he turned into a wide paved driveway and stopped in front of a set of tall black security gates, Alanna knew their home would not be some ordinary little house, certainly nothing like the two-bedroom fibro cottage she'd lived in with Darko.

But as the gates swung slowly open she saw that her home was not a house at all, but a mansion. A huge white cement-rendered mansion with three garages on the side, a fancy fountain in the front yard and a double storey façade that screamed multimillionaire status.

'I didn't realise you were *this* rich,' she said.

'I haven't always been,' came his offhand reply. 'And I might not always be. The real-estate business is fickle.'

'You sell houses?' she asked as he drove through the gate, down a rather steep incline towards one of the garages, the door of which was automatically opening.

'I used to. I'm a property developer now. I buy land and build bigger buildings than houses these days. Mostly apartment blocks. But I've also dabbled in resorts and retirement villages.'

'You must have worked very hard to achieve so much at your age. I mean…you can't be all that old. You only look about thirty-five.'

'Close. I'm thirty-six, going on thirty-seven. And, yes, I have worked hard. Which reminds me, I have to go into the office today for a few hours. There are some urgent things which need my immediate attention. I hope you don't mind. I thought you might like some time by yourself, anyway. Of course, I'll show you through the house first. I do realise you won't remember where anything is.'

'No, don't do that,' she said swiftly. 'Dr Jenkins said to test myself wherever possible, see what I instinctively remember.'

'Do you remember your car?' Reece said, nodding towards the silver Lexus that they'd just drawn alongside.

She stared at the sleek, sporty-looking sedan and shook her head. 'No. I don't.'

'You keep the keys in the zippered side pocket of your handbag,' he told her. 'The one you have at your feet.'

She picked up the brown leather handbag.. the very expensive brown leather handbag.. and sure, enough, in the side pocket was a set of car keys, along with a natty little mobile phone. She'd already inspected the other contents of the bag back at the hospital so she knew she wore Pleasures perfume these days and had developed a penchant for mints. Her purse hadn't contained much cash, but she had one hell of a lot of cards, including two credit cards.

'Do I work outside the home?' she asked her husband.

His head turned to look at her. 'Do you feel that you do?'

'No. No, I don't think I do.'

'You had a good job in public relations at the

Regency Hotel when we met. But you resigned after we married.'

'So I'm an idle rich bitch,' she said, startling herself with her self-accusing tone. But, really, marrying for money was not, in Alanna's opinion, a nice reason to marry anyone.

'Absolutely not,' her husband said quite sharply. 'You're a career wife. And a darned good one.'

A career wife…

Alanna thought about that job description as she followed Reece through an internal entry door that opened into a wide hallway, leading down to an even wider foyer.

As she glanced around at the expanse of grey marble flooring Alanna supposed looking after a home like this *would* take some doing. The floor-cleaning job alone would be considerable.

But then she realised she would probably have a cleaner come in. Rich bitches always had cleaners.

'You didn't open any of the doors on your left as you passed,' Reece commented. 'What do you think was behind them?'

'I have absolutely no idea.'

'The servant's quarters. And the laundry.'

She stared at him. 'We have live-in servants?'

'Actually, no, we don't. You said you didn't want that. A woman does come in twice a week to do the heavy cleaning and the laundry. And you do occasionally hire a catering firm you like when we have a party. But only the large parties. You like to cook yourself for our smaller dinner parties.'

'Thank God I do something!'

'You do a lot, Alanna. I lead a very busy professional and social life. You are my right hand.'

Now she sounded more like his personal assistant than his wife. Alanna began to wonder if they *did* sleep together. Not that she was about to ask. Just the thought of sharing a bed with this man, this...*stranger*, disturbed her considerably.

Reece might be a very handsome man. But she still couldn't see herself enjoying sex with him. Or any man, ever again.

'Anything seem familiar to you at all?' he asked.

Alanna glanced around from where she was standing in the middle of the foyer. To her left and right were dual staircases leading upstairs to she knew not what. Bedrooms, she supposed. Straight ahead, a wide step separated the foyer from an enormous living area that opened out onto an equally huge terrace.

Beyond the terrace, on a slightly lower level, lay the most beautiful kidney-shaped swimming pool, complete with spa. Further on were lawns and gardens sloping down to the water. In the distance on the right was the harbour bridge. Straight ahead across the water lay the northern suburbs of Sydney, with lots of apartment blocks whose views would be almost as spectacular as this one.

Everything about this home was spectacular, from the marble floors underfoot to the Italian leather furniture to the magnificent artwork on the clean white walls. Hanging high over her head in the vaulted ceiling was a chandelier that would not have looked out of place in a palace.

But nothing felt familiar to her, least of all the man asking her the question. The only thing she remembered about him so far was his laugh.

And that might not have been a memory but a new attraction. She hadn't consciously been with a man who laughed in years.

'What do you think is down there?' Reece asked, pointing to the hallway that led off to the right beyond the staircase.

'Sorry. I simply have no idea.'

'My study, and the guest wing.'

'And what about these two doors over here?' he said, pointing to one on each side of the foyer, underneath the staircases.

'A powder room and a coat closet?' she tried.

'Close. They're both powder rooms, one for our male guests and one for the ladies.'

'Oh.'

I should have known, she thought ruefully. His and her toilets. I haven't just married money. I've married pots of money.

Suddenly, a wave of weariness washed through Alanna. Maybe it was physical, but she suspected it was more likely an emotional tiredness.

'Why don't you get back to work?' she suggested. 'I'll be fine here by myself.'

'Are you absolutely sure?'

'Yes. To tell the truth, I'm rather tired. I might have a lie down for a while. I...oh, no,' she groaned.

'What? What is it? Have you remembered something?'

'I forgot to bring home the lovely flowers you gave me in the hospital,' she said, genuinely disappointed at having left them behind. They'd been a huge basket of assorted flowers, with lots of Australian natives that would have lived on for quite some time.

He smiled softly at her. 'Don't worry. I'll get you some more.'

'Goodness, you don't have to do that.'

'Yes, I do. That's my job. To make my wife happy. As you have made me happy, Alanna,' he finished.

She stared at him. 'We're truly happy together?'

'Yes.'

'In bed, too?' she plucked up the courage to ask.

'In bed, too.'

Alanna swallowed. She found it impossible to get her head around the concept of ever finding pleasure in a man's body again.

But then she realised that this thinking was false. Five years had gone by since Darko had reduced her to a petrified wreck, incapable of feeling anything much but fear. Clearly, she'd emerged from that unnatural state to rediscover what she'd once been. A girl who, at the age of nineteen, had been shown the delights of the flesh by a man much older than herself. A girl who'd thrilled to the feel of her first orgasm. A girl who hadn't needed to be in love to enjoy being made love to.

Maybe she'd married Reece Diamond, not for his money, but for the most basic reason of all.

Sex.

Alanna recoiled at the idea. Really, that reason wasn't any more acceptable than marrying him for his money.

What if you married him for both those reasons? her merciless mind persisted. His money *and* his sex appeal. He sure has plenty of both.

'What on earth are you thinking?' he said, taking a step towards her, his eyes turning anxious.

Alanna blinked, then swallowed. 'I…I guess I'm still confused over why I went to that introduction agency you told me about. Becoming a career wife seems an unlikely choice for me. Given my first experience at marriage.'

'I see. Well, your mother might be able to help you with that. Why don't you give her a call?'

'No,' Alanna said immediately. 'I don't want to talk to my mother. Not yet.'

'Then perhaps you should have a talk with Natalie. Natalie Fairlane,' he added when she must have looked totally blank. 'The lady who runs the Wives Wanted introduction agency. Would you like me to call her for you and explain the situation? I'll see if she can pop in to see you tomorrow. Not today. I can see you're too tired for visitors today. You can ask her anything you want to know about who you were and what you wanted when you came to her. She would have done a very in-depth interview with you. Besides, talking to her might spark off something in your memory.'

'Yes. Yes, that would be a good idea,' Alanna said,

although not sure if she'd be pleased to discover what kind of woman she'd become. She seemed to be getting the picture of a very mercenary creature who'd gone into her second marriage for what she could get out of it. Reece might proclaim they were happy in bed together, but what if she was just pretending to enjoy sex with him, in exchange for living the life of Riley?

'I'll call her as soon as I get back to the office,' Reece offered kindly.

'Thank you.'

'My pleasure,' he said, and smiled one of those incredible smiles of his.

No wonder he was successful, with a smile like that. It made you want to do anything for him.

Anything but that, Alanna thought with a shudder.

It was no use. When she looked at her husband she saw a very attractive, very sexy-looking man. But she didn't want to go to bed with him. The thought he might expect her to share a bed with him tonight brought a stomach-churning panic.

'One thing before you go,' she blurted out.

'Yes?'

'About our sleeping arrangements,' she said, her face flushing with embarrassment. 'I mean…I…I don't want to…to…'

'It's all right, Alanna,' he said gently, his expression carrying both regret and understanding. 'I've already moved my things into another room. We'll wait till you get your memory back for that.'

'But…but what if I never get it back?'

His expression became quite steely, and stubborn. 'The doctors said you would remember everything in time.'

'But when? Tomorrow? Next year? In ten years' time?' She couldn't imagine a man like him waiting that long to have sex with his legal wife. Darko hadn't been able to go a day. He'd forced himself on her even when she'd objected, claiming there was no such thing as rape in marriage. A wife was her husband's possession. He could do with her as he willed, when he willed it.

'Soon,' Reece said optimistically. 'Now I have to go. Don't forget to eat something. There's lots of food in the kitchen.'

She had to smile. He really was a most considerate man. So different from Darko. Whatever her reasons for marrying Reece Diamond, she had chosen well.

'I'll be fine,' she said, and, without thinking, reached out to touch her husband lightly on his arm. 'You don't have to worry about me.'

He stared down at her hand, then up into her face. For a split second, she could have sworn she saw torment in his eyes. But then he smiled and patted the back of her hand.

'That's what you always say,' he said.

'Do I?'

'Yes. You are a very independent woman.'

'Am I really?' The concept amazed her.

'Trust me.'

Trust him…

Alanna didn't want to admit that she found it almost impossible to believe that she would ever trust another man.

Yet she must have. And, strangely, it felt right.

'I'm sorry,' she said as she withdrew her hand from his arm.

He frowned. 'Sorry for what?'

For forgetting you, she was tempted to say.

'For causing you so much trouble. It must be awkward having a wife who doesn't remember you.'

He laughed. Not an entirely happy sound. 'You could say that.'

'When do you think you'll be back today?'

He glanced at his watch. 'Mmm. It's already eleven. Probably not till six.'

'Do you want me to cook you dinner? I mean…is that what I normally do?'

'In the main. Though we do eat out quite a bit. Look, how about I bring something home with me? You do look tired. What would you like? Chinese? Thai? Italian?'

Her mouth pulled back into a wry smile. 'You tell me. What *do* I like these days?'

Again, something flickered across his eyes. Not torment this time. Something exciting. Something almost…wicked.

What *was* it he was thinking of that she liked?

Alanna swallowed. Surely not something sexual. Surely not *that*. Alanna had liked the taste of a man once, but it was difficult to like something when your husband forced you to do it, all the while twisting your hair and calling you a whore.

'I'll surprise you,' Reece said. 'If you need to ring me, my private number is the first one in the menu of your phone. The one in the bag you're holding. Now I have to go, Alanna.'

Reece stepped forward to take her shoulders and lightly brush his lips against her cheek. Only the briefest and most platonic of kisses, but it sent her heart racing in her chest. Goose-bumps broke out all over her skin.

'See you around six,' he added, and was gone, whirling on his heels and striding off the way they had come.

Her hand lifted to touch her cheek as she stared after him. One thing was certain. Her mind might not remember her husband, but her body was beginning to.

CHAPTER TEN

REECE'S office was in the centre of the city, on the twelfth floor of a high-rise building that overlooked the harbour.

His suite of rooms was plush, but not overly large. Diamond Enterprises only had three permanent employees on staff. Reece himself. His personal assistant, Jake Wyatt, a gung-ho young tyro, and a female secretary/receptionist to front the reception desk.

Her name was Katie. She was thirty-eight years old, an ex-real-estate salesperson who'd wanted a change from the pressure of selling. She was blonde. Attractive. Diplomatic. Pragmatic. And best of all, happily married.

Reece liked to prevent personal problems at work.

'No calls for half an hour, Katie,' he announced as he swept through Reception shortly after eleven. 'And before you ask, no, Alanna hasn't got her memory back yet and, yes, I am not in the best of moods.'

'You don't want me to send out for your usual coffee and bagels, then?' she replied without batting an eyelid.

Bagels and coffee did sound good. He hadn't exactly been caring about eating lately and his stomach was beginning to rebel.

Reece stopped at the door of his office and threw

Katie a belated smile. 'You know how to tempt a man, don't you?'

She shrugged. 'Man cannot live by bread alone,' she quipped. 'But bagels are a different story.'

'You're right there. Get me two. And make the coffee strong. But not for twenty minutes. I simply must make a couple of calls first.'

'What about Jake?'

'What about Jake?' Reece repeated somewhat wearily. He wasn't sure if he could tolerate too much of Jake this morning.

'He wants to give you an update on that house-hunting job you gave him. You know…the one for your banker friend?'

'Ah, yes.' Before going on his honeymoon, Richard had given Reece the job of finding a suitable family home for himself and Holly, Reece promising to have several possibilities lined up for him to inspect by the time he came back.

But that wasn't for another four weeks. At this precise moment, he had other priorities.

'Look, tell Jake I'll talk to him about that some other time. Okay?'

'You're the boss.'

Reece forged on into his office, closing the door behind him and striding over to the highly polished, rosewood desk that had once graced an Englishman's residence, but which now sat sedately in front of a panoramic view of Sydney Harbour.

When Reece had leased this office eighteen months

earlier, he'd given considerable thought to the elegant décor, and the impressive view.

Today, he noticed neither. His thoughts were totally consumed with one subject and one subject only.

And it wasn't work.

Plonking down into the black leather swivel armchair, he snatched up his phone and selected Mike's number from his automatic dial menu. As much as he would prefer to be in a bar somewhere, drowning his sorrows, the time had come for him to follow through on the main promise he'd made to God last Sunday: to give financial assistance to the poor and underprivileged.

Maybe if he were extra generous, God might have more mercy and bring back Alanna's memory on top of saving her life. Because if she didn't ever remember him… If she decided she couldn't bear being married and wanted a divorce…

Both possibilities made Reece feel physically ill.

'Mike Stone,' Mike answered on the third ring.

'Mike, it's Reece.'

'Reece!' Mike sounded both surprised *and* wary. 'Look, mate, I hope you still haven't got your nose out of joint about last Saturday night. It wasn't *my* idea for Alanna to teach me to dance, you know.'

Reece had forgotten all about that. Last Saturday night seemed so long ago. Yet it had been less than four days.

'Yeah, I know, Mike. I'm not ringing about that.'

'Brother, I've never heard you sound so serious. I hope there's nothing wrong.'

As briefly as he could, Reece filled his friend in on what had happened to Alanna.

'Hell, Reece!' Mike protested after he finished his sad and sorry tale. 'Why didn't you tell me about this days ago? I might have been able to help. I could have at least taken you out for a drink or something. Got your mind off things for a while. You must have been worried sick.'

That was the understatement of the year!

At this point, Reece told Mike about the bargain he'd made with God.

'That's admirable, Reece,' Mike said. 'But…er… what has this got to do with me?'

'I thought I could do what you do. With poor kids. You know, buy them stuff they can't afford. Computers and sports gear. And pay for them to go on holidays. That kind of thing.'

'You mean that?'

'Sure I do. But I want you to decide how the money is spent. You'd know exactly where it's best needed and what to do with it.'

'How much money are we talking about here?'

'How about one million for starters? And one mil every year after that. Provided I'm still in the black. You know me, Mike. My finances go up and down like a flag on a flagpole.'

'I don't know what to say.'

'Just say thanks, mate. Then tell me where to send the money. I'll do it today.'

Two minutes later, Reece was off the phone, Mike's bank account number jotted down.

That was what he liked most about Mike. No bull. Just straight down to business.

He suspected his phone call to Natalie Fairlane would not be as brief.

Fortunately, he still had her number in his diary. Also fortunately, she answered. Reece knew that Natalie was the entire staff at Wives Wanted, which meant that when she was out of her office..her office being the downstairs front room in her Paddington terrace house..her secretary was her answering machine.

'Reece Diamond here, Natalie,' Reece said brusquely.

There was the smallest of hesitations at the other end before she replied.

'Reece! Hello. Don't tell me this is bad news and your marriage to Alanna isn't working out.'

'My marriage to Alanna has been working out fine,' he reassured her, surprised by her sentiments. He'd tabbed Natalie as an extremely pragmatic businesswoman, not anyone who would ever become personally involved in the marital matches she made.

Although a striking redhead with a knockout figure, she came across as cold and forbidding in the flesh. Yet just now, over the phone, she'd sounded quite warm, and genuinely concerned about his marriage.

'Then how can I help you?' Natalie asked, this time in a more puzzled tone.

He told her the situation with Alanna, pleased when she didn't interrupt him with a myriad silly questions.

Not that she was a woman who would ever ask

silly questions. Reece had never met a female quite like Natalie Fairlane. Highly intelligent, but one tough cookie!

He found it hard to imagine her ever getting married, despite her physical attractions. It would be a perverse man who found her daunting persona to his liking.

'How very distressing for you both,' she said when he'd finished his explanation. 'But for Alanna most of all. I had no idea that her first marriage had been bad. It's really rather odd. Women who have bad first marriages rarely back up for a second.'

'That's what's bothering Alanna the most,' Reece said. 'She can't believe she'd ever get married again. I was thinking you might be able to fill in that gap for her, but it seems you can't. Apparently, she didn't tell you the truth, either.'

'It seems so. But you know…I was always a bit worried about her.'

'Why was that?'

'I can't put my finger on it. Sometimes, I have an instinct for women who've been hurt. I sensed something in Alanna the moment I met her. But I mistakenly thought I had the answer when she told me that her first husband had been tragically killed. I should have gone with my gut feeling. I will, in future.'

Reece had a good idea at that moment why Natalie was as she was. At some stage in her life she'd been burnt by a man. Very badly.

'I wonder if you might still come and visit Alanna,' Reece asked. 'The doctors say she needs to be surrounded by people and things from the five years she's lost. You might spark some memory in her. It can't do any harm.'

'I'd be happy to,' Natalie replied crisply. 'When?'

'How about tomorrow? She's pretty tired today and still getting used to the house all over again.'

'Give me a time and I'll be there.'

'Shall we say ten in the morning?'

'Will you be there?'

Reece hesitated. He wanted to be with Alanna. Hell, he'd much prefer to be with her right now. But he wasn't stupid. He could see how stressed she was over the situation. He had to give her some space. Not hover over her. She'd had enough hovering from her first husband to last her a lifetime.

'No, I have to come in to work,' he said. 'I'm way behind. But the cleaner will be there. Her name is Jess. She'll let you in.'

Jess was a nice woman. She wasn't likely to upset Alanna. Or harass her with too many questions.

'Is the address the same as the one I have in my files?'

'Yes.' Reece had bought the house the day he'd decided to get married again. It had come totally furnished and decorated, the previous owner having moved overseas. 'Thanks a lot, Natalie. You'll have to let me take you out to lunch one day, as a thank-you.'

She laughed. 'Thanks, but no, thanks, Reece. I gave up having lunches with married men some years ago.'

Ah, so that was who had burnt her. A married man.

'I wasn't trying to come on to you,' he said. 'I love Alanna. Oh, damn,' he bit out immediately. 'For pity's sake, don't tell Alanna I love her. The last thing she wants is to hear that. Promise me you won't say anything.'

'All right. I promise. Poor Alanna,' Natalie went on with genuine sympathy in her voice. 'Once bitten that badly, for ever shy. And you're right. She wouldn't want to hear that you love her. Not with words. But that doesn't mean you can't show her how much you love her, Reece. I don't think that would be out of place.'

'Are you crazy?' he retorted. 'I daren't lay a finger on her at the moment.'

'Oh, dear.' Natalie's sigh carried exasperation. 'Do men always have to think in terms of sex? I wasn't talking about making love to her, Reece. I was referring to considerate little things you can do. Like taking her flowers…'

'I was already going to do that,' Reece said, though silently thanking Natalie for the reminder. He had a tendency to forget things when he was distracted. There was a florist in the foyer of this building. He'd dash down there shortly and buy some before that could happen. *And* send some to his mother.

'I have to go, Natalie,' Reece said when there was a soft tap tap on his office door. It would be Katie with the bagels and coffee. He knew her knock. 'I'll tell Alanna to expect you at ten. Thanks again. Bye.'

Reece glanced at his watch as he called out for Katie to come in. Twenty to twelve. He wondered what Alanna was doing.

Hopefully, getting her memory back.

CHAPTER ELEVEN

ALANNA was standing at the sink in the beautifully appointed white kitchen, washing up the mug she'd just used for coffee, when suddenly she sensed someone close behind her.

All the hairs on the back of her neck stood up, her mouth falling open as a scream bubbled up in her throat.

She whirled around, but no one was there.

She was alone.

Alanna leant back against the sink, her heart still racing.

Déjà vu?

But if that were the case, why didn't anything else in this house feel familiar? She'd had to search all the cupboards just now to find the wherewithal to make coffee. She hadn't been able to put her hand straight on a mug. Or the jar of instant coffee. Or the sugar.

None of the rooms downstairs had rung a bell in her brain. Neither had the outside. She'd wandered through the gardens for a while, staring at the pool and its surrounds before going down to the jetty and looking back at the house from that angle.

Nothing. Not a single flash of memory. Not even a flicker.

Shaking her head, Alanna decided that the time had come to go upstairs, to the master bedroom. She'd been putting it off. Why, she wasn't sure. Really, it was the one place where she would be most likely to remember something.

But, once again, she felt reluctant. And nervous.

Swallowing, she forced her legs to move, taking her from the kitchen back into the main living room, then up the wide marble step to the foyer. Once there, she delayed things a few minutes further by ducking into the ladies room.

The sight of herself in the vanity mirror brought her up with a jolt. She looked a fright.

'Lord, Alanna,' she said, pushing her hair back from her face. Okay, so she'd been blessed with wavy, naturally blonde hair that didn't need never-ending trips to the hairdresser to look good. It still could do with some love and attention. So could her face. Another good reason to go upstairs. She needed to shower, shampoo her hair and change her clothes. Her jeans and jumper felt grubby and her underwear was not on the comfortable side.

The bra was one of those underwired, half-cup contraptions that pushed her breasts up and together, her nipples in danger of popping out. The matching panties were terribly high-cut at the front, with just a thin strip of pink satin at the back.

Surely she owned some ordinary cotton underwear.

'Up those stairs you go, Alanna,' she lectured herself. 'And no more of this silly procrastinating.'

Emerging from the powder room, she turned and

walked more purposefully round to the right-hand side of the split staircase. As Alanna mounted the marble steps she passed by several large black and white pictures hanging on the white walls. Seascapes, they were. Very striking.

Had she chosen them? Or had they come with the house? They looked like something a professional decorator would have selected.

Actually, everything in the house looked like something a decorator would have chosen. Which meant what? She couldn't be bothered decorating her own home? Or was she happy these days to pay to have everything done for her?

Once again, Alanna felt weighed down by the amount of information she simply didn't know. It was extremely frustrating. Reece must be finding her memory loss frustrating as well.

Sighing, she continued up the curving staircase, which led to a rectangular-shaped landing. Straight ahead lay a pair of double doors with large silver knobs. In the centre of the wall on the left was a single door. Another door centred the wall on the right.

Logic told Alanna that the bedroom she'd shared with her husband lay behind the double doors straight ahead. But, once again, she checked the other rooms first.

Both were bedrooms. Both had *ensuite* bathrooms. The last one Alanna looked into..decorated in blue and white..had been slept in recently. The bedding was askew and there were some clothes hanging on the back of a chair. A black leather jacket. And a pair of stonewashed jeans.

Clearly, this was where Reece was sleeping at the moment.

His consideration for her was touching, but rather amazing. She wasn't used to her feelings being considered.

By the time Alanna pushed open the double doors, she was very curious to see what kind of room they shared, especially what kind of bed.

It was simply huge. A four-poster, but not an antique. The frame was painted white, which was proving to be the main colour throughout the whole house. The quilt was luxury itself, made in white satin, and padded, the squares sewn with a silver thread.

Considering the size of the room, there wasn't a lot of furniture in it. Two white bedside chests. Two white cane chairs and a white dressing table, showing an array of cosmetics and perfume that would have a cost a small fortune.

Alanna walked over to the dressing table and pulled open the top two drawers, her eyes widening at the contents. She'd never seen so many matching sets of bras and panties.

All echoed the style of the pink satin set she had on today. Half-cup bras and G-string panties.

The second set of drawers was devoted to other sexy garments. Silk pyjamas, lacy teddies and satin corselettes, as well as stay-up stockings with lacy tops.

It seemed that the Alanna who'd married Reece Diamond wasn't into cotton underwear.

Clearly, her second husband liked his wife to look sexy, an observation that should have already been obvious to her by the pictures on the bedrooms walls.

She'd been avoiding looking at them. Black crayon drawings on white paper, they were, with silver frames. The subjects were all women in various states of undress. None was an actual nude but all were exotic and highly erotic.

Now *these*, Alanna felt sure she hadn't chosen.

Yet, there again, how *could* she be sure?

She shook her head again. Losing chunks of your memory was a dreadful thing, Alanna decided as she moved on into the biggest and most luxurious *en suite* bathroom she had ever seen.

Floor-to-ceiling marble. Silver fittings. His and her vanities, not to mention a spa bath, toilet and bidet.

The long mirror above the vanities slid back, Alanna soon discovered, revealing shelves full of an array of medicines and toiletries.

She frowned as she picked up a packet of sleeping tablets prescribed to her. Did she have trouble sleeping? Wasn't she happy as Mrs Reece Diamond?

Reece had said they were happy, but maybe he was lying.

But why would he lie?

If they weren't happy, he had the best excuse possible now to get rid of her. Yet all he'd been since the accident was kind and considerate and caring.

It crossed Alanna's mind that maybe he didn't know she was unhappy.

Alanna sighed. She was sick and tired of speculating. Aside from being frustrating, it was emotionally exhausting.

Sliding the mirrored door back into place, she turned to glance one last time around the bathroom, but nothing sparked any memory in her. Not the packet of sleeping tablets. Or the large corner spa bath. Or the shower recess. Or the…

Alanna's eyes whipped back to stare at the shower recess.

Built for two, it had twin shower heads, along with his and hers shelves, filled with personal hygiene products. Shampoos. Conditioners. Shower gels.

Her mouth dried as she tried to imagine having a shower in there with her husband.

Did they do that? Did they wash each other's backs, and other places? Did she let him do other things to her in there? Was that what he'd been thinking of when he'd smiled over what she liked?

Alanna could not imagine liking anything of a sexual nature ever again.

Yet her heart was racing.

Was it fear of such intimacies making it do that? Or a subconscious excitement?

Annoyed with herself for continuing with these useless speculations, Alanna spun on her heel and marched from the room, telling herself not to be such a masochist.

One step at a time, Alanna, the doctor had said to her. Don't try to hurry things. Don't stress.

All she had to do today was reacquaint herself with this house, and her personal belongings. Which she was in the process of doing.

One last door in the bedroom called to her. It led into a walk-in wardrobe, again of the his and her variety, and very spacious.

On the right side were rows of neatly arranged suits, shirts, trousers and jackets—all expensive looking—confirming the opinion Alanna had already formed that her husband was a snappy dresser.

The left side was devoted to women's clothes.

Her clothes, Alanna had to tell herself as she stared at the many racks.

The first thing that struck her was the lack of bright colours. That *had* to be a hangover from her marriage to Darko, who'd hated her wearing anything that brought attention to her.

But as her eyes began to scan the huge array of outfits in closer detail Alanna soon realised that she dressed very differently as Mrs Reece Diamond from when she'd been Darko's wife.

Her evening clothes had her eyes almost popping out of her head. One gown in particular brought a shocked gasp to her lips. It was a long slinky number in champagne-coloured satin.

The front was daring enough with its low-cut neckline and unlined bodice. The back was beyond daring. Because there was no back. Nothing down to the waist. And further!

No way could you wear any underwear at all under that dress. Everything would show, even the tiniest G-string.

Alanna tried to get her head around her wearing such a dress in public. Darko would have killed her rather than let her wear something like that!

Shuddering, Alanna shoved the dress back along the rack and looked at the next dress. It was made in white satin and wasn't much better.

Suddenly, she spotted something in red peeking out at the far end of the rack of evening dresses.

Oh, no, she thought despairingly. A scarlet dress to go with her new scarlet soul!

But when she pulled the red dress out, Alanna was relieved to see that it wasn't a case of more of the same. The red dress was bright in colour, but quite modest in style.

When she checked the rest of her wardrobe, however, any relief reverted back to agitation. Nothing was quite as revealing as the first dress she'd looked at. But a lot of her going-out clothes were still very sexy. Short, tight skirts and figure-hugging jackets. Slinky-looking trousers and a range of low-cut tops made in sensual materials. Silk. Satin. Even see-through. Her shoes were show-stoppers as well, strappy and sexy, with high, high heels.

To say Alanna was stunned was an understatement. Wearing such clothes was as unbelievable to her as remarrying and enjoying sex. What kind of woman had she become?

Fortunately, her casual wardrobe wasn't of the

same ilk, consisting of track suits, jeans, shorts and an assortment of T-shirts, pastel coloured blouses and lightweight jumpers.

At least she wouldn't have to greet Reece tonight dressed like some tart. Or a tease.

Although perhaps that was what he liked.

Another shudder ran through her. This was all too alien. Too different. Too stressful.

One moment, she'd been an abused doormat of a wife who hardly dared step outside her front door. The next she was some property tycoon's trophy wife who dressed to kill, and to thrill.

Who could blame her if her overriding emotion at this moment was confusion? Alanna didn't know whether to scream, or to cry.

Shaking her head, she grabbed some casual clothes—a navy track suit and white T-shirt—and was heading back to the bathroom when the phone sitting on the nearest bedside chest began to ring.

The sound brought her to a shaky halt, her eyes darting nervously over at the darned thing. She didn't want to answer it. What if it was someone she should know but didn't?

But what if it's Reece?

She *had* to answer it. He'd worry if she didn't.

Tossing the clothes onto a chair, she hurried over to pick up the phone.

'Hello?'

'Alanna? Is that you?'

Alanna cringed. Her worst fear had just materialised. She had no idea whom she was speaking to, except that it was a woman with a rather posh voice. Sinking down on the side of the bed, she clutched the phone to her ear and prayed for inspiration.

'Er…yes, it's me.' No way did she want to launch into some lengthy explanation about the accident and her loss of memory. If she could bluff her way through this call, she was going to.

'You sound odd. Are you ill?'

'I was lying down,' she invented. 'I have a migraine.'

'You poor thing. You get those a lot, don't you?'

Did she?

'At least that explains why you weren't at the gym today,' the woman rattled on. 'I knew something had to be wrong for you not to show up two days in a row. I presume you won't be coming out with us tonight as well. The girls are going to be *so* disappointed.'

Alanna blinked. So she went to the gym quite a bit, did she? And had nights out with the girls. Maybe she *was* happy.

Pity she didn't know whom she was talking to. But Reece would probably know. She'd ask him tonight.

'I don't think I should,' she said. 'Sorry.'

'Oh, darn. Our nights out are never the same without you, darls. You're such fun to be with. Oh, well. Next time. I hope you feel better soon. Bye.'

'Bye…'

Alanna hung up, feeling even more amazed, and confused. Not only did she dress sexily these days, she was an exercise junkie and a life-of-the-party extrovert.

Yet she was nothing like that at all!

Suddenly, it was all too much for Alanna. Tears of utter frustration filled her eyes. She wanted her memory back. Not tomorrow. Or next week. Or next month. She wanted it back today, this afternoon, *before* Reece came home tonight. She wanted to be able to greet him at the door and say, 'Hello, honey. I'm so glad you're home. I remember you now, and yes, you were right. We *are* happy. And, yes, I am a good wife.'

But Alanna was afraid that might not be the case. Afraid that she might have gone into this marriage out of some kind of sick revenge.

Please God, don't let me have become a cold-blooded bitch, she prayed as the tears spilled over and streamed down her face. Or a mercenary cow. Or, worse still, a heartless whore!

CHAPTER TWELVE

REECE had been watching Alanna toy with her Thai beef satay for quite some time before he decided he could no longer ignore her mood. When he'd first arrived home, she'd seemed happy and appreciative of the flowers he'd brought her, as well as the wine and the food, but now she looked distracted and her appetite was zero.

'Is there anything wrong, Alanna?' he asked quietly.

They were sitting on either side of the breakfast bar on stools, Alanna having refused to eat in the formal dining room.

'No, no,' she said, glancing up at him. 'The food's delicious. I'm just not very hungry.'

'It's your favourite,' he said.

'Is it?' she said rather listlessly, and moved her meal slowly round the plate again.

Reece wasn't sure what to do. He could understand her feeling down. It must be dreadful, losing five years of your life, especially when you found yourself back in a part of your life that was awful.

In the end, he decided not to press.

'More wine?' he said, scooping the bottle out of the ice bucket and refilling her glass. 'This is your favourite, too,' he added. 'You simply adore New Zealand whites.'

Alanna picked up her glass and took a sip, her expression appreciative, then thoughtful.

'Do I drink much?'

Her question surprised him. So did the sudden edge he heard in her voice.

'You like your wine,' came his careful reply. 'But I've never seen you drunk. No, I take that back, you did get seriously sloshed one night.'

'What night was that?'

'Our wedding night.'

'Oh,' she said, and a fierce blush scorched her cheeks.

'We didn't sleep together before we were married,' he explained. 'You didn't want to. Knowing what I know now,' he added gently, 'I imagine you might have been nervous.' And then some. Judy had told him when they'd been discussing Alanna just last night that, before her marriage to him, she hadn't been to bed with a man since the dreaded Darko.

Her eyes searched his, curiosity finally overriding any embarrassment. 'What was it like...our first night together?'

'It was fine.'

His answer seemed to trouble her. But there was little point in giving the event glowing compliments when she'd hopefully recall the event herself one day.

To be bluntly honest, he'd had to work very hard to get her to relax. Her first orgasm had taken him an hour, plus every ounce of lovemaking skill he had. Then, afterwards she'd passed out like a light.

'That doesn't sound too good,' she said.

'It got better.'

She frowned at him. 'How much better?'

'A lot better. Look, Alanna, let's talk about something else,' Reece said sharply, his body having automatically responded to thinking of her and sex in the same breath.

Alanna's back stiffened at his curt tone.

'God, I'm sorry,' Reece immediately apologised. 'I didn't mean to snap to you like that. It's just…damn it all, there are no excuses. I'm sorry.'

'No, no,' she said swiftly. 'Tell me. I want to know what I did that annoyed you.'

'What *you* did? You didn't do anything. It's me.'

'What about you?'

He looked at her and shook his head. 'You don't want to know.'

'But I do. You've been so kind. Bringing me those flowers,' she said, nodding towards where they were sitting down the other end of the breakfast bar, an elegant display of multicoloured flowers in a basket. 'Not to mention this lovely food and wine. I've never known a man quite like you. No, that's not altogether true. You do have some of the attributes of a man I knew once.'

'Not Darko, I hope.'

'Lord, no!'

'Who, then?'

She smiled a rather shamefaced smile. 'He was my tutor at university.'

'And?' Reece prompted.

'He was my first lover. I was nineteen. He was forty.'

'Ah. The experienced older man.'

'Very,' she said, and blushed once more.

Reece now knew where she'd learned some of the tricks she'd shown him last Saturday night.

Damn. They were back to sex again. He was never going to get to sleep tonight. Best change the subject.

'By the way, I rang Natalie Fairlaine today,' he said. 'The lady from Wives Wanted? She's going to drop in tomorrow morning around ten. I've explained the situation so you won't have to go into that. It's the cleaner's day tomorrow, too, by the way. Her name's Jess.'

Alanna looked unhappy at this news. 'I don't mind about this Natalie woman coming. But does the cleaner have to come? I'm more than happy to do the cleaning till I get my memory back. Please put her off, Reece. Please.'

Reece sighed. 'Very well. I'll cancel the cleaner. But only until you get your memory back.' He supposed it was better she kept busy, rather than just mope around.

'Thank you. I simply hate the thought of having to deal with people who seem like perfect strangers to me. Some woman rang me today and it was so awkward.'

'You never mentioned that. Who was it?'

'I have no idea. Someone I go to the gym with. She had a posh voice.'

'Ah, that would be Lydia. There's quite a group of you who go to the local gym together. You go out with them on a Wednesday night as well. I should have warned you. I forgot. I suppose she was calling about that.'

'Yes, she was.'

'What did you tell her?'

'Nothing. I was able to bluff my way out of the situation by saying I had a migraine. The funny thing is, she said I get lots of those.'

'I wouldn't say lots. But you do get them occasionally.'

'I see… So, is this Lydia my best friend?'

'No. You don't really have a *best* friend. Although you've become quite close to Holly over the last few weeks.'

'Holly,' Alanna repeated, frowning. 'No, that name means nothing to me, either. Who's Holly?'

Reece explained about Holly and the wedding last Saturday, and how Holly and Richard would be away on their honeymoon for the next month.

'I have to say you looked absolutely gorgeous in your red bridesmaid dress,' he said, then wished he hadn't, the compliment taking his mind right back to Saturday night.

'Oh!' she exclaimed. 'I saw that dress today when I was going through my clothes. So that's why it was so different from all my other dresses. It was a bridesmaid dress!'

'Not quite your usual taste,' Reece said. 'But it suited you.'

'Yes, I…er…I noticed what my usual taste was,' she said. 'I dress rather provocatively, don't I?'

'I *like* the way you dress.'

'Darko would have ripped most of those clothes off me,' she said.

'Well, I'm not Darko,' he ground out, feeling angry for her. And sad at the same time.

'No,' she replied, her eyes searching his face. 'You certainly aren't…'

Reece found himself gripping his fork as if he were a drowning man holding onto a scrap of wreckage. The way she was looking at him. Not with love, or mindless desire. But with the most ego-stroking admiration, and heart-rending gratitude.

He'd never wanted to kiss her so badly. Just kiss her, and hold her. Comfort and reassure her.

His love for her expanded from his heart outwards in ever-increasing circles till it filled every pore in his body.

'I would never hurt you, Alanna,' he said with a fierce tenderness. 'Never.'

Suddenly, tears filled her eyes.

'I just wish I could remember you,' she choked out.

'You will. In time.'

'How can you say that?' she cried, dashing the tears away with her hands. 'I might never get my memory back. Doctors don't know everything. They could be wrong.'

Reece could well understand her feelings of distress

and panic. It would be easy to surrender to panic himself. But they couldn't both start falling apart. Alanna needed him to be strong for her.

'We'll cross that bridge when we come to it,' he said firmly. 'Meanwhile, you're not frightened of me, are you?'

'No...'

Damn. She could have sounded a bit surer. He'd done everything he could not to alarm her.

'Then everything will be all right. Trust me.'

'Trusting a man doesn't come easily to me, Reece.'

'I can imagine. But you *have* learned to trust again, Alanna. Otherwise, why would you have married me?'

'I suppose you're right,' she said with a frown.

'Talk to Natalie tomorrow,' Reece said. 'She'll tell you the kind of woman you were when you went to her agency, searching for a husband.'

'That's what worries me.'

'What do you mean?'

'I'm not sure I'll like that Alanna.'

'I don't see why not.'

Her face carried agitation. 'She's nothing like me.'

'In what way? Give me any example.'

'The clothes I wear, for starters. There's this one particular dress in my wardrobe. An evening gown. I mean, all my clothes are rather sexy, but this one is positively indecent!'

'Ah yes, I know the one you mean. It's made of satin. In a pale fawn colour.'

'Yes, that's the one. I can't imagine ever buying a dress like that, Reece, let alone wearing one.'

'You wore it all right. But only the once. And you didn't buy it. *I* did.'

She stared at him.

'It was a bit over-the-top, I admit,' he said ruefully. 'But you have the body to carry it off.'

'But I couldn't have worn any underwear with a dress like that!' Alanna protested, her tone horrified.

'True.' Not a good reminder. Reece recalled being turned on to the max during that party. He was turned on now, just thinking about it.

'And that didn't bother me?' she questioned him, her expression sceptical.

'Maybe a little. You told me later that night that you wouldn't be wearing it again till you had the straps shortened.'

'I doubt that would make much difference. It would still be a slut's dress.'

Reece came close to dropping his fork. So *this* was what was bothering her. She equated sexy clothes with being immoral.

That was certainly not *his* Alanna's way of thinking. She believed a woman had the right to wear whatever she liked.

The Alanna of five years ago, however, must have been brainwashed into a far more prudish frame of mind.

That appalling Darko had a lot to answer for!

But even as Reece blamed Darko for Alanna's present qualms he struggled to put aside his own guilt over why he'd chose such a dress for his wife. He was also pretty sure he wouldn't be letting her wear that satin number again.

Still, that wasn't the point at the moment. The point was to reassure Alanna over the woman she'd become.

'Alanna, you are in no way a slut,' Reece said firmly. 'In the last five years, women's fashion has become increasingly glamorous and sexy. You are not the only woman wearing such dresses. It's quite acceptable to dress provocatively for a party, especially when the wearer has a body as slender and beautiful as yours.'

She flushed again. 'Darko always said I was too skinny.'

The bastard. Reece's teeth clenched down hard in his jaw.

'You're perfect in every way,' he insisted, perhaps a little too passionately.

Reece decided to change the subject once more. Get right away from Alanna's perfect body.

'If you're not going to eat any more of that,' he said, 'why don't I get rid of it and make us both some coffee?'

Her eyes showed surprise. '*I* should be getting the coffee. You've been at work all day.'

'Do you think you can manage? I mean…you might not know where everything is yet.'

'I know where the coffee is,' she said rather drily. 'That's the first thing I looked for.'

He laughed. 'You're not too good without your coffee.'

'That's another thing which is strange. I never used to like coffee at all. Now I can't seem to get enough.'

'Our tastes change as we get older,' Reece said carefully.

'I suppose so. But I still find it hard to believe how much I've changed in five years. I can't recognise myself at all.'

'Try not to think about things too much, Alanna,' Reece advised her. 'Try to relax.'

'Relax! How can I possibly relax?' she threw at him in a burst of frustration. 'Or not think about things! My mind doesn't stop. It just goes round and round. I don't know who I am any more!'

'You're Alanna Diamond,' Reece said as he slipped off the stool and stood up. 'My wife.'

His wife.

Alanna swallowed, her gaze dropping away from his handsome face as those feelings swamped her again, feelings that made her face grow hot and her skin tingle all over.

The moment he'd walked in the door tonight, carrying those lovely flowers, she'd felt different with him. More aware of herself as a woman. And as his wife.

Whenever she looked at his mouth, she thought of him kissing her. Whenever she looked at his hands she thought of them touching her. Whenever she didn't look at him at all..such as now..her mind flooded with far more explicit images, images that made her mouth dry and her heart race, images that she hoped were memories, and not fantasies.

Alanna's head spun with the intensity of her desire, every muscle in her body stretched tight as a drum.

Try to relax, he'd said.

No way was she ever going to relax whilst in his presence. She had to find some excuse to leave him. To be alone.

'I…I seem to be coming down with a headache for real,' she said, and finally looked up at him again.

His frown carried concern. 'I hope it's not a migraine.'

'I hope not as well. Is there anything special I take when I get one?'

'I'll get them for you,' he replied, walking over to open a built-in cupboard high above the fridge.

When he reached up to rifle through the contents, his blue business shirt stretched tight across his shoulder muscles. Alanna found herself staring at him and wondering if he looked as good naked as he did in clothes.

By the time he turned back round with a packet of pills in his hand, she hoped she wasn't blushing again.

'You usually take a couple of these,' he said, putting them down on the granite benchtop next to her. 'Then you lie down in a darkened room and try to sleep it off. Sometimes, you take a sleeping tablet as well. There's a packet in the cabinet in the bathroom.'

'Yes, I saw them and wondered what they were for. Would you mind if I skip the coffee and just go do that?' she said, hoping she didn't look as guilty as she felt.

He shrugged his broad shoulders. 'Why should I mind? I'm just sorry you have a headache on top of everything else.

'No, I'll do that,' he said sharply when she stood up and started clearing away the plates. 'You just go and look after yourself. But why don't you try a relaxing bath before you start popping pills? It might be a tension headache more than a real migraine.'

Alanna found a polite smile to hide her shame. 'Yes, I'll do that. And thanks again, Reece. For everything.'

'My pleasure,' he said, then did the worst thing he possibly could do to her. He smiled.

And there they were again. Those feelings. And those mental images.

With a strained smile, Alanna snatched up the painkillers and hurried from the kitchen, increasing her pace across the living-room floor, hardly drawing breath till she was safely out of Reece's sight and climbing the staircase.

By the time she reached the master bedroom, her lie was fast becoming a reality, wavy-edged circles dancing in front of her eyes.

Punishment, Alanna decided, for being a liar *and* a slut.

Groaning, she dashed into the bathroom and took a couple of the painkillers, post-haste. Then, because it was still so early, she ran herself a bath, adding some of the bubble bath and bath salts and turning on the spa jets.

Half an hour later, she emerged from the triangular-shaped bath, her body all perfumed and pink, but still with the most dreadful headache. In desperation, she popped a couple of the sleeping pills and went in search of something to wear to bed.

But all of the sexy negligee sets in the walk-in wardrobe screamed slut to her. So she went to the dressing table and pulled out the set of pink silk pyjamas she'd seen there earlier in the day. They were less outrageous, though still very sensuous to wear and the silk felt cool against her water-warmed skin.

Her headache had intensified by the time she crawled into the huge four-poster bed, but her mind was definitely becoming fuzzy. Those sleeping tablets were finally working, thank God. She desperately needed some respite from the pain in her head and the confusion in her mind. She needed to feel nothing but peace. Or, better still, nothing at all.

Fifteen minutes later, Alanna's wish seemed to be granted as with a small sigh she slipped off to sleep.

But there was no escape from emotional torment, even in sleep. Dark dreams awaited Alanna in the night, dreams of danger and Darko, of hurt and horrors, of love betrayed and trust destroyed.

CHAPTER THIRTEEN

REECE was in bed, reading a book, trying to make himself tired enough to sleep, when he heard the scream.

'Alanna!'

Jumping up, he dashed for the master bedroom, turning on the overhead light as he burst through the door and raced over to the bed.

She was curled up in a ball in the middle of the bed, her eyes squeezed tightly shut, her head bent almost to her chest.

'No, please, Darko,' she whimpered. 'Please...'

Reece's heart almost broke to see her like that. It was one thing to hear Alanna's mother tell him about what that monster had put Alanna through. Another to hear for himself how frightened she had been.

The poor darling. No wonder she suffered from migraines.

He had to wake her. Bring her back from the horrors of her past. Make her see again that Darko was dead and she was safe. With him.

'Alanna,' he said as he shook her gently by the shoulders.

Her eyes flew open, terror still in their green depths.

'It's me,' he said swiftly. 'Reece. Your husband. Remember?'

'Reece. Oh, Reece!' she sobbed, her hands coming up to cover her face, her shoulders shaking uncontrollably as she began to weep.

Reece's heart filled to overflowing with love, and the need to show that love. Not sexually. Just physically.

'It's all right, darling.' Without a moment's hesitation he lifted the bedclothes and slid in beside her. 'You're safe,' he said, and wrapped his arms tightly around her.

For a split second, she stiffened, but then she sank against him, still weeping, but not quite so hysterically.

'Reece,' she choked out once more, and wound her arms around his back. 'Not Darko.'

'No, not Darko. I'm nothing like Darko. Hush, my darling,' he murmured as he stroked her hair. 'Hush.'

How long did he hold her like that, soothing her, stroking her, making her feel safe? It might have been fifteen minutes. Maybe longer. He couldn't be sure.

Neither was he sure of the moment when his soothing started to change to seducing.

Desire for her had snuck up on him. Slowly. Seditiously. Before he knew it, he was fiercely erect and he was kissing her mouth, softly at first, then with more purpose, and passion.

For a few moments, her mouth froze under his, but then it relaxed and melted and turned to liquid heat, Reece's mind blazing with male triumph at the speed of her surrender. She might not remember him consciously, but her body did. It was telling him so in no uncertain terms, her tongue as avid as his as they entwined with each other.

She moaned softly when he withdrew.

He levered himself up on one elbow and looked down into her flushed face.

'Alanna, I want to do more than kiss you,' his conscience compelled him to say. 'Tell me now if you don't want me to continue.'

She said nothing. Just stared up at him.

Reece smothered a groan, his gaze dropping to where her nipples were outlined like little rocks against her pink silk pyjamas. Yes, her body wanted him. But what about her mind? Could he even say she was in her right mind at this moment? Wasn't he taking advantage of her need for someone.. possibly anyone.. to comfort her?

Man and woman had been using sex as an instrument of comfort since Adam and Eve.

'Say something,' he insisted, his voice raw with his own need.

He would stop if she wanted him to. He loved her too much to risk causing her any hurt, either emotional or physical.

'Yes,' she said, her voice low and quivering.

Yes? Yes, what?

Reece groaned. 'You want me to stop?'

'No!'

No.

His loins leapt at the news. She didn't want him to stop.

Never had a woman admitting she wanted him meant so much to Reece.

'Oh, Alanna,' he whispered, his right hand trembling as it stroked down her lovely face.

He almost said he loved her then. Almost. But, luckily, he bit his tongue in time, bending his mouth to hers instead.

With her permission, the urgency of his own need had lessened. Giving Alanna pleasure was what he wanted most. Making her *feel* loved without his having to say it.

Natalie was right about men. They did prefer to express their love physically.

But sometimes that was the best way for them. Most men weren't wonderful at words, or sentimental gestures. Besides, that type of thing could just be a cover for lies, or con-jobs. When a man made love to a woman, his real feelings for her came through in his actions.

Reece had quite recently thought his feelings for Alanna were mainly lust. But that was certainly not true any more. He didn't want any kinky positions tonight. Or for her to do *anything*. Just to let him love her.

His head lifted again, leaving her eyes clinging to his in the most heart-stopping way. He watched her face as his hands went to the small pearl buttons on her pajama top, alert for any sign of protest, or returning panic.

But all she did was take a deep breath.

His fingers fumbled a little on the last button, his own breath becoming suspended as he bared her chest to his eyes.

It was almost as if he were seeing her body for the first time. *Feeling* it for the first time.

When his right hand brushed lightly over the tips of her breasts, she sucked in sharply. Reece glanced up to make sure it was all right for him to go on.

Her eyes were big on him, her lips apart, her breathing shallow and quick.

Encouraged, he bent his mouth to her right nipple, licking it gently with his tongue.

She gasped, her back arching.

He looked up again. This time, her eyes were tightly shut but her lips had fallen even further apart.

Taking this as a good sign, he resumed his attentions on her breasts, moving his mouth from one nipple to the other, licking them softly, then sucking them oh, so gently.

Her moans of pleasure thrilled him. And aroused him. Reece began finding it harder to be gentle, and patient.

But gentle and patient he remained.

It was she who became impatient, surprising him when her hands reached to push down on the elastic waistband of the satin boxer shorts he was wearing, then at the bottom half of her own pyjamas.

Reece was only too happy to comply with her wishes by then, stripping himself, then her in double-quick time.

'Are you sure, Alanna?' he asked her one last time before his control totally deserted him.

'Yes,' she said, and reached for him.

They both gasped as they came together, Reece stunned by the emotion that welled up in him as his flesh filled hers.

He'd never felt anything quite like it.

'Don't close your eyes,' he said thickly as he began to move inside her.

She didn't. They just grew wider and wider.

He kept his rhythm slow, withdrawing as far as possible before surging back into her as deep as he could go. His eyes didn't leave hers. He saw the pleasure build in them. And the tension. A tension he also felt.

A groan escaped his lips when her flesh began squeezing his, gripping it for dear life.

Dear God, don't let me come before her.

'Reece,' she said suddenly, her voice choked.

He stopped moving.

'No, no,' she moaned. 'Don't stop. Don't stop.'

He smiled. 'Whatever you say, Babe. Move with me this time. Go with the flow.'

In no time she came, her hips lifting from the bed as her body splintered apart.

Answering cries burst from Reece's throat. His shoulders shook. His back arched. His mind exploded, along with his body.

And it was whilst her flesh was milking his, over and over, that Reece realised something even more wonderful than the experience they'd just shared.

Today was the day Alanna had marked on the kitchen calendar with the biggest red circle. Today was the day when she was most likely to conceive.

She might never remember him. She might never love him. But after tonight, she was going to have his baby.

Reece was sure of it.

CHAPTER FOURTEEN

ALANNA woke with a start. And total recall.

'Oh!' she cried out, her heart racing with joy and relief. 'Oh, thank you, God.'

She could hardly believe it. She could remember everything!

Better still, all the confusion and worry that had been pressing in on her the last few days was totally gone. She no longer felt afraid. She no longer felt as if she didn't know who she was. She was her old self again.

Reece! She had to tell Reece!

But his side of the bed was empty and...

'Heavens!' she exclaimed on seeing the time on the bedside clock. Nine-fifteen.

Her excitement was dampened a little as she realised Reece had left for work. She had so wanted to tell him.

But then she saw his business card propped up against the side of the clock.

It wasn't the first time Reece had left her a note this way. Alanna snatched it up and turned it over.

'Glad to see you sleeping so well,' she read aloud. 'Will ring to check up on you around lunch-time. Take it easy. Love Reece.'

She sighed her pleasure in the note, her gaze travelling back from the clock to where his body had lain next to her, the imprint of his head still in the pillow.

Had it been his tender lovemaking that had done the trick? Broken through that veil of fear that she'd been living under since their car accident? Made her really relax and have such a sound sleep?

It must have been that.

Reece was going to be so glad. It couldn't have been easy being married to a wife who didn't remember him. Yet he'd been incredibly kind and sensitive.

She had to ring him. Tell him. Thank him.

Yet when she reached for the phone, an unexpected shyness overwhelmed Alanna. Her stomach went all fluttery and she found herself blushing as she recalled the way she'd acted last night.

One moment weeping with fear, the next clinging to Reece like a vine, quivering with a passion that had been as urgent as it had been powerful. Stunningly powerful.

Stunning, but not totally surprising, Alanna conceded.

She'd been having sexual feelings for Reece earlier in the evening, when he'd been totally dressed, not half naked in bed with her, holding her close and stroking her so sensually. By the time he'd kissed her, she could not have said no if her life had depended on it.

At the time, she'd been a bit shocked by her feelings. Now that she had her memory back, however, Alanna happily blamed her physical responses to Reece on her subconscious mind. Last weekend, after the wedding, he had finally tapped into the woman she probably would have become if Darko hadn't entered her life.

That woman had still been there, despite her memory loss, her newly liberated libido ripe and ready for more lovemaking. There was no need to feel awkward about it this morning, she told herself. Or embarrassed in the slightest.

If she were frankly honest, it had been a wonderful experience. Reece had been wonderful. There was no getting around that fact. Her mother had been right when…

'Oh, my God!' Alanna burst out. Her mother. Her poor mother.

Alanna groaned as she swept up the phone. Ringing Reece would have to wait. She had to ring her mother first and apologise.

'Mum, I'm so sorry!' Alanna blurted out as soon as her mother answered.

'Alanna!' Her mother sounded both relieved and delighted. 'You've got your memory back!'

'Yes. When I woke up this morning, everything was back to normal. Oh, Mum, do you forgive me?'

'Don't be silly, dear. Reece explained the situation and I understood entirely.'

'I do hope so. I hate to think I might have hurt you. You were so good to me when I came home after Darko's death. If it hadn't been for you I don't know what would have become of me.'

'You would have been fine. You're very strong, Alanna.'

'How can you say that? I stayed married to a pig for three years. I should have left him.'

'You loved him.'

'Only in the beginning...'

'You and I know why you didn't leave him, Alanna. You have to go through something like that to understand.'

'I suppose so. I just wish that..'

'Come on, now,' her mother interrupted. 'Don't start going over old ground. You've moved way past that. You have a good life now, and a very good husband. Reece really cares about you, Alanna. Forget the past and concentrate on the present, and the future.'

'I'll do that, Mum,' Alanna said, and glanced at the clock again. Twenty to ten. Suddenly, alarm bells began to ring in her brain. 'Oh, my goodness, I just remembered I have a visitor coming soon and I'm not even dressed.'

What an understatement! She was stark naked. Another reminder of her behaviour the previous night.

'Off you go, then,' her mother was saying. 'Glad to see that you're back to your old self. Give my love to Reece when you speak to him.'

'I'll do that, Mum. Bye,' she said, and hung up.

She had twenty minutes before Natalie arrived.

Not long.

So what was she doing lying back down in the bed, angling herself into the imprint of Reece's body and thinking about how it had felt when he'd made love to her last night? She could almost feel him now, thrusting deep into her, pulling back oh, so slowly, then thrusting deep again.

Her breath quickened. Her belly tightened. Her hands curled into fists by her sides.

Suddenly, she didn't want to ring him. She wanted to tell him in person. She wanted to be with him.

Tonight was too long to wait.

But first she would have to throw some clothes on and get rid of Natalie. That shouldn't take too long. After all, the reason for Natalie's visit was no longer relevant. Alanna knew exactly what kind of woman she'd been when she went to Wives Wanted.

A woman who had finally moved on from victim to survivor. A woman whom she was proud to be. A woman who'd decided what she wanted out of the rest of her life and was determined to get it.

Financial security. A physically attractive husband who respected her.

And a baby.

Alanna sat bolt upright.

A baby!

She didn't bother with clothes. She bolted downstairs, charging into the kitchen. On the wall next to the fridge was a calendar, one where she jotted down appointments and social obligations, plus the days she was most likely to conceive.

Her heart leapt into her mouth when she saw that yesterday had a big red circle around it, preceded by two days with little red circles around them, and two days with little circles afterwards.

Last night had been the very best night for them to make a baby!

Had Reece known that?

Possibly not. He wasn't as wrapped in having a baby as she was. Alanna sometimes got the feeling he was just going along with her plans for a family to please her.

A quiver of sheer joy rippled down her spine as she stared once more at that big red circle.

Maybe she shouldn't say anything. Not yet. For one thing, she didn't want to start getting her hopes up again.

But she had a good feeling about last night. A very good feeling.

Her hands lifted to rub softly over her stomach.

'Are you in there, my darling?' she whispered. 'Yes, you are, aren't you? It's Mummy here. Daddy's at work at the moment but we're going in to visit him soon. We're going on a ferry,' she rattled on more loudly as she whirled and hurried from the room. 'It's much quicker than driving. I hope you don't get sea-sick…'

Natalie eased her car into the kerb outside the Diamond house right on ten. Punctuality was a virtue of hers. Not that it got her anywhere these days. No one ever seemed to be on time for anything. When she was, and complained of the tardiness of others, she was accused of being anally retentive, or some such gobbledegook.

'The trouble with you,' her one true love had once said to her, 'is that you take life far too seriously.'

Possibly, that was true. But she didn't think it was unreasonable at the time to go ape when she discovered that the man she'd wasted the best years of her life on turned out to be married, with two children.

Natalie had begun Wives Wanted three years ago as therapy for herself, more than a means of making money. She gained a savage satisfaction every time she matched one of her female clients with a man who would, not only marry her, but give her children and provide for them all in style.

There'd been a time when she'd entertained the hope of finding such a man for herself.

Unfortunately, the experience of a grand passion betrayed had given her once softer personality a hard and very cynical edge that men didn't find attractive.

So it looked as if she was condemned to spend the rest of her days playing matchmaker.

A job she did very well, she thought as she pressed the front door bell. The Diamonds were only one of her many successes.

When no one came to the door, Natalie rang the bell again. Maybe the cleaner had the vacuum on. Or was upstairs. The house was simply huge! Alanna had certainly done very well for herself.

This time, the front door was yanked open reasonably quickly. But not by the cleaner. Alanna stood there, wearing jeans and looking utterly gorgeous, despite not having a scrap of make-up on.

'I'm so sorry to have dragged you out all this way

for nothing, Natalie,' she said with a wide smile. 'You've no idea what's happened. I woke up less than an hour ago from a simply fantastic night's sleep and it's back. My memory.'

'Well, isn't that marvelous?' Natalie said, genuinely pleased for her. She liked Alanna. 'Reece must be happy, too.'

'I haven't had the chance to tell him yet.'

Natalie was taken aback. Almost an hour ago, hadn't she said? Couldn't she have picked up the phone and called? The man *loved* her.

Damn it all, didn't she know how rare that was?

Natalie was tempted to tell her. But, of course, she didn't. A promise was a promise. And Reece was right. Alanna didn't want to be loved.

Natalie understood the reasons behind this. And empathised with it to a degree. Brandon had claimed to love her till the cows had come home. And she'd believed him. Believed everything he'd told all, all his excuses for not spending more time with her. Plus his reasons for delaying their marriage.

All lies.

Okay, so he hadn't physically hurt her. But the damage to her psyche had been enormous.

She would find it hard to believe that a man really loved her ever again.

Alanna, however, was *afraid* of being loved. Natalie could appreciate her fears. But it seemed a shame. Reece was such a nice man.

'Yes, I know what you're thinking,' Alanna said

swiftly. 'Why haven't I rung Reece already? The thing is...I want to tell him in person.'

Natalie blinked her surprise. 'That's a bit romantic for you, isn't it?'

She'd sussed out Alanna's personality when she'd interviewed her at length. They were sisters in cynicism when it came to romance.

Alanna laughed. 'I feel romantic today,' came her breezy reply.

The sheer happiness shining in her eyes stunned Natalie.

And then the penny dropped.

Did Alanna realise she'd fallen in love with her husband? Should she risk Reece's anger and say something now about his loving her back?

'Would you think me horribly rude if I didn't ask you in?' Alanna said before Natalie could make up her mind what to do for the best. 'I want to make myself presentable, then catch the next ferry. I only have forty minutes.'

Natalie decided that Alanna would discover the truth herself in time. There was no need for her to extend her matchmaking services to outright meddling.

If Natalie had known what was to transpire later that day, she might have decided differently.

'No, don't worry,' she answered. 'Go get ready. Glad you've got your memory back, Alanna. Give my regards to Reece when you see him.'

'I'll do that. And thanks again, Natalie. Sorry about this.'

'No need to apologise. I understand. Totally.'

CHAPTER FIFTEEN

THE breeze off the harbour ruffled Alanna's hair. But she didn't care. Her hair was pretty wind-proof, needing only a quick brush through to settle her natural waves back into place.

She was standing on the foredeck of the ferry, wishing it would go faster. She couldn't wait to tell Reece she remembered him, and their marriage, and everything!

It wasn't till the ferry docked at Circular Quay and she was moving down the gangway that Alanna realised Reece might not *be* in his office. Admittedly, he was between building projects at the moment, but that didn't mean he might not have dashed out to inspect a site he was thinking of buying. Or have left for lunch with some architect he was courting. Or engineer. Or client.

He was always doing that.

Still, it was a little early for lunch. Reece rarely ate before one. It was only noon and his building was just a short walk away. Hopefully, she'd find him sitting behind his desk.

But the possibility that he might not be there took some of the wind out of Alanna's sails. She hastened her step, oblivious of the second glances she received from every male who passed her by.

Frustration set in when the lights turned red on the corner opposite Reece's building, leaving her to tap her foot impatiently against the kerb.

Her eyes lifted to the twelfth floor as she waited, willing Reece to be there. Of course, she could always catch him on his mobile if he wasn't, but telling him over the phone just wouldn't be the same.

At last the lights turned green and she dashed forward, her long legs carrying her as quickly as they could with what she was wearing.

The outfit she'd chosen to meet Reece in was quite new. A chocolate suede suit that had a short, tight skirt and a three-quarter-length jacket, which she had left undone. Underneath she wore a lightweight polo in a caramel colour, which clung to her figure and made her small breasts look bigger. Her shoes were ankle-height black boots. Her natty handbag was black as well, with stylish wooden handles.

Her make-up was minimal. She only ever wore a skin-coloured sunscreen during the day. Her lipstick today was a bronze gloss and her eye-shadow a smoky green that matched her eyes. A touch of black mascara and that was it.

Alanna's heart was thudding in her chest by the time she stepped up onto the kerb on the other side of the street. Rushing plus the anticipation of seeing Reece again had put her into a highly excitable state. She hurried past the trendy coffee shop that sat right on the corner.. and which she'd gone to occasionally with Reece.. pushing through the revolving glass doors that led into his building.

She was crossing the expanse of black and white tiled floor, heading for the bank of lifts at the back of the cavernous foyer, when an idle glance to her right sent her heart skittering to a halt, much the same way as her legs did.

For there, sitting just behind the mainly glass wall that separated the foyer from the coffee shop, sat her husband. With a woman. A blonde woman.

Not Katie. Alanna wouldn't have minded Reece having coffee with Katie.

The sight of him sitting opposite *this* blonde, however, had the hairs on the back of her neck standing upright.

For it was Kristine. Reece's ex-fiancée.

Alanna had never met Kristine, but she'd come across a photo of her early in her marriage to Reece. It had been sitting on Reece's desk. Not framed or anything. But not hidden, either. When she'd asked Reece who it was, he'd told her without a trace of guilt.

At the time, she hadn't overly cared that he kept a photo of his ex-fiancée. That was his personal and private business. The Alanna who'd gone into marriage with her head and not her heart wasn't about to tell her husband what he could and couldn't do.

But she'd taken a good, long, hard look at the woman he'd been madly in love with, curious over what she looked like.

Very sexy, that was what. One of those flashy blondes with big hair and big eyes and big lips.

Alanna could not stop staring at her through the

glass wall, her eyes glued to the way Kristine's hand was stretched out across the café table, covering one of Reece's in a highly intimate fashion. He wasn't pulling it away, either.

The emotional storm that immediately brewed up within Alanna's chest took her breath away. Her jealousy was fierce, as was her hurt.

He was *her* husband. *Her* man. *Her* lover.

She would not share him. She *loved* him.

The realisation floored her. Then appalled her.

She didn't want to love him, especially not in the way that evoked such a dark and powerful jealousy.

It was a curse, that kind of love. It warped minds and destroyed lives.

But even as she told herself not to be jealous her jealousy increased, fuelling an explosive anger within her tightened chest.

Yet Reece wasn't really doing anything wrong, she tried telling herself. Just having coffee with an old flame. And in a public place, for heaven's sake. It wasn't as though he'd whipped the woman off to a hotel room for the afternoon.

And it was Kristine who was doing the pawing. She was probably one of those touchy-feelie women.

Then let her be touchy-feelie with some other man, came the savage thought. *Not mine!*

The temptation to barge in there and slap the bitch's face was acute. *Too* acute.

Horror that she was acting the way Darko had acted propelled Alanna across to the lifts where she practically fell into one, grateful that it was empty. She didn't want anyone seeing the ugliness in her face.

For jealousy *was* ugly. Ugly and destructive.

By the time the lift opened on the twelfth floor, Alanna had pulled herself together sufficiently to walk into the head office of Diamond Enterprises in what she hoped was her usual manner.

'Hello, Katie,' she said breezily as she came through the door.

The receptionist looked shocked. 'Alanna! My God, you *know* me!'

'Yes. I've got my memory back. Isn't it wonderful?'

'It certainly is. When did this happen?'

'When I woke up this morning. I was going to ring Reece, but then I thought I'd come in and surprise him.'

Alanna tried not to read anything in the flash of worry that zoomed into Katie's eyes.

'He...er...isn't in his office at the moment. He stepped out for some coffee. But he should be back soon. I'll give him a buzz on his mobile and tell him you're here.'

Alanna could feel her smile turning brittle. Were women employees always this protective of their bosses? Did Katie lie for Reece on a regular basis? What other times had she covered for Reece since their marriage? Maybe he'd been having affairs behind her back all along.

It was possible.

He didn't love her, after all.

'Yes, please do that,' she said, hoping she sounded polite and not as vicious as she was suddenly feeling towards the woman. 'I'll wait for him in his office,' she added, and headed straight in there, closing the door firmly behind her.

Best she be alone for a while with the way she was feeling. She couldn't trust herself to continue to act normally.

Yet she *must* by the time Reece arrived. To start questioning him over where he'd been and whom he'd been with would be the kiss of death to their relationship. He would not tolerate such behaviour. He might leave her.

Losing Reece was an even worse fate than loving him. She had to learn to hide her love, and to control her jealousy. Really, she had no evidence that he'd been unfaithful to her, either with Kristine or any other woman.

But if he were totally innocent, wouldn't he *tell* her he'd just been having coffee with his ex?

Hopefully, when he arrived, he would.

She spent some time brushing her hair, then pacing the office, then staring out of the window at the view. But all she could think about was how long it was taking Reece to tear himself away from his beloved Kristine. He was only just downstairs, after all. How long did it take to say goodbye and get himself up here?

Finally, the door to the office burst open and there he was, looking as drop-dead gorgeous as ever, his handsome face beaming, his eyes showing nothing but delight at her visiting him here.

'Alanna! How beautiful you look today!' he said as he closed the door and came forward. 'Better still, you've got your memory back, haven't you?'

Alanna stiffened a little as he slid his arms around her back, underneath her jacket.

'How did you know?' she threw up at him. 'Did Katie tell you?'

Reece grinned and pulled her closer. 'Nope. I put two and two together. After all, how else could you have known where my office was?'

'The business card you left me had the address on it,' she pointed out rather frostily.

He looked startled for a second, then he laughed. 'Stop teasing me, you saucy minx. You've remembered everything all right. Why else would you have come here to me in person, dressed like this? You're my old Alanna again. As well as my new Alanna,' he murmured, his voice dropping low and husky.

His kissing her made her forget her jealousy for a few moments, but the second his lips lifted it was back with a vengeance, digging away at her.

'I was disappointed when you weren't here,' she heard herself say. 'Where were you?'

'Just downstairs, having coffee.'

'All by yourself?'

'No. I was with an old friend.'

'Oh? Who?'

'No one you know.'

His twisting of the truth was like a dagger in her heart, making it bleed tears of blood.

'What say I take you somewhere swish for lunch?' he offered. 'The Rockpool. I'll get Katie to make us a reservation.'

Alanna bit her bottom lip. This was it. One of those moments when you had to decide the path your life was going to take. She could confront Reece about having seen him with Kristine. Or turn a blind eye.

It was then that she remembered the baby. The baby she was almost sure she'd conceived last night. A baby deserved two parents.

'Alanna?' Reece said. 'Is there something wrong?'

Alanna made up her mind. 'Not at all. I was just wondering if you realised last night was the most fertile time of my cycle.'

'I did, indeed,' he replied, the warm glitter in his eyes reassuring her.

Maybe he'd just run into Kristine by accident. Maybe his sidestepping her identity meant nothing.

And maybe not…

'You *really* want to have children with me, Reece?'

'What a strange thing to say! Of course I do. Come on, let's go have a fabulous lunch to celebrate you remembering everything.'

Alanna felt reasonably happy as Reece swept her out of his office and through Reception. If only she hadn't taken that last glance over her shoulder at Katie when she said goodbye.

The receptionist now had an extremely relieved

look on her face, as if some major crisis had just passed.

What crisis could possibly have just passed, unless it was that the boss's wife hadn't found out that the boss was still meeting his ex, and that.. oh, God, not that. Surely not that. He couldn't still be madly in love with Kristine, could he?

Alanna could cope with Reece not loving her. But not with his being madly in love with someone else.

CHAPTER SIXTEEN

SHE wasn't quite her old self again, Reece realised as he watched her through lunch. She was too bright. And way too bubbly.

The Alanna he'd married was a coolly confident creature. Very sure of herself. She wasn't a try-hard.

Alanna's recent memory loss had changed her.

Was it because the dark memories of her marriage to Darko were now fresher in her mind? Maybe she was trying to push them aside too quickly by pretending to be more extroverted than usual. Maybe she was afraid of slipping back into the victim mentality that she'd lived with for so long, and which must have taken an enormous effort of will to overcome.

Alanna had no idea how much he admired her for what she'd accomplished in her life. To throw off such a past was not easy.

By comparison, *his* past had been very easy to throw off.

Seeing Kristine again today had underlined that fact.

What a stupid, shallow, superficial female she was, thinking she could turn up at his office, just like that, and get him back. He'd only taken her downstairs for a cup of coffee because she'd started acting like a fool, throwing her silly arms around him and trying to kiss him, right in full view of Katie.

As it was, she'd still grabbed his hand over coffee, holding on so hard that it had been easier to leave it there than pull it away. His only emotion as he'd listened to her abject apologies had been amazement. Amazement that he'd ever thought he'd loved her.

When she'd claimed that she still loved him and she *knew* he still loved her, Reece had put her straight in no uncertain terms. At which point, she'd started to cry.

Katie's phone call to say that Alanna was in the office had been a godsend. It had still taken him a few minutes to extricate himself without Kristine making a big scene. He'd ordered a taxi for her and put her in it, making sure that she couldn't do anything crazy like follow him up to the office. He might not be able to tell Alanna that he loved her, but he didn't want her thinking he was being unfaithful to her.

Women were sometimes quick to jump to conclusions like that, especially where another attractive woman was concerned. As much as Reece didn't think Kristine was a patch on Alanna, she was still a sexy-looking woman. Not the kind of ex you wanted floating around your office when the wife you loved was there.

'I simply don't know what to order for dessert,' Alanna said with a shrug of her slender shoulders as she inspected the menu.

'Something delicious and fattening,' Reece advised.

Her upward glance projected instant worry. 'You think I'm too skinny?'

Reece smothered a groan as he recalled Darko used to tell her she was too skinny.

'Not at all,' he replied. 'But you might be eating for two, remember?'

True joy gleamed back at him.

Now this was a subject that always made her happy.

Babies.

'I don't want to get my hopes up too soon,' she said.

'Why not? Life is all about hope, isn't it?' He hoped that one day she'd fall in love with him. Judy had told him the other night her daughter had a lot of love to give, which was why she was so keen about having children.

Hopefully, Alanna might have some left over for him one day, too.

The sound of his cell phone ringing made Reece swear under his breath. He should have turned the darned thing off.

Pulling it out of his pocket, he flipped it open and put it to his ear. 'Yes?' he said rather impatiently.

'Jake here, Reece. Sorry to bother you at lunch, but you remember that land up at the Gold Coast you've been wanting to buy for ages? I just got a tip from a friend that it's coming on the market this weekend. It's being advertised in tomorrow's paper. If you fly up there today, you could snap it up before anyone else gets the chance.'

'Today,' Reece repeated, glancing over the table at Alanna.

'We're talking prime real estate, boss. Right on the beach. It won't last, even in the present climate.'

'Yes. I know that. But today's almost over. What about tomorrow?'

'There are no early-morning flights to the Gold Coast.'

'I see.'

'Shall I get Katie to book you an afternoon flight, then? And a car? And an apartment at Coolangatta Court?'

Reece didn't want to leave Alanna alone tonight. At the same time, a chance like this might not come again. If he was going to have a family he had to think about the future. They'd be financially secure for life if he bought this land. On top of that, it would give him more money to do good work with. God had really come through for him today, so he had to reciprocate.

'Okay,' he agreed.

'Great.' Jake said, and hung up.

Reece pulled a face as he slipped his phone back into his pocket. 'This is unfortunate timing,' he said. 'I have to go away. This afternoon. To the Gold Coast. It should be for only one night, but possibly two if I don't clinch the deal tomorrow.'

He almost asked her to go with him. But he never had before. She might think it odd.

'Oh,' Alanna said, a momentary cloud crossing her

eyes. But then her eyes grew bright again. 'Oh, well, it can't be helped, I suppose. That's your job. I might ask Mum to come down. I did ring her, you know, and apologise for my not wanting to see her, or talk to her.'

'That's good. I was a bit worried about that.'

'No need. Mum understood. Look, under the circumstances I think I'll skip dessert,' she said, putting the menu down on the tablecloth. 'You'll want to be getting home to pack.'

'I don't think I'll have the time. I'll use the emergency bag of clothes I keep at the office. I should get going.' He called for the waiter and the bill. 'I'll get them to order you a taxi as well.'

'All right,' she agreed.

Five minutes later Reece was waving her off and resenting what he had once appreciated. He didn't want Alanna being so damned agreeable any more. He didn't want her not really caring about where he went and what he did whilst he was there.

He could have sworn that the Alanna he'd discovered last weekend..and last night..might have insisted on coming with him.

She was an enigma, all right. There again, she always had been. Even now, knowing everything about her, he still didn't totally understand her.

But he did love her. More than he could have ever thought possible. He hated leaving her, even for one night.

He'd close that damn deal tomorrow and get back by tomorrow night, or his name wasn't Reece Diamond!

CHAPTER SEVENTEEN

ALANNA'S agitation increased as the afternoon wore on. She could not settle to anything. She paced around the house, still wearing the same clothes she'd worn into town. All she could think about was Reece up on the Gold Coast, not to buy land, but to have a romantic rendezvous with Kristine.

It was too much of a coincidence, his having coffee with her and then dashing off like that the same day.

Jealousy bored away at Alanna like an insidious worm.

Yet she hated jealousy. Hated it with a vengeance.

Darko had been jealous all the time, right from the moment he'd discovered on their wedding night that she wasn't a virgin. Jealousy had eaten away at him, making him irrational and violent in the end.

'But this is different,' Alanna muttered away to herself. 'Darko had no reason to be jealous. I do!'

Because Reece didn't love her. That was the trouble.

Alanna moaned. She couldn't bear the thought of her husband being in that woman's arms. Not for a minute, let alone a night. Maybe two.

But then another thought came to her. Maybe this wasn't the first time. Reece had gone away a lot during their relatively short marriage. Maybe Kristine had been going with him for a while. Or all along.

Then why had he married *her*?

The conversation she'd had with Mike last Saturday night popped into her head. Mike knew much more about Reece's relationship with Kristine than she did.

She would *make* him tell her what he knew, Alanna resolved as she raced into the kitchen, snatched up the phone and pressed number two. The numbers of all Reece's best friends were programmed in. Richard was number one. Mike number two.

Frustration set in when Mike didn't answer straight away. He did work from home, but maybe he was out. If it kept on ringing, in a moment it would cut into his answering machine. If it did, she would just hang up.

'Mike Stone.'

'Oh, Mike. Thank God you're home.'

'Alanna? Is that you?'

'Yes, yes, I..'

'You've got your memory back!' he exclaimed.

Alanna grimaced. 'Reece told you about that, did he?'

'Well, of course. The man was worried sick.'

'Was he really?' she said, far too drily.

Her tone brought silence from the other end of the line.

'I don't want to talk about that,' she went on abruptly. 'Look, Mike, remember last Saturday night, when you wouldn't tell me about what happened the day Kristine left Reece?'

'Yeah. Why?'

'You have to tell me now. I have to know.'

'Alanna, I..'

'I think he's gone away with her. With Kristine.'

'*What?* I don't believe that.'

'I saw them having coffee together today in town and they looked very cosy indeed. I'd gone in there to tell Reece my memory had come back. Then later, over lunch, he gets this phone call and he suddenly decides he has to go to the Gold Coast for a day or two on business. I don't believe in that kind of co-incidence, Mike. He still loves her, doesn't he?'

'No, damn it. I don't think he does.'

'Tell me what happened that day,' she insisted.

Mike sighed.

'Tell me, Mike. And tell me why you think he married me. You know. I know you do.'

'Hell, Alanna, that's all in the past. Things have changed since then. *Reece* has changed.'

'Mike, stop trying to protect the man. Give it to me straight. I can cope with the truth. I can't cope with lies.'

More silence from the other end.

'Mike, *please*,' she begged.

'Oh, all right,' he said with a disgruntled sigh. 'But I still think you're barking up the wrong tree.'

He told her how Kristine had made love to Reece that final day, all day, in ways that most men only fantasised about. Afterwards, she'd risen from his bed, dressed, then coolly told him that she was leaving him and that when he was lying alone in his bed at night he could think about her doing all those things with her new lover.

The last thing she'd said as she'd walked out the door was that she still loved him.

'But why did she leave him if she still loved him?' Alanna asked, confused.

'Because he wouldn't sell this huge parcel of land he'd sunk all his money into,' Mike explained. 'The rates alone were gradually sending him bankrupt. He could have sold it.. at a loss.. but he wouldn't. He told me he knew it would be worth a fortune in another year or two. He didn't mind being poor for a while. But Kristine did. She wanted the good life. If she'd only waited with him, she could have had both. Reece *and* the good life.'

'I see. And his marriage to me?' Alanna asked, although she had a sinking feeling what Mike was going to say.

'In the beginning, I think it was a kind of revenge on Kristine. To show her he'd moved on without her, in every way. I guess he wanted to make her jealous, too. As jealous as she'd made him.'

'Jealous?' she repeated a bit blankly.

'You're a very beautiful woman, Alanna. More beautiful than Kristine. It would have been a blow to her vanity to see Reece married to someone as stunning as you.'

Alanna's heart sank. So that was why he dressed

her the way he did. Why he was always so pleased when their photos were in the papers and magazines.

All to spite Kristine.

'I'm sure Reece doesn't think like that now,' Mike went on, an urgency on his voice. 'Remember how jealous he was of you the other night when I danced with you? He doesn't give a damn about Kristine any more. I'd put my money on it. Look, let me ring Reece on his mobile and talk to him. I'll bet he..'

'No,' Alanna cut in firmly. 'No, please don't do that. This is my affair, Mike. Or possibly Reece's affair,' she added with a cold little laugh. 'I have to deal with it myself. Promise me you'll stay out of it.'

'But..'

'*Promise* me!'

'I didn't realise you could be so tough.'

'I'm a survivor too, Mike.'

Brave words. She didn't feel like much of a survivor at this moment. More like another victim.

But only temporarily. Because she would not live with fear again, even if that fear was only in her mind and heart. She certainly would not live with jealousy, especially her own. She'd rather confront the truth than ever live like that.

The time had come to take action.

'Bye, Mike,' she said.

'Before you go, promise *me* something.'

'What?'

'Call me when you find out you're wrong.'

CHAPTER EIGHTEEN

RECCE couldn't work out where Alanna was. He'd rung her at home as soon as he'd checked in. But there was no answer. When he'd tried her mobile, she had it turned off. He'd left a message, but so far there'd been no answer from her, which was odd.

They'd never lived in each other's pockets, but he always kept in touch when he was away. And Alanna never went out on a Thursday night. Not alone, anyway.

Maybe she'd gone to the gym for a long workout to make up for the days she'd missed. Or maybe she'd decided to drive home to visit her mother, instead of the other way around.

Reece contemplated ringing Judy to find out, but decided that was carrying things a bit far. He didn't want to start acting like that creep Alanna had been married to, checking up on her all the time.

No. He'd have a shower, then go to bed and read. He'd picked up one of those blockbusters at the airport and started it during the flight up.

Reece had just switched off the water in the shower when he thought he heard someone knocking on the door. Pulling on the hotel bathrobe, he hurried through the bedroom into the sitting area, finger-combing his wet hair back from his face on the way.

Someone was very definitely knocking at his door.

'Who is it?' he demanded through the door, puzzled. Hotel employees always announced themselves. But no one was saying Room Service, or Housekeeping.

'It's me, Reece,' came the truly amazing reply. 'Alanna.'

'Alanna!' Reece whipped off the security chain and pulled open the door.

And there she was, looking beautiful but extremely uptight.

He didn't know whether to be delighted, or worried.

'What on earth are you doing here?' he blurted out.

'I caught the eight-twenty flight,' she said, all the while looking him up and down in the strangest fashion.

Not sexually. Assessingly.

'Yes, I can see that,' he said with a slightly awkward laugh. 'But why?'

'Aren't you going to invite me in?'

Her chilly tone stunned him.

She didn't wait for any invitation. She just forged past him, turning left and heading straight for the bedroom.

And then it twigged. She thought he was here with someone. She'd followed him, hoping to catch him out with some woman.

Bloody hell!

Reece banged the door shut and charged after her. By this time, she'd reached the bedroom, which was a typical hotel room, with few places to hide a partner in adultery. Reece watched her frown as she glanced around.

'Perhaps you'd better check out the bathroom,' he threw at her. 'She might be hiding behind the shower curtain.'

'If there was a stupid shower curtain,' he muttered under his breath when she actually did as he suggested.

By the time Alanna returned to the bedroom, Reece was almost gratified to see that all the blood had drained from her face, leaving her skin even more pale than usual.

'You're alone,' she said, her eyes wide with surprise.

'Are you sure?' he ground out. 'She might be running late. Whoever *she* is.'

'Kristine, of course. The woman you're still in love with.'

'Kristine! Are you mad? I'm not still in love with Kristine.'

Colour zoomed back into her cheeks. 'Don't lie to me. I saw you together. Today. Holding hands.'

'She was holding *my* hand. I can't stand the woman.'

Alanna's eyes flared wide. 'You can't?'

'No. I...'

Reece broke off and just stared at her.

For the rest of his life, he would never forget this wondrous moment, when Alanna's uncharacteristic actions suddenly made sense and he realised that his dearest wish had come true.

'You were jealous,' he said, his voice as stunned as his suddenly joyous soul.

Her face twisted, her eyes tormented. 'I... I... I was wrong.'

'No, not wrong, my darling,' he said as he came forward and drew her into his arms. 'You've never been more right in all your life. You love me, don't you?'

'Oh, God,' she cried. 'I'm such a fool.'

'If you're a fool, then I'm one too. Because I love you.'

Her eyes turned to liquid pools as she stared up at him. 'You love me?' she choked out.

'With all my heart. I nearly died last Sunday when I thought you were hurt. Then, when you couldn't remember me, I was in sheer hell.'

'But you were so wonderful!'

'That was the new me.'

'The new you? What do you mean by that?'

Reece felt a little embarrassed, telling her about his bargains with God. But he did it all the same.

He was touched that she was so touched.

'But you always *were* a good man,' she complimented him.

'Not good enough for you, Alanna. You deserve the very best.'

'Oh, Reece, that's so sweet.'

'I've been dying to tell you all week that I love you, but I was afraid to.'

'*You*, Reece? Afraid? You're never afraid.'

'I was afraid of losing you, my darling. You always said that you never wanted to be loved again. When I realised last weekend that I'd fallen in love with you, I was worried sick.'

'Oh, Reece…'

'I wanted to ask you to come away with me today,' he told her. 'But I didn't dare. I was afraid you might think it odd. I had no idea you'd seen me with Kristine. Or that you might think what you did.'

Her smile was softly rueful. 'If you were in hell last Sunday, then I was in hell today. When I saw you in that coffee shop with that woman, it took all of my will-power not to charge in there. I've never experienced that kind of jealousy before, Reece. I wanted to do dreadful things to her. I can't tell you how appalled I felt at the time. Appalled and ashamed. I hate jealousy of any kind.'

'I can understand that,' he said softly, though privately thinking he'd rather liked hers.

'Jealousy is a terrible thing,' she went on. 'It feeds on itself and becomes more and more irrational. I mean…you weren't doing anything wrong in that coffee shop. Just having coffee. And you're right. I could see it was her hand covering yours, not the other way around. Yet the more I tried telling myself you were totally innocent, the more I started seeing deception in everything you said and did, especially when you took so long to come back after Katie contacted you.'

'I was worried that Kristine might follow me up to the office and cause a scene in front of you, so I called her a taxi and waited with her till she was safely gone.'

'It's all right, Reece. You don't have to explain yourself.'

But Reece felt he did owe her an explanation. Otherwise she might always worry and wonder. He knew he would, if Alanna's ex were still alive and well.

'Do you know, Kristine seriously thought she could just show up in my life after all this time and get me back? She even imagined I was still in love with her. The woman has to be totally deranged!'

'But you did love her once,' Alanna pointed out. 'You were still in love with her when you married me.'

'I thought I was. But, looking back, I'm not sure that what I felt for Kristine was ever love. Frankly, I don't think I knew what real love was back then. I was too young, and way too selfish. But I know now, my darling,' he said, pulling his lovely Alanna even closer. 'It's what I feel for you. I adore you, Alanna. And I do so admire you. You are an incredible woman to survive what you survived with that monster. I can't imagine too many other women having the courage to move on and make a new life for yourself after what you went through. I feel so grateful that you chose me to trust, and to marry. I am one lucky man.'

She shook her head at him, her eyes shining. '*I'm* the lucky one. I never thought I would say I was happy to lose my memory, but I am saying it now. It made me step back and take a good look at the man I married. Having Darko fresh in my mind made me see why I chose you as my second husband. I think I've always loved you, Reece. I just didn't realise it till today. No, I subconsciously knew it last night, when you made love to me so beautifully. That's why I remembered everything when I woke this morning. Because it was safe to do so. You made me feel safe, Reece. That might not seem such a big deal, but it is to me.'

And there it was, that look he'd always wanted her to give him. The look of true love.

Reece's heart turned over.

'I'm so sorry I was jealous,' she said as she lowered her head to his chest, her arms tightening around him at the same time.

'I'm not,' Reece returned warmly. 'Because if you hadn't been, you wouldn't be here and we'd still be pretending not to love each other. Which wouldn't be a good idea,' Reece added with a smile in his voice, 'now that we've become parents.'

Her head whipped up, her eyes bright. 'You believe that, too?'

'Yes, I do.'

'We might be wrong.'

'Well, tonight's the second best night for you conceiving, you know. How about we make sure?'

Alanna was lying in Reece's arms afterwards, savouring the moment and thinking that happiness like this only came once in a lifetime. Then again, a man like Reece only came along once in a lifetime.

'Reece,' she said softly.

'Mmm?'

'I have to make a phone call.'

'What, *now*? At this hour?'

'Yes.'

'Who to?'

'Mike.'

'Mike!'

'Now none of that. We love each other and trust each other. We don't ever need to be jealous. I just have to tell Mike something. I promised him.'

'Promised him what?'

'You can listen in.'

'Oh, all right,' Reece grumbled, and reached for his mobile, flipping it open and pressing a couple of buttons.

'It's ringing his number,' he said by the time he handed it over.

'Mike Stone,' Mike finally answered in a gruff tone. 'This had better be important. It's bloody late and I was working.'

'It's important,' Alanna told him. 'You were right and I was wrong. Reece doesn't love Kristine. He loves me, almost as much as I love him. Now you can go back to work.'

'And you can go back to whatever you were doing,' Mike said with a low chuckle.

'Oh, yes,' she said, her eyes sparkling up at Reece as she handed him back the phone. 'I fully intend to.'

EPILOGUE

POSITIVE. It was positive.

Alanna cried out her joy, then burst into tears.

Reece dashed into the bathroom, panic in his eyes.

'What is it? What's happened?'

Tears streamed down her face as she held the indicator out to him.

'I bought one of those home tests,' she choked out. 'It turned blue.'

'Is that good news or bad news?'

'It's wonderful news,' she sobbed, and grabbed a handful of tissues.

All of a sudden, Reece wanted to cry himself.

Alanna was having a baby. *His* baby.

He'd thought he wanted her to get pregnant just for her sake; to give her what she most wanted in the world. He hadn't realised how much it would mean to him on a personal level.

She smiled through her tears. 'You should see the look on your face.'

'I'm feeling unexpectedly overwhelmed,' he said faintly. 'I might have to lie down.'

'*I'm* the one having the baby.'

'I'm the one who gave it to you,' he retorted. 'Clearly, it's taken it out of me.'

'You poor thing,' she said, still smiling. 'But you

can't lie down. There isn't time. Richard and Holly will be here soon to look at the house.'

Richard and Holly had arrived home from their honeymoon the previous day, and were delighted with Reece's news that he'd found them just the house to buy.

'Needs a few renovations,' Reece had told his best friend over the phone last night. 'But it's a bargain at the price they're asking. Better yet, it's only three doors up from us!'

Reece couldn't wait to see his best friend again. *And* to tell him about the baby.

'You're right,' he said with a glance at his watch. 'They'll be here in less than ten minutes. Just time enough for you to ring your mother and me to ring mine.'

Ten minutes later, it was a beaming Reece and Alanna who answered the door to Richard and Holly.

It only took Richard a couple of minutes to see the change in his best friend and his lovely wife. Holly seemed to sense something, too.

'If I didn't know better,' Richard whispered to Holly as they followed Reece and Alanna into the house, 'I'd think *they* were the ones who'd just come back from their honeymoon.'

'I was thinking exactly the same thing,' Holly whispered back. 'Do you see the way they're looking at each other?'

'They've fallen in love,' Richard said.

'Madly, I'd say,' Holly agreed.

Just then, both Alanna and Reece stopped and

turned to face their friends. Reece slid his arm tightly around Alanna's waist and pulled her close.

'Before we have coffee or go along to see your new house, we have something to tell you,' he announced.

'You're pregnant,' Holly said, smiling at Alanna, who was positively glowing.

'Yes! How did you guess? I haven't put on any weight yet. I'm only a few weeks gone.'

'I only had to look into your face. I've never seen you so happy. You too, Reece.'

'We're very happy,' Reece replied. 'And very much in love.'

Both Richard and Holly laughed. 'We could see that, too,' they chorused.

'Mike's never going to believe this, you know,' Richard added ruefully.

'Oh, I think he will,' Alanna said. 'Mike's not quite the hard nut he pretends to be. It wouldn't surprise me if, one day, he falls in love himself.'

Richard and Reece looked at one another and roared with laughter. Holly and Alanna looked at one another, and smiled.

A Scandalous Marriage

CHAPTER ONE

MIKE was grimly silent during the taxi ride from Mascot to his apartment in Glebe. He wasn't at all happy with the way his business trip to the States had turned out, or the course of action he'd rather impulsively decided to take.

But it was too late to change his mind now. He was locked in.

Once home, Mike stripped off the Italian business suit that he'd bought for his meeting with Helsinger and headed for the bathroom. After a shower and shave, he pulled on blue jeans and a T-shirt, then set about cooking himself a decent breakfast. The breakfast they'd served him on the plane as they'd approached Sydney hadn't touched his sides.

Mike ate the plate of bacon and eggs out on the sun-drenched balcony, which was north-facing and had a great view of Sydney's inner harbour.

The balcony was one of the reasons Mike had bought this particular apartment. Water relaxed him, he'd discovered. He liked nothing better than to sit out here in the evening after a hard day's work on the computer, sipping a glass of whisky whilst the water distracted and calmed his mind.

Nothing, however, was going to calm his mind at this moment.

He ate quickly, his aim just to fill his stomach before driving into the city to meet with his best friend—and banker. As Mike scraped the leftovers into the garbage disposal he wondered what Richard's reaction would be.

Mike suspected he'd be supportive of his rather unconventional decision. Richard might look conservative, but underneath he was anything but. You didn't get to be CEO of an international bank before the age of forty by being meek and mild. Richard had his ruthless side, especially when it came to making money. And as crazy as Mike's scheme might sound, if it succeeded, it was going to make both of them very wealthy men.

Five minutes later, Mike slipped on his favourite black leather jacket and headed for the front door. Half an hour later, he was sitting in Richard's office.

'What do you mean you didn't see Helsinger?' Richard's tone was more confused than angry. 'I thought you'd lined that meeting up before you left Sydney.'

'Unfortunately, Chuck was called out of town the day I arrived in LA,' Mike told him. 'He left his apologies. A family emergency.'

'Hell, Mike. That was bad luck.'

'No sweat. I met with his managing director, instead. He assured me Comproware were still very interested in my new anti-virus, anti-spyware program.'

'Yes, I'm sure they are,' Richard said drily. 'It's brilliant.'

Mike wholeheartedly agreed with Richard. It *was* brilliant, especially the way it could track back to see where the virus—or the spy—came from, then deliver a counter-strike of its own. Mike had known, right from the first day he'd started work on the ground-breaking program, that his own relatively small, Australian-based software company didn't have the power to do such a product justice. He needed an international company with marketing clout to launch it, worldwide.

After doing some indepth research, he'd come up with Comproware, a relatively new American soft-ware company that had great marketing flair, and which also had a reputation for offering generous con-tracts to the creators of new programs and games, paying royalties instead of a flat sum.

After some not-so-successful negotiating via the in-ternet and the telephone, Mike had flown to Comproware's head office in America to meet the owner face to face. He'd expected to pin Helsinger down to a contract during his two-day stopover. He certainly hadn't expected what had transpired, or the path he'd now set himself upon.

'I didn't get a contract,' he admitted. 'What I did get, however, was the offer of a possible partnership.'

'A partnership!' Richard exclaimed excitedly. 'With Chuck Helsinger? You've got to be kidding. That man's a retail legend. Everything he touches turns to gold. A partnership with him has to be worth millions.'

'Actually, Rich, more like billions. If I can close

this deal, your fifteen per cent of my little company is going to make you an even richer man than you already are. Reece is going to be pretty pleased with his fifteen per cent, too.'

And *my* seventy per cent share means I'm going to be able to do all those things I've always wanted to do, Mike thought, not for the first time. A boys' club in every city and big town in Australia. Lots more summer camps. And scholarships.

The possibilities were limitless!

If he got the partnership.

Richard shook his head in amazement. 'I can't believe it. This is incredible.'

'There was one small catch. But I can fix that.'

Richard immediately looked wary. 'What catch?'

'Chuck Helsinger has a hard-and-fast rule about the men he goes into partnership with.'

'What rule is that?'

'They have to be married. Settled men with solid family values.'

'You're joking.'

'Nope.'

Richard groaned, then leant back in his leather office chair, his elbows on the padded arm-rests, his hands steepled together in front, his dark brows drawing together. 'And how, pray tell, are you going to fix that?'

'I've already started. I immediately emailed Chuck that I'd recently become engaged to a wonderful girl and that we were getting married before Christmas.'

Richard's eyebrows formed a sardonic arch. 'That

was very inventive of you, Mike, but I don't think that's going to cut it. A man like Chuck Helsinger is sure to have any prospective business partner of his thoroughly investigated. He'll soon find out that you lied to him.'

'I did think of that. But it's not going to be a lie for long.'

Richard shot forward on his chair. 'You mean you'd actually get married!'

Mike could understand his friend's shock. Mike was, after all, a confirmed bachelor. He'd told Richard many times that marriage would never be on his agenda.

Still, he'd never anticipated a deal such as this coming his way. Sometimes, a man had to do what a man had to do.

But on his own terms, of course.

'If I want this partnership,' Mike said matter-of-factly, 'I'm going to have to. And as soon as possible. Helsinger is going to be in Sydney on the fourth of December to pick up a luxury yacht he's having built here. It's a Christmas present for his family. He and his wife want me and my new bride to join them for a couple of days for a getting-to-know-you cruise around Sydney's waterways. I presume, if I pass muster as a happily married man with solid family values, the partnership will be mine.'

'Good God!' Richard exclaimed.

'Look, I don't intend to *stay* married,' Mike informed his friend. 'It will just be a business arrangement, played out till the partnership is signed and sealed.'

'That's a bit cold-blooded, isn't it, Mike? Even for you.'

Mike shrugged. 'The end justifies the means. After all, what right does that hypocritical old buzzard have to insist on such a ridiculous requirement? Being married has nothing to do with being a good businessman. I'm proof of that.'

'Maybe, but that doesn't make him hypocritical.'

'You reckon? I did some investigating myself before I decided on Comproware, delving into its owner's professional and personal background. Did you know that Chuck's on his third wife, a woman, I might add, who's a good twenty-five years younger than his own seventy years? Okay, so they *have* been married for sixteen years and she's given him children. Two boys. But does that make him a decent man with solid family values?'

'I see what you mean,' Richard muttered.

'His wife can't be much better. Do you honestly think she married him for his charm? Hell, no. She hitched herself to a gravy train, like lots of women do with wealthy guys. You know how it is, Rich. Money is one hell of an incentive when it comes to some members of the fairer sex. Since I became a millionaire, I've never been lacking for female company. I'll have no trouble finding myself a temporary wife. I just have to wave the right amount under the right girl's mercenary little nose.'

'You sound like you have someone in mind. One

of your ex-girlfriends, I suppose. You've had enough of them.'

'Hell, no. None of those will do. The last thing I want is complications, or consequences. I need a wife who knows exactly what I require from her, right from the start. Which is absolutely nothing but appearances. This will be a marriage in name only, to be discreetly dissolved at a later date. There will be no consummation of this union. Be assured of that!' Mike finished up forcefully.

He was sick and tired of women claiming emotional involvement with him, despite his up-front warnings. They seemed to accept his 'just-company-and-sex' rule to begin with. But once he took them to bed a few times, they changed. Mike couldn't bear it when a woman started telling him she loved him. For one thing, he just didn't believe them. Women trotted out those three little words all the time to manipulate men. And to try to trap them.

Little did they know that telling Mike they loved him was the kiss of death.

That was the reason for his many exes. As soon as they began to get clingy, that was it. His latest ex had been a dedicated career girl. A lawyer, chosen because he'd thought she might be different. But no...she'd soon become just as possessive as all the others.

Mike had given up dating for a while, because he simply couldn't stand the scenes. Lately, he'd been spending his spare time with his charity work, instead. And putting in more hours at the gym.

'And where do you think you're going to find this super mercenary creature, Mike? Girls don't walk around with signs on them saying they'll marry for money.'

'What a short memory you have, Rich. I'll get her from an internet introduction agency, of course. Didn't you tell me yourself that you tried Wives Wanted before you found Holly? And didn't you confess to me over a bottle of Johnny Walker that that particular matchmaking service had loads of good-looking gold-diggers on their books?'

Richard frowned. 'You're right. I did say that. But, in hindsight, maybe I misjudged them. I was in a pretty cynical state of mind at the time I dated those women. They probably weren't as bad as all that. I mean, Reece found Alanna using that agency. No one in their right minds would call her a gold-digger.'

'There are always the exception to the rule,' Mike said, his mind momentarily going to Reece's lovely and very loving wife. 'Alanna is that exception. Wives Wanted will have what I'm looking for. What I need from you, Rich, is their contact number. Do you still have it? If you don't, I could ask Reece.'

'I have it here somewhere,' Richard admitted.

No use protesting further, he realised as he opened the top drawer in his desk and went through the pile of business cards he kept in the corner, looking for the one from Wives Wanted. Mike was clearly determined to do this. And who could blame him? A partnership with Chuck Helsinger was the chance of a lifetime.

Still...

Holly wasn't going to believe him when he told her about this tonight. Mike was the most anti-marriage guy they knew. Anti-marriage. Anti-love. And anti-women.

No, that was going too far. He wasn't anti-women. There was always some beautiful dolly-bird on his arm. Women buzzed around Mike like bees to the honeypot. Richard wasn't too sure why, since Mike wasn't conventionally handsome. Holly said it was because he was tall, dark and dangerous-looking.

Richard conceded that Mike's macho appearance might be the main contributing factor to his attractiveness. He had wall-to-wall muscles. And then some.

He also rarely dressed in suits, favouring jeans and leather jackets. Black, like the one he had on today.

Whatever it was, Mike was never lacking in female company. Fortunately, Holly didn't go for that type. She preferred his own more conservative, well-groomed style. Thank God.

'Here it is,' he said as he picked up the card and handed it across to Mike. 'The woman who runs the place is called Natalie Fairlane. Her name and number are on the back. She'll want you to come in for an interview before she matches you up with anyone. She never takes on a client over the internet. I suggest you don't tell her up front what your agenda is. Ms Fairlane takes her matchmaking services very seriously. One other little word of warning, too. The women on the Wives Wanted database whom I dated were all drop dead gorgeous. It might be wise if you didn't pick one who's too beautiful. Otherwise, it could be hard for a man like you to keep your hands off.'

Mike bristled. 'What do you mean, a man like me?'

'You like your sex, Mike. Don't pretend you don't. You've had more girlfriends in the few years I've known you than the stock market has ups and down. I think you're very wise not consummating this marriage. But will you be able to resist temptation? The reality is that during the time that you're going to be…''married''—' Richard made quotation-like signs with his fingers '—you and your new bride will be together quite a bit. You'll have to share a cabin on Helsinger's yacht, for starters. If she's too pretty, you might find it hard to keep your hands off the merchandise.'

'You underestimate me, Rich. I can do celibate. No problem.' He'd been doing it for a few weeks now. 'For the amount of money at stake here, I'd become a monk for life.'

Richard didn't look too convinced. 'If you say so. Now don't forget what I said about Natalie Fairlane,' he added when Mike stood up. 'Watch what you say to her.'

'I think you're being a bit naïve about the owner of Wives Wanted,' Mike replied. 'Ms Fairlane is in the marriage business strictly for the money, just like ninety-nine per cent of her female clients. Wave the

right amount under *her* nose and the old bag'll find
me the right girl before you can say Jack Robinson.'

A wry smile pulled at Richard's mouth as he
watched Mike leave. He'd love to be a fly on the wall
when his friend met the formidable Ms Fairlane.

Mike might be right about her being as mercenary
as some of the women on the Wives Wanted database.
He didn't know her well enough to judge. But an old
bag, she was not.

CHAPTER TWO

'MUM, this is terrible,' Natalie said. 'How on earth did you and Dad let your finances get into such a mess?'

Even as she asked the question Natalie already knew the answer. Her father had always been attracted to get-rich-quick schemes. He wasn't a gambler in the ordinary sense of the word. He didn't waste money at casinos or on the racetrack, but he was a sucker for the kind of investment or business idea that sounded too good to be true, and usually was.

Natalie hadn't realised what a poor businessman he'd been when she'd been growing up. She'd never lacked for anything. As an only child, she'd actually been rather spoilt.

It wasn't till Natalie had grown up that she'd realised her parents lived mainly on credit.

She'd been helping her mother out with her housekeeping budget for quite some time—slipping her a hundred dollars or so every time they saw each other. But now, it seemed that things had really hit rock-bottom. Her father could no longer continue with his latest venture—a lawn-mowing franchise he'd foolishly borrowed money on top of his already hefty mortgage to buy, and which required a fit young man to run.

Natalie's dad was reasonably fit. But he was fifty-seven.

Last month, he'd fallen and broken his ankle. Naturally, he hadn't taken out any income-protection insurance. What sane insurance company would have given it to him, anyway?

The bank was threatening to repossess their house if they didn't meet their mortgage, which was already running months in arrears. Natalie could cover a couple of months' payments, but not the many thousands of dollars they were behind.

Which meant her parents would shortly have no money and no place to live.

Natalie shuddered at the thought of having them live with her. She was thirty-four years of age, long past the time when you enjoyed living with your parents.

On top of that, she ran her business from home, using one of the two bedrooms in her terraced house as an office-cum-computer room, and her downstairs living room as her reception and interviewing area. Things would get very difficult with two more adults in the place. Especially two miserable ones.

'Don't you worry, dear,' her mother said. 'I'm going to get a job.'

Natalie rolled her eyes. Her mother was as big a dreamer as her father. She hadn't been properly employed for over twenty years. She'd been busy helping her silly husband with all his crazy schemes. On top of that, she was even older than Natalie's dad.

No one was going to employ a fifty-nine-year-old woman with no certifiable qualifications.

'Don't be ridiculous, Mum,' Natalie said more sharply than she intended. 'It's not that easy to get a job at your age.'

'I'm going to do cleaning. Your father ran off some fliers on that old computer and printer you gave him and I put them in every postbox in the neighbourhood.'

Natalie wanted to cry. It wasn't right that her mother had to become a cleaner at her age.

'Mum, I could get a second mortgage on this place,' Natalie offered. 'It's gone up quite a bit in value since I bought it.'

'You'll do no such thing,' her mother said firmly. 'We'll be fine. I don't want you to worry.'

Then why did you tell me? Natalie groaned silently.

The sound of her doorbell ringing brought Natalie back to her own life. 'Mum, can I ring you back later? I have a client at the door.' Her first in a fortnight. Business at Wives Wanted had dropped off a bit this past month. She hadn't had any new female clients, either. Maybe it was time for another series of magazine ads. It was a rare business that could survive on word of mouth alone.

'You go, dear. But do ring me back later.'

'I will. I promise.'

Natalie hung up quickly, buttoning up her suit jacket as she rose and headed for the front door.

A quick glance in the hallway mirror as she passed

by assured her she looked every inch the professional businesswoman. Her thick auburn hair was pulled back tightly into a French pleat. Her make-up was minimal and her jewellery discreet. Just a slimline gold wrist-watch and simple gold studs in her ears.

It wasn't till her hand reached for the knob that Natalie wondered what Mr Mike Stone looked like.

He'd been referred to her by Richard Crawford, a merchant banker who'd been a client of Wives Wanted earlier this year. Natalie suspected, however, that Mr Stone wasn't in the banking business. He hadn't sounded like executive material over the phone. He'd sounded less polished than Richard Crawford. Hopefully, that didn't mean less rich. Most of her male clients were well-off, professional men.

But beggars couldn't be choosers, especially not right now. If Mr Stone was willing to pay a few thousand for her to find him a wife, then he could be a truck driver for all she cared.

Better, however, if he were a *rich* truck driver. Most of her girls weren't in the market for working-class husbands.

Natalie turned the knob and opened the front door, her eyes widening when she saw the man standing on her doorstep.

Never, during the three years she'd been running Wives Wanted, had she had a client quite like this.

He wouldn't have looked totally out of place behind the wheel of a truck, she supposed. Not if it was an army truck and he was wearing a military uniform instead of the jeans and black leather jacket he was currently wearing.

Mike Stone was soldier material through and through.

Not an ordinary soldier, Natalie decided as her assessing gaze travelled all the way up his impressive body to his hard, dark eyes and close-cropped brown hair. A commando, one of those highly trained soldiers who went on covert missions and killed people without making a sound or turning a hair's breadth.

He wasn't classically good-looking. His features lacked symmetry. His nose had obviously been broken at one stage and his mouth was way too cruel.

But, for all that, Natalie found him extremely attractive.

Natalie smothered an inner sigh of frustration, at the same time making sure that not a single hint of interest showed on her face.

Ever since she could remember, Natalie had been attracted to men like this. Men who didn't fit the conventional mould. Men who exuded an air of danger. Men who both intrigued and aroused her.

Ten years ago, she would have gone openly gaga over this guy. Today, the inner twanging of her female antennae irritated the life out of her.

'Ms Fairlane?' he enquired, his rough, gravelly voice matching his appearance.

'Yes,' she returned, annoyed with the way her heart was racing. And with the way *he* was looking *her* up and down, his expression somewhat surprised. What on earth had Richard Crawford told him about her?

'Mike Stone,' he said at last, and held out his hand.

She hesitated before she placed her own hand in his, steeling herself not to react to his touch in any way.

But when his large male fingers closed firmly around her much smaller, softer hand, there it was. That spark. That automatic zap of sexual chemistry, running up her arm, leaving goose-bumps in the wake of its highly charged current.

Thank God her jacket had long sleeves, and that she had anticipated something like this.

'Pleased to meet you, Mr Stone,' she said, her outer coolness belying her inner heat. If she'd met Mike Stone anywhere else, she would have walked away. No, she would have *run*. But she could hardly do so at this moment. He was a potential paying client. A potential five grand in her pocket. Money she was in desperate need of today.

'Mike,' he said. 'Call me Mike.'

'Mike,' she repeated, her mouth pulling back into a plastic smile. 'Well, come on in, Mike,' she said, waving him past her into the hallway. 'The first room on the left. Go right in and find a place to sit.'

Natalie pressed herself hard against the wall as he stepped inside. No way did she want his broad-shouldered body accidentally brushing against her chest as he walked along the narrow hallway. But once he did move safely past her, she watched his back view far too avidly and for far too long before she pulled herself together and flung the front door shut, rolling her eyes at herself as she followed him into the living room.

By this time he was settling himself in the middle of her sofa, his long legs stretching out in front of him whilst he leant back and glanced around.

Natalie knew it was an oddly furnished room, filled with pieces that didn't match but that she personally liked. There were three large squashy armchairs covered in an assortment of prints, plus a seductively long brown velvet sofa, which stretched across under the front window and on which her client had just made himself very comfortable.

On the wall opposite the sofa was a state-of-the-art home theatre system, which she was still paying for. The wall to the right of her visitor had built-in floor-to-ceiling bookshelves, in front of which sat an ancient mahogany desk, with the latest laptop sitting on one end and an old-fashioned green desk lamp on the other. The floor was polished boxwood, a colourful circular rug providing warmth and a touch of the orient.

There was no coffee-table to bump into, just an assortment of side tables in all shapes and sizes on which sat ornaments and curios bought from flea markets and garage sales. Two standing lamps with gold-fringed lampshades flanked the sofa, providing subtle light at night when she was watching TV.

A friend had once commented to Natalie that the décor of her living room was very much as she was. Hard to pin down.

'You're very punctual,' she said brusquely, glancing at her watch as she headed for the upright chair behind her desk. It was right on five, the time they'd agreed upon for his interview.

'I'm always punctual when I'm not working,' he replied.

Natalie ground to an instant halt. 'I'm sorry,' she said sharply. 'But I don't take on male clients who are unemployed.'

Again, he looked her up and down, his expression this time annoyingly unreadable.

'I didn't say I was unemployed. I said I wasn't working at the moment. I am self-employed. I own a computer software company.'

Natalie could not have been more surprised. He didn't look at all like a man who spent most of his life sitting at a computer. He was far too fit-looking. Far too tanned.

As Brandon had been.

His reminding her of Brandon sent her irritation meter up even higher.

'I see,' she bit out. 'Sorry,' she added before proceeding over to her desk, where she sat down and turned on the laptop.

Natalie took her time pulling up the page into which she would enter his personal details and requirements, not looking up till she was good and ready.

'So what happens where you *are* working?' she finally asked.

'I sometimes don't show up at all,' he returned.

Charming, she thought.

It seemed men who looked like this were true to type.

Brandon had never been on time for anything. There again, Brandon had had lots of reasons for running late for his dates with her. Or for not showing up at all.

His job as an anti-terrorist agent for one. Plus the wife and two children that she'd never known he had, came the added caustic thought.

She wondered what Mike Stone's excuse was.

'Sounds like you're a workaholic.'

'It's not the first time I've been called that,' he replied with an indifferent shrug.

Natalie liked him less with each passing second. 'Is that why you haven't had much luck finding a wife so far?' she asked rather waspishly.

'No. I could have married any number of women.'

'Really.' Natalie added outrageously arrogant to his rapidly increasing list of flaws.

Finding Mike Stone a wife was going to prove difficult, despite his impressively masculine physique. Her girls all wanted amenable husbands, not up-themselves egotists. Most of them had had unhappy relationships in the past, with difficult and selfish men who hadn't delivered. By the time they came to her, they usually knew exactly what they wanted, and had no intention of settling for anything less.

Natalie suspected that the likes of Mike Stone would not find favour with any of them.

But it wasn't her problem if none of her girls wanted to marry him. She charged her male clients five thousand dollars up front, whether they found a wife at Wives Wanted, or not.

For his money, Mr Stone would be matched and introduced to five very attractive and intelligent women who fitted his criteria the best, and vice versa. After that, it was up to him.

But he'd have to show a bit more charm on a date than he was currently showing if he wanted a wife. Just being sexy was not enough for her once-bitten, twice-shy girls.

Still, that wasn't her problem.

'Since you own a computer software company, Mike,' she said matter-of-factly, 'you'll be familiar with the type of program I use to match up my clients. It's quite basic, really. Mine, however, does have a security check built in, which validates that my clients are exactly who they say they are. I presume you have no objection to that?'

'Nope.'

'Good. Let's get started, then. Your full name.'

'Mike Stone.'

'No, your *full* name,' she said, a touch of exasperation creeping into her voice. 'The name that's on your birth certificate and driving licence.'

'Mike Stone.'

Natalie gritted her teeth. 'Not Michael?'

'Just Mike.'

'Fine. Your address and phone number, please? Mobile as well.'

She typed them in as he rattled them off, thinking to herself that his address of an apartment in Glebe could be good news or bad news. Glebe had become a trendy suburb of late. Its proximity to the inner city and Sydney University was highly valued. But some parts of it were still a bit dumpy.

'Your work address?'

'I work from home.'

Oh-oh. Now that was *definitely* bad news. Okay, so there were some small businesses that were quite successful. But not too many.

'Age,' she said.

'Thirty-four.'

Now *her* eyebrows lifted. She'd thought him older. There was a wealth of life's experience *within* those eyes.

'I'll be thirty-five in December,' he added. 'December the fifteenth.'

'So you're a Sagittarius,' she said as she tapped in that information.

'I don't believe in crap like that.'

'Really.' She should have known. Brandon had said something very similar when she'd claimed the stars deemed them a reasonable match. She was a Virgo, which wasn't a bad match with a Scorpio.

But Natalie wished she'd taken notice of the part that said Scorpio was the sign of dark secrets.

'Marital status?' she went on.

'What?'

'Have you ever been married?'

'Nope.'

'Lots of my clients have been,' she remarked.

'Not me, sweetheart.'

Natalie stiffened before shooting him a wintry glance. 'My name is Natalie,' she said in a voice that would have cut frozen butter. 'Not sweetheart.'

His black eyes glittered for a moment, as though her correction amused him. 'My mistake. Sorry.'

She could see he wasn't. Not at all. But at least she'd made her stand. She couldn't bear men who called women generic names liked sweetheart and honey. It was condescending and demeaning.

'Well, nothing has come back to say that you're not who you say you are,' she told him after a few seconds' wait. Neither was there a warning that he'd ever been arrested, or in prison. 'Now on to your physical description. I can see for myself that your hair is dark brown and very short, and that your eyes are black.'

'They're not black. They're dark brown. They just look black because they're deeply set.'

Deeply set and infuriatingly sexy.

'Right,' she said. 'Height?'

'Six four. Six five, maybe.'

'What's that in centimetres?'

'Lord knows.'

'Never mind. I'll put six five. I'm five ten and you're a good bit taller than me.'

For weight/bodytype, she typed in 'fit and muscly'. She wasn't the only female in the world who liked well-built men.

'Do you smoke?'

'Nope.'

'Do you drink?'

He laughed. 'Do ducks swim?'

'How much do you drink?'

'Depends.'

'On what?'

'On whether I'm working or not. I don't drink when I'm working.'

Natalie sighed. 'And when you're not?'

He shrugged. 'I'm a scotch man. But I like a nice red with evening meals and a cold beer on a hot day.'

'Would you classify yourself as a problem drinker?'

'Certainly not.'

'Hobbies.'

'Hobbies?' he repeated.

'What do you enjoy doing during your leisure hours?' she asked, and looked up from the laptop.

Their eyes met momentarily before his left her face to drift down to where her jacket was straining across her breasts.

'Besides that,' she snapped.

His eyes narrowed on her, and she wondered if he was wondering why she was letting him get under her skin so much.

'I like to work out,' he replied. 'And to go out.'

'Where to?'

'Clubs. Pubs. Wherever I can have a drink with my mates and meet women.'

He'd have no trouble picking up women, Natalie conceded. He wouldn't even have to speak. His hard, sexy body and those hard, sexy eyes would do all the talking for him.

'Are you a good lover?'

The question was out of her mouth before she could stop herself. It was not one of her usual questions. But, thankfully, he didn't know that.

'I've never had any complaints,' came his nonchalant reply.

She almost asked him how much sex he would want from his wife, but she pulled herself up just in time. She'd already overstepped the mark.

'Religion?' she asked instead.

'Nope.'

'An atheist?'

'Nope.'

'What, then?' she asked through gritted teeth.

'The Lord and I haven't had much to do with each other so far, but who knows what the future might hold?'

'Fine. I'll put open-minded on the subject of religion. Education?'

'Not much.'

'Could you be more specific than that?'

'I attended school till I was seventeen, but I didn't sit for my school certificate or my HSC. I've never been to college or university. I'm a self-taught computer genius.'

'*Genius?* My, let's not be too modest here.'

'I'm not being modest. I'm saying it as it is.'

'Fine. But I think I'll enter computer expert. You wouldn't want to put off a potential wife by sounding a little…shall we say…arrogant?'

'I'm not arrogant. I'm honest. But put what you like.'

She intended to. Lord, but he was the most irritating man. 'What's the name of your software company?'

'Stoneware.'

'Stoneware?' She rolled her eyes at him.

'The name amused me,' he said, and actually smiled.

Not a big smile. More a lifting of the corner of his mouth.

'You do have a sense of humour, then?'

'It's not one of my best qualities.'

'Somehow I gathered that,' she muttered. 'Now, Mike, I will understand if you do not want to give me a precise figure, but approximately what is your annual income?'

'I don't mind telling you. Last year Stoneware made six point four million dollars profit. I own seventy per cent of the company, so my share was four point four eight million. I expect this next year to be a much better year, however.'

Natalie swallowed her surprise and said, 'How much better?'

'A *lot* better,' he replied drily. 'We released a couple of new games which have really taken off.'

'I see.'

'I presume that improves my chances of finding a wife?'

His question—and his tone—had a decidedly cynical flavour, which ruffled Natalie's feathers.

'Money alone will not secure you a wife from amongst *my* girls,' she told him crisply.

'Are you sure about that?'

'Quite sure.'

'Pity.'

'What does that mean?'

He stared hard at her, making her squirm on her chair.

'You know, you're not quite what I expected,' was his next, rather cryptic comment, 'but I can see you're still a no-nonsense businesswoman. Like I said, I'm a truthful man. I don't like to con people. I also don't have the time to muck around. The thing is, Ms Fairlane,' he continued as he sat forward on the sofa, his elbows coming to rest on his knees, 'I need a wife before the first week in December.'

CHAPTER THREE

'THE first week in *December*!' Natalie exclaimed. 'But December's just over a month away!'

'That's right,' Mike said, feeling perversely pleased that he'd got a real rise out of her.

He'd met females like Natalie Fairlane before. For some reason they were sour on life, and on men. That was why they tried to hide their femininity behind masculine-looking clothes. They lived in constant denial of their sex, and their sexuality.

Yet a man would have to be blind not to see that Natalie Fairlane was a looker. With the right make-up and the right outfit, she'd be a knock-'em-dead type. She had all the basic equipment. Gorgeous red hair. Striking blue eyes. A sultry mouth. And, if he was not mistaken, hiding behind that simply awful grey trouser suit was a darned good figure.

'But that's impossible!' she informed him agitatedly. 'It takes a month and a day to get a marriage licence, unless you have a special reason for a special licence. *Do* you?' she demanded to know. 'Oh, this is quite ridiculous. *Why* do you have to be married by then?'

Natalie watched as he sighed, then leant back again, stretching his arms along the back of the sofa, his leather jacket coming apart as he did so.

Natalie did her best not to stare. But, brother, did that man have a chest on him!

'Do you want the long version or the short version?' he said.

'Any version will do,' she told him. 'Provided it makes sense.'

'Fair enough. The thing is, Ms Fairlane, I'm in negotiations with an American company named Comproware who are very interested in a new firewall program I've written. Interested enough to offer me a partnership.'

'And?' Natalie prompted when he stopped talking for a second. Patience was not one of Natalie's virtues.

'Such a partnership would earn my company many millions over the coming years. Unfortunately, the owner of Comproware is a sanctimonious, self-righteous old buzzard named Chuck Helsinger who refuses to go into partnership with any man who isn't married. Married with solid family values, I've been informed.'

'Aah, I'm beginning to see. But why do you call Mr Helsinger self-righteous?'

'He's seventy years old. And his wife is in her forties. His *third* wife.'

'At least he *married* her!'

'Trading your wife in on a younger model every once in a while hardly demonstrates solid family values. Not that I feel all that sorry for any of his wives.

No doubt they only married him in the first place for his money.'

'Which is exactly what you're planning to do,' she pointed out tartly. 'Marrying for Mr Helsinger's money.'

'Right in one, Ms Fairlane. Glad to see you've got the picture.'

'Oh, I've got the picture all right, Mr Stone,' she countered, a furious indignation simmering away inside her. 'Now let me give you *my* picture. If you think I would insult any of my girls by matching a man like you up with any of them, then you can think again. They wouldn't enter into the kind of loveless marriage you're wanting, for all the money in the world. They want real marriages with real husbands and the possibilities of a real family, which I presume wouldn't be on *your* agenda.'

Her tirade didn't seem to have affected him in the slightest. He continued to lounge back in that nonchalantly relaxed pose, his expression as poker-faced as ever.

'You're quite right, Ms Fairlane. I certainly wasn't planning on being a *real* husband. This would be a business arrangement only, with a discreet divorce in the foreseeable future.'

'A business arrangement?' she repeated a bit blankly. 'You mean...no sex?'

'Absolutely no sex.'

Somehow she found that hard to believe. Mike Stone oozed testosterone from every pore.

But then she realised what he meant. Just no sex

with his bought bride. He'd probably still be having it off with other women.

'I'm sorry,' she said stiffly. 'I would still not entertain the thought of putting such an outrageous proposition to any of my girls. It's not what they came to Wives Wanted to get. They would be offended and none would accept.'

'You're quite sure of that?'

'Absolutely.'

'I will pay one million dollars up front. And a further one million if the partnership goes through.'

Natalie gaped before she could stop herself.

'Naturally, I will also cover all expenses associated with the wedding,' the object of her gaping went on before she could regather her composure. 'The marriage will have to look real. Mr Helsinger could be having me investigated.'

'I see,' she said after her mouth finally snapped shut. 'That's a very…generous…offer.'

Generous and tempting.

'It's fair for the amount of work and inconvenience involved. Aside from the bother of going through with a wedding, and making it look the goods, my temporary wife will have to be available to spend a couple of days with me aboard Mr Helsinger's yacht early in December. He's coming here to Sydney to pick up this brand-new luxury boat and look me over at the same time.'

Natalie frowned. 'Yachts don't have huge bedrooms. If you're supposed to be newly-weds, you'll have to share a cabin.'

'I can see the way your mind is working, Ms Fairlane, but I can promise you there won't be any hanky-panky. I don't want to create any problems afterwards. This marriage will not be consummated, so please don't match me up with any female who might fancy herself a *femme fatale*, or who might imagine that I will fall in love with her. I won't,' he finished up with a flash of steel in his hard, dark eyes. 'I don't fall in love and I won't be staying married.'

'You don't have to worry about some poor deluded creature from Wives Wanted trying to seduce you, Mr Stone,' she said, thinking his name reflected his nature. He was made of stone. 'I still have no intention of matching you with *any* of my female clients.'

Natalie would later question why she did what she did next. Was it just for the money, or were there other, darker forces at work?

The money was certainly very tempting. She would be able to pay off her parents' mortgage and give them a lump sum to help with their retirement. Then, when she got the second million—she didn't doubt that the ruthlessly ambitious Mike Stone would get his partnership—she could pay off her own mortgage and maybe go on an overseas holiday. She was getting tired of matching other women to men who actually wanted to marry them. It had once given her a kick to see two of her clients happily wed. Lately, however, a measure of envy had been creeping in.

Despite her disastrous relationship with Brandon, Natalie had always believed she would marry one day. And have a family of her own. When she'd started Wives Wanted three years back, she'd still harboured the hope that one day her Mr Right would walk through the door.

But something had happened to her, post-Brandon. She'd become defensive and aggressive where the opposite sex was concerned. The bottom line was she just didn't trust them.

Men were not attracted to her harder, more cynical persona. She hadn't had a date, or a single lover, since Brandon.

'How about me?' came her curt offer.

That got his attention. He sat up straight, his arms falling off the back of the sofa.

'*You?*'

The shock in his voice piqued her considerably.

'Yes, me,' she snapped. 'What's wrong with me?'

What was wrong with her was that he fancied her.

Keeping his hands off the provocative Ms Fairlane might prove difficult, especially on those nights they were thrown together on the yacht. On the other hand, it was clear she wasn't about to help him find a wife from amongst her precious 'girls'.

Suddenly, he understood why. She wanted the job—nope, she wanted the *money*—for herself.

'I suppose you were looking for someone younger,' she said with a flash of those cut-glass blue eyes of hers.

'How old *are* you?' he asked.

'The same age as you. Thirty-four.'

His eyebrows lifted. He would have tagged her as

a couple of years older. But that was probably due to the dreary clothes she was wearing.

'I can look younger,' she said with a proud toss of her head. 'And prettier. If that's what you want.'

'What I want, Ms Fairlane, is a wife who can convince Chuck Helsinger that she's genuinely in love with me. Can you do that?'

Her chin lifted. 'For two million dollars? I'll convince him I adore every single hair on your head.'

Mike smiled as he ran his hand over his very thick crew cut. This, he'd like to see.

His smile faded, however, when he realised he might find it even harder to keep his hands off when Ms Fairlane started playing the besotted bride. He would have to keep reminding himself that she was just doing it for the money.

Damn, but that thought really annoyed him. He hated gold-diggers with a passion.

'I presume you won't entertain any romantic fantasies that I might fall in love with you and want to stay married to you?' he threw at her.

'Don't be ridiculous! You'd be the last man on earth I'd fantasise over.'

'I'm not your type?'

'Only a fool would fantasise over a man who obviously doesn't believe in love and marriage. I am not a fool, Mr Stone,' she finished up firmly.

'In that case, it's a deal, Ms Fairlane.'

Even as he said the words Mike suspected he was going to regret marrying this tough-talking but rather temperamental redhead. But what alternative did he have? Instant wives didn't grow on trees. December would be here before he could blink.

For the first time since they'd met, she suddenly looked uncertain, her hand coming up to her throat in a decidedly vulnerable gesture.

She had a long throat, he noticed. Long and pale, as if she hadn't been out in the sun for ages.

An image popped into Mike's mind of her lying naked on a bed, her whole body pale and soft, her gleaming red hair spread out on the pillow. Her wide eyes would be locked with his, just as they were now, but more so, their expression expectant, yet at the same time excited.

'So...what do we do now?' she said, breaking into his fantasy.

Why don't I take you to bed? he wanted to say.

Because that was what he wanted to do. Right now.

It had been too long, Mike realised ruefully, since he'd been to bed with a woman. Richard was right. Celibacy did not sit well with him, not when he was in the company of a woman he fancied.

But there was nothing he could do about it now, certainly not with Ms Fairlane. She'd blow a gasket if he started coming on to her. Nope. He was trapped into a no-sex existence for another couple of months at least. He couldn't even sneak a bit on the side. Cunning old Chuck might find out about it and any partnership would fly out the window.

Just think of the money, he told himself. The same as the mercenary Ms Fairlane is doing. And stop thinking about her being naked, and willing. The odds of her ever being naked and willing with you, Mikey, are about as high as your staying married to her.

Which reminded him. He had a marriage to arrange, and there was no time to lose.

'It's Thursday night,' he returned, glancing at his watch. 'The stores don't close till nine. First, we'll go get a quick bite to eat. After that, I'm taking you engagement-ring shopping.'

CHAPTER FOUR

'WHAT?' Shock propelled Natalie to her feet. 'Did you say engagement-ring shopping?'

'Absolutely,' Mike replied, rising to his feet also.

'But surely that's not necessary!' She couldn't bear the thought of going into a jewellery shop with him and pretending to be lovers.

'Of course it is,' he returned. 'When I present you to Mr Chuck Helsinger as my wife you're going to have everything my wife should have. That includes a rock on your ring finger and a wardrobe which will knock that dirty old devil's eyes out.'

'But…'

'No buts, please, Natalie. Sorry, but I do have to call you Natalie, since sweetheart and honey and, I presume, darling is out. Unless, of course, you want me to call you Nat.'

She winced at the shortened form of her name, which she'd been called in high school and which she still hated.

'Natalie will be fine,' she bit out.

'Okay. And don't you forget to call me Mike. It wouldn't do for you to address me as Mr Stone.'

'I guess not. Now, about this wardrobe business…'

'Yes?'

'I don't always dress like this, you know. These are just my work clothes.'

'That's a relief.'

Natalie bristled. 'There's no need to insult me.'

'I wasn't insulting you. I was being truthful again. That pant suit you're wearing is simply dreadful. The colour does nothing for you and the cut is far too masculine.'

'I thought you were a computer genius,' she snapped. 'Not the fashion police.'

'I'm a man. And I know what looks good on a woman. The fact that you would even consider buying that outfit in the first place speaks for itself. I'm taking you clothes shopping before December, whether you like it or not.'

'Whatever,' she said, privately conceding that her wardrobe possibly didn't have the clothes necessary for a weekend cruise with the jet set. 'You're paying for it.'

'Good. That's one thing I like about you, Natalie. You know what side your bread is buttered on.'

Natalie tried not to take offence. But it was a bit much, having him criticise her clothes, then tell her that the only thing he liked about her was her mercenary side.

She was tempted to throw at him that the only reason she'd made this appalling deal with him was because of her parents' dire financial position.

Which reminded her.

'I have to make a quick phone call before I leave,' she told him.

'Fine. I'll wait for you out in my car. It's parked just down the street. It's a four-wheel drive. Black, with the number plate STONE. You can't miss it.'

He was gone before she could think of a suitably caustic comment.

Natalie rolled her eyes, then snatched up the phone on the desk. But as she punched in her mother's number she wondered what on earth she was going to tell her.

Nothing, Natalie decided, till the first million was in the bank.

In that case, you'd better stop being so darned prickly, came a sharp warning from her head. Or your would-be benefactor might back out of the deal.

If he wanted to buy her an engagement ring, then fine. If he wanted to buy her a whole wardrobe, that was fine, too. She was not in a position to look this particular gift horse in the mouth.

'It's me again, Mum,' she said when her mother answered. 'Some good news. I've got another client at last.'

'That's good news. Is he rich?'

'Rich enough.'

'Good-looking?'

'Sort of.'

'Do you think you'll be able to find him a wife, more to the point?'

'Yes. No trouble. Which means I'll be flush soon, so don't you go doing anything foolish like pawning things, or borrowing more money from some loan shark. Meanwhile, give me the name of the bank which holds your mortgage.' Her mother always took care of the banking.

She did so, Natalie making a mental note of it as she thought up a strategy to satisfy her parents till she could take care of the whole mortgage. Though Lord knew what she was going to tell them then. Maybe that she'd won the lottery.

'I'll go see the manager tomorrow and organise to have your mortgage refinanced at a lower interest rate,' she offered. 'Rates have come down considerably since you took out that loan. And I'll cover your first few months' payments. Give you some breathing space.'

'Would you? Oh, darling, that would be wonderful. I've been so worried.'

'Yes, Mum, I'm sure you have been. But you don't have to be any longer. I would never see you tossed out of your home. You must know that.'

'You are such a good girl.'

Natalie grimaced. That all depended on one's definition of good. Was it good to marry a man strictly for money?

She supposed it wasn't bad, if the money was for a good cause and you didn't prostitute yourself as well by sleeping with him.

It *was* bad, however, to secretly wish that you were doing just that.

Natalie smothered a groan. It was no use. She had to confess, if only to herself, that just the thought of sleeping with Mike Stone was insidiously exciting.

It was just as well that he was firm on the 'no sex'

part of their arrangement. *And* that he wasn't attracted to her.

Natalie would hate to think what would happen if he fancied her. She would make a fool of herself all right. Not in the way she'd been a fool over Brandon. She would never fall in love with Mike, or think he was anything other than the ruthless, arrogant, mercenary devil that he was.

But she didn't want him lumping her together with all the other silly women he'd obviously bedded and not wedded. In her case, Natalie was determined it was going to be a case of wedded, and not bedded.

'I still can't stay and chat, Mum,' she said. 'I'm going out to dinner with my client.'

'I hope he's paying.'

'Mum, this is me you're talking to. Miss Budget-wise. Of course, he's paying.'

'In that case, eat up, dear. You're getting too thin, you know.'

Natalie had to laugh. Thin, she was not. But her mother always thought she was.

'I'll ring you tomorrow night,' she promised. 'Let you know how I went with the bank. Bye.'

'Bye, dear. And thanks again.'

Natalie resisted the temptation to primp and preen before joining Mike outside. She just grabbed her black carryall, locked the front door and launched herself out into the street.

His car was as macho as he was, she thought as she hurried towards it. An all-black four-wheel drive with darkly tinted windows that exuded a faintly menacing air.

A shiver ran down her spine when the passenger door suddenly swung open, propelled by a black leather-clad arm that disappeared as swiftly as it had appeared.

'You are a most unusual woman,' he said as she climbed in and shut the door behind her.

'In what way?'

'You don't keep a man waiting.'

'Is that a good thing or a bad thing?'

He looked her up and down again. 'That depends.'

'On what?'

'On what we're doing and where we're going.'

'Where *are* we going?'

'This is your turf, Natalie. Where do you suggest we go to get a quick meal?'

'There's a small Italian café a couple of blocks down this street. Bertollini's. They give quick service and serve great pasta and pizza.'

'Sounds just the thing. I'm starving,' he said, and gunned the engine.

'So am I,' she said truthfully.

He shot her a sharp, sidewards glance. 'Don't tell me you're not on a diet. Every female I've ever dated is always on a diet.'

'I never diet.' And she'd never been overweight. She had a high metabolism and a tendency to lose her appetite totally when she was stressed. She'd fallen to a shockingly thin forty-five kilos after Brandon, which had taken her some years to recoup.

But she was fine now, weighing a pleasing fifty-three kilos.

'Stranger and stranger,' he muttered, then said no more till he pulled up outside Bertollini's.

The Italian mamma who owned and ran the café fussed over Natalie in a way she never had before, possibly because she had a man by her side. They were given complimentary glasses of wine and even better service than usual, Natalie feeling embarrassed by the knowing looks all the staff gave her. She had been coming there regularly for three years by herself, so she supposed they thought she'd finally landed herself a boyfriend.

'So how come you're not married yourself?' he asked over their plates of spaghetti Marinara. 'And don't tell me no one has ever asked you,' he added drily. 'You might be a shocking dresser, but you're a good-looking woman.'

Natalie opened her mouth to make some smart crack, then closed it again. If she was going to marry this man—and pretend to adore every hair on his head—then perhaps he should know the truth about her. He claimed to be big on the truth.

'Actually, no one *has* asked me,' she admitted. 'I spent the best years of my life on a man whom I hoped would ask me one day. But he never did. I found out why after four years of loving him, and making endless excuses for him.'

'Don't tell me,' Mike said drily. 'Let me guess. He was already married.'

'How did you know?'

'Sweetheart, it's written all over you. Oops, sorry. That just slipped out.'

'What do you mean, it's written all over me?' she demanded to know.

'For Pete's sake, just look at you.'

'There's nothing wrong with me!'

'There's everything wrong with you. If you still want to get married for real. And I suppose you do. Most females do, for some reason. Then it's just as well I came along.'

'Meaning?' she said stiffly.

'You need someone to tell you as it is, woman. And to sex you up at bit.'

'Sex me up?' she choked out, glad that no one was standing near their table at that moment.

'Yep. You're never going to catch a guy looking and acting like you do, Natalie. They might give you a bit occasionally, but they won't stay the night, and they sure as hell won't ask you to marry them.'

Natalie was torn between asking him if he'd give her a bit and telling him to shut his appallingly in-sensitive mouth.

'You're an expert on the subject, are you?' she said tartly.

'Yep.'

'My, aren't I the lucky one!'

His eyes narrowed thoughtfully on her across the table as he forked some spaghetti into his mouth and chewed it slowly. At last, he put down the fork and picked up his glass of Chianti.

'I'm often told that I'm far too blunt,' he said after

he took a decent swallow of the wine. 'But sometimes you have to be cruel to be kind. Would you rather I lie to you?'

There was an oddly touching sincerity in his words, and his face. Clearly, he hadn't meant to offend her, even though he had.

Natalie could do one of two things. Go back to prickly, or embrace his advice. In truth, she did still want to get married. And have a family. Especially have a family.

The thought that she might never have a child was too depressing for words. And whilst she'd known for some time that her lack of success with the opposite sex was entirely her own fault, perhaps it needed a man like Mike to make her face her off-putting ways. And to make her try to change them.

She couldn't successfully carry off the role of his besotted new bride, dressing and acting as she had been. Why not use this opportunity to try to become a different woman? A softer, sexier, less aggressive woman.

She sucked in a deep breath and let it out slowly. 'I'm well aware that I've fallen into some bad habits. I never used to be this hard and cynical. But when I found out Brandon not only had a wife, but two children as well, I totally lost it.'

'How did he get away with it?' Mike asked. 'I mean, how did he hide a wife and two children from you for...how long was it?'

'Four years.'

'Bloody hell. That's a long time. Surely you must have suspected something.'

'I should have, but I didn't. His work gave him the perfect excuse for when he had to go away, and when he couldn't tell me where he was going, or why I couldn't contact him. He was a spy, you see.'

'A spy!' Mike exclaimed. 'Lord, Natalie, you didn't fall for that old chestnut, did you?'

'He was—*is*—a spy,' she ground out firmly. 'He works for ASIO in their anti-terrorist unit. I know this for a fact, Mike. I was working in a government position myself at the time.'

'What as?'

'I was personal assistant to one of the ministers in the Premier's Department. I took six months long service leave after the fiasco with Brandon. And I never went back. I started up Wives Wanted instead.'

'Why?'

'Why?'

'Yes, why? No lies now. Give it to me straight.'

'I guess there were lots of reasons. A few weeks into my long service leave, I started looking up introduction agencies on the internet. I was only thirty, after all. And terribly lonely. But after some simply awful email experiences with men who just wanted to get into my pants, I decided to start up an agency of my own, one which fulfilled my own requirements for a husband. I soon discovered there were lots of other women out there like me, and lots of men too who'd been burned, but still wanted wives and children.'

'Makes you sound like a do-gooder. Admit it, Natalie. You started Wives Wanted to find *yourself* a husband.'

She sighed. 'I suppose so. Unfortunately, it didn't work out that way. But it still satisfied something in me to see women get what they wanted where men were concerned. I guess it was a form of revenge and therapy rolled into one.'

'Yeah, I can understand that.'

'What about you?' she asked, sick of talking about herself. And going over such painful old ground.

'What about me?'

'What made you so sour on love and marriage?'

'I'm not sour on love and marriage. Good luck to those who find happiness in both, I say. They're just not for me.'

'But why? And don't lie to me. Tell me the truth, like you say you always do.'

The muscles in his jaw stiffened, then twitched.

'There are some truths better left unsaid,' he muttered, and returned to his meal.

Natalie stared at him, unrequited curiosity destroying her own appetite. 'That's it? You're not going to tell me?'

He never said a word till he finished his food. 'Nope,' he said as he put down his fork.

'Well, thank you very much,' she snapped.

'You don't need to know all the ins and outs of my life. It's not as though we're getting married for real.'

'I told you mine,' she threw at him.

'Women like to talk about themselves,' he said brusquely. 'Men don't.'

Natalie's frustration level zoomed up to maximum. She couldn't stand men who did this to her. It reminded her too much of Brandon, who'd been the sneakiest, most manipulative bastard in the world, worming every single detail of her life out of her, then telling her virtually nothing about his own life.

If and when Natalie ever married, it would be to a man who kept nothing from her, who told her everything that was in his head, and in his heart. He would trust her with his secrets, and his soul. He would never play her for a fool in any way, shape or form. Because love wasn't cruel. It was kind, and tender, and sensitive.

Natalie stared at the man sitting across the table from her and realised he was incapable of being kind, and tender, and sensitive. His so-called truthfulness was nothing more than ill-disguised rudeness. He disliked and disrespected women for some reason. And had no intention of telling her why.

She'd made a deal with the devil agreeing to this marriage. But there was no backing out now.

Still, she didn't have to do what she didn't want to do.

'I'm already well aware that men don't like to talk,' she told him coldly. 'Which is a pity. It might do them some good. Women, on the other hand, don't like being made to look foolish, so I won't be coming engagement-ring shopping with you tonight. I know I will have to pretend devotion in front of Mr

Helsinger. I won't, however, pretend in front of some simpering salesgirl. My grandmother willed me all her jewellery. I will wear her engagement ring. *And* her wedding ring, when the time comes. Take it or leave it.'

Again, he just shrugged, his indifference annoying Natalie considerably. 'Whatever. Provided they're nice rings. Not cheap ones. A man in my position would not buy cheap rings for his wife.'

'They are beautiful rings,' Natalie ground out through gritted teeth.

'In that case, good. It saves time and trouble. But I won't back down on the clothes issue. Still, that can wait till a later date. Getting that marriage licence, however, can't wait. You said it takes a month. Where do you go to get it?'

'The registry office. In the city. You'll need to take your birth certificate with you. I presume you have a copy.'

'Nope.'

'You'll have to get one, then, won't you? If you go into the department of Births, Deaths and Marriages personally, you can pick it up over the counter. That's in the city, too.'

'Good. We can get it all done first thing tomorrow morning. I'll pick you up at nine.'

Natalie bristled. 'You might like to ask if I'm busy tomorrow morning.'

'Are you?'

'I have a hairdressing appointment. I go every Friday morning.' It was an indulgence, she knew. But it was the most relaxing thing she did all week. Natalie especially enjoyed the head massage after the shampoo.

His eyes lifted to her hair. 'In that case I suggest you dump your present hairdresser before December and find someone with a bit more pizzazz.'

Natalie glared at him across the table. 'And I suggest *you* find someone else to marry.'

He seemed startled, as though he wasn't aware that he was being abominably tactless. 'You *like* the way your hair looks?'

'*I* did my hair this way today. Not my hairdresser.'

'Oh, I see. So you *deliberately* make yourself look as unattractive as possible whenever you're interviewing a new male client.'

Did she? Perhaps. She had a tendency to be self-destructive when depressed. And she'd been depressed with her personal life for several months.

'What time will you be finished at the hairdresser's?' he asked abruptly.

'Around twelve.'

'I'll pick you up at your place at one-thirty.'

'Fine. I'll be ready.'

'Good. That's it for tonight, then,' he said, and called for the bill.

He left a hefty tip, Natalie noticed.

Brandon had been a big tipper. He'd been a big man, too. There were lots of similarities between the two men, Natalie realised. Too many for comfort.

When he slid the four-wheel drive into the kerb outside her house, she refused to let him get out of his car and walk her to the door. She didn't want to stand next to him on her doorstep, dying to ask him to come in, hating herself for already feeling excited about tomorrow.

She didn't like him. But she was wildly attracted to him. Just sitting next to him in that car for less than three minutes had rendered her breathless.

She could feel his eyes still on her as she unlocked her door. He'd said he wouldn't move off till she was safely inside.

That reminded her of Brandon also, the way Mike's male presence made her feel protected. Was it just because of his size, and his strength? Whatever, being around Mike Stone gave her that same slightly help-less and very feminine feeling that was as irritating as it was seductive.

Natalie hated the fragility of that feeling. And the frustration it inevitably evoked.

At the same time, she suspected that come one-thirty tomorrow she would open this same door look-ing totally different from the way she looked at this moment. If nothing else, Natalie would have the sat-isfaction of seeing those hard, dark eyes widen with surprise.

Not that it would change anything. Mike still wouldn't like her. And she wouldn't like him.

But sexual attraction wasn't always about liking, Natalie was not totally surprised to discover. Nor was it linked to common sense. It had a mind of its own. A powerful and primitive mind, which didn't listen to logic; which was compelled by base and basic instincts; which reduced a woman to little more than an empty vessel, aching to be filled.

Natalie lay in bed later that night aching to be filled by Mike Stone.

'What a fool I am,' she muttered to herself as she tossed and turned.

But the fierceness of her physical frustration served the purpose of changing her mind about the following day. She would not wear grey, but neither would she doll herself up for this man. Her pride would not let her, regardless of what her ego—or her treacherous body—wanted.

Such a transformation could backfire on her, anyway. Mike might look at her very askance, perhaps jumping to the wrong conclusion. He might think she was a closet *femme fatale*, with designs on making him fall for her and stay married to her.

If he thought that, he'd run a mile.

To risk losing two million dollars for the sake of a moment's triumph was ridiculous. If she had some chance of actually seducing the man, it might have been worth it. But Mike had been very adamant on the score of the 'no sex' clause in their contract.

Which reminded her. Perhaps she should make him actually sign a contract. After all, what guarantee did she have that he would give her the two million? A man like him wouldn't care if he ever got a legal divorce. Remarrying didn't interest him. He might just walk away when he got his partnership and give her nothing.

On the other hand, he wouldn't want a nasty legal

fight on his hands. Or bad publicity. From the sounds of things, Chuck Helsinger wouldn't be impressed.

Still, she would be stupid if she didn't bring the subject up. Yes, that was how she had to continue dealing with Mike. In a very practical and pragmatic fashion. None of that silly, soft female stuff.

Now if she could only get to sleep...

But Natalie found it very difficult to sleep. She didn't drop off till well after two, and then it was to dream of a faceless man whom she allowed to use her body in the most shameless fashion. He turned her this way and that, taking her repeatedly, making her cry out with the darkest of possessions. The dreams—and the ravagement—seemed to go on for hours. Then, when she was totally spent, he began to walk away, without a word.

But at the last moment he glanced over his shoulder, and she saw his eyes. They were deeply set, and dark, and horribly hard.

'Mike,' she called out in her dream.

But he just kept on walking.

CHAPTER FIVE

MIKE smiled wryly to himself as he drove towards Natalie's place the next day.

Richard's response when Mike had called this morning to tell his friend whom he'd secured for his wife still amused him.

'You're joshing me!' Richard had exclaimed. 'Natalie Fairlane! Madame Tough-nut herself?'

A very funny but apt description in Mike's opinion.

Richard's initial surprise had quickly subsided once Mike had explained the lucrative terms he'd offered the owner of Wives Wanted.

'Amazing what some women will do for money,' Richard had remarked in a cynical tone that echoed Mike's opinion.

Still, there was no doubt she would impress old Helsinger, once he got her wearing some decent clothes. Natalie couldn't have *always* dressed as she'd been dressed yesterday. She'd had a lover for four years. Married guys who had women on the side went for sexy pieces of skirt, not uptight, women's-lib types who hid their female assets behind unflattering gear.

Mike couldn't wait to re-uncover Natalie's female assets. He'd glimpsed a more-than-adequate bust stretching that awful grey jacket. And she was tall

58

enough to have good legs. He'd noted slim ankles when she'd sat down at the café and crossed her legs.

Pity about her shoes, though. Black pumps with thick heels didn't do a thing for any woman. Nor did grim grey trouser suits.

He'd love to see her in tight hipster jeans that hugged her body and left absolutely nothing to the imagination. He'd team them with a sexy top and some come-to-bed stilettos.

The sudden awareness of a hard-on reminded Mike that this was not a sensible train of thought at this moment, muttering a steely reproof at his wayward flesh as he slid his car into the kerb outside Natalie's place.

It was a terraced house, one in a long line of identical houses that stretched down her street. The only difference between them was the paintwork.

Some of the others were a bit on the garish side, but Natalie's was painted in traditional federation colours. Cream walls, with forest-green roof and ironwork, and a splash of burgundy here and there. The front door and window sill were burgundy, plus the guttering. The tiny front yard was totally paved in old-fashioned terracotta tiles, with green glazed pots filled with palms sitting in each corner.

Mike stayed where he was for a further five minutes before climbing out from behind the wheel and making his way slowly to her door, before finally ringing the brass bell.

'You're late,' she snapped as she swept open the door.

'I don't consider five minutes late,' he retorted, thinking all the while that the improvement in her appearance was only minimal.

She was still wearing trousers, this time a black linen pair, topped by a crisp cream shirt that resembled a schoolgirl's blouse. Her hair was somewhat schoolgirlish as well, tied at the nape of her neck with a black ribbon.

Mike did not have a schoolgirl fetish. He liked his women to look like women.

Only her face got his approval. She seemed to have taken some trouble there, make-up making her big blue eyes look bigger and bluer, and her full mouth look…

Better not look at her mouth, he told himself sternly. Lush lips enhanced with scarlet lipstick did wicked things to him at the best of times.

Her perfume was on the seductive side as well.

'Shall we get going, then?' he said abruptly.

'I'll just get my bag and jacket.'

'You won't need a jacket. It's twenty-eight degrees.'

She set decidedly cool eyes on him, making him wish he'd brought *his* jacket.

'I always take a jacket with me. You never know in Sydney when a southerly change is going to sweep in.'

'Fine,' he said, with a nonchalant shrug.

'Are you always this impatient?' he grumbled when she returned with a black handbag.

*   *   *

No, Natalie wanted to confess, shame and self-disgust bringing a guilty colour to her face. Only when I've been sitting there for the last fifteen minutes like a cat on a hot tin roof, forcing myself not to run to the front window with every passing car. Telling myself I was crazy to feel like this over a man who wanted nothing from me but an act. Hating myself for feeling physically sick when one-thirty came and you hadn't arrived.

'I guess I'm a bit nervous,' she bit out by way of an excuse. 'It's not every day that I agree to marry a man I hardly know.'

'Not having second thoughts, are you?' he asked.

Natalie suppressed a shiver as her gaze swept over him. She'd found him attractive in blue jeans and leather jacket yesterday. Today, she found him devastating.

Was it her dream of last night that had heightened her hunger for him? Or was it the tight black jeans and equally tight black T-shirt that made her crave to touch his magnificent body?

Nothing was hidden from her eyes today. She could see it all, from his broad shoulders and incredible biceps down to his flat stomach and slim hips.

Natalie worked out at a gym herself three times a week and was used to seeing good male bodies. But Mike's was something else.

He made Brandon look like a weakling, which he hadn't been. He'd been very fit and toned.

'No,' she said. 'Your being a friend of Richard Crawford's is an excellent reference. He's a very reputable man. But I got to thinking last night and I want a pre-nuptial agreement which guarantees what you promised me.'

If she was worried that he might react negatively to her request, then she shouldn't have.

'Fair enough,' he said with one of his now-familiar shrugs.

'You agree?'

'Absolutely. Money matters are best not left up to chance. I'll have Rich line up a meeting with his legal team at the bank. They can organise a pre-nup which stipulates the terms I outlined.'

Mike's mentioning the word bank brought a gasp to her lips. 'Oh, Lord, I forgot.'

'Forgot what?'

'I promised to do a job for my parents today at their bank. They're having some money problems,' she added, then wished she hadn't. 'It clean went out of my mind.'

'So where is their bank? I can drive you there after we're finished.'

'Would you? It's not in the city. It's in Parramatta.'

'No trouble. It won't take for ever to do the marriage licence bit. Not if we get moving.'

Natalie was rather relieved to get moving, till Mike climbed up into his black vehicle next to her and shut the door after him. Once again, the enclosed space combined with Mike's overwhelming maleness quickened her breathing, making her regret the foolishness of asking him to drive her to Parramatta.

Whatever had possessed her?

Silly question. The answer was sitting right next to her with all his disturbing machismo.

Natalie drew in a deep breath, then let it out slowly, telling herself it wasn't a crime to look, even to lust. Men did it all the time. The crime would be to let Mike know how he affected her.

She was very glad now that she'd dressed sensibly today. She would have despised herself if she'd tried to make herself into a *femme fatale*.

As it turned out, fate—and Friday afternoon—let her off the hook where any trip to Parramatta was concerned. Parking problems plus long queues meant it was four by the time they'd secured Mike's birth certificate, and then their marriage licence.

'It's too late to go to Parramatta now,' she said as they left the registry office.

'Is this problem of your parents' urgent?' Mike asked. 'Can it wait till Monday?'

'It'll have to, I suppose,' she replied, not happy with herself for having forgotten to fulfil her promise.

'What is the problem, exactly?' Mike asked as they walked together back towards the parking station.

Natalie bit her bottom lip. She knew it had been a mistake to mention that. The last thing she wanted was for Mike to know why she was marrying him. Telling him some sob story about her doing it for a noble cause would sound so lame now. And so Hollywood.

Far better Mike continue to think she wanted his money for herself. No way did she want his pity. Pity was the last thing she wanted from him, she thought with perverse amusement.

At the same time, she had to come up with some plausible explanation. Mike was no fool.

'Dad's got behind with the mortgage a bit. But if they refinance their loan at the current rate—which is much lower than when they took it out—they should be able to manage better.'

'You sound like you know what you're talking about. Are you an accountant?'

'Not certified. But I have a business degree.'

'I thought you said you were a secretary.'

'I was a personal assistant, not a secretary.'

Mike suddenly took hold of her arm and pulled her to a halt. 'Rich's bank refinances loans. He'll help you out if I ask him to. He owes me a favour.'

'How's that?'

'He owns shares in Stoneware.'

'Ah-h-h.'

'So now you know my secret,' he said with a wry smile. 'I'm not just marrying you to get Helsinger's money for myself. I have other, less selfish motives.'

'We all have more than one motive for what we do,' she replied, thinking of her parents again.

'That sounded deep. So what are *your* other motives for marrying me?'

'Oh, no, you're not going to do that to me again.'

'Do what?'

'Make me reveal all my personal secrets, then tell me absolutely nothing about yourself. We both know the main reason why this marriage is going to happen.

The bottom line is money. That's all you have to know, Mike Stone.'

His dark eyes actually twinkled at her, making his face look softer for a moment. 'Fair enough. Look, Rich's bank is just around the corner from here. Come on. He'll still be in his office, being the workaholic that he is.'

Natalie found herself being propelled back along the pavement at considerable speed, giving her a glimpse of Mike's physical strength.

'But we can't just barge in there!' she protested breathlessly as they dodged people going the other way.

'Besides, isn't his bank a merchant bank? They wouldn't handle home mortgages.'

'He'll do it for me.'

'But—'

'For pity's sake, woman, let me help you out here. Or does letting a man help you out go against your women's lib creed?'

That silenced her. Because she'd never thought of herself as a women's libber. And she didn't like the tag one bit.

'That's better,' he muttered as he ushered her silent self into a solid grey-stone building that looked old enough to have been built by convicts.

Inside, however, the décor of the foyer was spacious and plush, exuding the sort of rich yet sombre atmosphere Natalie associated with Swiss banks.

Mike steered her past the security guards who flanked the lifts, actually saying, 'Hi,' to them as if he was an old friend. They were soon exiting on the fifth floor, Natalie's shoes sinking into thick red carpet as they walked along a wide corridor dotted with heavy wooden doors. The one right at the end had a gold plate with Richard Crawford's name on it, plus CEO underneath.

By the time Mike reached for the knob on this door, Natalie's agitation had increased considerably. This was going to be so embarrassing. And awkward. How was she going to keep her parents' dire financial situation from Mike if he accompanied her into his friend's office?

Which he would.

The first door opened, not into Richard Crawford's office, but his secretary's.

'Hello, Pattie,' Mike said to the middle-aged brunette who was busy tapping away on her computer. 'Is the boss in?'

'Where else?' she replied with a dry glance. 'Do me a favour, Mike, and take him out somewhere for a drink, would you? I have visitors coming tonight and need to get home before dark.'

'Will do, sweetheart,' Mike said.

Natalie rolled her eyes at his calling the woman sweetheart. Still, at least he was consistent.

'Aren't you going to introduce us?' the secretary asked with a quick smile towards Natalie.

'Sorry. Forgot my manners. Natalie, this is Pattie Woodward. Pattie, this is Natalie Fairlane,' he said. 'My fiancée.'

Natalie was glad she smothered her gasp in time.

'Thought I'd pop in and tell Rich the good news,' Mike rattled on whilst the secretary just stared at Natalie.

Natalie wondered if Pattie's shock was due to Mike getting married at all, or the woman he'd chosen to marry. Clearly, she wasn't his usual type.

'Well!' Pattie exclaimed at last. 'Congratulations to you both. And when's the wedding to be?'

'As soon as possible,' Mike replied. 'And, no, it's not a shotgun wedding. We just can't wait to be man and wife,' he added, shocking Natalie when he snaked one of his arms around her waist and pulled her hard against him. 'Isn't that right, darlin'?' he added, his large fingertips rubbing along her ribcage just under her right breast.

This time she did gasp, her heart fluttering in her chest as her nipples tightened in the most exquisitely pleasurable way. Without thinking, she lifted her eyes to his, her lips parting to say 'yes' in the most horribly breathless fashion.

His eyes narrowed before dropping to her still-parted lips, Natalie's heart lurching when he swung her round and his head began to descend.

My God! He was going to kiss her. Right here. In front of Pattie.

And she was going to let him.

CHAPTER SIX

'AHEM!'

Mike whirled round to see Richard standing in the open doorway of his office, giving him the sternest of looks.

Mike supposed he should have been grateful that his friend had stopped him from kissing Natalie.

But, damn it all, she'd felt so good in his arms. A few more seconds and he'd have found out what she tasted like. And what she kissed like.

Now he'd never know.

'Hi there, Rich,' he said, frustration still fizzing along his veins. 'Guess what? Natalie and I are engaged. Thought we'd come and tell you the good news personally.'

Richard, who looked his usual banker self in a navy pinstriped suit, didn't turn a hair. 'Really. How nice. My congratulations to you both. We'll have to have a celebratory drink together. You can have an early mark, Pattie.'

'I won't say no to that,' his secretary replied with a quick smile and some instant bustle. 'Thanks, boss.'

'My pleasure. Come on inside for a sec, you two. I have a few things to finish up before we can leave.'

As Mike pushed her ahead of him into Richard Crawford's office Natalie was wishing that the floor would open up and swallow her. She knew her face was still burning. And so were her nipples.

What would have happened if Richard hadn't interrupted them?

The prospect didn't bear thinking about.

Thankfully, Mike steered her over to a chair before pulling one up for himself. She really needed some breathing space from him. He was still fairly close, but not as close as he'd been out there in front of Pattie's desk.

Natalie sucked in some deep breaths whilst Richard closed the office door and walked round to sit behind his own impressive desk.

The whole office was impressive, Natalie finally had the presence of mind to notice. And the view through the window behind Richard's desk was second to none, overlooking Hyde Park and the Botanical Gardens.

'Did you have a reason for telling Pattie that you and Natalie were engaged?' Richard said straight away. 'I thought you would both want to keep your marriage confidential.'

Natalie couldn't have agreed with Richard more. She glanced over at Mike for his explanation.

He seemed annoyingly unperturbed by everything. 'If Helsinger is having me investigated, I thought it best that everyone—other than my closest friends, of course—thinks this is a genuine love match.'

'I see,' Richard said. 'So you and Natalie were just pretending out there.'

'Of course.'

Natalie just stopped herself from staring over at him. Because what she'd felt pressing into her stomach hadn't felt like pretence.

Richard turned his businesslike gaze on her. 'Natalie? You don't mind pretending you're in love with Mike?'

'Only when it's necessary,' she replied, pleased that she sounded nicely composed.

'Which it will be when we're on the yacht with the Helsingers,' Mike pointed out. 'So we need a bit of practice beforehand. By the way, Natalie wants a proper pre-nup.'

Richard nodded. 'Sensible of her.'

'Could you have one drawn up for us both to sign?' Mike went on, leaving Natalie trying to look suitably sensible and pragmatic about everything.

'I can.'

'The first million is to be paid into her account on the day of our wedding. The second when the partnership becomes a reality.'

'Fine,' Richard returned. 'So when will this wedding be?'

'Just over a month from today is the earliest it can be,' Mike said. 'Isn't that right, Natalie?'

'Yes. You need a special licence to make it any earlier. But that might look suspicious.'

Richard began flipping over his desk calendar. 'Today's the twenty-eighth of October,' he said. 'The third of December is a Saturday.'

'The third of December it will be, then,' Mike said.

Richard frowned. 'That's cutting it pretty fine. Didn't you say Helsinger arrives in Sydney on the fourth?'

'Yep.'

'When do you have to join him and his wife on the yacht?'

'From the fifth till the seventh.'

'Given you'll only have been married two days by then, you'll have to act like newly-weds.'

Natalie grimaced. How on earth was she going to endure pretending to be Mike's blushing bride?

'Just think of the money,' Mike said with a glance at her face.

'Just look like you two did out in Pattie's office a few minutes ago,' Richard said drily, 'and you'll convince the devil himself that you're madly in love. Now, are you planning on a church wedding?'

'No,' Natalie jumped in. 'I wouldn't like that.' She would not mock God with such a scandalous marriage.

'A celebrant, then,' Richard suggested. 'You could use my penthouse for the ceremony. Holly and I have moved into our new house, but we've kept the penthouse as a getaway. It would make a nice setting for a wedding.'

Natalie remembered that when Richard Crawford had signed up with Wives Wanted, his address had been a new swish apartment in East Balmain.

'You could stay there together till you have to board Helsinger's yacht,' Richard offered.

'We won't say no to that,' Mike said. 'Much better

than a hotel where we'd be on show all the time. Thanks, Rich.'

'Yes, thank you, Richard,' Natalie concurred. *Much* better than staying in some honeymoon suite at a city hotel. That could have been awkward, and seriously embarrassing. Richard's penthouse was sure to have more than one bedroom.

'I'll ring Reece and get the number of that celebrant he and Alanna used,' Mike went on.

Natalie blinked, then swivelled to face Mike. 'Are you talking about the Diamonds?'

'Yep. The one and the same couple you brought together. They're close friends of mine.'

Natalie could not have been more astounded. 'Good heavens!'

'Why so surprised?'

'They…er…just don't seem like your type of people.'

Reece Diamond was a property tycoon, with more looks and charisma than any man had a right to. He was famous for throwing glamorous parties where the women wore designer gowns and the guests were served caviare and champagne.

She couldn't imagine Mike mixing in that crowd.

'I met Reece through my dealings with Rich here,' he explained. 'He lent us both money when we needed it. The three of us have been friends ever since.'

Natalie actually knew Reece and Alanna better than most of her clients. She'd been genuinely happy when their rather pragmatic marriage had blossomed into a true love match.

'Alanna hasn't had any recurrence of that memory loss she had a while back, has she?' she asked, regretting that she hadn't kept in touch since Alanna's accident.

'Nope,' Mike said. 'She's fine. They're having a baby, did you know? So is Holly. Rich's wife.'

'How lovely for you,' Natalie managed to say, even whilst a huge wave of depression swamped her.

Everyone she knew seemed to be having babies. One of her old girlfriends from work had rung her this week to say that she and her husband were expecting. Her hairdresser had regaled her with similar news this morning.

Babies, babies everywhere. But not for her.

Well, certainly not till you stop wasting your time on the Mr Wrongs of this world, she lectured herself.

Still, her marriage to Mike wasn't going to last for too long. There was still time for her to find Mr Right, she decided with a return to more positive thinking.

'Actually, the main reason we popped in to see you, Rich,' Mike continued, 'was because Natalie's parents have a problem meeting their mortgage. She was going to go to their bank today about refinancing, but we ran out of time. I suggested you might be able to help her out.'

'Be glad to. I presume they've run into arrears?'

'Somewhat.'

'Is their bank threatening to repossess?'

'Yes,' she admitted reluctantly.

'Why didn't you tell me things were as bad as that?' Mike demanded to know.

She turned a cool face towards him. 'It wasn't any of your business.'

'It is if this is the reason you agreed to marry me.'

'What does it matter why I agreed to marry you? The end result will be the same. You will hopefully get your partnership and I will get two million dollars. What I do with it should not concern you, just as what you do with your money doesn't concern me.'

'She's right, Mike,' Richard said matter-of-factly.

Yes, she was, Mike appreciated. But that didn't make any of it more palatable. He much preferred thinking of her as a tough-talking, mercenary creature, not some sweet, self-sacrificing daughter.

Still, he supposed two million dollars was a lot more than what was owed on that mortgage. She would still reap in a considerable sum for herself. That still made her reasonably mercenary.

'Okay,' he said. 'I won't quibble. Can you arrange some refinancing, Rich?'

'Not right away. But if Natalie comes in to see me on Monday morning with all the particulars and a letter of authority from her parents, then I can make sure their home is safe till she can pay off the mortgage in total. Will that be satisfactory to you, Natalie?'

'Perfectly. Thank you, Richard. This is very good of you.'

'I'm glad to be of help. On principle, I hate it when

banks start threatening to repossess. There is always another way. What time would you like to come in Monday morning. Ten suit you?'

'Ten is fine. My time's my own on the whole.'

'Good. You can both sign the pre-nup at the same time. Now are we still going to have that celebratory drink? I can't stay too long. I want to get home to Holly.'

'I'm sorry,' Natalie jumped in, 'but I can't. I have to be getting home myself. I have things I have to do.'

'What things?' Mike asked in the lift on the way down.

'Female things.'

Like what? Mike thought irritably. Wash her hair? Paint her toenails? Shave her legs?

His mind suddenly filled with the image of her lying back naked in a bath with one bare leg propped up provocatively on the side whilst she ran a razor in long, languid strokes from her ankle to her knee, then up her thighs.

The lift doors opening broke into his fantasy, startling him. For Mike was not a man given to such fantasies. When he thought of sex, it was in more basic terms.

Natalie, however, seemed to be inspiring him to think in more seductive scenarios.

Was it just the challenge her prickly self presented?

Probably. He never could resist a challenge.

But he aimed to this time. No way was he going to risk rejection, or spoiling the deal of a lifetime. His male hormones would just have to behave themselves for a while.

'You don't have to drive me home,' Natalie announced snippily as she stepped out of the lift. 'I can just as easily catch a taxi.'

He looked at her hard, then shook his head. Damn, but she was an annoying woman. He was constantly torn between wanting to seduce her, and strangle her.

'Don't be ridiculous,' he ground out, taking her by the elbow and urging her across the foyer. 'I might not quite be in Rich's mould, but I'm gentleman enough to know that when you take a lady somewhere, you take her home afterwards.'

CHAPTER SEVEN

NATALIE could not wait to get out of Mike's car. This time, however, he insisted on walking her to the door.

'What are you going to tell your parents?' he asked whilst she fumbled for her house keys.

'I have no idea,' she muttered, sighing her frustration when she dropped the darn things. 'Maybe I'll say I won the Lotto,' she said as she bent to pick them up.

But Mike swooped up the keys just before her, their faces staying level for a long moment, his dark eyes boring into hers.

'You should tell them the truth.'

His penetrating gaze kept hers prisoner as they both rose to their feet, her keys still in his hands.

'You have to be kidding,' she said. 'My mother would have a pink fit.'

Actually, Natalie wasn't too sure about that. Her mother had probably reached the stage where she'd be happy with the role of mother of the bride under any circumstances. She was always bemoaning the fact that her daughter could find rich husbands for other girls but not herself.

'My father wouldn't like it, either,' she added.

'I'm sure both your parents would be supportive,

once you explained the situation. They're going to benefit substantially, after all.'

'There's more to life than money,' she snapped.

'Only when you have it,' he countered just as sharply, making her wonder what hardships he'd once encountered in his life.

'With your parents in on everything,' Mike argued, 'our marriage would be even more convincing. We could have proper family photos taken to show Helsinger.'

Natalie winced. 'But that would mean a proper wedding dress.'

'You were always going to have that.'

'*Was* I?'

'Absolutely. And a proper honeymoon wardrobe.'

His eyes ran down her black trousers, right down to her black pumps, then back up again, his expression disapproving. No, worse than disapproving, Natalie conceded. Closer to disgusted.

'You have a great figure, Natalie. Why do you hide it?'

She stiffened. 'I don't hide it.'

'Yeah, you do. And I think I know why. You're scared.'

'Scared of what?'

'Of some man wanting you and using you again.'

'My! A pop psychologist as well as a fashion expert and a computer genius!' she scoffed, even whilst she knew he was dead right.

He stared at her with hard, unfathomable eyes,

making her long to know what he was thinking. Probably that she was a total bitch.

But that was all right. She wanted him to think that, didn't she? Because right at this moment she was afraid of *him*, afraid of what he could make her feel and want, afraid of what might happen if she abandoned her defences and started dressing as she had once dressed for Brandon.

'Could I have my keys, please?' she asked with prim politeness.

He stared at her some more before finally dropping them into the palm of her outstretched hand. Then, before she could stop him, he reached out and picked up a long strand of hair that had come loose earlier.

She stiffened as he fingered it, her skin breaking out into goose-bumps when he slowly looped it behind her ear.

'How long is it, I wonder,' he said in a low, husky voice, 'since you really let your hair down?'

Natalie's head whirled at the thought of doing just that. With him.

Their eyes met, and held.

'Have a good weekend,' he said abruptly, then turned on his heels. 'I'll see you Monday morning,' he threw over his shoulder as he strode towards the front gate.

'Oh, and Natalie...' He turned back again at the gate. 'Start wearing your grandmother's engagement ring.'

She clenched her teeth and sucked in some much-needed air. 'Anything else?' she bit out.

He looked her up and down again. 'Some new clothes wouldn't go astray. But I guess that can wait till I take you shopping. I don't trust your taste. Now off you go and do your female things. I have some *male* things I have to do. See you.'

Natalie found herself gripping her keys with white-knuckled intensity. What kind of male things?

But deep in her heart of hearts she knew, didn't she?

He was going to have sex, with one of those many females he could have married, but hadn't. He would probably spend the whole night with her—maybe the whole weekend—making love in all sorts of ways.

By the time Natalie managed to insert her key into the deadlock and let herself inside, a dark and self-destructive jealousy had taken possession of her. The temptation to do anything to spoil Mike's plans for a sex-filled weekend almost extended to telling her parents the truth.

Because she knew how they'd react.

Her mother would be consumed with curiosity and her father with worry. They would both demand to meet this man who planned to marry their daughter, but not stay married to her. The money angle might sway total objection up front, but they would still want to look Mike over before letting their precious child put pen to paper and sell herself like that.

Which was only sensible, of course. There were a lot of weirdos in this world. And whilst Natalie didn't think for one moment that Mike was a weirdo—just a ruthlessly ambitious, impossibly sexy man—she relished the idea of her parents giving him the third degree.

And they would. Both of them!

In the end, however, Natalie was forced to abandon that idea. It would be more trouble than it was worth. One look at Mike and her mother would start imagining that there was more to this marriage than met the eye. She knew her daughter's taste in men.

But she would still have to ring her mother tonight and tell her something to explain how she would soon have the means to pay off their mortgage.

A version of the truth came to her that just might work.

After she'd made herself a bite to eat Natalie made her way into the living room and reached for the phone.

CHAPTER EIGHT

MIKE was sitting on his balcony with his feet up, sipping a glass of Glenfiddich and watching the night lights blink on all over the city, when his mobile phone rang. Putting his scotch down on the side table next to him, he lifted his right hip up and slid the phone out of his back pocket, flipping the phone open on its way to his ear.

'Mike Stone,' he said, wondering who it could be. One of his contract programmers perhaps? No, not on a Friday night. It was probably Richard, warning him again to keep his hands off his prospective bride.

'Mike. It's Natalie.'

'Natalie!' His eyebrows arched in surprise. 'I was just thinking about you.'

'I'm sure you were,' came the caustic retort. 'Where are you?' she demanded to know with a degree of puzzlement in her voice. 'Wherever it is, it's rather quiet.'

'I'm at home.'

'Oh. I needn't have rung your mobile, then. Not that it matters. Well, I did what you wanted me to do. I told my parents the truth. You'll be pleased to know that we're expected at their place tomorrow for a barbecue lunch.'

'What?' Mike's knee-jerk reaction had his feet falling off the chair onto the floor with a thud.

'I could have warned you this might happen,' she went on blithely. 'My parents happen to care about me. Naturally, they want to look you over, make sure you're not a psychopath, or a pervert. Which you might well be, come to think of it. I don't know all that much about you.'

'I am a lot of things, but a pervert is not one of them. I'm not a bloody psychopath, either.'

'How do I know? I only have your word for that.'

Mike bristled. 'I'm no saint, but I never lie. Ask around. You'll find that Mike Stone is a man of his word.'

'And who should I ask? Besides Richard Crawford, whom you admit has shares in your company and will benefit if I marry you and you get that partnership. That could be called a conflict of interest.'

'*If* you marry me? I thought it was a done deal.'

'That was before you brought my parents into it. Now, you'll have to pass muster with my mum and dad first. If you do, I'm all yours.'

The provocative words were out of Natalie's mouth before she could snatch them back. She should never have made this call. Never have decided to torment Mike with what would have happened if she *had* told her parents the truth.

Thankfully, he was on the end of a phone and not able to see the guilty heat spreading over her cheeks.

Because, of course, those provocative words echoed her secret desires. She'd *love* to be all his.

No, that wasn't quite right. She'd much prefer for him to be all hers. Her own private toy boy, to be played with till these cravings he evoked in her were satisfied.

But that was a pipedream. Total fantasy world stuff. The real world didn't allow women that kind of privilege. Women always paid for their sexual pleasure, with emotional involvement and the most soul-destroying pain.

It was only the men in this world who could take what they wanted, then walk away without turning a hair. Natalie didn't doubt that Brandon hadn't lost any sleep over her. He'd have just gone back to his wife, then eventually found another gullible female to sleep with on the side.

'The trouble with you,' Brandon had said to her scathingly when she'd told him to leave, 'is that you take life too seriously.'

Remembering those words reminded Natalie that she wasn't capable of playing sexual games. For her, lust and love inevitably became entwined. Whenever she went to bed with a man, she ended up falling in love with him. Brandon had not been her first disaster. Just her last.

Definitely her last, she reaffirmed.

'Before your testosterone gets any ideas,' she added in what she hoped was a suitably droll tone, 'that was just an expression.'

'I think my testosterone is quite safe around you, Natalie.'

Oh, that hurt. That really hurt.

'I'm very relieved to hear that, Mike. But perhaps you should be careful when choosing my new wardrobe. Men are renowned for being notoriously shallow when it comes to sex. In the olden days it only took a flash of an ankle and they were frothing at the mouth.'

He laughed. 'I'd need a lot more than a flash of your ankle, sweetheart. Not that I'm a frothing-at-the-mouth kind of guy. I've had women stand in front of me stark naked and it hasn't got me going.'

'Poor Mike. You have a problem in that area?'

He laughed again. 'I sure do at the moment. But I aim to fix it later tonight.'

Natalie thought as much. He was going out on the town to pick up some little dolly-bird.

'Hope you use protection.'

'Honey, I always use protection.'

'Do you realise that you've called me both sweetheart and honey in the last thirty seconds?' she threw at him. 'I thought we had an understanding about that.'

'That's the trouble with you, Natalie. You think too much. You'd be far better off putting on some glad rags, going out and getting yourself laid.'

'Like you, you mean?'

'I have no intention of going out anywhere tonight.'

'But I thought…'

'See what I mean? You think too much. Incorrectly as usual.'

'You are an extremely irritating man.'

'And you are an extremely irritating woman.'

Her sigh carried total exasperation. 'I have better things to do than try to mix words with you. Before this goes any further, I have a confession to make.'

'That sounds ominous.'

'The thing is, I didn't really tell my parents the truth. There is no barbecue lunch tomorrow at their place.'

'Sorry. I don't get it.'

'I wanted to show you how complicated things could become if we start telling all and sundry that we're getting married. I realise you want our wedding to look real. But I'd like to be able to get a quiet divorce later without having to explain anything to my family. Wouldn't you?'

'I don't have any family to explain my actions to,' he replied, making her wonder about him again.

'What, none at all?'

'None at all,' he ground out in a way that stopped her from asking any more questions on the subject.

'What about your friends?' she asked instead.

'I only have two close male friends. Rich already knows the situation and Reece soon will. I'll be asking him and Alanna to our wedding.'

'What on earth for?'

'The photos. And the kudos. Reece is a very high-profile businessman and Alanna is having a baby.

Helsinger will be impressed that I have friends with brains, and solid family values.'

'Maybe, but I'll be embarrassed.' As much as Natalie liked Reece and Alanna, they were former clients. She didn't like them knowing she was marrying Mike for money.

'You? Embarrassed?' he scoffed. 'Never! You're tough as teak.'

Natalie stiffened. If only Mike knew.

'Not nearly as tough as you,' she countered tartly.

'True,' he agreed. 'So what *did* you tell your folks?'

'As much of the truth as I could. I told them all about you and your potential partnership deal with Mr Helsinger and that you were willing to pay me a million-dollar bonus if I could find you a wife in a day. Which I happily told them I did. I just didn't tell them that it was me.'

'That was very clever of you.'

'Yep, that's me. Clever as well as tough. So you're right, Mike. Your testosterone is quite safe with yours truly. Clever and tough are not attributes in a woman which turn men on.'

Mike wished that were true. Unfortunately, his male hormones hadn't been this stimulated in a long time.

Of course, his recent celibacy had to be part of his problem. But it wasn't the only reason for his constant state of arousal. That sassy mouth of hers turned him on no end. Not to mention her deliciously repressed body.

Mike smiled a darkly rueful smile. She'd really had him going there for a while over that barbecue business. He'd actually started to worry over what he'd tell her folks about his background.

As much as Mike preferred the truth, he'd have been forced to lie. Because the truth would have seen any normal, loving parents advising their darling daughter to have absolutely nothing to do with him, no matter how much money was involved!

The truth might send Natalie running for cover as well. He'd have to be careful with her, and around her, in many ways. Perhaps he should restrict seeing her till their wedding, cut down the odds of anything happening that might spoil things.

Yep. That was what he would do.

'By the way, I can't make it to the bank on Monday morning,' he said straight away. 'I'll drop in later in the day and sign the pre-nup.'

'Fine,' she said in her usual snippy fashion.

'We'll make the following Saturday our clothes-shopping day. I have to find out from the Helsingers what you need first. But we might as well make a time now. How about nine?'

'You mean I won't be seeing you till then?' came her astonished reply. 'What happened to making this engagement look like a real one? Shouldn't we spend a bit more time together? Go out to dinner occasionally. *Visit* each other.'

Mike could not think of anything worse. He was sure to end up making a pass.

'I don't seriously think Helsinger is having our

every move watched,' he said firmly. 'A man of his ego will rely on his own personal judgement. It's what we do on the yacht which will count, not our behaviour beforehand. See you next Saturday, Natalie.' And he hung up.

Natalie stared into her dead phone. She wasn't going to see him for a whole week.

That was seven whole days.

And seven whole nights!

'Good,' she muttered, and slammed the phone down.

CHAPTER NINE

NATALIE could not believe how slow time went that weekend, and then the following week. She tried to keep busy, organising ads in magazines for Wives Wanted, as well as doing some spring-cleaning around the house. She visited her parents more than usual, delighting in their happiness over having their financial problems solved, but at the same time resenting Mike and his damned money every single moment.

The man was a menace all right. Not only had he revved up her hormones something rotten, he'd made her see how empty her life was. And how lonely.

She no longer enjoyed reading as much, or watching television. Yet she'd once really looked forward to sitting down with her latest best-seller, and watching her favourite TV shows. Suddenly, such activities seemed nothing more than futile time-fillers. Going to the gym felt pointless as well. Why shape and tone a body that no man ever saw?

As for working with the clients of Wives Wanted…

Matching people up together had seriously lost its gloss. Natalie decided that, once she got that second million, she would do something else with her life.

Meanwhile, her mind returned to tomorrow morning, as it had many times that day.

Nine, he'd said he would pick her up. Less than fifteen hours to go. So why did it feel like an eternity away?

Natalie found herself wandering through the house in a highly restless state, not settling to anything, her thoughts as agitated as she was.

At six-thirty, she decided to stop pacing and go down to Bertollini's for some pasta. Cooking herself something did not appeal.

Stopping in front of the hall mirror on the way out, Natalie scowled at her hair, which was up in a rather severe French pleat. Okay, so it was glossy and healthy-looking from a treatment the hairdresser had put in this morning. But Mike was right. Her hairstyle was boring. And ageing.

He was right about something else, too. She hadn't let her hair down—not in the way he meant—in a long time.

She shook her head and walked on to the front door, before grinding to an unhappy halt. The thought that Mamma Bertollini might ask her questions about her missing boyfriend was unbearable. So was the prospect that she might not ask at all, just look at her with pity in her eyes.

Natalie groaned.

The temptation to call Mike was acute, but she resisted.

Tomorrow was only one sleep away now. She could last. She *had* to last.

So where else could she go? Who else could she call?

She still had friends from her old job, she supposed. But she'd said no to their invitations to go to drinks on a Friday night with them so often that they'd stopped calling. Kathy had been her only close friend at work, but she was married now and expecting a baby. Natalie didn't want to visit her and see how happy she was.

Maybe she should go down to the local video shop and get herself a couple of new releases, as well as half a dozen chocolate bars. Boost her spirits that way. She might pick up some wine as well, and get plastered.

Her own phone ringing interrupted her waffling and sent her heartbeat into the stratosphere.

It wouldn't be her mother. Her parents always went to the club on a Friday evening.

It had to be Mike.

As Natalie raced to answer it it came to her that maybe he was going to put off tomorrow. If he did, she'd just die!

'Natalie Fairlane,' she said in a much less crisp voice than the one she usually used for answering the phone.

'Natalie. It's Alanna. Alanna Diamond.'

'Alanna!' Natalie exclaimed whilst she struggled to contain her disappointment that it wasn't Mike. 'What a nice surprise. How are you?'

'Marvellous.'

'Your memory is obviously still fine.'

Alanna laughed. She had a very nice laugh. Very

feminine. There again, she was a very feminine woman.

Unlike me, Natalie thought wretchedly. No wonder Mike avoids me like poison. If I were a man, I would, too.

'You know, I don't think I ever thanked you properly for dropping in that day,' Alanna said.

'It was the least I could do.'

'Not everyone would have bothered. Anyway, Natalie, that's not why I'm ringing. The thing is, I had a call from Mike earlier today.'

'Oh?' Natalie said tentatively.

'He told me about your coming marriage.'

'Did he?' He'd warned her that he would, but she still wished he hadn't.

'He's asked Reece and myself to help Richard and Holly with the arrangements for the wedding.'

Natalie tried not to feel hurt. And totally left out. But, darn it all, marriage of convenience or not, she was still the bride, wasn't she?

'I hope he explained that our marriage is just a temporary business arrangement,' she said sharply. 'Not some silly love match.'

'Yes. He was very emphatic about that.'

'I can imagine,' Natalie said drily. 'Mike made it perfectly clear right from the start that he's allergic to love and marriage.'

'I can just hear him saying that. But is that the case with you too, Natalie? Are you allergic to love and marriage? I mean…why start up a matchmaking service if you don't believe in romance?'

'I do believe in romance,' she confessed, 'but the reality of life has dented my faith in the opposite sex somewhat.'

'Yes, I know what you mean,' Alanna agreed, perhaps thinking of her first, rather horrific marriage. 'So this marriage to Mike is strictly a matter of money for you as well, then. You don't secretly fancy him, do you?'

Alanna waited for Natalie to say *of course not* in her usual businesslike fashion. But when there was no immediate answer from down the line, Alanna realised that maybe—just maybe—there was more to this marriage than met the eye. At least on Natalie's side.

'Natalie?' Alanna probed gently.

The sigh she heard was rather telling. It looked as if Holly *had* been right, Richard's wife having immediately put a romantic spin on Mike's coming marriage to Natalie.

'No decent girl marries a man just for money,' Holly had pronounced when they'd discussed the situation over the phone. 'If this Natalie is as nice a person as you say, then she must be attracted to Mike.'

'You do fancy him, don't you?' Alanna persisted.

Natalie sighed again. 'I have no idea why. He'd have to be the most irritating man I've ever met.'

'He is a hunk, though.'

'True.'

'So would I be mistaken in saying that the no-sex

side to this marriage doesn't meet with your approval?'

Natalie didn't deny it. 'It's no use wishing for the moon, Alanna. Mike's not attracted to me at all.'

'How do you know that?'

'He said so.'

'Oh, dear. He can be so tactless at times.'

'Tactless. But truthful. So tell me, Alanna, just out of curiosity, what kind of female does Mike usually date?'

'Difficult to say. They come from all walks of life. But they're always good-looking, with good figures.'

'I see…'

'*You* have a good figure,' Alanna pointed out.

Natalie laughed. 'I don't think it's a question of my figure, but my whole package. Aside from my too cynical and assertive manner, he thinks my hair lacks pizzazz and my clothes are appalling. He says he's going to have to take me clothes shopping before the wedding because he doesn't trust my taste.'

'Actually, no, he's not,' Alanna said.

'Not what?'

'Not taking you clothes shopping. I am. That's the other reason I'm ringing. Mike doesn't have the time. He's working.'

'But he said he was between projects!'

'Not any more. He's found some bug in his new program and he has to fix it. Sorry.'

'He could have at least called and told me personally!' Natalie snapped.

'You're absolutely right. He should have. I suppose

you were looking forward to Mike taking you clothes shopping.'

That was such an understatement. Natalie suddenly felt like a balloon that had lost all its air.

'I wanted to show him he was wrong about my being such a dag,' she confessed wearily. 'My silly pride again.'

'I don't think pride is silly at all. You can still show him, starting with your wedding day. I'd bet you'd like Mike's mouth to fall open when he sees you in your wedding dress, wouldn't you?'

Natalie didn't know what to say to that. She'd spent every moment since meeting Mike fighting her desires and telling herself not to make a fool of herself over him. But where had that got her? She was downright miserable.

If there was even a slim chance she could make Mike want her—even for one night—she was going to take it.

'Yes,' she admitted with a sigh. 'But do you honestly think that's possible?'

'Sweetie, you could knock him for a six. No trouble. By the time I've finished with you, Mike won't be able to keep his hands off. Aside from anything else, I have it on good authority that, come the first week in December, your groom will have been celibate for quite a few weeks, a most unusual occurrence for Mike. His testosterone level is going to be sky-high.'

Natalie winced. Did she really want Mike taking

her to bed just because his frustration had reached breaking-point?

The answer was as scandalous as their marriage.

Yes.

'I'll take your silence to mean you like the idea of Mike being unbearably randy, come your wedding day. Okay, so tomorrow morning we're going to start on our makeover mission. There's no time to lose. I'll pick you up at eight-thirty. Sharp. Ooh, this is going to be such fun.'

Fun. Natalie considered the word. It had been a long time since she'd had fun. *And* since she'd surrendered totally to the female within herself.

Suddenly, she felt more alive than she had in four long years.

CHAPTER TEN

MIKE glanced at his watch. Ten past three and still no sign of the bride.

'Holly, go and see what's keeping Natalie, will you?' he said impatiently.

'Okay,' Holly returned amicably. 'But she's only ten minutes late, Mike. Brides are often much later than that.'

'But she's not a *real* bride,' Mike muttered after Holly left.

'Legally she will be,' Richard said by his side. 'Till you divorce her.'

Mike shot his friend a savage glare. 'Don't remind me.'

'What's the problem, Mike?' Reece asked from where he was standing on the other side of Richard. 'You're beginning to sound like you're having cold feet, like a *real* groom.'

'He will be a real groom,' Richard piped up again.

'Not exactly,' Reece said drily. 'He won't have a real groom's rights tonight. Which might be a problem.'

'And what does that mean?' Mike growled.

'I gather you haven't seen Natalie lately.'

'Haven't seen her in over a month.' He'd rung her twice, suggesting that he drop by, using the excuse of supposedly checking on her new wardrobe. But she'd always had some reason why it hadn't been convenient for him to visit, impossible woman that she was!

'Well, I have,' Reece said ruefully. 'She stayed over at our place last night. And all I can say is... good luck.'

When the bedroom door opened, both Alanna's and Natalie's heads whipped round to see who it was.

'Don't worry,' Holly said as she waddled in, her floaty pink dress doing its best to conceal that she was very, very pregnant. 'It's only me.'

'Just as well,' Alanna said, thinking to herself that her own bump was quite small compared to Holly's. Still, Holly was seven and a half months compared to her six.

'Wow, Natalie,' Holly gushed, her hands clutched across her big belly. 'You look simply fabulous! Doesn't she, Alanna?'

Alanna stood back to inspect the bride, smiling her satisfaction of a job well done. The dress was a triumph, the woman in it even more so. Amazing what the right clothes, make-up and hairdo could do.

Of course, she'd been working with excellent basic equipment. Natalie had a great figure, much better than her own slender curves. Her face had always had the potential to be striking, too, with the right make-up.

Changing her hair, however, had been the *coup de grâce*. Alanna had found an old picture of Rita

Hayworth and taken it along to a top city hairdresser to reproduce. The end result was a very sexy style, which fell in bangs and waves from a side parting to Natalie's shoulders. Her naturally auburn colour had been deepened with some more red, making her pale skin glow by comparison.

'I couldn't agree more,' Alanna said. 'If Mike doesn't go for you in this outfit,' she whispered in the bride's ear as she adjusted the ivory chiffon scarf around her head, 'then I'll go jump off the penthouse balcony.'

'You and me both,' Natalie murmured back.

'I can't believe you didn't buy that dress in a bridal shop!' Holly exclaimed. 'It *looks* like a wedding dress. Yet it's so original. I love the idea of the scarf instead of a veil.'

'Yes, it's most unusual,' Alanna replied. 'Ready, Natalie?'

Natalie looked away from where she'd been staring at herself in the mirror.

'As ready as I'll ever be,' she returned, and picked up the small spray of orchids that she'd chosen as her bridal bouquet.

God, she was nervous. Yet excited at the same time.

She felt, not so much like a bride, but how she imagined an actor felt on opening night on Broadway. For what was this but a performance? She was going out there, not just to marry a man, but to seduce one.

She hadn't set eyes on Mike since that Friday over

a month ago. She'd made sure she hadn't, deflecting him on the two occasions when he'd wanted to check on the clothes she and Alanna had been buying, then, today, making sure that the men didn't come to Richard's penthouse for the ceremony till she was safely in the guest bedroom, getting ready.

She and Alanna had been like two conspirators, plotting and planning.

Alanna had been right, though. It *had* been fun. Natalie was over the moon with the clothes they'd bought, not just her wedding dress, but her entire wardrobe. There was one evening gown in particular that she couldn't wait to wear.

Mrs Helsinger had emailed Mike their social itinerary on the yacht, which included this really swish yacht-warming party on the second night of their stay on board. Mike had given this itinerary to Alanna, telling her to make sure his future 'wife' had everything she needed.

On his part, Mike had taken Reece shopping with him to make sure *he* wouldn't let down his side in the clothing department. According to Alanna, Mike now had a wardrobe second to none.

'What does Mike look like?' she asked Holly.

'Fabulous. Just as good as Richard and Reece. Truly, it's amazing what a tux can do for a guy. But he's not in the best of moods. Very antsy. Shall I tell him you're ready?'

Alanna and Natalie exchanged meaningful looks.

'I think another five minutes, don't you, Alanna?' Natalie said, her heart thundering in her chest.

Alanna grinned. 'Maybe even ten.'

'Not that long,' Holly wailed. 'Please. I don't think *I* can stand it.'

Natalie smiled at Holly, whom she now counted as one of her friends. What a lovely girl she was. But such a hopeless romantic. She really thought something might come of this marriage.

Natalie suspected Alanna was harbouring a few secret hopes in that department, too.

But Natalie knew better. Even if she succeeded in making Mike want her sexually, he was not going to fall in love with her. A brief affair whilst the marriage lasted was all she could hope for. Even that was not a foregone conclusion.

Mike might take one look at her today and be downright furious. He'd told her at their first meeting that he didn't want to marry some *femme fatale* type who thought she could get him to change his mind about divorcing her afterwards.

Natalie's excitement took a nosedive with this train of thought, along with her confidence.

'That's all right,' she said, a sudden burst of nerves making her voice tremble. 'I don't think I want to wait that long, either. Tell Mike I'll be out in a sec.'

Mike frowned at Holly when she returned. 'Well?'

'She's coming out in a sec,' he was told. 'You'd better get ready.'

The three men and the celebrant—a dignified gentleman in his fifties—took up their positions near the railing of the penthouse terrace, which was a truly glorious setting for a wedding, especially on a warm summer afternoon with the sun shining and only the lightest of breezes. The view of the harbour and the bridge behind them was truly magnificent.

There would be no excuse for the photographer not getting great snaps of the bride and groom. Wedding photos were essential, if Mike was to convince Helsinger that the marriage was genuine.

At the moment, it felt all too genuine for Mike.

He'd been insane, coming up with this idea.

He didn't want to get married. He didn't want a wife, even a temporary one. And he sure as hell didn't want that wife to be a woman he wanted to take to bed as badly as this one.

Mike sucked in sharply.

Oh, my God!

That *couldn't* be Natalie Fairlane walking towards him, not in that long, slinky, stunningly strapless dress.

She didn't look like any bride he'd ever seen, despite the ivory colour. She looked like a temple goddess with that sexy scarf wrapped around her pale throat, then swathed around her simply stunning red hair.

Mike's feelings for Natalie had been controllable when she'd been dressed like a legal-aid lawyer. Suddenly, nothing was controllable. Not his desire. Or his anger.

She'd done this on purpose. Transformed herself in secret to catch him unawares. Perhaps to make him look a fool. She was a witch, like all women.

But she'd made a big mistake, taking him on.

He never made a fool of himself over a woman.

If she thought she could turn him on, then spurn him, she was in for a big surprise. If anyone did the turning-on and the spurning here, it would be him.

Natalie's step faltered when Mike smiled at her. She much preferred his shock of a moment before. That had been most gratifying.

His smile, however, was unnerving. Because it was the wickedest, sexiest smile she'd ever encountered.

Not a large smile. Just a small lifting of the corner of his mouth, accompanied by a look that most women only dreamt about. His dark gaze smouldered as it travelled slowly down her body, then up again, bringing a dryness to Natalie's throat and a swirling lightness to her head.

She swallowed, then carefully continued her journey across the terrace to where the ceremony would take place, forcing herself to project a cool façade, even whilst waves of heat rippled through her tensely held body.

Thank the Lord the bodice of her gown was heavily lined and boned, otherwise her scorchingly erect nipples would have betrayed her.

The photographer, she noted, was busy taking pictures, both of herself and the three men waiting for her. Holly had been right about them. They all looked great. But Natalie's eyes were only for Mike, who looked simply incredible. Still not handsome in the traditional sense, but sophisticated and suave and, yes, too sexy for words.

Natalie swallowed again.

'I see you've been hiding your light under a bushel,' Mike murmured as he held out his hand to her, his eyes locking with hers.

'I did tell you that I could look prettier,' she returned, struggling to keep her cool as she placed her hand in his.

How big it was, his fingers dwarfing her own, his palm feeling large and hard against her own soft, slightly clammy skin.

'Honey, pretty is not the word for you today,' he said with another of those sexy smiles. 'As you very well know…'

She might have rebuked him for calling her honey if she'd been capable of speaking. Instead, she just stared up at Mike, her heart pounding behind her ribs as she realised that she'd achieved her objective.

He wanted her. Really wanted her. She could see it in his eyes.

His fingers tightened around hers as he drew her round to face the celebrant, giving her another glimpse of his strength.

His physical power both frightened and excited her. He would be a dominant lover. Powerful and passionate and primal, taking no nonsense from her. She could see him now, stripping her quite roughly before throwing her onto the bed.

Such thinking robbed her of her breath, and her brains.

The celebrant launching straight into the ceremony was a relief, giving Natalie time to scoop in several deep breaths. But her thoughts remained totally scattered during the next ten minutes. She must have made all the right verbal responses. But she had no memory of their marriage at all. Not till that moment when the celebrant told Mike that he could kiss the bride.

That woke her up.

Mike was holding both her hands by this stage, the spray of orchids having long been handed to Alanna. He turned her to face him, staring deep into her eyes as he slowly, very slowly, lifted her hands to his mouth, pressing his lips, first to her grandmother's wedding ring, and then against each startled fingertip.

Shivers ran down her spine with every touch, her eyes widening with surprise.

This was not the kind of lover she'd imagined earlier. This was a man with finesse. And lots of erotic experience. As much as Natalie had thrilled to the fantasy of Mike acting like a caveman with her, what he was doing at that moment was also very effective indeed.

Already, she craved for him to take one of her fingers into his mouth, to suck on it. Her mind whirled with the mental picture of his sucking on other, far more intimate parts of her body, her lips falling open to provide more air for her suddenly panting lungs.

His eyes narrowed on her mouth, oh, so knowingly, his hands dropping hers to cradle her face. He was going to kiss her now. Properly.

Her lips stiffened at first contact with his—perhaps out of some lingering, long-held fear—but all too soon they softened and trembled apart, inviting him in. When his tongue slid down deep into the warm, wet orifice behind her teeth, her arms slid around his back, wanting him close, then closer still.

Natalie totally forgot where she was. This was what she'd thought about and dreamt about for the last month. Being in Mike's arms. Being able to kiss him and touch him.

His body felt as good as it looked. And he kissed even better than she could have possibly imagined.

Mike's abruptly putting her aside only a few seconds later came as a shock. So was the cold glare he gave her before turning away to accept everyone's congratulations, leaving Natalie to struggle helplessly with the aftermath of his kiss. Her heart was racing, her face felt hot, and her nipples were like bullets inside her dress.

She didn't know where to look or what to do.

Alanna and Holly producing some nibbles, plus trays laden with champagne-filled glasses, was a godsend, Natalie scooping up a glass brimming with the sparking liquid. She desperately needed something to help her regather her composure and face the depressing reality that she'd got carried away with herself earlier on.

Sure, Mike might think she looked sexy today. And, yes, he'd been very convincing in the role of besotted bridegroom in front of the celebrant and the photographer.

But it was now obvious that that was all it had been. A role. An act. He couldn't wait to stop kissing her. Or to leave her to her girlfriends and talk to his mates. Alanna had been wrong and she'd been right. She wasn't Mike's type. Never would be, no matter how much she tarted herself up.

'A toast to the bride and groom,' Richard proposed.

Natalie groaned a silent groan. So did Mike, by the look on his face. If only the celebrant and photographer would leave, she thought wretchedly, they could stop all this awful pretending.

More photos followed, and more toasts, Natalie's only relief coming from being able to replace her now-empty glass with another full one. She was infinitely grateful that she'd refused point-blank to have a wedding cake. Cutting it with Mike's hands clasped around hers in mock love would have been intolerable!

'I hate to hurry you,' the celebrant said at long last. 'But I have another wedding later this afternoon and have to drive some considerable distance to get there. So if we could please just sign the papers, I can be on my way.'

After he left, the photographer was despatched also, leaving the six friends alone. The atmosphere, however, was still not very relaxed. Mike had a face like thunder and Natalie just wanted to crawl into a bed somewhere and cry.

'I don't want to be rude,' Mike suddenly threw at his friends, 'but you've done your bit. The wedding's over. So could you please just go home?'

Natalie's mouth dropped open when his friends immediately did just that. Left.

Alanna and Holly did manage a brief parting hug, with Alanna whispering a hurried, 'Ring me in the morning,' but in no time flat she was alone with Mike.

'You might not *want* to be rude,' she snapped after he flicked the lock on the front door, 'but you *are* rude. A word of thanks might have been in order at least. Not a summary dismissal.'

His expression was equally dismissive of her. 'For pity's sake, don't be such a drama queen. My friends know the kind of man I am. *And* what I think of having to get married like this. The last thing they want is to be around me when I'm in a filthy mood.'

'I don't think much of it, either.'

'Too bad. You're stuck with me. Just think of the money, honey. You're getting well paid to put up with my moods for a while.' He snatched up an untouched glass of champagne and swigged back a hefty amount before glowering over at her. 'I do realise you thought today would end differently to this. But you thought wrong.'

Natalie stiffened. 'What do you mean—end differently?'

He walked slowly towards her across the thick blue rug that separated them, his eyes doing what they had done earlier, only much less respectfully.

'You thought you could play games with me,' he ground out. 'Teach me a lesson that my testosterone wouldn't forget.'

'I don't know what you mean,' she lied breathlessly.

He stopped right in front of her, his eyes now glittering and cold as he glowered down at her. 'You know exactly what I mean,' he ground out. 'You're a smart girl, Natalie. Smart and devious.'

'I wasn't playing a game,' she defended, the champagne having given her some Dutch courage. 'I just wanted you to see that I could look attractive, and sexy. Call it female vanity, but I didn't like you criticising the way I looked.'

'Let's call a spade a spade, Natalie. You wanted to turn me on. That's the bottom line.'

'All right,' she blurted out. 'Yes! I wanted to turn you on!'

'Well, you succeeded.'

Her whole insides contracted at his gruff admission.

'Not that it's going to do you any bloody good,' he added angrily.

Natalie was to wonder, afterwards, if it was the champagne that opened her mouth so boldly.

'I'm not after your heart, if that's what you're thinking. I just want your body!'

His lips pulled back into a cynical sneer. 'That's what lots of women say. But it's not what they mean.'

'Well, *I* do,' she insisted. 'Remember what you said to me the first day we met? You said that I needed you to sex me up a bit. You were so right. After the fiasco with Brandon, I'd fallen into shocking habits, with my dress and my attitude towards men.

But my worst habit was not staying sexually active. I was in danger of becoming a dried-up old maid. But when you came into my life, my female hormones got a wake-up call. You're a very sexy man, Mike.

'Not a man I could ever fall in love with, mind,' she hurriedly pointed out. 'Or want to stay married to. But a man I would like to go to bed with. Trust me when I say I *will* divorce you, once you've got your precious partnership.'

CHAPTER ELEVEN

MIKE could not have been more taken aback. Damn it all, that was *his* speech. *He* was the one who usually said he wouldn't be falling in love, etc. etc. etc.

He should have been pleased, he supposed. The temple goddess had just given him the green light to sleep with her, without any strings attached.

So why wasn't he jumping at the chance? Why wasn't he already ripping that infuriating dress right off her and getting down to business?

Darned if he knew what was going on in his head. Or was it hers he was still worried about? Women could never be totally trusted. Mike didn't like it that Natalie had already got under his skin. He sure as hell didn't like it that he was going to ignore his misgivings and do what she wanted.

Resisting her, now that she'd offered herself to him, no strings attached, was impossible. He looked at her mouth and couldn't wait to make it melt under his—as it had when he'd kissed her earlier. He couldn't wait to hear her moan.

He'd liked the way she'd clung to him earlier as well. Liked it when her fingertips had dug into his back.

You like her too much, came the warning.

Too late!

'Fine by me,' he muttered, and reached out to start unwinding that tantalising scarf from her head.

By the time he tossed it aside, she was breathing heavily, her chest rising and falling. His own heart was going like the clappers. As he twisted her round to attack the zip at the back of the dress he told himself to calm down, to take his time. After all, she was his, not just for tonight, or a mere week, but till he divorced her. His to play with and to possess. Over and over and over. He could make all those fantasies he'd been having about her come true. Every single one.

By then, he should have had enough of her. *More* than enough, he reassured himself.

Mike breathed in deeply and glanced around, his hands stilling on Natalie's silky shoulders. Richard's penthouse was a fabulous place. Big, bright and airy, with a relaxed décor and a holiday atmosphere.

But the living room wasn't the ideal place for the kind of sex Mike had in mind. The tiled floor was cold-looking, and the cane furniture wasn't big enough for two people in the throes of passion, especially one his size.

His eyes dropped briefly to the blue rug underfoot, which was quite large and thick. The thought of pulling her down onto the floor had his flesh twitching. But he resisted the urge to indulge in something that could be counter-productive. Lots of women didn't go for that sort of thing. No, he needed a bed. King-sized.

There was everything he needed in the master bedroom. He'd been in there earlier, dropping off his overnight bag. The bed was huge, and the *en suite* bathroom spacious, with a corner spa bath and a shower built for two. Ideal settings for the sexy scenarios that had been tormenting Mike ever since he'd met Natalie Fairlane.

Mrs Stone now, he reminded himself. Mrs Mike Stone.

She was his, legally.

His.

A shudder ran through Mike at this thought, his hands tightening possessively over her bare shoulders. His mouth descended to push aside her hair and brush against the soft skin at the base of her throat, his nostrils flaring at the musky perfume she was wearing. When her head tipped back against his shoulder with a soft moan, he almost lost it, and, yes, almost dragged her down onto the rug with him.

But he steeled himself against temptation just in time, whirled her round and scooped her up into his arms.

Natalie gasped.

'Where are you taking me?' she asked breathlessly as he began to carry her in the direction of the bedrooms with considerable speed.

His smile was the smile of the devil. 'Somewhere a little more comfortable.'

'Oh…'

'Unless, of course, you like your sex on the rough side. *Do* you?' he demanded to know, grinding to a halt in the middle of the hallway. 'Be honest with me. Best I know right from the start what you like and what you don't like.'

She stared up at him, her mind flooding with lots of different scenarios, some rough, some tender, some slightly kinky. *All* of them exciting.

'I think I'm going to like everything,' she confessed, shocking herself, *and* him.

But Mike's shock only lasted a second or two before he laughed, a deep, throaty, sexy laugh. 'You're my kind of girl, then,' he said, and strode on down the corridor, steering her through the last doorway into what had to be the master bedroom.

When Natalie had first arrived at Richard and Holly's penthouse earlier in the day, she hadn't been interested in any grand tour. Her entire focus had been on getting herself ready and in steadying her nerves. So she hadn't been in here before.

Her eyes darted round the room, which was spacious and summery-looking, with the same cream tiles on the floor that ran through the whole penthouse, and the same cream walls. The furniture once again was cane, but painted white, not left natural. The bed was huge, with a blue satin quilt the colour of the sky. The wall that faced the terrace was totally glass, no doubt with built-in doors that slid back. Gossamer-thin curtains rested at each end, fully drawn back, the abundance of light reminding Natalie that the sun had not yet set.

Nor would it for several hours, Natalie thought with a swallow.

She was about to be made love to in broad daylight, by a man who was her legal husband, but whom she didn't really know.

Was that what made the prospect so exciting? Was it simply a version of the *sleeping with a stranger* fantasy? Or was it something else, a place where Natalie didn't really want to go for a second time in her life?

Concentrate on the sex, she told herself as Mike lowered her feet to the fluffy white rug that stretched along beside the bed. Don't think about the man, or the future. Think about the here and now. Focus on the pleasure of his touch. The feel of his male body. And what it can do for you.

A lot, she thought with a shiver when his hands ran lightly up and down her arms.

'You can't be cold.'

'No,' she admitted tautly. 'Please don't talk, Mike.'

His eyebrows lifted. 'You don't like to talk during sex?'

'No.'

'Mmm. You really *are* my type of girl.'

Secretly, Natalie suspected she wasn't, but she was going to try to be. For what was the point of being anything else? She might have made Mike want her in a physical sense today, but he didn't want her in any other way.

'Got any objections to my undressing you?' he asked abruptly.

Did she?

What would his type of girl do?

She recalled Alanna having told her that one of Mike's girlfriends had been an exotic dancer. Certainly no shy violet when it came to exposing her body. Natalie's stomach contracted as she whirled to boldly present her back to him.

I can do this, she told herself. I was once the mistress of a spy!

But the moment he started running the zip down her back and the tightly boned bodice was released, her hands grabbed at the gaping top, pressing it back against her swollen breasts.

But he would have none of her modesty, removing her hands quite forcibly and pushing her dress down till it pooled at her feet, leaving her standing there in nothing but a lacy white G-string and open-toed ivory high heels.

Natalie didn't know if she felt excited, or embarrassed. Whatever, her face was flaming.

'That's better,' he muttered, his hands zeroing in on her breasts, his outstretched palms rotating over her nipples.

'Oh,' Natalie gasped.

She could not remember her nipples ever feeling so big, or so tight. They kept lengthening and stiffening, two exquisite peaks of sensations that began screaming for more.

He gave them more, taking them quite firmly between his thumbs and forefingers, twisting then tugging till they were burning. Till *she* was burning.

When he abandoned her breasts to scoop her up

into his arms once more, Natalie was beyond worrying about anything.

The satin quilt was cool against her back. Cool and sensual. He arranged her in the middle of the bed with her head resting on a mound of pillows, stopping to plant a hungry kiss on her mouth before standing up and just staring down at her.

'You are one very beautiful woman, Mrs Stone,' he muttered, then began ripping off his own clothes.

She watched, fascinated, as he exposed his magnificent body to her eyes. It was everything that—and more than—she'd imagined. He had superbly developed muscles and a shape to emphasise them. Broad shoulders and chest, a six-pack stomach, slim hips and the legs of a gladiator.

But it was what rose up between those legs that drew her eyes the most, and held them.

'And you are one very beautiful man, Mr Stone,' she couldn't resist saying, her voice low and husky.

'I thought you said you didn't like to talk.'

'I've changed my mind.'

He shrugged his broad shoulders. 'Whatever turns you on.'

Just looking at him turned her on.

He stood there and stared down at her some more, then down at her lace panties, then further down to where she was still wearing her high heels.

'Those heels are lethal weapons,' he growled, sitting on the edge of the bed and reaching for her feet. 'They have to go.'

'The panties too,' he added after her shoes hit the floor.

Natalie held her breath as he hooked his fingers under the sides of her lacy G-string and levered them over her hips, peeling them swiftly down her legs, leaving her with nothing to hide her sex but a small vee of damp curls. She found herself pressing her thighs tightly together, embarrassed, suddenly, by her total nakedness.

Thank God he bent down and kissed her again, kissed her and kissed her till all her shyness melted away again, replaced by a fierce need to have him on that bed with her, on top of her, inside her, filling that part of her that needed to be filled, oh, so desperately.

'Mike,' she moaned against his mouth when he finally let her come up for air.

'Mmm?' His lips rubbed over hers, one of his hands around her neck, the other trailing down to tweak a still-tender nipple.

'Just do it.'

His head lifted, his eyes searching hers.

'You sure?'

'Yes,' she choked out.

'I won't be a sec.'

It took him more than a sec to retrieve a condom from his wallet. More like thirty seconds. But Natalie didn't mind. Despite the intensity of her need, she enjoyed lying there, watching him, admiring his male beauty, thrilling to the thought that, soon, he'd be really making love to her.

No, not *really* making love, she told herself with a small lurch to her heart. Having sex with her.

The brutal reminder dampened her excitement a little, till she accepted that honesty was better than deception, especially self-deception. This had nothing to do with love. It was all about sex.

But that didn't mean it wasn't special. Already she felt more of a woman than she had in years. A beautiful, desirable woman, a woman another man might want to get to know and love and possibly marry some time in the future. Being with Mike was going to be a changing experience in her life.

She was smiling up at him. Not a saucy smile. Or a sexy smile. A warm, soft, glowing smile.

Mike wasn't used to women smiling like that at him in bed. Not *before* he had sex with them. He wasn't sure what it meant.

He climbed onto the bed and kissed her again, obliterating the smile, bringing his mind and his body back to what he did understand. She wanted him to do it to her. Right now. No more foreplay. No fancy moves. Just straight into it.

Well, that was fine by him, he thought as his mouth turned savage on hers and his right knee wedged between hers, levering her thighs open. He could do that.

One hand twisted in her hair, holding her mouth captive under his whilst his other hand guided his straining erection into her.

Was it her moan he heard? Or his own?

Her flesh enclosed his like a soft leather glove. Restricting. Delicious. Exciting.

Too exciting.

Once buried in her to the hilt, Mike forced himself to lie still, lifting his mouth from hers and levering himself up onto his elbows.

She looked up at him dazedly, her beautiful blue eyes dilated with desire.

How seductive she looked, with her glorious red hair spread out around her flushed face; her lips wet and shining, and provocatively apart.

'Put your arms up above your head,' he told her.

She blinked once, then did it, the action raising her lush breasts, bringing her long, hard nipples closer to his mouth. But he didn't kiss them. Or lick them. Even though he knew she would have liked it. He didn't want to give her too much too soon. Or himself, either. He wanted to savour her. Like a wonderful meal. This was just the first course. The entrée. There would be many more courses to come. To hurry would have been a crime.

If only she hadn't moved her hips, and her bottom, her restless need compelling *him* to move, at first with creditable control, but then more urgently as hot blood rushed through his body, bringing him swiftly to that point of no return.

Soon, he was balancing on that knife edge, trying desperately to hang on, to satisfy her first. Her eyes were now tightly shut and her head had started twisting from side to side. Suddenly, her body lengthened under him, her arms stretching up till her fingers reached then slipped through the cane bedhead. She moaned, her back arching, her flesh squeezing tightly around his. The effect was electric and instantaneous. He could not possibly last much longer. Any second now he was going to explode.

She gave a tortured cry, then started spasming wildly around him.

Mike had never felt a woman come so intensely. His own answering orgasm stunned him as well, releasing his physical frustrations with a raw rush of pleasure that far exceeded anything he'd ever experienced before. Suddenly, he needed her closer, his arms sliding around her back to scoop her up from the bed. He sat back on his haunches and pulled her hard against him, her bottom balancing on his thighs. His mouth burrowed into her hair, pushing it aside so that he could suck on the base of her throat. She shuddered in his arms, her head tipping sideways to give him better access to the pulse in her neck, like a victim offering herself up to her vampire lover.

Eons later, they collapsed on the bed together, lying there for ages without saying a word, their ragged breathing taking a long time to calm.

'No, don't go,' she pleaded when he eventually went to withdraw.

Normally, once he'd had a woman, especially for the first time, Mike made a point of distancing himself, either by rolling over and going to sleep, or going to the bathroom.

Experience had taught him that danger lay during the blissful time of post-coital satisfaction. Women were extra vulnerable after sex and prone to misinterpreting his feelings for them. They invariably wanted to cuddle and to talk. Mike was not a talker, or a cuddler. The one time he'd been fool enough to do that—out of teenage gratitude—the girl had declared her love for him before he could say boo.

Mike couldn't stand being told by a woman that she loved him.

So why wasn't he bolting for the bathroom right now? Why was he stroking Natalie's hair gently back from her face and kissing her lightly on the lips?

Because this situation was different, he reassured himself. Natalie would never tell him she loved him. He didn't have to tread any careful line with her. He could relax and just do whatever he liked.

And he *liked* doing what he was doing at the moment.

'Want to come to the bathroom with me?' he suggested.

She looked slightly taken aback, as though no man had ever suggested such a thing to her.

'Er...what did you have in mind?'

'There's a great corner spa bath in there.' And he nodded towards the *en suite*.

'Well, I...'

'You get the champagne and nibbles,' Mike commanded. 'And I'll run the water.' He wasn't going to let her do what *he* usually did. Run for cover. 'We're married, remember? Having a bath with your husband is pretty normal behaviour for newly-weds.'

She laughed. 'Nothing about this marriage is normal, Mike.'

He shrugged. 'So? We might as well have some fun while it lasts. Isn't that what you want? To have fun? I'll let you wash me all over, if you'll let me return the favour.'

'You're wicked; do you know that?'

'Yep.'

She sighed voluptuously as she wriggled a little, making Mike aware that he was already on the road to recovery.

Hopefully, there'd be some more condoms in the bathroom. He only kept two in his wallet.

'Bingo!' Mike exclaimed five minutes later.

There was an open box in one of the vanity drawers, with several left inside. He began whistling as he turned on the bath taps and tipped in some bubble bath that was sitting on a shelf, then went in search of a few more fantasy-fulfilling items.

The very well-appointed bathroom supplied everything Mike had in mind.

All he needed now was Natalie.

'Natalie?' he called out. 'Where in hell are you?'

She came sailing through the open bathroom door, wearing an ivory silk robe, which she must have brought with her but that did little to hide her nakedness underneath.

'I can't open the champagne,' she said a bit breathlessly. 'I'm utterly hopeless at that kind of thing. Oh! Bubble bath! How lovely!'

She didn't look at him. Not directly. Mike didn't

think it was his nakedness bothering her so much as his erection.

Her sudden shyness was a bit of a worry. Maybe she wasn't as sexually experienced as he'd been imagining.

But that didn't make sense. Natalie had been a married man's mistress. They must have got up to some tricks together.

'Why don't you pop yourself into the bath?' he suggested smoothly. 'I'll get the champagne.'

'Oh, would you?' she said, looking at him at long last.

'Anything for you, beautiful,' he returned.

Her blush enchanted him. But he wasn't going to be totally fooled by it. She was one hot babe, once she got going. And he aimed to keep her going.

Reaching out, he undid the sash on her robe and slipped it back off her shoulders, letting it drop to the tiles. She sucked in sharply, but she didn't try to cover herself with her hands.

'I prefer you naked,' he pronounced, snaking an arm around her waist and pulling her against him.

She didn't say a word. Maybe she couldn't. Her eyes looked dazed. Mike felt somewhat rattled himself.

One feel of her lush body and his desire soared. He wanted her again. Now. Fast.

Thank the Lord the condoms were handy or he might not have bothered.

He didn't ask permission, her lack of protest confirming what he'd begun to suspect about her. She liked a man to be the boss in the bedroom. To take, not to talk.

He hoisted her up and onto the vanity in a flash, spreading her legs and pushing into her with one almighty thrust.

The silken glove of her flesh encapsulated him once more, holding him tight before drawing him in even deeper. He groaned to find that his orgasm was already building. He grabbed her hips, determined to slow things down a little. Instead, his rhythm was urgent, his eyes fixed on that spot where his flesh entered hers.

When she moaned, he glanced up at her face, then simply could not look away again. Her eyes were shut, but her mouth was open, her head tipped back so that her hair fell away from her back.

She looked utterly abandoned and totally beautiful.

He was still watching her when she came, her back arching away from him, her palms pressing flat on the marble vanity top as her naked cries of pleasure echoed off the tiled walls.

His own orgasm surprised him, being no less powerful, despite his distraction. He shuddered into her with force, his body not stilling for ages. Finally, he was done, his forehead dropping to her chest as a huge sigh rattled from his lungs.

And he was like that when her arms wrapped tenderly around his head, her lips brushing against the top of his head.

'That was incredible,' she whispered. '*You're* incredible.'

For a few moments, Mike wallowed in her warmth, and her flattery. He might have wallowed more if his wariness about women hadn't warned him not to get too carried away.

Her delicious body had already acted like a powerful aphrodisiac on him, making him lose control. He didn't want to start losing his head as well.

'Thanks for the compliment,' he said, lifting his head, then lifting her off the vanity.

Now it was time to slow things down before the next course. Time for that long, leisurely bath together, and the task of discovering exactly how far his sexy new bride would let him go.

CHAPTER TWELVE

'NATALIE! At last!' Alanna exclaimed. 'I've been dying for you to ring me all morning. Still, I suppose it is only ten o'clock. Well? What happened after we left yesterday? Did he or didn't he?'

'Did he or didn't he what?' Natalie teased.

'For pity's sake, girl, don't torment me. I can already tell something happened. You sound too chipper for all our efforts to have failed. I want to know every single detail.'

Natalie laughed even as she blushed. No way would she be telling Alanna *every* single detail. *She* could live with the knowledge that Mike had rendered her absolutely shameless. But she didn't want anyone else to know.

Still, there was no point in pretending that she and Mike hadn't become lovers. He'd probably tell his friends. Men did like to brag about their sexual conquests.

And, brother, she was a sexual conquest to end all conquests! Was there anything she hadn't let him do last night? If there was, she didn't know about it. By the time he'd carried her out of that decadent bath, she'd been totally corrupted.

'Okay, okay,' she admitted. 'Yes, all our efforts worked. Mike and I did go to bed together last night.'

My, what a delicate way of putting it, considering their sexual escapades hadn't been exactly confined to the bed.

'I knew it!' Alanna exclaimed. 'Reece said he wouldn't be able to resist you. He said Mike and celibacy just don't go together.'

Natalie winced. As much as she knew she would never have been Mike's first choice of partner, she still didn't like to think it was just frustration that had compelled him to accept her offer of sex.

'So, what do you think of him now?' Alanna persisted. 'Do you like him any better?'

Natalie grimaced. She should have known Alanna would start asking questions like that. Natalie had suspected all along that both she and Holly had been harbouring hopes about this marriage.

But Natalie refused to encourage her friends. Or her own silly self.

'I guess so. But we have absolutely nothing in common.'

'Opposites attract, you know.'

'Attraction is not enough for marriage, Alanna.'

'It's a start. Do you think you might fall for him in time?'

'I don't think that's likely,' came Natalie's hedging answer.

Sexually obsessed with him, yes.

Addicted to his body, yes.

Falling in love with him?

Oh, dear, she sincerely hoped not. To self-destruct a second time over a man would be the final straw.

But Natalie suspected that, down deep in that place where unbearable truths tried to hide, she was already treading a fine line between being in lust and falling in love.

'Unlikely, but not impossible?' Alanna suggested.

'Nothing's impossible.'

'Where is he now?'

'He drove over to his place to collect the rest of his clothes for our stay on the yacht. And to buy some supplies.'

'Really? What kind of supplies? Holly said the penthouse had everything you might need for a short stay.'

Natalie could hardly say more condoms. That would be a dead give-away and lead to more awkward questions.

'Just the Sunday paper,' she replied. 'And some milk. We both like fresh milk in our coffee.'

'See?' Alanna said. 'You do have something in common.'

'You are an eternal optimist, Alanna.'

'Life without optimism is dreadful. You have to always have hope. I know what it's like to live without hope and it sucks. Holly and I were talking last night and we both think you're the right kind of woman for Mike.'

'Good heavens, why?'

'You're smart and sexy and extremely sensible. I'll bet you're a good cook, too.'

'I'm competent enough in the kitchen,' she admitted.

Brandon had been keen on cordon bleu food, but not so keen on paying for it. She'd spent hours making elaborate meals for him, often having to eat them alone when he hadn't turned up at the last minute.

'Just as I thought,' Alanna said. 'You're perfect wife material, Natalie. Now, all you have to do is make Mike appreciate that having a wife like you would be a bonus, not a burden.'

'What if I don't want Mike as my husband?' she retorted.

Alanna laughed. 'I've spent the last few weeks with you, Natalie. I think I know you quite well by now. Do you know how much you talked about Mike?'

Natalie groaned. 'How much?'

'Endlessly. Every time you tried on an item of clothes, it was…would Mike like me in this? Will this turn Mike on?'

'That's just sex, Alanna.' If she kept saying it, she just might believe it.

'Till it turns into something else. Mike's a good man, Natalie. And terribly lonely. He needs someone to love him.'

'He doesn't think so. He couldn't have been more adamant about not wanting love and marriage.'

'Try looking past that macho, loner act to the real man underneath. He's not as tough as he pretends. Do you know about all the money he spends on under-privileged boys? Boys who don't have much in the way of family, or money.'

'No,' Natalie said, startled by this piece of news. 'He's never mentioned that.'

'He wouldn't. But he gives heaps to these kids every year. Pays for them to go to summer camps. Buys computers for them by the bucketload. Goes to their schools and gives free computer classes. Recently, he started a new project, building community clubs for them. The kind that have indoor sporting facilities and games rooms and lots of other activities. Reece and Richard help out with donations, but Mike's money is the main source of finance. If you think he's going after this partnership deal to increase his own personal wealth, then you're dead wrong.'

Natalie was stunned. 'Why didn't you tell me this before?'

'I just didn't think of it. We were too busy trying to make you over into a sexpot. But now that you know, does Mike being a closet philanthropist make any difference to your feelings for him?'

'I...I...well, it sure makes me want to know more about him. I mean, what drives him, Alanna? What happened during his own childhood to make him the way he is? Do you know?'

'No. He never talks about it. Not even to Reece or Richard.'

'Must have been pretty bad.'

'*Very* bad, I'd say. Why don't you ask him one day, when he's...shall we say...vulnerable to a bit of pillow talk?'

'Mike's not into pillow talk.'

'Maybe you should ask him straight out?' Alanna suggested. 'After all, you will need to know something about his past before your stay on that yacht. Mr Helsinger or his wife might ask you about Mike's background, and it would look funny if you knew nothing.'

'Yes, I guess it would,' Natalie agreed, sounding calm whilst inside she was anything but.

Alanna was beginning to agitate her. And to make her think too deeply about Mike, plus her feelings for him.

Natalie refused to start acting as she had in the past, always thinking she was in love, always wanting more than the current man in her life was prepared to give. Common sense told her to settle for enjoying whatever time she had with Mike, especially this coming week.

Meanwhile, she didn't want to talk to Alanna any more. Or anyone else, for that matter.

Natalie felt infinitely relieved that she'd told her mother she was going away on a week's driving holiday down the coast and was turning her mobile off. She'd emailed the same thing to all her clients at Wives Wanted.

'I must go, Alanna,' she said. 'Mike'll be back any moment. Look, I won't ring again till next weekend. I'm not taking my mobile on the yacht with me and I'll be with Mike all the time. It could be awkward.'

'That's all right. You have a good time, now. Can I tell Holly about you and Mike?'

'Only if you don't romanticise the situation.'

'But it *is* romantic, Natalie. You just can't see it yet.'

'No, it's you who can't see it, Alanna. I'm *not* in love with Mike. It's just sex. Okay?'

'If you say so,' Alanna trilled whilst Natalie rolled her eyes. Some people just wouldn't listen.

'Goodbye, Alanna.'

'Bye, sweetie.'

Natalie hung up with an exasperated sigh. 'That girl,' she muttered.

'Alanna trying to do your trick, is she?'

Natalie whirled to find Mike standing in the doorway of the kitchen, his dark eyes watchful and wary.

'I didn't hear you come in,' she said before realising that she wouldn't have. The penthouse was huge and the kitchen quite a way from the front door.

On top of that, Mike's feet were bare.

A good lot of him was bare this morning, his only clothing a pair of bone cargo shorts, slung low on his hips.

'What do you mean?' she added with a frown. '*My* trick?'

'Matchmaking.'

Natalie pulled a face. But there was no point in denying what he'd obviously overheard. 'She only wants the best for you, Mike. She thinks you could do with a real wife. She also thinks I'm in love with you, just because I slept with you. I tried to tell her that she had it all wrong.'

'Yeah, I heard you say it was just sex.'

If that was the case, why didn't he look happier about it? Just sex was all he wanted from her, wasn't it?

'What is it with you women?' he ground out, marching over and plonking the milk and paper down onto the black granite counter top. 'Do you have to tell each other *everything*?'

Natalie's chin shot up. She would not be spoken to like that, certainly not by Mike.

'Pretty much,' she said. 'We women have this awful tendency to need people in our lives. For things other than sex, that is. We need companionship and caring and children and, whoops, oh yes, occasionally we need love. We are such silly fools! But don't you worry, Mike. I won't be looking for love with yours truly. I'm not that much of a fool. I can see you're frightened to death of the word. You couldn't love anyone if your life depended on it!'

He glared at her, his eyes glittering, his hands balling into fists at his side.

'You don't know what you're talking about.'

'Then tell me. I'd like to know. What drives you, Mike? Why are you generous with your money but not with your feelings? What happened to you when you were a boy to make you the way you are?'

He looked furious for a second, but then he laughed. 'I see Alanna has been telling secrets out of turn.'

'Being generous and kind shouldn't be kept a secret!'

'What I do with my money is my business and my business alone.'

'Which is what you're always going to be, Mike,' she snapped. '*Alone.*'

'That's my choice.'

'It surely is. I'm sorry, but I don't think I can continue with our sexual relationship.' Even as she said the words, she wished she hadn't.

His nostrils flared. 'Why not?'

'I...I'm not sure I can handle it.'

'You handled it well enough last night.'

'Don't be nasty.'

'I'm not being nasty. I'm telling the truth. Here,' he said, snatching up both her hands and spreading them over his bare chest. 'You couldn't get enough of this last night. Or of me. Nothing's changed this morning, Natalie. I'm still the same man and you're still the same woman.'

But I'm *not*, she wanted to scream at him. And you're not.

Something's changed between us, can't you see it? Can't you *feel* it?

'I certainly haven't had enough of you,' he growled.

Even as he said the words his eyes betrayed more needs than sexual ones.

Alanna had said how lonely he was, how he needed someone to love him. She was right. Natalie saw the truth in his face, glimpsing the emotional bleakness behind his physical passion.

But he would never admit it. She knew that, too. The wounds of his past—whatever they were—had never healed properly. All she could offer Mike was comfort in its most primitive form. She could not tell him she loved him, but she could show it.

'That's nice to hear,' she murmured, trailing her fingertips over his male nipples till they tightened into tiny marbles.

When her head bent to lick them he groaned, taking an unsteady step backwards till his back was pressed up against the kitchen benchtop.

'Is this what you want?' she whispered as she went down onto her knees before him, her eyes lifting up to his tortured face.

He sucked in sharply when she unsnapped the waistband of his shorts, moaning softly when her lips pressed against his navel. She swirled her tongue around it whilst her hands pushed his shorts and underwear to the floor.

How different it felt from when she'd done this last night. This was not an act of lust, but an act of love. Her hands cupped him gently whilst her lips ran lightly up and down his length. Every lick. Every kiss. Every touch. All done with love. And when she took him into her mouth, her head was swimming with emotion.

'No,' he ground out as he carried her from the kitchen in the direction of the bedroom. 'That is *not* what I want. I just want *you*, Natalie.'

Natalie didn't say a word as he swept her into the bedroom. She was too busy fighting with the futile hopes that his passionate words evoked in her.

Because he didn't *really* want her, did he? Not for ever. Just for the time being.

But the time being *was* exciting, she told herself as he lowered her to the bed.

Enjoy it, Natalie.

And who knew what might happen in the future?

Alanna had said that life without hope sucked.

Natalie had to agree with her.

So she began to hope.

CHAPTER THIRTEEN

NATALIE was doing some last-minute primping and preening with her hair when she spotted Mike in the bathroom mirror. He was standing in the bathroom doorway, watching her.

Dear heaven, but he did look gorgeous in his new clothes. His cream trousers were superbly tailored, lending an elegance to his long, muscular legs. And she did so like the colour of his shirt. It was a deep fawn with a cream collar and arm bands that highlighted his tan. The shirt was short-sleeved, of course, showing off Mike's wonderful arms.

Reece had chosen well.

'Ready?' Mike asked her.

'As ready as I'll ever be,' Natalie replied as she whirled away from the vanity mirror. 'I didn't realise I'd be this nervous.'

'No need for you to be nervous. You look fabulous.'

'You like me in this?'

She'd wondered momentarily if Alanna had got it wrong, worried that she should have been wearing something more casual for her first meeting with the Helsingers. The white Capri pants she had in her case, for instance, not a calf-length skirt and matching top that were dressy enough for a day at the races.

139

'Blue suits you,' Mike said, pleasing her.

Wait till he saw the dress she'd bought for the party tomorrow night. It was bluer than blue.

'Pity about the bra,' he added as his gaze swept over her.

'But I'm not wearing a bra!' she said, confused by his comment.

'I know,' he said drily, his eyes zeroing in on where her naked nipples immediately peaked against the silk lining.

'Stop staring at me like that,' she told him agitatedly. This was what he was always doing to her. What he'd done continuously all yesterday. Turned her on with just a look. 'We…we have to be going in a minute.'

'No, we don't,' he growled. 'I can cancel and Helsinger can go fly a kite. There are plenty of other companies who'll want my program. I don't need Comproware.'

'But they won't give you a partnership,' she protested, thrown by this sudden change of attitude. 'Mike, you *married* me to get this deal. This is where the big money is, money you can do so much good with.'

His eyes narrowed on her. 'Are you sure you're thinking of my good works, or your own second million?'

Natalie stiffened. 'That's not fair.'

'No, you're right,' he said, actually looking a bit guilty. 'I apologise. I'm not myself today. It's just that I hate jumping through hoops for any man, and

Helsinger has been making me do that. He wanted me married so I got married. Something I said I'd never do. I was thinking this morning how much I like being my own boss. I hate the thought of kowtowing to Chuck Helsinger.'

'You'd never kowtow to any man, Mike,' she said, and meant it.

'But I already have,' he grumped. 'And probably all for nothing!'

'What do you mean?'

'If Helsinger *has* been having me investigated, then we're already busted. I mean…any PI worth his salt would have found out that my new bride runs an agency called Wives Wanted. What do you reckon Helsinger would make of that? Only a fool would think our marriage was the real McCoy.'

'In that case he *isn't* having you investigated,' Natalie reasoned aloud. 'Or he'd have cancelled the invitation to join him on his yacht and taken back the offer of a partnership. I'll bet my house on it.'

'I hope you're right, Natalie. But I have a negative feeling about this. Maybe Helsinger likes to play with people's lives. Maybe he's bored with being a billionaire.'

'Life is full of maybes, Mike. We've gone this far. We have to see it through.'

Mike stared at her. She was right, of course.

But he still didn't want to. Helsinger wasn't the only problem in his head today. *She* was. This beautiful and intriguing woman who'd got under his skin right from the start, and who was fast becoming an obsession. A dangerous obsession.

Dangerous to his peace of mind, not to mention the peace of his body. He was different with her from how he'd been with other women. The more he had Natalie, the more he wanted her. His desire had become a compulsion. He was beginning to *need* her, with the same desperation that a man dying in the desert needed water.

Mike had once vowed never to need a woman. Not like that. Never like that.

'Mike?' Natalie prompted, her lovely forehead wrinkled into a frown.

'You're right,' he said sharply. 'We have to see it through.' Even if it drives me insane. 'But I'm not going to put up with any bulldust.'

'At least we don't have to *pretend* to be lovers,' she said, and smiled a softly seductive smile.

The effect on him was stunning, as if he were suddenly wrapped in a warm blanket on a freezing cold night. Hot blood charged along his veins, stirring his flesh.

Thank God they had to get going right away, otherwise he might have pounced on her.

'No more titivating,' he ordered her abruptly. 'Let's get out of here.'

'I have to get my handbag first,' she said. 'And the wedding photos.'

'No. Not the photos.'

'But you paid extra for a brag book to be delivered this morning so that you could show the Helsingers!'

'I've decided I do not wish to show them to the Helsingers. They're not close friends. They wouldn't expect it.' In truth, he'd hated the way the photographer had captured the way he'd looked at Natalie before and during the ceremony. Like some infatuated, fatuous fool.

'I'll meet you at the front door,' he said brusquely as he walked off.

He'd already taken their cases downstairs to the concierge of the building, there at the ready for when the hire car arrived. It was due at ten-thirty, booked and paid for by their host to escort them to where his yacht was moored at a pier at Darling Harbour.

A glance at his watch showed it was ten twenty-nine.

'Mike, what will I say if the Helsingers ask me questions about your family background?' Natalie queried on the way to the lift.

'Just tell them the truth,' he told her bluntly.

'But I don't know anything about you.'

'Exactly,' he said, and hustled her into the lift. 'Tell them you don't know anything about me.'

'But I can't say that. They'd think I'm crazy to marry a man I don't know anything about.'

'Mmm. They could be right.' He hit the button and the lift doors closed. 'Say I had a horrible childhood, but I don't like to talk about it.'

He could feel her looking at him, but he refused to look back at her. Things happened when he looked at her. Bad enough that her perfume was enveloping him in that closed space.

'And *did* you? Have a horrible childhood?'

He dared to look at her now that he had a reason to be annoyed. 'You're an intelligent woman, Natalie. You already know I did. Let's leave it at that, shall we?'

Natalie shivered under his harsh voice and suddenly cold eyes, so different from the way he'd looked at her earlier.

Any lingering excitement she might have been feeling over spending two romantic days with Mike on board of a luxury yacht faded to nothing. If he didn't change his mood, this was going to be more than difficult. It was going to be miserable.

But the sight of a white stretch limousine waiting for them outside the apartment building lifted Natalie's spirits.

Impossible not to feel some excitement when confronted by such luxury, plus the added little thoughtful touches inside. Champagne. Caviare. And a welcome message on the built-in television that the driver set into motion as soon as they were under way.

Even Mike smiled when their larger-than-life host filled the screen, introducing himself and his very pretty blonde wife before congratulating them on their recent marriage and saying how much he and Rosalie were looking forward to meeting them both.

'So what do you think?' Natalie whispered once it was over and the television went blank.

Mike pressed the button that operated the privacy screen, waiting till it slid into place before answering.

'I think any man who wears a navy blazer with brass buttons has *not* been having me investigated.'

Natalie laughed. 'He did look like an escapee from the fifties, didn't he? But I rather liked him.' Okay, so he was fat *and* bald. But he had a nice face. And happy eyes.

'What did you think of his wife?' Mike asked.

'Hard to form an opinion. She didn't say a single word.'

'I would imagine that making conversation is not Mrs Helsinger's role in Mr Helsinger's life,' Mike said drily.

'They might be very much in love,' Natalie suggested.

Mike's face showed a wealth of scepticism. 'You saw the size of him. She married him for his money and he married her for what she does when she's not talking.'

Natalie recoiled as her mind shot back to what she'd done for Mike a few times when she hadn't been talking.

'What is it?' he said sharply. 'What did I say?'

'Nothing. I...nothing.'

'No, it's not nothing. You look upset.'

Her eyes searched his. 'I...I just didn't want you to think that anything I've done with you has anything to do with money. Because it hasn't. I...I like you, Mike. I like being with you. Honestly.'

Natalie didn't know how else to put it without saying that she loved him.

He turned his head away to stare through the tinted window next to him. 'It *has* been fun, hasn't it?'

Natalie swallowed. He was talking in the past. Was that it, then? Had the boredom begun to set in? He certainly hadn't been bored with her earlier this morning.

Still, she'd sensed a change in him later. A cooling. And a distancing. He hadn't held onto her hand in the lift. Or touched her in any way for a while. Yesterday, he hadn't been able to stop touching her.

'Are you trying to tell me something here, Mike?' she asked him, determined not to cry. Or make a scene. If it was over for him, then it was over.

His head turned slowly back to face her. 'Like what?'

'Like we might have to *pretend* to be lovers from now on?'

'I don't think I could manage that,' he muttered.

'Manage what?'

'To be with you in such close quarters and not have sex with you.'

'Gee. I'm that irresistible, am I?' she threw at him.

He looked hard at her, his dark eyes glittering. 'Actually, yes, Natalie. You are.'

She sucked in sharply, her mind spinning at his admission.

'Nevertheless, come Thursday, I'm calling it quits,' he added, suspending her breathing altogether.

'But why?' she choked out.

'Because.'

'Because *why*?' she demanded to know.

'I have to stop this before you get hurt,' he ground out. 'I'm no good for you, Natalie. I'm nothing but a twisted, heartless bastard. I'm not interested in love. I'm not interested in anything but having sex with you.'

'So? You haven't heard me objecting, have you?'

He glared at her before suddenly reaching out to grab her upper arms and yank her hard against him.

'God damn you, Natalie,' he growled, his eyes cold and hot at the same time. 'God damn you to hell.'

But it was Mike who took her to hell, right there, in the back of that limousine. He didn't even undress himself. *Or* her. But she still came, with the same savage swiftness that he did.

Afterwards, he slumped back against the leather seat, total torment in his eyes.

'Why don't you ever say no?' he raged as he fixed his clothes. 'Why don't you ever stop me? You should have stopped me this time, Natalie. I didn't even use a condom!'

She just stared at him, her mind racing to dates, her heart jolting once she realised the possible consequences of his uncontrollable passion. No, not possible, *probable*. She was right in the middle of her cycle.

Surprisingly, no panic followed this discovery. Instead, a strange calm stole over her. A sense of karma.

'It's all right, Mike,' she told him as she opened her handbag and set about repairing any damage to her appearance. 'It won't be a problem.'

'You're sure?'

'Absolutely. I ovulated a while back,' she said. A minute ago, hopefully. 'You don't have to worry. Truly.'

And that *was* the truth. She would not burden him with a child he didn't want. If she was lucky enough to become pregnant, she would have his baby all by herself and love it to pieces for the rest of her life, just as she loved him.

'Oh, do stop scowling at me, Mike,' she added, her new resolves having brought a boldness with them. 'I'm not trying to trap you into anything. Okay, so I admit I'd like our relationship to continue for a while longer. You really are *very* good at sex. But I can see you're determined to end things when we leave the yacht. I won't argue with you. But there's no reason why we can't enjoy our time left, is there?'

He just shook his head at her, his expression approaching bewildered.

'I'll take that as a no,' she went blithely. 'Now, could you pour me a glass of that very expensive champagne? No point in wasting it.'

CHAPTER FOURTEEN

THE Helsinger yacht was what was called an ocean-going super yacht. It was sixty-five metres long, with an aluminium hull, twin engines, computerised navigation systems and a top speed of seventeen knots. It accommodated twelve guests and fourteen crew. There were six deluxe guest cabins, a formal lounge and dining room as well as a large saloon and a home cinema with tiered seats and surround sound. The teak decks incorporated informal dining and entertaining areas along with a swimming pool, a spa, a games area, a heliport—complete with helicopter—and a twelve-metre launch, which doubled as a game-fishing boat.

Their host supplied all this mind-boggling information within minutes of Mike and Natalie boarding the *Rosalie*.

Chuck proved to be even larger in the flesh than he'd appeared on television. But he was holding his age well, as big men sometimes did. His wife didn't look a day over thirty. Clearly, she had an excellent plastic surgeon.

Mike actually didn't mind when Chuck swept him off for a hands-on, man-to-man tour of his pride and joy, leaving Natalie to be shown to their cabin by Mrs Helsinger, who'd swiftly proved she could talk.

Frankly, some time away from Natalie was just what the doctor ordered. Mike still hadn't totally recovered his equilibrium from the interlude in the limousine. He had never, ever been that carried away before that he hadn't used a condom. Aside from that, Natalie's ready agreement to their separating on Thursday did not sit well on him. Which was perverse. Neither did the way she was suddenly acting. As if she was on some kind of high.

Admittedly, she'd downed a tall glass of champagne before they'd pulled up on the pier at Darling Harbour. But that shouldn't have set her cheeks aglow the way they were glowing.

She'd never looked more beautiful, or more desirable.

Yes, best he keep away from her every chance he got during the next two days. Or at least make sure one of the Helsingers was around when they were together. There'd be no afternoon naps down in their cabin. Or watching movies alone in that incredible home theatre. Mike vowed to stay on deck as much as possible, in full view of the crew.

'You have to have a look at the bridge,' Chuck insisted after showing Mike the pool with its swim-up bar and huge spa.

The bridge was amazing, resembling something you might imagine gracing a spaceship. Mike was soon blessedly distracted with boy stuff, chatting away to the captain who pointed out all the electronic gadgets and gismos.

'So what do you reckon, Mike?' Chuck asked after

they left the bridge. 'It's a great boat, isn't it?' he added, waving his hands around the deck in an arc as expansive as his waistline.

'You're a lucky man.'

Chuck's laugh was as big as he was. 'You're the lucky man, from what I've seen. That wife of yours. Wow. She's a living doll.'

'Natalie's a wonderful girl.'

'How did you meet her?'

Mike looked into Chuck's far-too-sharp eyes before deciding he wasn't going to lie. As much as he did want the billions a partnership with Comproware might bring, he couldn't stand the deception. Or the pretence.

'Actually, Chuck, Natalie runs an introduction agency called Wives Wanted,' he said matter-of-factly. 'When I was told you wouldn't consider a business partnership with any man who wasn't married, I decided to find myself a wife, quick smart. So I gave Wives Wanted a call.'

Chuck looked totally taken aback. 'You mean you were prepared to get hitched, just to get a partnership with me?'

'It seemed a good idea at the time.'

'And?'

'Natalie refused to find me a wife on the basis of a business-only arrangement.'

Chuck was beginning to look a bit confused, which rather confirmed what Natalie had said. He hadn't had Mike investigated.

'I see,' his host said. 'Sort of. So what happened

next? Nope!' Chuck held up both his hands in a stop-ping gesture, his eyes twinkling. 'You don't have to tell me. I can guess. You took one look at each other and fell madly in love.'

Mike opened his mouth to deny it, then closed it again. It was perfectly clear Chuck didn't want to hear the truth. He wanted to hear romance. The man was an incurable romantic!

'How did you guess?' Mike said.

'Same thing happened to me. With Rosalie. One look and pow! She was driving this car—a snazzy little red convertible—and we pulled up next to each other at a set of lights. Her eyes slid over my way and that was it. Love at first sight. I had that girl in bed before the afternoon was out. Three days later, we surfaced and headed for Vegas.'

'Weren't you worried it might not last?'

'Nope. I knew it was the real deal, you see, the same way you knew. I'd already been married and divorced twice. To girls who had dollar signs in their eyes when they married me, not love. I knew straight away that what Rosalie and I had together was dif-ferent. It wasn't just the sex. It was how I felt when I was with her. Like we were soul mates. I've never talked so much to a woman in all my life. Never felt so happy, either. Nope, neither of us had any doubts, despite our age difference. And here we are sixteen years later, as happy as pigs in mud, with two great kids and a lifestyle second to none.'

'Looks like you have it all,' Mike said.

'No need for you to envy me, my boy. You play your cards right and you'll have it all, too.'

'If playing my cards right means sucking up to you and your rather late-in-life moral standards, Chuck, then you've got the wrong man.'

Chuck threw back his head and laughed a big belly laugh. 'I'll have to tell Rosalie that. She'll crack up. She always said that one day I'd meet my match in the business arena. I think today might be that day. But don't worry, Mike. If anyone has to do any sucking up around here, it's going to be me. I'm told that this new firewall program of yours is going to revolutionise the worldwide web. Going to make someone a mighty big parcel of money, too. My lawyers are already working out a deal which will give both of us the best of that world.'

'I'll look forward to having *my* lawyers look at it,' Mike said, playing it cool.

But he couldn't wait to tell Natalie.

'I suppose you'd like to tell your little lady the good news,' Chuck said, making Mike wonder if he was a mind-reader.

'Yes, she'll be pleased.' *Very* pleased.

Now, she wouldn't have to wait long for her second million. Not the most inspiring thought.

Natalie would be the one who ended up having had it all. A satisfying sexual fling with him. And a nice pot of money to take with her afterwards, making her an even more desirable catch for some man who wanted what she wanted. Marriage and children.

Mike's jaw clenched down hard when he thought

of her marrying some other man. Of her smiling at him, and getting pregnant by him and being happy with him.

And where would he be whilst all this was happening? He'd be alone, as she'd said he'd end up being.

But wasn't he better off being alone? You didn't hurt anyone when you lived alone. You didn't destroy lives.

'I think it's time we joined the girls for lunch,' Chuck said. 'It's being served on the upper deck where we can get a good view of everything. The plan is to cruise around your magnificent harbour during lunch. After that, we'll be heading out through your heads and up the coastline to Pittwater. I'm told that's one of Sydney's most panoramic waterways. I dare say you've already seen it, being Sydney-siders, so while Rosalie and I act like typical tourists you two newly-weds might like to have a little lie-down.' And he winked at Mike.

When Chuck strode off in the direction of the steps that led down to the next deck, Mike shook his head. Everyone was conspiring against him. But what the hell? A little lie-down with Natalie might be a necessity by then, given he had to endure sitting next to her during what would probably be a long lunch, looking at the size of Chuck.

Launching himself after his fast-disappearing host, Mike decided not to fight the situation any longer. He was here with Natalie for the next two days. He might as well enjoy them, as she said.

*   *   *

'So what do you think of the Helsingers now?' Mike asked as he rolled over and picked up the remote control of the huge plasma-screen television that was built into the wall opposite their bed.

It was their first actual conversation since they'd retired to their cabin after lunch. Talking had not been an immediate priority on Mike's agenda, and, as usual, Natalie had been with him all the way.

When he rolled back, she snuggled up to him, running her fingers lightly through the smattering of curls that covered the centre of his chest.

'I really liked them,' she said. 'Impossible not to. Impossible not to like this boat as well. Just look at the size of this cabin. And the sheer luxury.'

Mike could not help but agree. The walls were wood-panelled in a rich, warm-coloured wood, the gold carpet on the floor thicker than any carpet he'd ever come across. The bed was simply huge, and, whilst its green and gilt brocade quilt was currently on the floor, Mike had to admit that it would not have looked stray in a palace. Neither would the *en suite* bathroom, which was made entirely in black marble with gold fittings.

The furniture all looked like genuine antiques, but possibly they were reproduction. Only the lighting was modern, being recessed to give the illusion of more space. The walk-in robe-cum-dressing-room was surprisingly large, and already hung with all their clothes by the time they'd come down, making Mike glad that he'd gone shopping with Reece.

'I like them too,' Mike admitted, flicking through

the satellite channels out of curiosity before turning the television off again. He had better things to do than watch TV.

'You were a big hit with Chuck,' he said, lying back and wallowing in the feel of Natalie's hands on him.

'That's nice,' she murmured.

'He virtually told me the partnership's mine.'

Natalie's head shot up. 'He *did*? Why didn't you tell me earlier?'

'Couldn't. My tongue was otherwise occupied.'

She laughed, then levered herself over to lie on top of him, resting her chin on her hands, which she'd folded over his heart. 'So it was. You know you're very good at that. Not all men are, you know?'

'Thank you for reminding me that I wasn't your first.'

'Don't tell me you're jealous.'

'Would that be a surprise?'

'Absolutely.'

'Then prepare to be very surprised. Because I'm very jealous,' he growled, rolling her over and pinning her underneath him. 'Of every man you've ever been with.'

'Don't make it sound like a legion. I haven't had all that many. Unlike you, Mike Stone.'

'Yeah, but I've never had a woman like you.'

'Is that a compliment?'

'It's a damned complication.'

'Why?'

'Because I don't want to let you go.'

There! He'd said it. Now let her make of it what she willed.

She stared up at him, her eyes stunned.

'Do you really mean that?'

'Unfortunately.'

'Why unfortunately?'

'Because I'm no good for you. You want a proper marriage. With children. I'm not cut out for anything proper. And I sure as hell don't ever want to be a father.'

'But *why*, Mike? You're wonderful to those boys you help. You obviously have a lot of love to give.'

'Love! I don't give them *love*. I give them help. And money. And opportunity. Love's got nothing to do with what I do.'

'Then what's it got to do with?' she threw up at him. 'That horrible childhood of yours, I suppose. You don't want other boys to go through what you went through, is that it?'

'Something like that.'

'So what *was* it that happened to you, Mike?'

'I told you. I don't like to talk about it.'

'Why not? It might do you some good.'

For the first time in his life, Mike was tempted. He sucked in a deep breath, but then shook his head. He just couldn't tell her. He didn't want to see pity in her eyes.

'What are you afraid of, Mike?' she persisted. 'I promise not to tell anyone else. This will just be between you and me.'

'Trust me. You don't want to know.'

He could just imagine how Natalie would react. She'd had such a normal childhood. She had no idea what it was like to live the way he'd lived as a kid. Okay, so her dad had obviously been a bit of a dill, money-wise. At least she'd *had* a dad. And a mother who'd been a mother. They actually sounded nice.

'Mike, I think it's important that you talk about what happened,' she went on, clearly determined to worm everything out of him. 'You've bottled it up for too long. If you're worried I might be shocked, then don't. I'm not some fragile flower. I've seen and read about lots of not-so-nice things in my life.'

He grimaced, then rolled over to lie next to her. Maybe he could do this if he didn't have to look into her eyes.

And maybe he couldn't.

'I wouldn't even know where to start,' he muttered.

'Let's start with your being born. Tell me about your mother and father. Who were they? How did they meet? Where are they now?'

He slanted her a wry glance. 'You're not going to shut up till I tell you everything, are you?'

'Nope.'

Mike would have been irritated to death if it had been any other woman badgering him like this. So why wasn't he with Natalie?

Because you *want* to tell her, that's why, supplied that inner voice that he'd been trying to ignore, but that would no longer stay silent. You want her to know what makes you tick. You want her to understand you.

'Don't say I didn't warn you,' he still felt compelled to say. 'Okay, so you want to know about my parents. Not much I can tell you about my father. I never knew him. Never knew his name, either. My birth certificate says father unknown. I gather he was an American marine, here in Sydney on R and R.'

'So your mother had an affair with a soldier and you were the result. That's not so terrible, Mike.'

'Look, let's not whitewash anything here. Mum was a junkie,' he told her harshly. 'Had been since she was fifteen. Her parents kicked her out of home around that time. Mum used to pick up all sorts of men when she needed money for drugs. Obviously, that night she was too high to think of using protection. That's how I came about.'

'Oh. I see.'

Mike read quite a bit in those softly delivered words. None of it good. He'd known she'd be disgusted.

'I told you it wasn't a pretty story,' he snapped.

'It's not an uncommon story, Mike. But it's still a sad one. Sad for you and sad for your mum. Poor thing.'

'Poor thing!' He sat up abruptly and glared down at this woman who dared to have sympathy for his mother.

'I was the one who was poor. Me and my poor little brother!'

'Brother!' Natalie sat up also, her hands lifting to push her hair back from her face. 'You said during your interview that you didn't have any brothers or sisters.'

'Tony was my half-brother. Lord knows who *his* father was. Mum admitted she didn't know. I reckon she only had us kids because we were good little money-spinners. Welfare pays single mums more for each child they have.' His face twisted as he battled the tortured feelings that always welled up when he thought of his mother. 'She was a hopeless mother. Nearly all of her money went on drugs. There was never much left for food, or clothes. Even worse, no money for medicine for Tony who was a sickly kid, right from the start.'

And there they were again, the memories of his boyhood, flooding back, bringing with them the dark demons that had haunted his dreams for years and that only went away when he was working, or having sex.

They'd been Mike's two escapes for years. Work and sex.

But there was no escape for him this time.

It had been a mistake to bare his soul. A *big* mistake.

Mike whirled round, swinging his feet over to the side of the bed, all the while battling the tumultuous feelings that were welling up inside him. Tears pricked at his eyes, but he refused to cry. Crying was for babies. And women.

'You have no idea what it was like,' he bit out. Had she ever gone to bed hungry at night? Or gone to school with no lunch, and wearing hand-me-downs that were too small? Or watched a little brother fade away before her eyes?

Her gentle hands on his shoulders almost unravelled him totally.

'No,' Natalie said softly. 'I don't. But I can imagine how unhappy you all must have been. You, your brother *and* your mother. Try to have some pity for her, Mike. Try to forgive.'

'I can never forgive her,' he grated out, his head shaking from side to side. 'She told us how much she loved us. All the damned time. She'd cuddle and kiss us, but she never looked after us. Her actions spoke a lot louder than her words.'

'She was sick,' Natalie insisted. 'And she had no support. Not everyone is as strong as you, Mike.'

'Don't make bloody excuses for her,' he snapped. 'She made her choices and Tony and I suffered for them.'

Natalie could understand his bitterness. Still, children did judge their parents harshly. She resolved not to be so critical of her own mum and dad in future. All in all, they'd been wonderful parents. Warm and loving and caring.

'So what happened to her?' she asked gently.

He laughed. A cold, empty sound. 'She died of an overdose, of course. I was nine at the time. Poor little Tony was just six.'

'What happened to you and your brother after that?' Natalie asked. 'Did your mum's parents take you in?'

'You have to be kidding. The authorities contacted

them, but they said their drug-addict daughter and her filthy offspring were dead to them. So we were fostered out. To different homes. I didn't get along with any of my foster families. So I ended up in a state institution.'

'An orphanage, do you mean?'

'Yeah. An orphanage.'

'Oh, Mike…'

God, he couldn't take any more of her pity. His head lifted, his back and shoulders straightening.

'It wasn't too bad,' he lied. 'There was this nice old guy there. A janitor. He was into computers in a big way and could see how much I liked them. Anyway, he gave me an old one of his one year for Christmas. Fred, his name was. Uncle Fred. I've never forgotten him.'

That part was true. He'd gone back years later to repay the man's kindness, only to find out that Fred had died a few months before.

'So that's how you got started in computers.'

'Yeah. I took to programming like a duck to water and never looked back. I never did get my higher school certificate. I refused to sit for exams. I was a rebellious beggar back then. But it didn't matter in the long run. I made it by myself.'

'That you did,' she said in a way that made him feel quite proud. 'But what happened to your brother, Mike?'

Mike grimaced. Women! They had to know the ins and outs of everything, didn't they? They couldn't let sleeping dogs lie.

'He died. When he was eight. Meningitis. His foster parents didn't recognise the symptoms till it was too late. They thought he had the flu. Poor kid never stood a chance.'

'That's terribly sad, Mike. I'm so sorry.'

'Now you know why I don't want to be responsible for a child's life. I couldn't bear it if I was a bad father.'

'But you wouldn't be. You'd be an exceptional father, for that very reason. You'd care more than most men.'

'Would I?' He could just as easily be a chip off the old block.

'Yes, you would,' she insisted.

Her arms wrapping tightly around him brought the most incredibly moving emotion. If only her seeming belief in him were real. If only he could trust it, and himself.

'Would *you* have a baby with a man like me, Natalie?' he heard himself asking her, his voice still holding scepticism. 'Would you, *really*?'

Her lips, which had been planting tantalising kisses over his back, stilled.

Mike could just imagine what was going through her head.

'I might,' she said at last.

Yeah…*right*.

He twisted round to look into her eyes. 'You're just saying that.'

'No,' she denied. 'I'm not. Do you *want* me to have your baby, Mike?'

His stomach swirled with a sudden nausea. 'Good God, no,' he denied gruffly. 'What I want is for you to stay with me after we leave this yacht. I want you to come live with me, not as my wife. As my woman.'

Her eyes searched his. 'For how long?'

'For as long as you like.'

She frowned. 'I can't promise to stay for ever, Mike.'

Mike knew exactly what she was saying. One day, she'd want more than he was willing to give her.

But that one day wasn't today, he thought with ruthless resolve as he pushed her back onto the bed.

'How long have we got before we have to get dressed for pre-dinner drinks?' he asked huskily as he wrapped her legs around him and thrust into her.

'About an hour,' she replied, moaning softly when he set up a powerful rhythm.

An hour. A day. A lifetime.

There would never be enough time, Mike realised on alternate waves of ecstasy and despair. Never!

CHAPTER FIFTEEN

'WILL I do, darling?' Natalie asked as she paraded herself in front of Mike in her electric-blue party dress.

Mike's dark eyes blazed when they fastened on her cleavage.

'No,' he growled. 'You certainly won't do. You look much too sexy. Do you realise how many billionaires will be at this party tonight? Chuck told me he's flying in his super-rich friends from all over the world. There's sure to be some playboys amongst them who think nothing of seducing other men's wives.'

'Ah, but this wife is not in the market to be seduced,' Natalie purred as she sashayed up to Mike, who was looking pretty yummy himself in the same black dinner suit he'd worn at their wedding. 'She's way too satisfied with her husband.'

'Seduction is not always a matter of sex, Natalie,' he retorted. 'And what's with this *darling* business?'

She reached up on tiptoe to plant a soft kiss on his mouth. 'You don't like it?'

'I didn't say that. But it isn't quite you. It sounds...superficial.'

That was because he didn't realise she meant it, Natalie thought as she turned away and walked over to where she'd put her earrings. He *was* her darling. Her darling, and, with a bit of luck, the father of her baby.

And what will you do if you *have* fallen pregnant? Natalie wondered as she slipped her earrings into her lobes. Tell him, or just leave him without saying a word about it?

It would depend, she supposed, on how their relationship developed once they moved beyond the honeymoon phase.

But for now that honeymoon phase was exactly where they were at, and she was loving every delicious, decadent moment. Mike's need for sex with her still bordered on insatiable, his lovemaking ranging from slow and sensual to fast and furious. He couldn't seem to get enough, his desire often inflamed by what she was wearing. Or *not* wearing.

Her new wardrobe had been a fantastic success, especially the wicked black bikini Alanna had insisted she buy, and which she'd worn by the pool this morning. Mike hadn't been able to take his eyes off her. He'd been very impatient to get her back to the cabin, supposedly to change for lunch. The shower they'd had together had been rather long. He'd also loved the tight white Capri pants she'd worn for lunch, then lounging on deck afterwards, if the glitter in his eyes had been anything to go by. Though it was probably the skimpy red midriff top that had turned him on again, the one she'd worn with a bra.

Right at this moment, her only underwear was the tiniest G-string, bringing a sensual awareness of her body that was exquisitely exciting. The design of the dress heightened that awareness, the strapless bodice being ruthlessly boned, pulling her waist in and pushing her breasts up and together into a stunning cleavage. The bell-shaped skirt didn't touch her skin from her hips downwards, leaving room for air to swirl around her bare legs and mostly bare bottom.

'I hope you're at least wearing panties under that dress,' Mike muttered.

Natalie smiled a saucy smile at him in the wall mirror that hung over the dressing table. 'That's for me to know and you to find out.'

His groan was telling. So were his eyes.

Natalie liked nothing better than making Mike desperate with desire for her.

Maybe this was because she knew he didn't love her. His lust for her, however, was the next best thing. She could pretend that he loved her when he was inside her, when he cried out uncontrollably at the moment of his release, when his body trembled and shook with the force of his passion.

'What about these earrings?' she asked as she whirled back to face him, the rapid movement setting the long diamanté drops swinging back and forth across her bare shoulders. 'Too sexy as well?'

His smile was wry. 'You're trying to get a rise out of me.'

'Yes, indeed,' she said, her eyelashes fluttering before dropping down to his groin area.

He laughed. 'If only I'd known that first day how

naughty you were, I would have whisked you straight off to bed, like I wanted to.'

Natalie blinked her surprise. 'You wanted to take me to bed, even when I looked like a frump?'

'You'd better believe it.'

Nothing he'd ever said had pleased her so much.

'I wouldn't have said no,' she confessed as well.

'*Now* she tells me.'

'I didn't like you much, but I thought you were a sexy beast.'

'I do so love your backhanded compliments.'

She reached up to stroke his cheek. 'I like you much better now. In *every* way.'

He took a step back from her so that her hand dropped away.

'I think we should go up to the party, Natalie. Much as I don't like the idea of you being fancied by every man there, I don't want to risk ruining that very beautiful dress you're wearing. And I might, if we stay down here any longer.'

'I love it when you say things like that.'

'I know. Shall we go?'

'Goodness me,' Natalie murmured as they walked along the deck towards the main saloon. 'Sounds like there's a hundred people in there.'

Mike's hand tightened around hers. He hadn't been kidding when he'd said he was worried about some of the men at the party making a play for her. She looked extra desirable tonight in that glorious blue evening gown. Strapless dresses did become her, especially with her sexy new hairstyle. Mike loved the way it waved around her face and brushed sensually against her shoulders when she walked.

Other men would love it, too. Men far more handsome than he was. And far, far richer.

'Chuck said he'd invited a few extra guests at the last minute,' Natalie told him. 'Look, there's the launch coming in again now, bringing more people.'

They stopped at the railing, watching with interest as the launch angled itself against the *Rosalie* and a member of the crew set about helping the latest party-goers disembark.

'Hey, it's Rich and Reece!' Mike exclaimed, surprised and relieved when he recognised the two well-dressed and very handsome men as his friends.

'And Alanna and Holly,' Natalie added excitedly. 'Oh, don't they look lovely?'

Mike didn't think they held a candle to his Natalie, but they did look pretty good for very pregnant ladies. Alanna was wearing some long white floaty number and Holly was in black, with a silvery shawl around her shoulders.

They called out to each other and soon the six friends were gathered together on the deck, exchanging handshakes and hugs.

'This is a pleasant surprise,' Mike said. 'But a mystifying one. How come you're all here tonight?'

'Got an invite this afternoon,' Reece answered. 'Chuck decided after going past Palm Beach yesterday that he wanted to buy a house there. He rang one of his business contacts, asking him for the name of the best man in real estate in Sydney. Which was *moi*, of course.'

'Do try not to be so modest, darling,' Alanna said with a warm smile.

'Modesty never gets you anywhere,' Reece tossed off with his usual *savoir faire*. 'Anyway, Mike, I told Chuck we were great friends, whereupon he insisted I come to the party tonight, along with my better half. At that point I said if he really wanted to please you— and it seemed he did—then he'd invite Richard and Holly here as well.'

'After all,' Richard said. 'If Chuck buys a house here, he'll need a local banker, won't he?'

'What a pair of opportunists you are,' Mike said wryly. 'By the way, the partnership is in the bag, too.'

'That's great, Mike,' Richard congratulated. 'So it was worth getting married, was it?'

Worth it?

Mike thought of everything that had happened over the last few days. Then he thought of the future, and the day when Natalie would no longer be in his life.

'You don't honestly expect Mike to say that anything is worth getting married for,' Natalie broke in laughingly. 'But I don't think he's too miserable, are you, darling?' Her upward glance was downright wicked.

'*Darling*, no less,' Reece returned with a lift of his eyebrows. 'Sounds like you two have been enjoying a real honeymoon.'

'I think we'd better terminate this conversation,'

Richard said quietly. 'Chuck Helsinger is on the horizon, heading this way.'

Mike was grateful for Chuck's intervention. He wasn't in the mood to defend his relationship with Natalie. He also didn't want to keep examining his escalating feelings for her.

But that was exactly what he found himself doing over and over again during the next hour, especially when one of the billionaires at Chuck's lavish party did try to chat Natalie up. He was around fifty. Suave, handsome, and rich as Croesus. Married, of course. But that didn't stop him.

The moment Mike's back was turned to say something to Alanna, the lecherous devil invited Natalie for a dance out on the deck, where a band was playing and several couples were already locked in each other's arms.

A powerful jealousy claimed Mike as he watched Mr Moneybags wind his slimy arms around Natalie's bare back like some octopus. When he drew her much too close for Mike's liking, he knew he couldn't stand idly by.

'Hold this,' he said, shoving his glass of champagne into a startled Alanna's empty hand. 'My wife needs rescuing.'

Natalie was thinking how much she hated being out there, dancing with this oily creep, when Mike suddenly materialised, tapping her partner none too gently on his shoulder.

'My turn,' he announced, muscling in immediately

and whisking Natalie off into his arms, leaving Casanova in their wake with his mouth wide open.

As Mike twirled Natalie down the deck to a more private area she sighed her pleasure, and relief.

'What took you so long?' she said, her eyes sparkling up at him.

'I'm a bit slow sometimes.'

'Not that I've noticed,' she said cheekily. 'I see you're a good dancer, too.'

'You can thank Alanna for that. She taught me.'

This news startled her. And worried her, a bit. 'You like Alanna a lot, don't you?'

'She's a great girl.'

'You're not secretly in love with her, are you?'

'What? Don't be ridiculous!'

'She's very beautiful,' Natalie persisted, jealousy worming its unexpected way into her psyche.

'She's Reece's wife.'

'So?'

'Look, I'm not in love with Alanna, all right?' he said sharply. 'I told you. I don't fall in love.'

But even as he said the words Mike knew them to be a lie.

The realisation that he'd fallen in love with Natalie brought a maelstrom of emotions. First came a weird elation—he *could* love someone, after all—swiftly followed by something close to despair.

Because she didn't love him back. How could she? What was there to love about him?

She'd only agreed to stay in the marriage for a

while longer because of the sex. Once his partnership came through and she had her second million, she'd be off to make a life for herself with a nice, normal guy from a nice, normal background.

Mike didn't begrudge Natalie a happy life. Hell, he wanted her to be happy.

But Mike wasn't a masochist. He couldn't continue making love to her, knowing that he loved her. He was a man of extremes. It was all, or nothing.

So far in his life, there'd been nothing, emotionally.

Nothing, he could handle. Nothing, he could live with.

Love was too hard. Too gut-wrenching.

In the morning he would tell her it was over. Meanwhile, they had one more night together. Difficult to deny himself when they had to share a bed.

Difficult?

Near impossible!

That was why he had to get right away from her as soon as possible.

'What are you thinking about?'

Her quiet question startled him out of his thoughts.

'Do you really want to know?' he muttered against her hair, his arms tightening around her.

'Yes.'

He stopped dancing and stepped back to look down into her lovely blue eyes.

I'm thinking that I would give anything to hear you say the three little words that I've always hated hearing on a woman's lips.

'I was thinking about your underwear,' he lied. 'Or lack of it. *Do* you have panties on, my darling wife?'

When she flushed, his lie swiftly became the truth.

'I do, actually,' she returned breathily. 'But they're easily removed.'

Her continual eagerness to oblige him sexually both annoyed and aroused Mike. He could almost hate her when she was like this. It was so close to what he craved for. Yet so far away…

'Go and remove them,' he ordered her. 'Then come back to the main saloon. I'll be waiting for you there.'

'But…aren't you going to come to the cabin with me?'

'No.'

He was going to make her wait. And wait. And wait.

Tonight, he was going to be cruel. Tonight, he was going to punish her for making him love her.

He whirled her in his arms, pulling her back hard against him so that she could feel his erection, his mouth dipping to her right ear, his intention being to whisper the darkest of desires to her.

But when her head tipped softly to one side and a trembling sigh escaped her lips, his own lips did nothing but kiss her ear. Then her cheek. Her jawline. Her throat.

'Oh, Mike…'

His name on her lips was like a caress, making him melt.

How could he possibly hurt her? Or punish her?

He loved her.

He would show her how much tonight. With tenderness, not cruelty. If tonight was going to be his last night with her, he wanted to remember it with pride, not guilt, or shame.

Natalie was a wonderful woman. A special woman. She deserved the best he had to give.

'We really should get back to the party,' he said, his tone gentle. 'Don't worry about the panties for now. I'll take them off later tonight, when we're alone.'

CHAPTER SIXTEEN

NATALIE woke to find Mike already up, fully dressed and packing.

'What…what are you doing?' she asked, pushing her hair out of her face as she sat up in the bed.

'Packing,' he replied. 'I thought that was obvious.'

His sharp tone shocked her. Where had the tender lover of last night gone to?

'But it's only eight-fifteen. We're not due to be dropped off at Darling Harbour till noon.'

His head lifted, his eyes hard and cold. 'I don't like to leave things to the last minute. Which brings me to something else.'

Natalie knew, before he said another word, that she wasn't going to like this something else.

'What?' she demanded to know, fear making her voice sharp as well.

'I've changed my mind, Natalie. Our living together isn't going to work for me. Sorry.'

Sorry.

Natalie's hands fell to the bed where she grasped at the sheet covering her lower half, holding onto it for dear life as she was holding onto her emotions for dear life.

Sorry.

One word, delivered without a care in the world.

Sorry.

One word, slashing into her heart and shattering all her hopes.

Of course, she'd been a fool to hope. But it was hard not to when the man you loved had made love to you half the night as if you were the most precious thing in the world to him and that he would never be able to live without you.

Sorry.

Her thoughts whirled as she tried to get her head around that one wretched word.

'For pity's sake, cover yourself up, would you?' Mike suddenly snapped.

Natalie blinked, then stared at him.

Cover herself up? This, from the man who had never been able to see enough of her. Who'd stripped her naked at every opportunity.

Suddenly, he was *offended* by the sight of her bared breasts? It didn't make sense.

Unless…

Dared she hope an even more outrageous hope?

Could it be possible?

'Why?' she asked him, leaving the sheet exactly where it was.

He scowled at her. 'What do you mean, why?'

'I mean why? Why do you want me to cover myself up all of a sudden? What are you afraid of?'

'I'm not afraid of anything,' he snarled.

'Then explain yourself. Last night was perfect between us. What's changed since then? You're a big one on telling the truth, Mike. But you're not telling me the truth now. I can feel it.'

'Can you just?'

'Yes,' she said, her eyes searching his.

He dragged his eyes away, slamming his case shut and zipping it up before glaring back at her.

'Don't be like all the others, Natalie. Don't make a bloody scene. Just accept what I say.'

'I'm not making a scene,' she countered. '*You're* the one making a scene. And I want to know why.'

'I'm going up on deck to have breakfast,' he told her harshly. 'You can please yourself what you do.'

Mike knew he had to get away.

Whirling, he strode swiftly towards the door, his hand lifting for the knob.

'You love me, don't you?'

Mike's hand froze in mid-air, his entire body stilling as well.

'That's what you're afraid of,' she threw at him. '*Loving* me.'

Mike closed his eyes for a moment. Then he turned, slowly, his insides churning, but his resolve strong. She wanted the truth. She would get the truth.

'No,' he denied. 'I'm not afraid of loving you. I'm afraid of hurting you. And of wasting your time. Yes, you're right. I do love you, Natalie. More than I ever thought possible. But you don't love me back. I know that. And I can understand why. I'm not a very lovable man. Far better you find someone you can love. Someone who'll give you everything you want, and deserve. A happy life. And children. You'd make a wonderful mother.'

'Oh, God,' she choked out, tears flooding her eyes.

'See what I mean? I've made you cry. And that's the last thing I wanted to do. I was trying to be cruel to be kind earlier. I was letting you go. But, like always, you couldn't let sleeping dogs lie, could you?'

'You don't understand,' she sobbed.

'What don't I understand? And, for pity's sake, *please* cover yourself up.'

Natalie scrambled to pull the sheet up, dabbing at her eyes whilst she struggled to find the right words to say to him. Her heart was so full. Of joy. And of fear.

How was he going to react when she told him she *did* love him? Would he believe her? And what about her possible pregnancy? He was sure to be angry with her, even if he did love her. Maybe he'd think she'd been trying to trap him all along. Oh God, she hoped not.

'But I *do* love you,' she blurted out.

His eyes widened, his face losing colour.

'Don't say that unless you mean it.'

'I do mean it. Oh, you've no idea how much I mean it.'

His face betrayed bewilderment. 'But you told Alanna over the phone it was just sex with you! I heard you.'

'I wanted to believe that was all I felt, because I thought you would never love me back. I was protecting myself.'

'You really love me?' he repeated, his expression still sceptical.

'Would I risk falling pregnant to you if I didn't?'

'*What?*'

'That day in the limousine. I lied to you. It wasn't a safe time for me. But it was a done deed, and once I realised I might have just conceived your baby I was so happy, Mike. I can't tell you how happy I was.'

'But you didn't know then that I loved you.'

'I was prepared to have your baby by myself, if I had to. Look, I haven't been trying to trap you, Mike. Honest. But I knew I wasn't going to fall in love again for a long, long time. And I wanted a child. Your child. Oh, please don't be angry with me. I know you always said you didn't want children, but I think you'd make a marvellous father. You have so much love to give, Mike. All you have to do is open your heart to the idea. And have faith in yourself. I have faith in you. You're a good man, Mike, even if you don't believe so yourself.'

She stopped talking at last, her heart pounding as she watched his face for his reaction.

Clearly, he was stunned. Then quietly thoughtful. When he started to walk back towards the bed, Natalie swallowed.

'You're not angry with me?' she choked out.

He sat down, his eyes no longer hard, or cold. He reached out to touch her face, wiping the tears from her cheeks with his fingertips.

'What are the chances of your being pregnant yet?' he asked softly.

'Um. Fair to middling.'

'But you might not be.'

'No,' she said, her heart squeezing tight. 'I...I might not be.' If he didn't want her to have his baby, she would just die!

'If you're not,' he said, a warm smile pulling at his mouth, 'we'll just have to keep trying, won't we?'

'Oh, Mike!' She dropped the sheet and threw her arms around him, kissing him. He kissed her back, for quite a long while.

'But we're going to have to make this marriage work,' he murmured as he pushed her back against the pillows. 'No child of mine is going to be raised by a single parent.'

'We'll make it work, Mike.'

'Yeah,' he said, his eyes shining as his head began to descend again. 'I reckon we will.'

EPILOGUE

'YOU really don't mind that it's a girl?' Natalie asked Mike.

They hadn't wanted to know the sex of the baby beforehand. They'd liked the idea of it being a surprise.

Mike bent over the crib and smiled down into his sleeping daughter's lovely little face.

'Of course not,' he said. 'I'm just glad our baby's healthy and that you got through everything okay. You were so brave, opting for no epidural.'

'I wasn't that brave. I screamed my head off when she was coming out.'

'Yes, I can still hear you,' he said, patting his right ear. 'Do you think you could stand trying for a second after you've forgotten how awful it was?'

Natalie's heart turned over. And this was the man who'd never wanted children. Just seeing the look on his face the first time he'd held his newborn daughter had been worth all the pain in the world.

What a lovely man he was. A real softie underneath that tough, macho façade. Alanna had been right about that.

'It might cost you,' she said teasingly.

His head shot up. 'You mean I have to *pay* you to have another baby?'

'Not with cash.'

'What, then?'

'I want you to rent Chuck's boat for the week from Christmas till the New year. Tess will be three months old by then so I should be right and ready for a second honeymoon.'

'You do realise how much Chuck charges for that, don't you? Four hundred thousand a week! Next year we'd be able to afford it, but we've spent a small fortune this year buying that big house Reece found us. My program's only been on the market six months and it takes time for the money to come in.'

'Yes, I do know that. But there are six double cabins for guests on the *Rosalie*. We don't have to rent the boat alone. I've discussed it with Alanna and Holly. They said Reece and Richard will pay their fair share. Holly said Richard will want to bring his mother and stepfather, but they've got scads of money and would be only too happy to contribute. Alanna wants to invite her mother and her new husband as well. They don't have much money, but she's a fantastic cook. Reece's mother won't be coming. Apparently, she spends every Christmas with her youngest son and his family.'

'When on earth did you organise all this?' Mike asked.

'Oh…last week some time. So is it all right?'

'How can I refuse? That boat has a decidedly erotic effect on you. Must be all the rockin' and rollin'. But what about *your* parents? We can't leave them behind. Not at Christmas.'

'Heavens, no. Their coming with us is a foregone conclusion. And Dad can well afford to pay something, too. They're quite flush since you gave him the job of managing the Sydney office of Stoneware and Comproware Inc. That six-figure salary you and Chuck pay him is ridiculously generous, you know.'

'You have to be kidding. He's a bargain!'

'You mean he's really good at his job?'

'You'd better believe it. That man's a brilliant manager and he's darned clever with computers.'

'I didn't realise,' Natalie murmured.

'You've been too wrapped up in having the baby to notice anything else.'

'You're right,' she said, and cast an adoring glance over at her daughter. 'Could you pick her up for me, Mike? I want to hold her again.'

She watched as Mike carefully scooped his daughter up into his large arms, rocking her gently back and forth when she woke up and started crying.

'I think she's hungry,' he told Natalie as he handed her over.

Natalie rolled her eyes. 'Four hours old and you're already anticipating her needs. I suspect your daddy's going to spoil you rotten, Tess, my girl,' she murmured to her baby, who stopped crying when her mother put her little finger in her mouth to suck.

'That's why you need to have another baby quickly,' Mike said. 'So that I don't.'

'Children are a lot of work, you know. You should listen to Holly. Her Andrew's just started to walk and she says it's bedlam most of the time.'

'That's because he's a boy. Alanna's little girl is much quieter. And easier to handle.'

'*We* might have a boy next time.'

'I won't mind that. I'd call him Tony, after my little brother. The one who died of meningitis.'

Natalie could already feel herself melting. 'Tony's a nice name.'

'So's Tess,' Mike said, his voice sounding a bit choked up.

It suddenly came to Natalie why Mike wanted to call his daughter that particular name.

'Tess was your mother's name, wasn't it, Mike?' she said gently.

He looked away as he did sometimes, when his emotions threatened to embarrass him.

'Yeah. Yeah, it was.'

'You loved her a lot, didn't you?'

'Yeah. I did,' he admitted gruffly.

Natalie's stomach tightened when she glimpsed tears glistening in the corners of his eyes. 'She did love you, Mike. She loved you *and* Tony. She just couldn't cope.'

'You're probably right. She was very beautiful, you know.'

'I'm sure she was.'

'Little Tess looks a bit like her.'

'I'm glad.'

He turned his head back to face her and, yes, his eyes were definitely wet.

The noises of impending visitors coming down the hospital hallway stopped Natalie from crying herself.

It was her parents, their faces beaming, their arms full of flowers and gifts.

'Oh, isn't she just beautiful?' her mother gushed when Natalie handed her daughter over to her grandmother. 'Look, John.'

'A real beauty,' her grandfather agreed. 'What are you going to call her?'

'Tess,' Mike answered, then added quite loudly and proudly, 'She's named after my mother.'

Wicked
– A novel steeped in darkness, danger and desire

The Earl of Carlyle was known as a beast.

Camille Montgomery is aware of the Earl's reputation. But as an expert in antiquities, she also knows his family's Egyptian artifacts are the finest in England. Unfortunately Camille's wayward stepfather knows this too. When he's caught in the act of robbing the 'Beast of Carlyle', Camille must swallow her fear and confront the man whose mask is said to hide a face too loathsome to behold.

Also available by Shannon Drake
Reckless – The spellbinding sequel to Wicked